Mieko Kawakami

BREASTS AND EGGS

*Translated from the Japanese
by Sam Bett and David Boyd*

Europa
editions

Europa Editions
214 West 29th Street
New York, N.Y. 10001
www.europaeditions.com
info@europaeditions.com

Copyright © 2019 by Mieko Kawakami
First Publication 2020 by Europa Editions

Translation by Sam Bett and David Boyd
Original title: *Natsumonogatari*
Translation copyright 2020 by Mieko Kawakami

Library of Congress Cataloging in Publication Data is available
ISBN 978-1-60945-587-3

Kawakami, Mieko
Breasts and Eggs

Book design by Emanuele Ragnisco
www.mekkanografici.com

Cover image: © David James Grinly – www.davidjamesgrinly.com

Prepress by Grafica Punto Print – Rome

Printed in USA

CONTENTS

BREASTS AND EGGS

BOOK ONE

1.
ARE YOU POOR?

If you want to know how poor somebody was growing up, ask them how many windows they had. Don't ask what was in their fridge or in their closet. The number of windows says it all. It says everything. If they had none, or maybe one or two, that's all you need to know.

I remember telling this to someone once. I can't remember who it was, but she really went off on me. "Come on, though. What if you have one window, but it's huge, with a garden view or something? You know, like one of those really nice big windows. How could that mean you're poor?"

But as far as I'm concerned, no one who's ever been poor could think like that. A garden view? A nice big window? Who has a garden, though? And what the hell could make a window "nice"?

For poor people, window size isn't even a concept. Nobody has a view. A window is just a blurry pane of glass hidden behind cramped plywood shelves. Who knows if the thing even opens. It's a greasy rectangle by the broken exhaust fan that your family's never used and never will.

You only know what it means to be poor, or have the right to talk about it, if you've been there yourself. Maybe you're poor now. Maybe you were poor in the past. I'm both. I was born poor, and I'm still poor.

What got me thinking about all of this again was the girl sitting across from me. The Yamanote Line was weirdly empty for a summer day. Everyone kept to themselves, staring at their phones or reading paperbacks.

The girl must have been eight, maybe ten. On her left was a young guy with a bag of sports gear at his feet, and to her right was a pair of older girls wearing headbands with big black ribbons. She looked alone.

This kid was way too skinny. Her dark skin made the patches of psoriasis even harder to overlook. Gray shorts, legs as skinny as the arms poking from her turquoise tank top. Her lips were tight and her shoulders were stiff—she reminded me of myself as a kid. That got me thinking about what it means to be poor.

I looked at the stretched neck of her tank top and her faded sneakers, which must have started off as white. How awful would it be if she opened her mouth and all of her teeth were rotten. I realized that she had no bag. No backpack, no handbag, no purse. Does she have her money and her ticket in her pocket? I had no idea how girls her age dressed when they had to take the train, but the fact that she had nothing with her left me worried.

I had the urge to get up from my seat and go say something to her, something no one else would understand, like the little notes you write down in a corner of your notebook knowing that no one else could read them. But what could I say? Maybe something about that coarse-looking hair of hers, stuck in place, or maybe her skin. Your psoriasis will clear up when you're older. Don't let it get to you. What if I asked her about her windows? I never had the kind of windows you could see out of. Do you?

I checked my watch. Noon on the dot. The train rolled through the languid summer heat. From the overhead speaker, a muffled voice announced that the next stop would be Kanda. At the station, the doors opened with a sound like something being punctured, and a drunk old man staggered onto the train. The passengers around him backed away instinctively. He let out a low moan. His gray beard, fraying like steel wool, hung in a tangled mass over the buttons of his punished uniform. He clutched a badly beaten clear umbrella in one hand and reached up for a strap with the other but stumbled when he missed. The door closed, and the train pushed off. When I looked back, the girl was gone.

Setting foot in Tokyo Station, I stopped short at the sight of all the people. Where were they coming from? Where were they going? It looked more like some strange competition than a crowd. I had the lonely feeling that I was the only one around who didn't know the rules. Gripping the strap of my tote bag for dear life, I tried to breathe.

My first visit to Tokyo Station was ten years earlier, the summer I turned twenty. It was a day like today, when you can never wipe off all the sweat.

I showed up lugging maybe ten books by my favorite authors, which I could easily have shipped ahead with the rest of my belongings, like any normal person, but insisted on keeping with me at all times, as if they kept me safe, carrying them inside this stupidly heavy-duty giant backpack that I stared at forever and finally bought at a used clothing store when I was in high school (and still use on occasion). That was 1998. Ten years now. I seriously doubt at twenty that I saw myself, in my vague dreams for the future, still being in Tokyo at thirty. No one reads my work (my blog, collecting dust in a corner of the internet, gets one or two visitors on a good day), and none of it has made it into print. Forget about readers, I barely have friends. I'm still in the same apartment with the slanted, peeling walls and the same overbearing afternoon sun, surviving off the same minimum wage job, working full time for not a whole lot more than 100,000 yen a month, and still writing and writing, with no idea of whether it's ever going to get me anywhere. My life was like a dusty shelf in an old bookstore, where every volume was exactly where it had been for ages, the only discernible change being that my body has aged another ten years.

I checked my watch again. Quarter past twelve. Since I had shown up a solid fifteen minutes early, I leaned against one of the thick stone pillars, cool against my back, and did some people-watching. Through the endless stream of voices and sounds, I watched a family rushing from the right side of my field of vision to the left, dragging what looked like all of their belongings. I saw a mother leading a little boy by the hand, an oversized water bottle hanging at his waist. A baby was screaming and young couples wearing makeup scuffled by, flashing their white teeth.

I pulled my phone out of my bag. No texts or calls from Makiko. They must have gotten on the Shinkansen from Osaka on schedule and should be arriving at Tokyo Station in five minutes. The plan was to meet up here, by the north exit of the Marunouchi Line. I'd mailed them a map so they'd know where to go, but now I was worried, and checked the date on my phone. August 20th. No issue there. The plan was to meet outside the north exit of the Marunouchi Line in Tokyo Station on August 20th—today—at 12:30 P.M.

Dear Journal,

Okay. So I've been eating eggs for my whole life. But today I learned that women have "ova," as in "oval," which literally means egg. How is it possible I knew about sperm first? That doesn't seem fair. Anyway, that was my big discovery for the day. I've tried the library at school a couple of times, but they make it so hard to check out books, not like they have a great selection anyway. Plus, it's small and kind of dark. If you sit at one of the desks and try to read, someone's always trying to see what you're reading. That's why I started going to an actual library. That way I can use the computer. Plus, being at school drains me. It's stupid. It's all stupid. But it's stupid to write it's stupid. At least everything at school just kind of happens. That's not at all how things work at home. They're like two different worlds. Writing is the best. You can do it anywhere, as long as you have a pen and paper. It's free, too. And you can write whatever you want. How sweet is that. I was just thinking about the different ways to say you hate something. You can call it disgusting, repellent, revolting. I looked up "disgusting" in the dictionary. The "dis" part means undo, and the "gust" part means taste. I guess that makes sense.

—Midoriko

Makiko, the one visiting me today from Osaka, is my older sister. She's thirty-nine and has a twelve-year-old daughter named Midoriko. She raised the girl herself.

For a few years after I turned eighteen, I lived with them in an apartment back in Osaka, when Midoriko was just a baby. Makiko and her husband had split up while she was pregnant, and as a single mother she was strapped for cash and needed help around the house. Rather than have me constantly running back and forth, we figured it'd be easier if I just lived there. Midoriko never met her dad, at least not that I've heard of. I don't think she knows anything about him.

I still don't really know why Makiko and her husband separated. I remember having lots of conversations with Makiko about her ex and whether they should get divorced, and I remember it was bad, but now I can't remember how it happened. Makiko's ex came from Tokyo, where he grew up. He moved to Osaka for work. They hadn't been together very long when Makiko got pregnant. One thing I kind of remember is the way he called Makiko "baby." Nobody talked like that in Osaka. They only said that in the movies.

We grew up on the third floor of a little apartment building near the ocean. Just two rooms, one more cramped than the other, no wall or anything between them. Izakaya on the ground floor. You could almost see the ocean. I remember going down to the water and staring at the leaden waves collapsing on the breakwater, retreating only to attack again. The whole town was ripe with salt and haunted by the action of the tides. At night it filled with boisterous drunk men. I remember seeing people crouched over by the side of the road, behind the buildings. Fistfights and screaming matches were an everyday occurrence. One time somebody even threw a bicycle in front of me. The stray dogs were always having pups, and as soon as the pups were big enough, they had pups of their own. We only lived there for a couple of years. Around the time I entered elementary school, my father left, and the three of us had to move in with my grandmother, who lived in public housing.

I only knew my father for those seven years. Even as a kid, though, I could tell he was a little man. He had the body of a schoolboy. He never worked. Just lay around the house, day and night. Komi—my mom's mom—despised my father for putting her daughter through so much. She used to call him "The Moleman" behind his back. He was always wearing the same stained tank top and long johns and lounging on his futon, a permanent fixture of the room. He never turned off the TV, even when the rest of us were sleeping. Tabloid magazines and empty cans surrounded him. He smoked all day, stinking up the whole apartment, and ashed into a can. He couldn't be bothered to sit up and would even use a little mirror to see behind him rather than turn around. Sometimes he cracked jokes, when he was in a decent mood, but he was fundamentally a man of little words. I can't recall a single time he played with us or took us somewhere. If something ticked him off when we were sleeping or watching TV, he'd scream at us, and when he got drunk, he lost his temper and beat mom. Once he got going, he'd find some reason to slap around me and my sister, too. Deep down, we were all afraid of him.

One day, when I came home from school, he wasn't there.

It was the same apartment, cramped and gloomy, dirty clothes on the floor, but without him, everything was different. I took a breath and went into the middle of the room. I tried using my voice. At first I was quiet, as if my voice was new to me, but then I let myself go and started saying whatever came to mind. There was no one else around. No one could stop me. Then I started moving, dancing. The more I used my arms and legs the lighter they felt. I could feel strength welling up inside of me. The layer of dust on top of the TV, the dirty dishes piled in the sink, the stickers all over the cupboard doors, the wood of the post where we had carved our heights. I saw these things every day, but now they gleamed, as if sprinkled with magic dust.

That scared me, because I knew the feeling couldn't last. Things would go back to the way they were. My father must have stepped out for a change, but he'd be coming back. I dumped my bookbag on the floor and took my usual seat in the corner and tried to breathe.

But he never came back. Not the next day or the day after that. Before long, strange men started showing up, and when they did, my mom chased them off. Then we started pretending to be out, but the next morning always found a pile of cigarette butts outside the front door. That went on for a while. Then one day, about a month after my father went missing— my mom finally dragged his futon, sheets and all, into the bathroom and stuffed it in the tub we hadn't used since the igniter busted. Crammed into that mildewy little space, and heavy with the smell of sweat and nicotine, my father's futon looked filthier than humanly possible. After staring at it for a while, my mom kicked the thing with everything she had. A month after that, my mom shook us awake in the middle of the night, saying, "Up, up, up." We couldn't see her face, but we knew she was serious. We got in a taxi and never saw that place again.

I had no idea why we were running, or where we were heading that time of night. Not even a guess. After a while, I tried to ask her what was going on, without pressing her, but I knew that my father was off-limits. I couldn't get an answer out of her. It seemed like we were driving through the dark forever, but finally we came to Komi's house, way on the other side of town, but still less than an hour away by train. Komi was the best.

I got carsick in the taxi. Mom emptied her makeup bag and held it up for me to vomit in, but nothing really came out. I wiped the spittle off of my face with the back of my hand. Mom rubbed my back, but all I could think about was my bookbag. It had everything I needed for Tuesday's classes, my notebooks, my stickers. Under them all, inside my sketchbook, I'd packed the picture of a castle that I spent days working on and finished the night before. My recorder was stuffed into the side pouch. My lunch pouch was dangling off the side. My new pencil case that had my favorite pencils and markers and scent balls and erasers. And my pink hat. I loved my bookbag. At night I kept it next to my futon, and whenever I left the house, I gripped the straps tight. It was everything to me. My bag was like a private room I could take with me wherever I went.

But I had left it when we ran out of the house. We raced into the dark, without my favorite sweatshirt, or my doll, or my books, or my bowl. I figured we were never going back. And that meant I would never have my bag again, or set my pencil case in its spot on the edge of the heated tea table and practice writing, or sit there and sharpen my pencils, or sit against the scratchy wall and read. It felt weird to think those things, like a part of my brain had fallen asleep. I couldn't find the power to move my hands and feet. I asked myself if this was really me. I mean, the real me would be waking up soon, and would walk to school, and have another normal day. The me who closed her eyes to go to sleep would never have imagined that a couple of hours later, I'd leave everything behind and jump into a taxi with my mom and Makiko and be running through the night, never to return. When I stared into the dark outside the window, it felt like that version of me, who had never seen this coming, was still asleep, under the covers. When I woke up the next morning and realized that I wasn't there, what would I do? Thinking about this brought me down. I nuzzled my shoulder into Makiko's arm. I was getting really sleepy. With my eyelids almost closed, I could see green digits glowing in the dark. The farther we got from home, the higher the number got, without making a sound.

We ran off and started a new life, living with Komi, but it didn't last long.

My mom died when I was thirteen. Komi died two years later.

Once it was just the two of us, Makiko and I worked like crazy. The only thing saving us from living on the street was the 80,000 yen that Komi hid behind the family altar. I remember almost nothing from the period between the start of middle school, when Mom found out she had breast cancer, and high school, when lung cancer took Komi. I was too busy working. One thing I remember is lying to the factory about my age every vacation, spring, summer and winter, all three years of middle school. The soldering irons hanging from the ceiling, and the hiss of sparks. Huge heaps of folded cardboard boxes. Most of what I remember from back then is from the bar. A little place run by a friend of my mom. Mom worked a couple of jobs during the day and worked at this bar at night. Makiko was in high school then and started there before me, washing dishes. Pretty soon I started working in the kitchen, serving sake and bar food while Mom kept the customers company. Makiko picked up a second job at a yakiniku restaurant and worked as hard as she could. She was only making 600 yen an hour, but in her best month, she managed to make 120,000 yen (which made her something of a legend in that place). For a few years after high school, they put her on the payroll, where she stayed until the place shut down. Then she got pregnant with Midoriko, and went from one job to the next, but after all these years, at thirty-nine, she still works at a bar five nights a week, living pretty much the same life as our mom. Another single mother, working herself to death.

It was almost fifteen minutes past the time we were supposed to meet, but Makiko and Midoriko still hadn't shown. I tried calling but Makiko wouldn't pick up or even text me back. Were they lost? Five minutes later, when I was just about to try her again, I heard a text come in.

"How do I get out? I'm on the platform."

I checked the arrivals display, found the train that I was pretty sure the two of them had taken out of Osaka, bought a platform ticket at the machine, went through the gates, then headed up the escalator. Up by the tracks, the August heat was like a steam bath. I was already sweating. After weaving through the people waiting for the next train and lined up at the kiosks, I finally found Midoriko and Makiko on a bench by the end of the platform.

"Hey!" yelled Makiko. "Look at you."

She smiled when she saw me, and I couldn't help but smile back. Midoriko, sitting beside her, was easily twice as big as I remembered her. I couldn't believe how much she'd grown.

"Midoriko!" I blurted out. "Where did these legs come from? Wow."

Hair pulled back tight in a ponytail, Midoriko was wearing a plain navy crewneck t-shirt and a pair of shorts. It could have been that she was slouching—but her legs looked way too long. I slapped her on the knee. She looked at me, embarrassed, but her mother cut in.

"I know, it's unbelievable, I can't believe how big she's getting."

Midoriko looked annoyed and turned away. She grabbed the backpack that was on the bench beside her and hugged it in her lap. Makiko looked at me with this pained expression and shrugged. That said it all.

Midoriko had not spoken to her mother in over half a year.

I had no idea why. One day, Makiko said something to her, and she didn't answer. That was it. At first she thought Midoriko was depressed, but that didn't seem to be the case. She had a healthy appetite, went to school, and talked like normal with her friends and teachers. Just not with her mom. It didn't seem like anything else was wrong. She just refused to talk at home. On purpose. Makiko had tried to figure out what was going on, treading carefully, but it was no use. Midoriko wouldn't give her any hints.

"We aren't talking. Just paper for everything."

Not long after it started, Makiko called me, exasperated, and told me what was going on.

"Paper?"

"Yeah. Pen and paper. Not talking. I mean, I still talk, but Midoriko writes me her responses. It's been like that for maybe a month now."

"A month?"

"A whole month."

"Every day?"

"At first, I didn't know what to do. I asked her a million questions but couldn't figure it out. Something happened, obviously, but she won't tell me what. Even when I yell at her, not a word. It's a pain in my ass, but apparently she talks to everybody at school like normal . . . I bet it's one of those things where kids blame everything on their parents. It's a phase. It can't last forever. It's fine, it's totally fine."

Makiko laughed into the phone, trying to sound cheerful. But now it had been half a year. This was the way things were, and there were no signs of them changing.

Dear Journal,

Today in health class we talked about "menarche." So basically, your first period. Pretty much everyone else has already had theirs, but that's what we talked about, how it works and what's happening in your body that makes you bleed. Then they told us about pads and showed us what the womb looks like. Lately, when other girls go to the bathroom, the ones who've had their period cling together and talk about things only they understand. Like they know the rest of us are listening and want for us to hear them. There must be plenty of girls who haven't had their period yet, but I feel like I'm the only one left.

I wonder what it feels like. I hear it hurts pretty bad, but that's not even the worst part. Once it starts, it keeps happening, for decades. How does that ever feel normal? I know Jun got hers. She told me. But it's weird how everyone knows I haven't. I mean, it's not like everyone goes around telling people when it happens. It's not like everyone waves around their little kits for all to see when they go to the bathroom. How can everyone just tell like that?

I was wondering about the "men" in "menarche." Turns out it's the same as the "men" in "menstruation." It means "month," which comes from "moon," and has to do with women and their monthly cycle. Moon has all kinds of meanings. In addition to being the thing orbiting the earth, it can involve time, or tides, like the ebb and flow of the ocean. So, "menarche" has absolutely nothing to do with "men." So why spell it that way? What happened to the "o"?

—Midoriko

When we started walking, I realized just how tall Midoriko was getting. She was still shorter than me, but her legs were clearly longer. I joked about how tall she was, but she just rolled her eyes and started walking behind us. Makiko was so skinny. I mean, her arms were like sticks. Her old brown overnight bag looked way too heavy. I kept reaching out to grab it, saying "I got it, Makiko," but she just said, "I'm okay, I'm okay," and wouldn't let me have it.

As far as I knew, this was Makiko's third time in Tokyo. Overstimulated, she kept on saying stuff like "Look at all the people," or "This place is huge," or "All the girls have the tiniest faces." When she almost ran somebody over, she apologized, "Sorry, sorry, sorry," way too loud. I was preoccupied with making sure Midoriko was still behind us, and I engaged with Makiko just enough to sound like I was listening—but the thing that really got me was her face.

Makiko looked old.

Everyone looks older as the years go by, but that's not what I mean. She wasn't even forty, but if she told you "I just turned fifty-three," you'd wish her happy birthday. She didn't look older. She literally looked old.

Makiko had never been curvy, but her arms and legs and hips looked way skinnier than the Makiko I knew. I guess it could have been her clothes. She wore a t-shirt she could have stolen off a girl in her mid-twenties, a pair of low-rise skinny jeans, and chunky pink mules, two inches at least. I guess she was one of those people you see a lot these days who looked young from behind, but the second that she turned around . . . Fashion faux pas aside, her face and body were way smaller than they should have been, and her skin looked a little pale. Her fake teeth were noticeably yellow, and the metal made her gums look black. Her faded perm had thinned so much that you could see the perspiration on her scalp. She was wearing way too much foundation. It made her face look washed out and more wrinkly than it was. When she laughed, the sinews of her neck popped out. Her sunken eyes called attention to their sockets.

She reminded me of Mom. I couldn't tell if it was just in the way that daughters start to look like their mothers over time, or if the things that happened to Mom's body were happening to her now, too. I can't tell you how many times I almost asked her, "Hey, how are you feeling? Are you doing okay?" but I always held off, not wanting to make her any more self-conscious. The weird part was, she had a ton of energy. She was used to her dynamic with Midoriko and talked to her like everything was okay, one-sided as it was. She gabbed away, so upbeat that it almost got to me.

"Maki," I asked, "how long do you have off?"

"Three days, including today."

"That's it?"

"We can stay tonight and tomorrow, but we've got to leave the next day, so I can get to work that night."

"Has it been busy or what?"

"I wish." Makiko groaned. "A lot of the other spots are shutting down."

Makiko was a hostess, but that can mean all kinds of different things. Some good, some not so good. Osaka is rife with drinking spots, but an address is enough to tell you what you should expect, in terms of clientele and atmosphere and host-esses.

She worked in Shobashi, the neighborhood the three of us worked in for years after we ran off that night and started our new life with Komi. There was absolutely nothing glamorous about Shobashi. Just rows of tired buildings, crooked and brown with age.

You can drink at a standing bar. You can get cheap noodles. You can sit down with a strong cup of coffee. Or you can find some company and spend your free time in one of the run-down inns more like a love shack than a love hotel. You can drink at Yakiniku restaurants that are long and narrow, shaped like trains, or at absurdly smoky Motsuyaki restaurants, by pharmacies whose jumbo signs for "DIABETES" and "HEM-ORRHOIDS" make them fit right in. No breathing room between the buildings, which means unagi restaurants rubbing shoulders with telephone clubs, and realtors sharing walls with sex shops. Busy electric signage and pachinko parlors waving banners. Seal-engraving businesses whose owners never both-ered coming in. Video arcades that looked anything but fun.

Aside from the people coming in and out or simply walking by, you'll find people slumped down motionless under the pay-phones, women who looked well into their sixties promising dances for 2,000 yen, and no shortage of vagrants and drunks, but you'll also find the whole of Osaka. Shobashi comes alive at night. From appearances, it's a dump. And from sundown to sunup, on the third floor of a building throbbing with karaoke reverb, you'll find the bar where Makiko works, five nights a week, from seven until midnight.

There are some seats at the bar and a few "box seats," which are just wrap-around sofas. Fifteen customers, and the place is packed. In one night, you'd have to really try to spend more than 10,000 yen. No one says it, but everyone knows that guests cover whatever their hostess orders, to pad their nightly sales. Since a hostess can't get shitfaced with her customers, she's supposed to stick to oolong tea. A tiny can for 300 yen. To cut corners, the bar makes their own brew, then chills it in the fridge and serves it up in empty oolong cans. When the hostess brings it to the table, she comes out with a look on her face that says, "I opened it in the kitchen right now." Once she's full of tea, she'll say, "I'm hungry," and ask her customer to order little sausages, or fried eggs, or some sardines, or fried chicken, stuff that sounds like the side dishes in a bento box, not something you'd want to snack on while sipping whisky. After that, it's time for karaoke, 100 yen a song. And all the hostesses sing, young or old, whether they can carry a tune or not. Even when the customers sing their hearts out, pushing their waterlogged and salt-clogged bodies to the limit, they usually go home spending less than 5,000 yen.

The owner of Makiko's bar was a short and heavy lady in her mid-fifties. Really nice, the one time that I met her. Her hair was dyed or bleached, more yellow than blonde, and gathered in a fat bun on her crown. Makiko told me how during her interview, this lady had asked her the funniest question, pinching a Hope cigarette between her chubby fingers.

"You know what Chanel is?"

"The brand, right?" answered Makiko.

"Yeah," she said, blowing smoke out through her nostrils. "You like Chanel?"

She pointed her jaw at the wall, where a pair of Chanel scarves hung like posters, under Plexiglas, lit up in a yellow spotlight.

"Honestly," the lady said, narrowing her eyes, "I love the stuff to death."

"So that's why you called the shop Chanel," said Makiko, admiring the noble scarves.

"Yeah. Women dream of Chanel. It's expensive stuff, though. Check out these earrings." She tilted her round chin to show Makiko an ear. Despite the flattering lighting, the ear-ring looked like it was decades old, but in its dull gold, Makiko recognized the telltale logo. She had seen it all over the bar. On the towels by the bathroom sink, on the thick paper coasters, and on the stickers slapped all over the glass door of the phonebooth in the corner. It was on their business cards, their welcome mat, and all the glasses. Apparently, everything was counterfeit, amassed over a long series of visits to the street vendors of Tsuruhashi and Minami. Even Makiko, who knew nothing about Chanel, could tell this was a bunch of crap, but this woman was seriously devoted to her collection. At the very least, the barrettes and earrings that she wore every day were the real deal. She splurged on them to commemorate the open-ing of the bar. It wasn't really Chanel she loved, so much as the sound of the word and the shape of the logo. One time, when a young girl at the bar asked, "Where was Coco Chanel from?" the lady answered "America," as if anyone who was white had to be American.

"How's Coco?" I asked Makiko.

"She's fine, never better. The shop's another story, though."

A little after two, we made it back to Minowa, the closest station to my place. Stopping along the way for a 210-yen bowl of noodles, we braved the heat and walked the ten minutes home, while the cries of cicadas smeared the atmosphere.

"You came from here to meet us?" Makiko asked.

"No, I had something else I had to do, I was already near the station. I'm just over this hill."

"Who needs a gym when you've got a hill like this?"

At first the two of us felt good enough to chat and laugh, but the heat soon got the better of us, and we stopped talking. The incessant spray of the cicadas clogged our ears, and the sunlight pinched our skin. The roof tiles and the trees and the manhole covers hummed with white-hot summer light, but the brighter it got, the darker everything appeared. By the time we made it to my apartment, the three of us were soaked in sweat.

"We made it."

Makiko sighed, and Midoriko crouched down by the potted plant at the building entrance and leaned in to get a better look at it. Then she pulled a notebook from her fanny pack and wrote [Whose plant is this?]. Her writing was oddly thick, pushed hard into the paper, like something etched in stone. It made me think of her when she was just a baby—when all she did was breathe, so tiny that she didn't seem real. It felt impossible to me back then that she would ever feed herself or write things on her own.

"I don't know. It has to be somebody's. My room's on the second floor. See that window? Upstairs and on the left."

Single file, we went up the iron stairwell scabbed with rust.

"It's not exactly spacious, but come on in."

"Hey, this is nice."

Makiko stepped out of her mules and practically skipped her way inside.

"Look at this apartment. Lucky you!"

Midoriko went straight to the back of the apartment. It was just a little kitchen and a pair of slightly larger rooms. I'd been there for nearly ten years, ever since I moved to the city.

"Did you put down the carpeting? What was it before? It wasn't wood, was it?"

"No, tatami. But it was stuffy when I got here, so I went with carpet."

Wiping the sweat from my brow with the back of my hand, I turned on the AC and brought it down to 72 degrees. Then I opened the folding tea table propped up against the wall and set down the three drinking glasses that I had I bought down the street for the occasion. Tiny grapes etched on the glass in a light purple. I filled each glass with ice-cold mugicha I made the night before. Makiko and Midoriko gulped it down like it was a race. Makiko leaned back and declared, "That's better!" I offered her the beanbag chair that had been sitting in the corner. Midoriko set her backpack in the corner and stood up. She looked around like she was on the moon. My place was nothing special. Small and underfurnished. What seemed to grab her attention was the bookshelves.

"You have so many books," said Makiko, like some sort of interpreter.

"Not really."

"Come on, this whole wall is books. Seriously, how many do you have?"

"I've never counted. A normal number, though."

To Makiko, who had never been a fan of reading, I'm sure it looked like I had tons of books, but I really didn't.

"If you say so."

"I do."

"It's kinda crazy how we're sisters. I couldn't care less about books. Midoriko reads them all the time, though. Right, Midoriko?"

No answer. Midoriko had her eyes glued to the shelves. She was reading every single spine.

"Hey," Makiko said, wiping a strand of hair stuck to her cheek behind her ear. "I know we just walked in the door, but you think I could take a shower?"

"Sure. The door for the bath's on the left. Separate from the toilet."

The whole time Makiko was in the shower, Midoriko gazed at the books. Her back was so sweaty that her navy shirt looked black. I asked her if she wanted to get changed, but after a few seconds she shook her head decisively.

I watched Midoriko browse the shelves, half-listening to the sound of running water. My apartment, so stubbornly familiar, was starting to feel like another place altogether. It felt like picking up a picture you had seen a million times and realizing it had changed entirely, without you ever noticing. I sipped my mugicha and thought about this strange sensation. But I couldn't figure out the cause of it.

Makiko emerged wearing a t-shirt with a stretched neck and a pair of baggy sweats.

"I used one of your towels," she said, patting her hair dry. When I saw her with all her makeup off, I felt a little better. On the platform, I felt like I wasn't even seeing my own sister. What a relief. I'd thought she was a walking skeleton, but she wasn't half as skinny as I'd thought. She'd worn the wrong foundation, and way too much of it. No wonder she looked pale. Maybe she hadn't really changed that much. It's just that it had been so long since I had seen her. Maybe I overreacted. It had sure been a surprise, but everyone grows old, and I started thinking that maybe she looked her age after all.

"Can I dry this somewhere? Where's your balcony?"

"I don't have one."

"You don't have one?" Makiko was baffled. Her tone made Midoriko turn around. "What kind of apartment doesn't have a balcony?"

"This kind," I laughed. "There's a railing outside the window. Don't fall."

"What do you do with your laundry?"

"We have a space for hanging laundry on the roof. Want to check it out later? Once it cools down a little. Because we're on a hill, it's actually a pretty nice view."

Makiko muttered "I bet" and reached for the remote. She switched on the TV and started flicking through the channels. First a cooking show, then an infomercial, but when she hit the news, the screen erupted. You could tell that something really bad had happened. A reporter wearing a grave expression spoke passionately into the camera, hands clamping a microphone. Behind her was a residential area, astir with paramedics and police and a plastic tarp.

"What happened?" Makiko asked me.

"No idea."

That morning, some guy had stabbed a college girl all over, not far from where she lived in Suginami. Her stomach, her chest, neck and face. The reporter said that she had made it to the hospital in critical condition, and that her lungs had stopped. She went on to explain that an hour after the attack, a man in his mid-twenties turned himself in at the nearby police station and was being questioned. Meanwhile, in a corner of the screen, they showed a recent picture of the girl who had been stabbed and displayed her full name. "Behind me," said the reporter, "You can't see it, but there's quite a bit of blood." She kept turning around. She looked nervous. A stream of police tape fluttered behind her, beyond which onlookers were taking pictures with their phones.

"Horrible," Makiko said. "Hey, didn't this just happen?"

"Yeah," I said.

Two weeks earlier, they had found what seemed to be part of a woman's body in a trash can at Shinjuku Gyoen. Pretty soon, they figured out it belonged to a seventy-year-old woman who had been missing for months, and before long they arrested an unemployed nineteen-year-old living in the area. The woman had no family. For years, she'd been living alone in a rundown apartment complex. The media went wild trying to figure out how the suspect and victim knew each other and what the motive could have been.

"That old lady, right? The one who got chopped to pieces."

"Right. They found her in the garbage at Shinjuku Gyoen."

"Shinjuku Gyoen?" asked Makiko. "Is that in Tokyo?"

"Yeah, just imagine the biggest park you've ever seen."

"The murderer was pretty young, right?"

Makiko scrunched up her face. Her voice turned pensive.

"How old was she, though? Seventy? Older? Wait, hold up.

That means she was the same age as Komi." She gasped at her own statement and opened her eyes wide. "And she was raped, right?"

"Pretty sure, yeah."

"Gives me the creeps. I mean, what if that was Komi? Who could do that to a woman the same age as Komi?"

The same age as Komi. Like all disasters, this would be old news within the hour, but Makiko's words would haunt me even after the TV was off. When Komi died, she looked her age, or even older. Which is what you would expect from someone hospitalized for cancer, but even before she got sick, Komi was old, without a doubt. I can only picture Komi as an old lady. As far as I was concerned, no part of her could be described as sexy; sex played no part in her existence. She was old. Not like I can claim to know the woman who was killed. Age is just a number; it can't tell you everything about a person. I know that this poor woman was a stranger, but the fact that she was seventy made it hard to separate her from Komi, or Komi from the rape. This really bothered me. The thought of making it to seventy, only to be raped and murdered by a teenage boy who could have been your grandson—I doubt in all her life that she imagined this would happen. Even in the moment, I bet she couldn't comprehend exactly what was happening to her. The TV anchors faced the camera and bowed. After a few commercials, a drama started—nothing new, just an old rerun.

Dear Journal,

Get this. Jun totally freaked out because she realized she's been wearing her pads backwards this whole time. OK, maybe she wasn't freaking out, not really. Part of what she said didn't make sense to me, but apparently there's a sticky part, and she had that part up against her body. I guess she didn't realize.

She knew something was wrong, though, like it wasn't absorbing properly. I bet it stung like hell to pull it off. Is that the sort of thing you can really get wrong? Is it that hard to understand?

I told Jun I'd never seen one before. She said she had tons of them at home, so we went to her house after school. The shelf above her toilet was stuffed with packs of pads. They looked like packages of diapers. We didn't have anything like that. I wasn't sure I wanted to see, but I wanted to be prepared, so I got up on the toilet seat to get a better look. There were all these different kinds, covered in discount stickers. Jun and I were talking about how you get your period because your eggs aren't fertilized, and how the puffy thing that's there to catch the fertilized eggs comes out with all the blood. Oh yeah, Jun also told me how she had been wondering if the unfertilized eggs were in the blood, so last month she picked her pad apart to see. I couldn't believe it. I gave her this horrified look and asked her what was in there, but Jun never gets upset at stuff like that. She said it was full of tiny beads, the color of blood. I asked her if they looked like little salmon eggs. She said yeah, but way, way smaller. I guess she couldn't tell if the egg was there or not.

—Midoriko

I was in the kitchen, boiling water in a stockpot for another batch of mugicha, when Midoriko came up with her notebook open.

[I'm going exploring.]

"Exploring?"

[Walking.]

"Fine by me, but let's see what Maki says, okay?"

Midoriko shrugged and sort of snorted.

"Hey Maki, Midoriko wants to go out for a walk. Is that okay?"

"I don't mind," she said from the other room. "You know how to get back? You won't get lost?"

[I won't go far.]

"You know how hot it is out there?" I asked. "What are you gonna do?"

[Go exploring.]

"Okay," I said. "Take my phone just in case. I guess you could check out the bookstore by the supermarket. Remember seeing that? There's also a boutique, or, what do they call those now? A select shop? There's a place with stationery, too. Have fun. Be careful, though. If you stand out in the sun too long, we'll have to peel you off the sidewalk. Look, here's how to redial. Press this to call your mom, okay?"

Midoriko nodded.

"And if anyone tries to talk to you, run and call us right away. Don't be long."

Midoriko slammed the door on her way out. Even though she hadn't said a thing, the room felt quieter without her. You could hear her stepping onto every stair on the way down. Further and further away, until she was gone. As if on cue, Makiko sat up from the floor and turned off the TV.

"Just like I said on the phone, right? It's been like this for months now."

"I can't believe she's kept it up." I was honestly impressed. "Half a year. But she's behaving normally at school?"

"Yeah. Right before summer vacation, I brought it up with one of her teachers. She said that she was fine. No problems with the faculty or the other kids. She asked me if I wanted her to talk to her, but I thought Midoriko would hate that, so I told her I'd just wait and see, you know?"

"Right."

"She's stubborn, huh? Like someone else you know."

"Come on," I said. "You were never that bad."

"I dunno. I was hoping she'd talk to you, literally talk. Oh well."

Makiko pulled her bag closer to her. She reached inside and pulled out a thick envelope.

"Anyway, let's talk about something else," she said and cleared her throat. "Natsuko. Check this out. That thing I mentioned on the phone . . . "

Makiko produced a colorful stack of brochures from the envelope and set it down on the table. That's when I remembered why she came to Tokyo in the first place. She sat up straight and put her hands on the stack, then looked me right in the eye.

2.
TO BE MORE BEAUTIFUL

I've been thinking about getting breast implants."

It had been three months since Makiko had called me up to make this declaration.

Initially, she asked me what I thought and actually listened to what I said, but things changed as the calls became more frequent, up to three nights a week, and always at one in the morning, after Makiko got home from work. It became increasingly clear that she wasn't looking for my opinion. She called me just to hear herself thinking out loud.

Her speeches had two refrains: "I'm gonna do it, I'm gonna get big boobs," and "Can I really go through with this?"

In the ten years I had lived in Tokyo, Makiko had rarely called me in the middle of the night, and certainly never made a habit of it. I wasn't ready for this. What was I supposed to say?

"Sure, why not," I said without much thought when she brought it up the first time, expecting that to be the end of it.

But saying "Sure, why not" opened the floodgates. It was a greenlight, and from there on out, I could barely get a word in edgewise. Meanwhile, Makiko gave me a first-class education on the state of breast augmentation surgery. Makiko explained the different costs, how and what would hurt, and all about the period of recovery that the clinics euphemized as "downtime." Now and then, we'd wind up at a kind of chorus, where Makiko became her own motivational speaker. "I can do it. I'm really gonna do it." Most of the time, though, she sounded like she was reading herself a list of all the information she'd gleaned over the course of the day.

Throughout these spirited updates, I tried remembering what Makiko's breasts were like, but kept drawing a blank. Which I suppose is only natural, since it's not like I can picture my own breasts, even though they're stuck to me. Makiko could gush forever about the ins and outs of getting implants, and share her every thought and observation, but I couldn't seem to connect Makiko with breasts, let alone breast augmentation. Listening to her talk, I felt something altogether separate from uneasiness or disinterest. I had to ask myself, "Whose breasts are we talking about right now, and why?"

Things between her and Midoriko were tense—as they had been for months. When Makiko fell into one of her "breast implant trances," I tried to snap her out of it by bringing up her daughter. But if I asked, "Hey, how's Midoriko?" she'd just say, "Yeah, she's good," in a voice that made it clear it was the last thing that she wanted to discuss.

You'd think that other things were on her mind. Makiko was going on forty. Where was her life taking her? How was she doing financially? What about her daughter? There were lots of other things she could have talked about, and all of them took precedence over the implants.

But who was I to judge? I'd moved to Tokyo so I could be alone, and I was single in the most literal way possible. I wasn't a mother. I had no right to tell her how to raise her child. If anyone was worried about Midoriko, it was obviously her mom.

I wish that she had money. Or a normal day job, something more sustainable. But if Makiko had any other choice, she wouldn't work nights at the bar or leave Midoriko alone. If she had it her way, she never would have let her daughter see her come home drunk, even if it was part of her job. She had no other prospects. Her only consolation was that she had close friends who would run over in a heartbeat if something ever happened.

But as bad as things were, I was honestly worried that things would get worse if they continued. Like working nights. As Midoriko got older, Makiko couldn't keep leaving her alone at night like that. It wasn't okay. Not by any stretch of the imagination. Things would have to change, and soon. But what else could she do?

Makiko had no skills, and it's not like I could help her out, working minimum wage. Midoriko was still a kid, and kids cost money. We had no relatives to call for help, and zero chances of marrying into money. Less than zero. Lottery odds. But there was always welfare—

We'd talked about it once, just after my move to Tokyo. Makiko got dizzy and fell, we never found out why. For weeks we thought she might have something, I mean something serious. She had to take all kinds of tests, basically living at the hospital. It completely wiped her out. When she couldn't make it into work, she lost her source of income. So we had to have a conversation about how to make ends meet for the foreseeable future.

"What about welfare?" I tried getting her to view this as an option, but Makiko wasn't having it. She actually resented me for making the suggestion, and we wound up saying some pretty mean things to each other. Makiko had decided "going on welfare" was something to be ashamed of. She thought that welfare made you some kind of a parasite, who leeched off of the government and put a burden on society—convinced it somehow marred your human dignity.

I saw things differently. To me welfare was just money, plain and simple, and had nothing to do with shame or dignity. I asked her what the government was for, if not to help you out in times of need. When things got rough, you ought to step right up and exercise your rights. It's called welfare for a reason.

But Makiko wasn't buying it. In tears, she told me it would undo all the work she'd done thus far in life. She cried and said she'd never asked for handouts, just worked as hard as she could, morning, noon and night. I stopped trying to tell her otherwise. Her tests all came back negative, and thanks to the money the bar had floated her, in no time things were back to normal. But normal was a far cry from sustainable.

"This is the place I'm thinking of getting them done."

Makiko showed me the first brochure in the stack.

"Trust me, I made the rounds in Osaka, and talked with all the different clinics, but this place is my number one."

I can't even tell you how many brochures she had. All shapes and sizes. She must have had well over thirty. Makiko still didn't own a computer. The thought of her locating all these different clinics without using the internet was so depressing I decided not to ask how she had done it. I held off on her top pick for the moment and flipped through some of the other brochures, more interested in all the clinics that had failed to meet her standards. Most of them had white girls with blonde hair on the front, wearing almost nothing, to give you an idea of what breasts looked like, and were embellished with pink ribbons or nice floral designs.

"I have my consultation tomorrow. Highlight of my summer. I brought these along to give you an idea of the process. I have way more back at home, but these were the best."

Inside one of the brochures, I found a doctor in a white coat staring back at me, with a deranged smile on his face. Even scaled down to this size, his teeth looked eerily white. The words "Experience is everything" were written in big letters over his head. I must have been staring, because Makiko said, "Forget that, look at this," and passed me the brochure for the clinic she had chosen.

"This is a clinic?" I asked. "Looks more like a luxury spa."

The brochure for her favorite place was glossy black,

printed on thick card stock. It had something the other brochures lacked. You could say it looked expensive, but I thought it looked aggressive. The lettering was thick and gold. No trace of the cutesy, happy, undemanding purity normally found in ads for clinics geared toward average women. Its style evoked all the drama of the red-light district and those who make their living there. Breast augmentation surgery is no simple affair. A woman has all kinds of questions, so you'd expect a bit more levity, a gentler touch, a sense of understanding, even if it's just for show. What would possess someone to go under the knife at a clinic with brochures that look like pamphlets for a VIP nightclub? My imagination got the better of me, but Makiko ignored my silence and went on.

"Like I told you on the phone, there are different ways to do it. Basically, though, you have three options. Remember?"

I was about to say no, but forced a nod.

"First, there's silicone. Then hyaluronic acid. Or they can take the fat from somewhere on your body and use that. Silicone's definitely the most popular. You get the best results, too, but it's also the most expensive. Here, this is silicone, see?"

Makiko tapped her nails against the photographs of flesh-tone silicone arrayed on the obsidian paper.

"The pouches come in different kinds, too. This is what I wanted to show you. Every clinic says something a little different, which makes it hard to choose, but this is the big one, the top of the line. Silicone gel, 100%. They call the next one gummy bear implants. Anyway, this one's a little bit more rigid than the gel type, so it's more resistant to leakage, but even if it ruptures, it's perfectly safe. It just looks a little hard. Some people think it looks unnatural. Then there's saline. The best part about saline is that they don't fill the bags until they're inside, so they can make a smaller cut. But most people get silicone gel. It's the future. So yeah, I've given it a lot of thought, and I want to go with silicone. This place is only 1,500,000 yen for both breasts. With general anesthetic, it's just another 10,000."

When she was finished, Makiko made this face like she was asking "Well?" and stared at me. At first, I just stared back, wondering why she was looking at me like that, but then I realized she had stopped so that I could share my thoughts. "Wow," I said, trying to smile. She was still staring, so I added, "1,500,000 yen though? That's a lot of money!" This wasn't so much an opinion as a fact, but as soon as I'd said it, I worried that I'd said the wrong thing.

I mean, 1,500,000 yen is serious cash. Hard to fathom. Neither of us had that kind of money. It didn't even sound like a real number. She said 1,500,000 like it was nothing, but I worried that the way I'd said it made it sound like it was too much for her breasts—I'd asked her "Are you really worth that much? Are your breasts worth that kind of an investment?" Which would have been a valid question, but I tried my best to sound supportive.

"Well, I dunno," I said. "I mean, it's a lot of money, but it's your body, right? Too bad that insurance doesn't cover it, but . . . maybe it's not so bad!"

"That's how I feel." Makiko smiled and nodded slowly, before continuing in a gentler voice. "Look at this one, Natsuko. The brochure says 450,000 yen, right? But when you actually show up at the clinic, there's no way that's all you're paying for. Their whole strategy is to get you in the door. Once you're there, things add up. Plus, if you go with the promo prices they list in the brochures, you can't even choose your own surgeon. Chances are good they'll hand you off to some twenty-two-year-old with no experience. There's a lot to keep in mind . . . It's a real long process we're talking about here, a real journey."

Makiko paused and closed her eyes, then opened them and looked at me.

"Yeah, at the end of the day, I decided this was the one! These things go wrong all the time. Outside the city, women don't have many options, so they go where they can. Those small-town doctors don't get enough practice, and it really is all about experience, you know? That's why people who are serious, and people who have their breasts redone come here, all of them."

"I hear you . . . but Maki, look. This one says that hylo, uh, hyaluronic acid is a simple injection. And the brochure says it's natural. That means no surgery, no cutting. Why can't you do that one?"

"The thing about hyaluronic acid is your body sucks it up and then it's gone." She pursed her lips. "For 800,000 yen? No thanks. You're right, though. It doesn't leave any scars. It doesn't even hurt. Honestly, it would be the best thing ever, if it lasted. It's more for models or celebrities. For those big moments when they need a little extra. It's more expensive in the long run, though."

It seemed like she had committed the entire brochure to memory. She didn't even look at the thing as she walked me through the cons.

"You see the part about the fat injections?" she asked. "The only reason they say they're safe is because the fat comes from your own body, but they still have to open all these holes in you. And they do it with the biggest needle that you've ever seen. It takes time and a whole lot of anesthetic. Seriously, they mess you up to make it happen. You know those power tools they use for ripping up the pavement? It's like that, but your body's the construction site. No joke. Things can go seriously wrong. Sometimes people die. Besides," Makiko tried to keep smiling, "I don't have any fat to spare."

After months of listening to this stuff on the phone, I was pretty sure I got the gist of it but hearing Makiko in person made me see things differently. It actually made me sad. It was the same feeling you get at a train station, or in a hospital, or on the street, when you stop a safe distance away from someone who can't seem to help but talk and talk, whether or not anyone is there to listen. Watching Makiko carry on like that, that's how I felt. It's not like I didn't care about Makiko or what she had to say, or like I didn't feel for her. But I realized I was taking pity on her in a way that had nothing to do with any of those things, and it made me feel guilty. Without thinking about it, I started picking at the skin of my lip with a fingernail, and when I licked my lips, I tasted blood.

"Oh, that reminds me. This is really important. They can put the silicone in two different ways. You have to choose. If you go with under the muscle, under the fat, it's way down there, so it's harder to tell that you had them done. The other one's way shallower. Just under the mammary glands. That one's easier on the body, and it's faster, but it's not a good idea for someone as skinny as me. Okay, you know how some women have these boobs that look like they've been sucked out with a plunger? You know what I mean? No meat anywhere else on their body, just the boobs. I can't do that. It looks so fake. So I made up my mind. I have to go under the muscle. At least I think that's what I'm going to do."

Dear Journal,

Once I start getting my period, every month, until it stops, blood is going to come out of my body. It's terrifying. I can't do anything to stop it from happening, though. I don't have pads at home, either. Just thinking about it is upsetting.

When it happens, I'm not going to tell Mom. I'll hide it. In most books where a girl "gets" her first period (they always make it sound like it's some kind of present), there's always this scene where the girl is like, great, now I can be a mom, thanks for having me, Mom, I'm a part of the circle of life now, I'm so happy. The first time I saw a story like that, I couldn't believe my eyes.

The girl is always overjoyed. She goes to her mom with a huge smile on her face. She tells her it happened, and the mom smiles back and says now you're a woman, congratulations. Please.

In some of those stories, the girls tell their families, or their classmates. There's one where the mom makes red rice and they eat it as a family, but that's going way too far. It feels like the books are trying way too hard to make it look like a good thing. These books are for girls who haven't had their period yet, right? It seems like all they wanna do is make girls think it's all going to be fine.

The other day at school, between classes, I forget who, but someone was saying, "I was born a girl, so yeah I definitely want to have a baby of my own eventually." Where does that come from, though? Does blood coming out of your body make you a woman? A potential mother? What makes that so great anyway? Does anyone really believe that? Just because they make us read these stupid books doesn't make it true. I hate it so much.

It feels like I'm trapped inside my body. It decides when I get hungry, and when I'll get my period. From birth to death, you have to keep eating and making money just to stay alive. I see what working every night does to my mom. It takes it out of her. But what's it all for? Life is hard enough with just one body. Why would anyone ever want to make another one? I can't even imagine why anyone would bother, but people think it's the best thing ever. Do they, though? I mean, have they ever

BREASTS AND EGGS · 45

really thought about it? When I'm alone and thinking about this stuff, it makes me so sad. At least for me, I know it's not the right thing.

Once you get your period, that means your body can fertilize sperm. And that means you can get pregnant. And then we get more people, thinking and eating and filling up the world. It's overwhelming. I get a little depressed just thinking about it. I'll never do it. I'll never have children. Ever.

—Midoriko

3.
WHOSE BOOBS ARE THEY?

Before we knew it, it had been almost an hour. Having apparently said all she had to say, and shared all she had to share, Makiko lovingly collected the brochures strewn all across the tea table, slipped the stack into its envelope, and stashed it in her overnight bag.

The clock said four, but the window was a flume of sunshine.

Beyond the glass, the entire world was seething with white light. The windshield of the red car parked in the lot across the way reflected the brightness like a pool of water. Light spilled off every surface. The light of day. I meditated on this phrase and stared into the radiance. At the far end of the street, I saw a tiny version of Midoriko, approaching with her head down. As she got closer, she looked up, like she was looking at me, so I gave her a big wave. For just a second, Midoriko froze and raised her hand, to show that she had noticed me, but then she dropped her head again and kept on walking, getting bigger with every step.

Makiko was in Tokyo for the consultation she had scheduled for the next day. That was the only thing she had on her mind. She had to leave a little before noon, which meant that I was watching Midoriko for the day. For ages, I'd been sitting on two free tickets to the amusement park, good for all the rides, which I'd been given as a freebie by this nice woman from the newspaper, but would a sixth-grade girl be into that? What was Midoriko into? All I knew is what Makiko had said, that she liked reading, but since she wasn't even talking, I wasn't sure if I could get her to physically agree to go with me. That woman from the paper was so nice. I still remember the way she smiled and said, "We don't sell newspapers. We spread the word." She told me that the newspaper was always looking to hire women, and that if I joined the team, I would probably make more money than whatever else it was that I was doing.

But that was tomorrow. We could worry about tomorrow when it came. What mattered most right now is how we would spend the remainder of today, even if it was half over. I'd figured we'd eat dinner at the Chinese restaurant around the corner, but we had a good three hours to kill before then. A whole lot of time. Makiko settled in to watch some more TV, with her head resting on the beanbag and one leg over her overnight bag. When Midoriko came inside, she sat down in the corner and started writing something in a notebook. According to Makiko, ever since Midoriko stopped talking, she never went anywhere without both of her notebooks. The first and smaller one was for answering people, but the second one was like a normal notebook, only thicker. From the way she was writing, it had to be something like a diary.

I didn't know what to do with myself, so I wiped down the tea table, then took a peek at the ice tray, which couldn't possibly be frozen yet, since I'd just filled it when I made the second batch of mugicha. Then I picked some lint off of the carpet. Makiko had made herself at home, just leaning back and laughing at the TV screen. Midoriko was focused on her writing. I could tell she felt relaxed, relatively speaking. No reason that we had to do something before dinner. This was plenty. We had tons of time. We may as well just do our own thing, each of us on our own. That was normal enough. Or at least, it was more comfortable that way. I decided to pick up the novel I was reading, but once I sat down and opened to the page where I'd left off, I couldn't concentrate, probably because of the company. I tried reading one line, then another, and even turned the page, but the words looked like nothing but meaningless patterns. I was all too conscious that the story wasn't taking shape. I gave up and put the book back on the shelf.

"Hey Maki, wanna check out the bathhouse?"

"Is it close?"

"Just around the corner," I said. "That way we can get all cleaned up before dinner."

Midoriko had been in her own world, absorbed in her writing, but now she popped her head up, grabbed the smaller notebook, and wrote [I'm not going] like she meant it. Makiko, who watched her from the corner of her eye, declined to comment, but turned to me and said, "Sounds good to me. Let's go."

I packed a plastic basin with everything we needed for the baths, including a couple of towels, and stuffed everything in a jumbo vinyl shoulder bag.

"Midoriko, you sure you don't wanna come?"

I knew she wouldn't, but figured I should ask again, just in case. She clenched her lips as tight as she could and nodded once, to make herself clear.

Night came, settling with the heat, and cast some things in stark relief and others into shadow. The world was saturated with regret and consolation, people and things that went before. As we walked along, something was asking me if I planned to keep on going, or if I'd finally had enough. Not like the world actually cared. This was nothing more than self-absorption. Narcissism. It was my dream to make a living as a writer, but was this tendency of mine to come up with sentimental narratives everywhere I went helping me or getting in my way? I honestly had no idea. Would I ever? I had no way of knowing.

The bathhouse was a ten-minute walk. This used to be our routine. Most nights, and sometimes on Sunday morning, Makiko and I would walk like this, two sisters heading to the baths. It felt more like we were going out to have some fun. And it was fun. We'd run into some girls we knew from down the street and play around in the baths for hours. Makiko and I were inseparable. I used to ride all over Osaka on the back of her bike. Since she was so much older, you'd think it'd be annoying, but Makiko never made me feel like she was hanging out with me just because she had to watch her little sister. I remember going by the park at night once, when she was still in high school, and seeing her just sitting on a bench, alone. We never talked about it, but I think Makiko always felt much more comfortable around younger kids than anyone her own age. What had come over me? The whole day I'd been running through old memories, getting lost in my own thoughts. But I guess that made sense. It was only natural. Despite Makiko being, in the present tense, my closest living relative, the bulk of our shared experiences were in the past, from another planet. In that sense, spending time with Makiko meant living in the past. Not like anyone had said this was a problem, but I couldn't stop myself from making up excuses.

"This isn't the way we went earlier, is it?"

"Nope, the station's down there."

The streets were empty. Along the way, we only saw one lady lugging groceries and a couple of old folks who were moving as slowly as turtles. The bathhouse was surrounded by homes, and the entrance was down an alley. I'd lived here for months before I even realized it was there. People in Osaka are always saying "Don't waste your time on bathhouses outside of Kansai." Which is a bit ridiculous. Still, most of the baths that I'd been to at that point in Tokyo were less than stellar, so I didn't get my hopes up, but when I checked this place out, I was pleasantly surprised. I mean, they had four giant bathtubs, plus another in the courtyard, and even had a proper sauna and a cold-water bath. I'm sure that all the homes in the area had their own bathtubs, and if people wanted a more luxurious bathing experience, there were fancier places they could go. It made you wonder how a place like this could stay in business, but all the times I went, it was packed. It reminded me of just how many people lived around here. Two years back, they went through an extensive renovation, and that was it. People from the surrounding area, and bathhouse maniacs from all over, started coming out in droves. The walls of the spacious front room were decorated with all kinds of crafts and dolls and photographs of the people who had made them, which made it hard to tell if they were slightly famous or lived nearby and did this as a hobby. Whatever the case, the bathhouse had become a local institution.

On a summer evening, an hour or two before dinnertime, you'd think it would be empty, but it was like the place was subject to entirely different forces than the lonely streets outside.

"This place is crowded."

"Yeah, people love it here."

"Everything looks so new. And clean."

A mom patted her baby dry at a changing table set up in the corner. Little kids darted around. Talking heads were nodding comprehendingly on a brand-new flatscreen, behind a chorus of hairdryers. The manager said hello from her perch between the changing rooms. Grandmas with stooped backs shared a couple of laughs. Women with towels wrapped around their heads sat naked on rattan chairs and chatted—the room was full of women. We found ourselves a pair of open lockers and undressed.

I couldn't care less how Makiko looked naked. I really didn't care. Still, regardless of my interest level, it felt like it was my responsibility to ascertain the situation. For months, the question of breast implants, and of course Makiko's breasts, had been central to our every conversation. I owed this to her, as her sister. Breast implants and Makiko's breasts . . . I had a hard time linking these two thoughts. I had to confront the problem at the source—the breasts she so desperately wanted to enlarge. What were we dealing with here? Like I said, back when we used to live together, Makiko and I were at the bath-house all the time, but I couldn't for the life of me remember what her boobs were like.

She undressed, back turned toward me, and stuffed her clothes inside the locker. I managed to sneak a few glances. She looked twice as skinny without clothes on—which distracted me enough I forgot all about her breasts.

From behind, I could see between her thighs where they should have pressed together. If she bent forward, her verte-brae and ribs, and the section of her pelvis just above her hips, poked out through her skin. My jaw dropped. Her shoulders were gaunt, her neck was thin, making her head look enor-mous. I had to look away.

"Let's go in," Makiko said, holding a towel to her chest.

She pulled back the sliding door into the bathing area, and we stepped into a wall of steam that soaked us instantly. The baths were just as crowded as the changing room, filled with a smell that can only be described as the aroma of the baths. At intervals we'd hear an echo bouncing off the cavernous ceiling, a sound you only ever hear inside a bathhouse. Each time it made me think of a huge version of the bamboo fountains that they have in gardens, the ones that fill with water until the pipe swings down with a hollow clack, except the one I was imag-ining was hitting a bare scalp. On stools by the wall of mirrors, women leaned forward to wash their hair. Others sat waist-deep in the tubs and chatted. Mothers called their kids back as they ran across the tiled floor. It was a room of bodies, coming and going, soaking wet and rosy from the heat.

After bringing stools and basins over to the mirrors, we had a seat and doused ourselves with steaming water, before heading to the hottest tub, where a panel gave the temperature as "104°" in red alarm-clock digits. Everybody knows you're not supposed to wear a towel in the bathtub, but Makiko didn't seem to care. She dunked herself into the water, her towel draped across her chest.

She turned to me and asked, "You call this hot? Is this what baths are like here?"

"Maybe it's not as hot as it says."

"Not even close. It doesn't even feel like it's a bath."

Without the slightest hesitation, Makiko scanned the bodies of the other women in the room, as if devouring them, especially the ones who stepped into the tub. It was embarrassing to sit beside her, to the point I wound up whispering, "Stop it, Maki," but I seemed to be the only one concerned that one of them might take offense. She barely answered me. She didn't care. At some point, I gave up and joined in her evaluation of the women in the room.

"So I was thinking about airplanes . . . "

I tried bringing up something entirely unrelated to the current setting, to take Makiko's mind off of the naked women. It's weird to think how safe airplanes supposedly are, out of all the ways to get around—so safe that you could probably live your whole life in the sky, from the second your mom has you till the day you die, say ninety years, and never fall. But even if it's not all that likely, airplanes still fall from the sky. How are we supposed to reconcile this risk against reality? I tried to get an answer out of Makiko, but she couldn't care less. And that was the end of that conversation. For a second, I thought about bringing up Midoriko, but decided that would be going too far; I didn't want to provoke her.

Just then, an old lady opened the sliding door. She moved so slowly you would almost think she was subjected to a different law of gravity. Hunching her fleshy body, she worked her way across the room and past our tub, lumbering like an elderly rhinoceros. It took her forever to reach the door at the back, leading to the bath outside.

"Did you see that woman's nipples?" Makiko asked.

"No, why?"

"They were really something." Makiko let out a reverent sigh. "It's a miracle for Asians to be born with nipples that pink."

"Really?"

"And with tips the same color as the areolas."

"Oh, yeah," I said, unsure of what to say.

"You know, these days you can use chemicals to lighten the skin and make it pink, but what's the point?"

"What chemicals?"

"First you use Tretinoin, to peel the skin off. After that, you use this bleach called hydroquinone."

"Wait, you peel the skin off?"

"It's not that kind of peeling. That's what the tret is for. It flakes off. It's a serious chemical peel."

"Wait, so first you peel, then you bleach?"

"Uh-huh."

"And that's what makes them pink?"

"Well, for a little while, yeah," Makiko said, with a faraway look in her eye. "But the dark skin comes from melanin, and that's in your genes. The hydro wipes the melanin out, but it'll always come back."

"Cells are always replacing cells."

"Yeah, exactly. See how hers were brown? You can make that less brown with the bleach, but it'll always come back. From the inside out. Because the melanin is always there. You can't change that, so if you want to keep your skin that way you have to make tret and hydro a part of your routine, but who can keep that up? I sure couldn't."

"Wait, you tried?"

"Yeah," she said, pressing her chest through the submerged towel. "It hurt like hell, too."

"Like hell? It hurt? Your nipples?"

"Yeah. Breastfeeding wasn't any better, though. I thought I was gonna die. It was just sucking and biting and blood and pus. All day long. I don't even want to think about it."

"Yikes."

"Your nipples burn like crazy. From the tret."

"They burn?"

"When you get out of the bath and brush it on, your nipples burn like you wouldn't believe. For an hour, at least. And once that calms down, you have to do the hydro, which makes them itch real bad. But you gotta do it every day."

"Did it work though?"

"Yeah, I guess," Makiko said. "After like three weeks or so. It was crazy, though."

"It better work," I said. "After that ordeal."

"I mean, they were definitely pinker. They were beautiful. I'd go into stores and use their dressing rooms just to look at my own nipples. That part was heaven. It's just . . . "

"What?"

"I couldn't keep it up." She shook her head, making a face like she had eaten something rotten. "First off, it's expensive. And the pain. I mean, it's torture. You need to keep all that stuff in your fridge, too. I couldn't stay on top of that. Worst part is, there's a good chance that you'll adjust to hurting all the time just as the chemicals stop being effective. Anyway, yeah, I had to stop. Three months was all I could take. I looked at my nipples, and somehow convinced myself that they were going to stay like that. Like, what if I was the exception, the only person on earth who could do it for a few months and keep my nipples pink forever? Of course, as soon as I stopped, everything went back to normal."

It appeared that the preoccupation, or shame, or insatiable curiosity that drove Makiko to fixate on her breasts was about more than size alone. Color was a major factor. I tried to imagine Makiko getting out of the bath, whatever time that was for her, and heading over to the fridge to grab the two small bottles of medicine, which she proceeded to apply to her own nipples, making them burn and itch like hell. These days even high schoolers are getting plastic surgery, so some people must think burning your nipples is a tiny price to pay, but this was my own sister. What had possessed Makiko to do this, at this stage in her life?

Not like I don't have hang-ups, or at least a lack of confidence, when it comes to my own breasts. *I'd be lying if I said it hadn't crossed my mind.*

I remember what it felt like when my breasts started getting bigger. How out of nowhere I had grown these things. It was incredible how much they hurt back then if anything bumped into them. As a kid, whenever I saw the naked women in the magazines that the kids in the neighborhood got their hands on, or saw a grownup woman expose her body on TV, I guess on some level I thought that someday all those parts of me would fill out, too, and I would have a body just like them.

Except that never happened. My monolithic expectation of what a woman's body was supposed to look like had no bearing on what actually happened to my body. The two things were wholly unrelated. I never became the woman I imagined. And what was I expecting? The kind of body that you see in girly magazines. A body that fit the mold of what people describe as "sexy." A body that provokes sexual fantasy. A source of desire. I guess I could say that I expected my body would have some sort of value. I thought all women grew up to have that kind of body, but that's not how things played out.

People like pretty things. When you're pretty, everybody wants to look at you, they want to touch you. I wanted that for myself. Prettiness means value. But some people never experience that personally.

I was young once, but I was never pretty. When something isn't there, inside or out, how are you supposed to seek it out? Pretty faces, gorgeous skin. The sort of shapely breasts that anyone would kill for. I had nothing of the sort. I gave up wishing I could look like that a million years ago.

What was up with Makiko? What made her so enthusiastic about implants? Why did she want to make her nipples pink? Try as I may, I couldn't think up a good reason. Not that she needed one. Wanting to be beautiful was reason enough.

Beauty meant that you were good. And being good meant being happy. Happiness can be defined all kinds of ways, but human beings, consciously or unconsciously, are always pulling for their own version of happiness. Even people who want to die see death as a kind of solace, and view ending their lives as the only way to make it there. Happiness is the base unit of consciousness, our single greatest motivator. Saying "I just want to be happy" trumps any other explanation. But who knows. Maybe Makiko had a more specific reason, not just some vague idea of how to make herself happy.

Both of us were spaced out. When I checked the clock hung high up on the wall, I realized we'd been in for fifteen minutes. The bath was decently comfortable, but like Makiko said, it wasn't the kind of heat that warms you to the bone. Tepid enough I could have stayed in there for another hour, maybe two.

When I checked to see if Makiko was still sizing up the other women, I caught her staring so hard she was scowling.

"You're right, Maki, this isn't hot at all," I said. "You ready to get out?"

" . . . I'm good," she muttered, apparently transfixed.

"Maki?"

When I said her name, Makiko shot up—sending water

everywhere. She pulled off the damp towel and pointed her bare chest at me. In a low voice that made her sound like some kind of martial artist, she asked me: "Well?"

"Well what?"

"The color, the shape."

Some words came to mind—small and dark, but big in their own way—but I held off. What would the other bathers think of this exchange? Two women splashing in the tub, one glowering over the other with her arms akimbo, like a warrior. The best I could do was nod repeatedly.

"Okay, forget about the size. I already know that," she said. "What about the color? Do they look dark to you? How dark? Tell me the truth."

"They're not dark, not at all," I said without thinking, or even meaning what I said, but Makiko had more questions.

"So they're basically normal?"

"Well, like, what's normal?"

"You know, whatever normal is to you."

"I don't think that's going to tell you what you want to know, though, if I'm just talking about what normal is to me."

"Come on, just tell me," she said plainly, leaving me little choice but to respond.

"Well, I wouldn't call them pink."

"I don't need you to tell me they're not pink."

"Oh, right."

"Right."

The next several minutes, we were quiet. My eyes may have been gazing off into the distance, but the image of Makiko's breasts had burned into my mind's eye. I kept imagining her breasts and her nipples rising up—in slow motion—from the surface of water, like Nessie, or a submarine.

Her breasts themselves were little more than a couple of mosquito bites, but her nipples were like two control knobs stuck onto her chest. Or like a pair of rubber tires on their sides. And the color. Imagine the softest pencil you could find—I guess that would be a 10B. Now imagine really bearing down with it and blacking out two little circles. These nipples were that dark. Darker than you're thinking—all questions of physical attractiveness aside, I thought that they could stand to be a little lighter.

"They're dark," she said. "I know. They're dark and they're big. No need to say it. I know they're not pretty."

"Everyone sees these things differently, though. Plus, it's not like we're white or anything. Of course they won't be pink." I tried to make it sound as if I didn't care about her nipples or their color, but Makiko's sigh told me I had failed.

"They weren't always like this," she assured me. "Not until I had a kid. Maybe they haven't changed that much. I don't know. But seriously, they were nowhere near this bad. I mean, what the hell are these? A couple of Oreos? Not even. More like black cherries. Black mixed with too much red. But these are worse than a couple of black cherries. They're the color of a flatscreen after you turn it off. The other day, I was shopping, and I saw one and I was like, shit, I know that color. Where have I seen that before? Oh, right. My nipples.

"And don't even get me started on how big they are. Even the doctor said, 'I'm not sure your baby will be able to fit her mouth around these.' No joke. And this is an expert. Do you know how many thousands of boobs this guy's seen? Then there's the fact that they're flat as pancakes. Or the plastic baggies they put goldfish in at festivals. Know how they're only half full? Like that. They're deflated. Everyone's different after childbirth. Some people go back the way they were, some people never even change. But me, I ended up like this."

The two of us were quiet for a while. Letting her words sink in, I thought about the temperature of the water. It couldn't possibly be over 100 degrees. The temperature display must have been busted. Then I thought about Makiko's nipples.

There was a lot going on with my Loch Ness Monster metaphor, but if forced to sum up what her nipples looked like in a single word, what would I say? I guess "strong" is the only word that did them justice. I could have told her, "Maki, your nipples look strong." But would she take that as a compliment? I doubt it. But what's wrong with having strong nipples? Or dark nipples, for that matter? Who wants their nipples to be cute or pretty? You'd think that, in the world of nipples, it'd be the strong, dark, big ones that would reign supreme. Maybe someday they'll have their moment. But probably not.

As I was wondering about this, the door rumbled open. I looked up and saw a pair of women—or so I thought, but something about them was off. One of them, who looked like she was in her twenties, had a typical woman's body, but the other one was something else. She had to be a man.

The one, still wearing makeup, whose slender neck and curves and blonde hair reaching down her back were unmistakably feminine, looped her arm around the bicep of the other—who had a guy's haircut and a thick chest that was basically flat, and a towel pressed over her crotch.

I didn't know if this was their first visit to the bathhouse, or if they'd been here before. All I knew was that I'd never seen either of them. All the other bathers tensed up, too. The place went painfully quiet, but the two of them didn't seem to notice. The blonde snuggled up to the tomboy, saying things like, "Ugh, maybe I should have put my hair up," but the tomboy plopped down at the edge of the tub, leaning slightly forward as she nodded.

They seemed to be a couple, but I couldn't be sure. From the looks of it, though, they were boyfriend and girlfriend.

I tried seeing what the tomboy had between her legs, but the way she held her towel made it impossible to tell. The two of them snuggled up on the edge of our tub, dipping their feet in the water. I knew it was none of my business, but I couldn't let it go, so now and then I'd pretend to stretch my arms and neck to try and catch a glimpse.

Was the tomboy actually a woman? I mean, this was the women's side of the bathhouse. If you tried hard you could find traces of a woman's body in her pink nipples, quite the contrast to her bulging shoulders, and there was something to the softness of her skin. At the very least, she was doing a great job of acting male.

In Shobashi, there were a million kinds of bars, including the onabe bars, where the hosts were born as women, but identified as men, and dressed like men, and interacted with their customers as men. The ones who were straight dated women, as guys. But Osaka is a big place. At the fancy clubs in Kitashinchi, the hostesses were of a different caliber, and your bill always had an extra zero at the end. At certain bars, you could find women who had had their breasts removed, lowered their voices by taking hormones, dyed their facial hair black, and even changed their genitalia. Or so I hear. Meanwhile, at the onabe bars back in Shobashi, no one had the money for all that. No one could afford to go all out. Plenty of people wished they could, but most of them had to settle for tying back or taping down their breasts, putting on a suit, gelling their hair, and acting like men, or like themselves. Whenever one of these hosts showed up with a customer—the sight of them gave me a feeling that I never got from any of the women at our bar. I guess it was a kind of femininity. It could have been their shoulders or their curves. Honestly, I'm not sure what made me feel this way, but this femininity, there's no other way to say it, always felt way stronger than what I picked up from the average woman. Staring at this tomboy's body, seated right across from me, the feeling that I'd felt so clearly but had never, until now, been able to articulate—this "femininity" I had never sensed from my own body, or from Makiko, or from our mother or my friends, felt like it was radiating from the tomboy.

It's not like I'd never met someone like this before, but it was my first time being naked with them, sharing the same tub. Soon it hit me—the crowded room had cleared considerably. Makiko and I were the only ones actually sitting in the water.

I started getting nervous. I knew that the tomboy had to be a woman, and that she belonged here on the women's side. But nothing about this situation felt remotely natural. I mean, I was seriously uncomfortable. Or could it be that I was wrong to feel this way? Should someone who acts like one of the guys be allowed on the women's side? If she identified as a man, was it alright for her to hang out naked, in a room of naked women?—But no, I had it backwards. The tomboy obviously had no problem with this arrangement. The real question was, "Is it okay for us to be naked in front of them?"

If she identified as male, and she was straight, that made her the opposite sex, even if she had no interest in our bodies. What made this any different from a "normal" guy being on the women's side? I sank down up to my chin and leered at the tomboy. What had started off as nervousness had lapsed into irritation. What business did a straight couple have barging into the women's side of the bathhouse? It wasn't right.

I seriously considered whether I should give the tomboy a piece of my mind. It was obviously a touchy subject, and I had no idea how things would play out. I'd have to be an idiot to invite that sort of mayhem into my life. I didn't need that, but I had a history of asking for it anyway—once I got stuck on something, wondering "Why is this happening," I couldn't seem to shake it, and wound up saying something anyway. It's not like it happened all the time, and it had basically no impact on my social life. It was just a tendency of mine. When I was in primary school, I wound up on a train with a bunch of people from some cult, on their way home from a gathering, and got in a huge fight with them when they came at me, all smiles, preaching about truth and the existence of a God (although by the time we were finished, they were smiling out of pity), and another time, in high school, after sitting through an outdoor demonstration by a group of nationalists, I called them out on all their contradictions, only for them to ask me if I'd join their side. Wondering what would happen if I spoke up to the tomboy, I sank up to my nose and ran through it in my head.

—Sorry to bother you, but I'm dying to know . . . are you a man?

—And who the fuck might you be?

Hold up. This isn't Osaka, and not every guy with a nice body and an icy gaze talks like he's about to rip your head off. My prejudice had biased my imagination. On both sides. I couldn't start things off that way. So how was I supposed to address the tomboy without insulting her, and get my point across, and find out what I wanted to know? Concentrating my awareness on my frontal lobe, I rubbed my thoughts together with ferocious speed, like a person rubbing sticks together to make fire, and waited for the smoke to trickle from the wood. Under the assumption that the tomboy was a decent person, I tried to think up a scenario where I'd say one thing and she'd respond agreeably, after which I'd make a joke and we would start a conversation, but then I noticed her checking me out.

I was the one with the questions. Why look at me? Was she so pissed that she was gonna deck me? The thoughts kept coming, but I couldn't look away. That's when I sensed something separate from her gaze, something inside of her. Whatever it was, it felt like it was pressing me. It went beyond unease and agitation. It was staring me down. The blonde said something funny. The tomboy turned to her and laughed. Seeing that side of her face—a voice inside my head asked, "Is that Yamagu?"

I called her Yamagu, but her full name was, hold on. Right, Chika—Chika Yamaguchi. We went to elementary school together. For a while we were best friends. Yamagu. She was popular, but not that popular. Her mother ran a little cake shop, by the bridge over the canal, where we used to hang out. Sometimes her mom made us snacks. When you opened the door, this sweet air swallowed you. A couple of times we waited for the grownups to go home and snuck back into the kitchen. The place was stuffed with shiny metal egg beaters, cake pans in all different shapes and sizes, and what looked like spatulas. The mixing bowls were always full of white or faintly yellow creamy substances that crested like the sea. One time, when it was just the two of us back there, Yamagu grinned at me, like this would be our little secret, poked her finger in a bowl and let me lick it. She always kept her hair short, and in sixth grade, she beat all the other students in the class at arm wrestling. She had thick eyebrows and chiseled features. I can still picture how she used to curl her upper lip whenever she smiled.

When I blurted out, "What are you doing here?" Yamagu worked the muscles of her shoulders, as if to say hello. At the sight of her complexion—the smell of custard cream enveloped me, and the two of us were peering over the rim of that gigantic bowl. It was hard to tell, by sight alone, whether the stuff inside the bowl was soft, what it would feel like. Yamagu dipped a finger in. I could taste the flavor that I knew so well. It spread over my tongue. Yamagu looked at me in silence. I tried saying, "Since when were you a man? I had no idea," but she didn't answer, just flexed her muscles. Then the bulging flesh sheared off, coming free like a hunk of dough, which morphed before my eyes into a bunch of tiny people. They ran over the water, skating across the tiles, whooping their way up and down the naked bodies of the bathers, like kids monkeying through a playground. Meanwhile, the real Yamagu had wrapped the hem of her shirt around the horizontal bar and was doing feet first somersaults ad infinitum.

I caught a stray homunculus by the neck and tickled him. I told him that he shouldn't be there. This bath was for women.

But the rest of them cried out "THERE'S NO SUCH THING AS WOMEN" and squirmed their little bodies. They sang those words over and over. They didn't care. Before I knew it, they had made a circle around me, and one of them was pointing at the ceiling. We all looked up to find the night sky over our camp. We were back at school. The panoply of blinking stars consumed our vision, and we cried into the open air. We had never seen anything like it. One of them picked up a shovel and spaded earth. Since coming to the camp, their guilt had died and left behind a husk, whose hair and flesh were crackly like onion skin. We buried the husks and covered them with dirt, each scoop sending them further away, to some far-off place. All of us were crying never-ending violent tears. Then over on the sunlit landing, somebody was cracking jokes. In imitation, or remembrance, we laughed back with our entire bodies. A nametag coming loose, vanishing words on a blackboard. "THIS IS IMPORTANT," one of the homunculi said to me. "THERE ARE NO MEN AND NO WOMEN AND NOTHING ELSE." When I looked closely, all their little faces looked familiar, like I had seen them all before, but because of the lighting it was hard to say. When I squinted, to see them better, I heard somebody call my name and saw Makiko staring back at me with a strange look on her face. At some point, the tomboy and the blonde had vanished. The baths had filled again with bathers.

Dear Journal,

Okay, so my mom asked me to go to Mizunoya today. I was thinking about going home but decided to go down to the basement level. There was something there I hadn't seen in years. Robocon. My mom brought me here sometimes when I was little. Robocon was the same as always, but it wasn't. It was so huge back then. Now it looked so small to me, I couldn't believe it.

I used to ride this thing a lot when I was little. You put a coin in, and it shakes around for a minute and a half or so. When you're inside, the eyes are like windows that you can see out of, but from the outside they look black. So basically, I could see my mom, but she couldn't see me. I remember how funny that felt. Like, all my mom could see was Robocon. But it was me, I was in there. Even after I got out, everything felt funny, the rest of the day.

My hands move. My feet move. I don't know how to move them, though. It's like everything is moving all these parts. It's funny. It's like I'm in there, somewhere inside myself, and the body I'm in keeps on changing, more and more and more and more, in ways I don't even know. I wish I didn't care. But I do care. And everything is always changing. Everything gets dark, and that darkness fills my eyes more and more. I don't want to keep them open. I don't want to see. I'm afraid, though. What if I close them, and I can't open them again?

—Midoriko

4.
Out For Chinese

S eriously, though, look at this menu."

Makiko practically sang the words. She was astonished, her eyes opened twice as wide as usual. "I've never had any of this stuff. It's just one guy working the kitchen, right? And that lady is the only person waiting tables?"

"Yeah, it's okay," I said. "At least they're super fast."

"Some places are like that, though, where they can make basically anything you want." Makiko was seriously impressed. "I've seen them on TV. These restaurants where you can get beef stew and okonomiyaki and hamburgers and sushi all off of the same menu. What's the kitchen even look like?"

After pondering the specials tacked up on the wall, we read through the entire menu on the table, before ordering ourselves a couple of beers, along with a few different kinds of squid, some plain noodles, and a plate of plump-skinned fried gyoza. Midoriko ordered with her finger, pointing at the steamed pork buns and some kind of a curly noodle made from tofu, but we shared everything.

The Chinese restaurant was ten minutes from my apartment. Built in the seventies, the building could only be described as a dump, but the restaurant was famous, on account of being dirt cheap. Apart from us, there was a family with an infant and a little boy, probably four or five, running around the table, making noise, a couple in their forties who barely seemed to be talking, and a crew of men in coveralls who were slurping up their ramen like their lives depended on it. An old-fashioned register sat right inside the door, along with a standing screen in brutal red and gold. The pride of the room was a framed piece of Chinese poetry, superimposed on an inky landscape. Its flatness gave the thing away as a print. Beside that was a vintage beer poster, so faded the entire thing looked turquoise. A smiling girl, relaxing in a swimsuit on the white sand, hoisted a mug of beer, running her hand through her hair, a style that used to be cool. The floor was slick with oil.

Once we were seated, Midoriko pulled her smaller notebook from her fanny pack, but thought twice and put the thing away again. She drank her plastic cup of water in one go. Above the ramen-eating workmen, a tiny old TV sat on a shelf blackened by years upon years of airborne grease. It was playing the innocuous kind of talk show that's always playing in a place like this. Midoriko, lips pressed tightly together, tilted her head slightly up, to watch the people laugh on screen, without palpable interest. The beers arrived at the table with the clinking of glass. Me and Makiko said cheers and took a sip. I asked Midoriko if she was sure she was fine with water, but she just nodded slightly, not turning from the TV.

We could see the kitchen through the counter set into the wall. As usual, the chef was dressed in thoroughly stained whites, moving quickly around the small space. Smoke plumed from his blazing wok, and fistfuls of ingredients crackled in the oil. From the grill where he was cooking the gyoza, we heard the violent sound of lots of water turning into steam. The outlets sunk into the wall above the counter were nasty with oil, the mesh basket that he used to scoop up vegetables from the bags by his feet, too low for us to see, was dirty and splitting, and the faucet spilling a constant stream of water into a stockpot was rusted beyond recognition. I remembered something. One time I came here with someone from work, this guy a few years younger than me. We'd been talking about grabbing food sometime, and when I mentioned that I had a place I liked, he said let's go. We'd been seated a couple minutes when I noticed he was acting kind of weird. I ordered for us, but he barely even touched the food. When I brought it up the next time that I saw him, he sort of winced and said he found the place a bit unsanitary, citing how the chef had wiped the wok down with a rag right before he fried our noodles. I had no idea how to reply.

"Hey, did you hear that Kewpie died?"

"Who?" I looked over at Makiko. As soon as I did, the lady showed up with a plate of gyoza and set them down in the middle of the table. "Kewpie?"

"You know, Kewpie!" Makiko took a sip of beer. "The scam artist with the guitar."

"Oh!" I said, so loud I was immediately embarrassed. "Wait, you mean that guy was still alive?"

"Yeah. He had a pretty good run."

In Shobashi, Kewpie was something of a local legend, known all too well at every bar in the vicinity.

He was essentially a busker, who went around with his guitar to all the bars and nightclubs, where he played for tips and took requests and let the customers do the singing, giving folks a break from the monotony of karaoke—but he had lived a double life as an extortionist.

The overpass for Route 2 runs north to south through Shobashi, splitting it in two. The station and most of the other stuff is on the south side, which is also where we used to work, and where Makiko still works. The main attraction on the north side is a run-down mental hospital with iron bars on all the windows. The north feels like a different city from the south. People only ever hang on one side or the other. The bars won't have anything to do with each other, either.

In that sense, Kewpie was a diplomat, frequenting both sides with his six-string slung over his shoulder, equally happy playing for a familiar face as for a stranger. Whether he was any good was hard to say. I guess he made a living. But sometimes, to earn a little extra cash, he'd wait until the busy streets had emptied out, and watch for license plates from out of town, then throw his tiny body on the hood of an oncoming car. On the days when Kewpie did a job, he looked like he had been to hell and back. He sure knew how to pick them. Good people, too. They cursed themselves for ever picking up their keys. They wailed and got down on their knees and said forget about the cops and begged for Kewpie to just let them take him to the hospital, promising that they would make it up to him, even if they had to work themselves to death. I don't remember ever hearing that the cops or insurance got involved. Kewpie made sure not to bang himself up too bad. He rolled up and off the hood, to make it look worse than it was. It always ended with a settlement, or else a couple of bills the driver palmed him on the spot—call it textbook extortion, but Kewpie wrote the book.

Kewpie was small, a peanut of a man. His head was pockmarked like a throwaway potato. His eyes were slits, and he'd lost more teeth than he had left. He had what sounded like a Kyushu accent, but he also had a stutter, on account of which he rarely said much. When he spoke with customers, all of his nouns and adjectives were followed by a question mark. I don't think I ever heard him form a complete sentence.

The two of us had never had a proper conversation, but he always popped his head out back and giggled at me and the other girls when we were doing dishes or preparing snacks. He was harmless, more of a kid than an adult. I liked that about him. It goes without saying that he never gave us any notice about when he would show up, but he usually rolled through the automatic door sometime around ten or eleven, toting his guitar. When the place was hopping, he would make himself at home and get the happy drunks to sing songs, even letting them drop coins in the sound hole of his guitar. But when the bar was quiet, or the customers were moody, he made this worried face and said "Goodbye." Most nights he didn't come back. If the boss was in high spirits, she'd sometimes treat him to a glass of beer, which he drank like it was a flute of champagne.

I remember Kewpie showing up once when the place was dead. Mom had gone out somewhere with the boss—sometimes she called a bar that she was friends with, and they'd try to bring some people back. All the other hostesses were off, and Makiko was getting busier with her other job, so it was only me and Kewpie. This was before Mom found out she was sick, so I was probably in sixth grade.

"Boss out?" Kewpie asked. I told him she'd be right back and popped the cap off of a bottle of beer, then poured him a glass and placed it on the bar.

"Oh, thanks," he said and drank it all. I poured him another glass. Kewpie said thanks again. A bit unsure of what to do, he sat over by the sofas on a stool reserved for hostesses, making that face of his, somewhere between a smile and a smirk. He held the little glass of beer with both of his hands like it was crystal. Without anyone around, the bar was way too quiet. The walls, sofas and pillows sucked up the awkward silence like a reef of sponges. They seemed to close in on all sides. Neither of us said a word. The phone didn't even ring.

After a while, Kewpie picked up his guitar to go, but stopped short by the door. After a moment's hesitation, he slowly turned around, making this face like he'd had a stroke of genius.

"How, how about singing a song?" he asked, looking straight at me. His eyes gleamed from their little slits like winning marbles.

"A song? You mean me?"

Kewpie jutted out his chin, pointing at me, and showed me the remainder of his teeth.

He held the neck of his guitar high above his shoulder and strummed a couple of chords. From the chest pocket of his polo, he produced a little whistle, which he held between his teeth to tune the strings. "I know, what about Soemon? I can do Soemon." Squeezing his eyes shut, he picked his way through the intro, layering on the vibrato and playing with the rhythm.

I was so embarrassed that I hid behind the bar. Mistaking my panic for glee, Kewpie nodded to the beat. He kept on strumming, saying "You can do it, you can do it," smiling ear to ear, but who can sing on command like that? Inside, I was shaking my head no like crazy, but for some reason, my voice found its own way out—I must have heard guests belting out "The Soemon Blues" a thousand times. I'd never sung it once myself, and yet the lyrics started spilling out of me.

As I stumbled through the melody, Kewpie smiled at me with his mouth completely open and kept time with his guitar, matching my speed to keep us going. When I botched the lyrics and looked like I was about to stop, Kewpie nodded patiently and played the vocal line to get me back on track. He played guitar with his whole body. I watched him closely, singing to the rhythm best I could.

Somehow I made it through. I had to fake most of the verses, but I landed the big line: "Show me your smile." Kewpie strummed the last chord really fast and smiled like a madman. He told me I did great and started clapping. I was so embarrassed I was positive that I was blushing. I covered my cheeks with my hands, but Kewpie kept on clapping. I had no idea if I was shy or mortified or thrilled. I hid it all behind a laugh. Then I poured Kewpie one more beer.

"Was he sick?" I asked Makiko.

"Maybe, but that wasn't what killed him," she snorted. "It was a job. Everyone knew he'd been in bad shape for the past few years. I guess he stopped making the rounds. The last time

I saw him was a while back. You know that coffee shop by the station? Rose Cafe. I saw him over there, standing by the door. He looked so frail at first, I didn't even realize it was him. I mean, he was always scrawny, but he was, I dunno. Scrawnier. I hadn't seen him at the bar in forever, and I wanted to ask how he was doing. I guess I was too late. He staggered off."

"Did he have his guitar with him?"

"I don't think so." Makiko took another sip of beer. "But a few months ago . . . Yeah. It was May, almost June, I think. There was this accident late at night, around midnight. Right in front of that Chinese place. You know the one I mean? We used to go there all the time. That's where he died. Later on, we were talking about it at work and one of my customers said that he'd seen Kewpie at the restaurant, maybe two hours before it happened. I asked him how he looked. He said he was the same old Kewpie, smiling, drinking, eating buckets of food. But after that . . . I don't know, things didn't work out."

Someone laughed out loud from the TV. I pinched another gyoza with my chopsticks. They were getting hard but tasted fine.

"Considering his health, I'm amazed he had an appetite at all," Makiko said.

Ignoring us, Midoriko fixed her gaze on the TV, jaw slightly tilted up. The face of Kewpie came to me, then vanished just as quickly. Then I saw the whole man, potato head and all. Sitting in the corner, huddled on the stool, clutching his beer in his hands. The pork buns Midoriko had ordered arrived inside a steamer—white, hot, and round. They made my eyes feel hot and itchy. I took a deep breath through my nose and sat up straight.

"Okay. Pork buns. Let's dig in."

I grabbed one of the steaming buns and smiled at Midoriko. She nodded slightly, drank another cup of water, and stared down at the pork bun on her plate. Makiko had one, too. When Midoriko bit into the doughy tip of hers, it was like the scene had changed—everyone relaxed. Reluctant to believe it, I finished my beer and ordered another. Seconds later they came back with the noodles and the stir-fried squid, filling out the table. Over the background noise of the TV, we ate and drank like a real family, our chopsticks clicking against the plates.

Makiko told the lady who was waiting on us that she was visiting from Osaka, and the lady mentioned all the spots in Osaka she knew. Meanwhile, Midoriko grabbed her first gyoza and chewed with her mouth open. Me and Makiko started talking about how good all the food was, then she ordered another beer. After Midoriko smiled a little at one of my jokes, I asked her what she did at night when Maki was at work. She pulled her notebook from her fanny pack and wrote [Homework. TV. Sleep until morning.] Right, I said, I guess if Maki left a little after six and came back around one, she wasn't really gone that long. Nodding, Midoriko bit into another chunk of the doughy mass that she had ripped to shreds.

Makiko had hit it off with our server. She announced for all to hear that we had come to the right place, then cleared her throat and joined our conversation.

"When I get home from work, there's one thing I always do," she said, with noticeable pride. "What do you think it is? The first thing that I do."

"Take your shoes off?"

"Nope." Makiko shook her head, as if we'd never guess. Her voice went giddy. "I watch this cutie pie sleep."

Midoriko shot her mom a look of disbelief, then grabbed another pork bun. Pressing her thumbs into the white cushion, she split the thing in half and gazed upon the filling, which she proceeded to attack with soy sauce. Then she ripped the halves in half, and ripped those halves in half again, and dipped each piece into her bowl of soy sauce, which turned the white dough black. I wondered how much sauce a single pork bun could soak up.

Makiko said my name to take my eyes off the pork bun. She had emerged from the bathhouse squeaky clean, but her face already gleamed with sebum, and the fluorescent lights were not doing her any favors. I could see the texture of her skin, down to the last pore. Makiko smiled wide. "I swear, though, listen, this kid's so damn cute sometimes I can't keep myself from kissing her while she sleeps." Waving at her with her chopsticks, she made a huge smile like she'd just given her daughter the sweetest birthday present. Embarrassed on Midoriko's behalf, I looked over and saw her staring at her mother with incredible intensity.

Makiko laughed this off, which made Midoriko double down. Her gaze deepened, as if her eyes were physically bulging from her face. After a silence so ridiculously awkward that the word awkward did it no justice, Makiko pounded her beer mug down on the table.

"What?" she asked Midoriko, without raising her voice. "What are you staring at?"

Midoriko turned away, then stared over at the Chinese poem on the wall. Then she set her smaller notebook down in the middle of the table, opened it up and wrote [YOU'RE GROSS] in jumbo letters, underlining the words multiple times. She bore down so hard that the tip of her pen ripped through the paper. Then she retrieved the pork bun that was marinating in the dish of soy sauce and tore her way through the entire thing, apparently unfazed that it was sopping wet. Makiko looked again and again at those two underlined words lines but had nothing to say.

After a brief pause, I asked Midoriko if the soy sauce wasn't too much, but I got no response. The noise continued in the kitchen, spiked now and then with "Thank you!" when the owner heard the server thank a group of customers. The three of us ate in silence, clearing our plates, enveloped by the colorful noise spilling from the TV set.

Dear Journal,

So I got in another fight with Mom, over money. This one was way worse than the last one. In the middle of everything, I asked, why'd you even have me? I ask myself that all the time, but it's a horrible thing to say out loud, I know. It just came out. My mom must have been really mad, but she didn't say anything back. It was so uncomfortable.

I dunno. I thought it would be better if we didn't talk for a while. I mean, we'd just end up fighting again, and I'd say something mean. I know it's partly my fault she has to work the way she does. Who am I kidding, it's all because of me. I get so upset thinking about it. I want to become an adult, right now. That way, I can work hard and help with money. I can't, though. Not yet. For now, all I can do is be nice to her, except I can't even do that. Sometimes I can't stop myself from crying.

I'm almost in middle school. That means three more years before I can get a job. But I don't want just any job. I need a skill. My mom never got a skill. That's why I need one. There are all these books in the library to help us figure out what to do with our lives. I'll start with those. Recently, when my mom asks me to go to the baths with her, I can't bring myself to go. After we had that other fight, the big one, it hit me. It was because of her job. It all started when she was riding on her bike, in that stupid purple dress she wears for work, the one with the gold fringe, when a boy from my class saw her and made fun of her in front of everybody. I wanted to be like shut up or I'll make you shut up, but all I could do was laugh along.

I laughed harder than anyone else, too. Then, when we were fighting, at the end, when she was mad but looked like she was about to cry, she shouted, "What can I do? We gotta eat, right?" That's when I said it. It's your fault for having me. I realized something after that, though. It's not her fault she was born.

I've already decided. I'm never having kids. No way. I was thinking about saying sorry. I really wanted to. But then it was too late. Mom had to go to work.

—Midoriko

5.
UP ALL NIGHT TALKING

Once we were back at my place, Makiko acted like nothing had happened. I did my best to go along with it, laughing and smiling. When I looked to see what Midoriko was up to, I found her sitting on the floor beside her backpack, with her notebook on her knees, not the one she used for talking, but the bigger one, running her pen over the pages.

"It's been a long time since we drank together," Makiko said to me. She went to the fridge and grabbed a few of the beers we'd picked up on the way home and set them on the tea table. "Night's still young," I said and dumped some snack mix and little jerky sticks into bowls. I rinsed the glasses that we'd used for mugicha that afternoon and was about to pour us each some beer, but then I heard the ding-dong of a bell, not something I was used to hearing.

"Is that your bell?" Makiko asked, staring back at me.

"I don't know," I said. "I heard a bell, though."

"Me too."

Then it rang again. Ding-dong. It was definitely my bell. I checked my watch. Just after eight. No one ever dropped in on me like that, day or night. We were just in my apartment, minding our own business, but without thinking I tried to make it look like nobody was home. Holding my breath, I tiptoed through the kitchen to the peephole. The fisheye lens had taken on a moldy tinge, which made it hard to see exactly who it was, but I could tell it was a woman. I thought about keeping up the act, but she must have heard our voices and the TV through the thin door. She wasn't leaving, so I finally spoke up.

"Who is it?"

"Sorry, I know it's late."

I cracked open the door. The woman had a short perm, like the kind you see on guys, only a little looser. Her entire forehead was showing. She was in her fifties or sixties. The brown eyebrows she had penciled on were maybe half an inch too high. Her sweatpants were torn at the knees, and even in the dark, I could tell that they were badly faded. Her white t-shirt was so brand-new that it practically glowed. The front had a huge picture of Snoopy, who was launching a heart with a wink. Over the image, in the Peanuts font, it said: "Nobody's perfect, except for me and you." Before I could ask her what was up, she cut to the chase.

"About your rent . . . "

"Ah." I turned around to whisper I would be right back and stepped into the hallway, closing the door behind me. "Okay."

"You have company?" The woman seemed preoccupied with what was going on inside.

"Just family."

"Sorry to drop in on you like this. I tried calling, but you didn't pick up."

"Sorry about that." The apology was automatic, but now that she mentioned it, I had received a bunch of calls from an unknown number over the past few days. "You must have just missed me."

"If you don't pay this month, you'll be three months behind."

"I know."

"It would help a lot if you could give me one month now."

"I'm afraid that won't be possible, but I can transfer it to you by the end of the month. Um, are you the landlord's . . . "

"Me? Yeah, that's right."

The landlord lived diagonally below me, in a unit on the far end of the first floor. He was a man of few words but came across as amicable enough. In the ten years that I'd lived here, I don't think we'd ever had an actual conversation. I'd fallen behind on more than one occasion, but he never harassed me about it. I always had my fingers crossed my good luck would continue. He must have been in his late sixties. His posture was so rigid that you'd think he was wearing a back brace. It was really something to see him on a bicycle. I'd never seen anyone else near his place. For no good reason, I'd assumed he was a lifelong bachelor.

She cleared her throat, which took some doing. "Look, I know he's been really lenient with you. But things are pretty tight on our end, too. Please make an effort to pay on time."

"I will, I will."

"I know, hon. The end of the month, right?"

"Yes, the end of the month."

"Okay. We have an agreement, then. I'll hold you to it."

Gazing at my feet, I waited for her to clear the metal staircase, until I couldn't hear her footsteps, before I went back in.

"Who was that?" Makiko asked.

"Landlord."

"Yeah?" Makiko giggled as she poured the beer. "About the rent?"

"Yep," I said, forcing a grin, I clinked my glass with hers and took a sip.

"How much do you owe?"

"Two months, I guess."

"They're really shaking you down, huh?" Makiko had drunk half of her beer down on the first sip, so she poured herself a refill.

"Not really. It's never been this way before. I've fallen behind a couple of times, but they've never come to my door or anything. I can't believe it. I've only ever dealt with this nice old guy. I mean, who does she think she is?"

"The lady just now?"

"Yeah, you should have seen her perm and her fake eyebrows."

"Maybe she's his ex," Makiko hypothesized. "That just happened, with a customer of mine. He's gotta be sixty. He's got one kid, a son, who's an adult now, but back when the kid started elementary school, his mom, this guy's wife, ran off with another man. She vanished, for maybe twenty years. They were in touch, I guess, but separated. She made a new life for herself, in a new place. So, you know, the kid grows up. His mom gets older, too, and somehow ends up on her own. Meanwhile, my customer's living with his parents, who were starting to go senile. Then, after like twenty years away, who waltzes in one day but the ex-wife."

"Crazy."

"Well, the guy's got his family's house. That means no rent. Plus, it isn't much, but his parents get a bit of pension money, and this guy's a pipefitter, so that's honest work right there. I guess she had nowhere else to go and was kinda giving him these puppy dog eyes, like she wanted to come back, you know? So he basically said, you can come back, as long as you look after the house and take care of my parents, however long they live, whatever they need, and I mean whatever they need."

"Holy shit."

"I know, right?" Makiko smacked her palm. "It's a sweet deal for him. It makes his life real easy. He's getting a live-in maid and a nurse, for nothing."

"What's it like for the son, though? I mean, she left when he was a kid. That's gotta feel weird. How do you get over something like that? And what about her? She didn't have a job or anything?"

"No way. If she had the money, she would never have come back."

"So what if she gets sick or something, and she can't do anything? That could happen."

"Course it could."

"So then what? He can't just kick her out, right?"

"I'm sure it's never crossed his mind. He probably thinks she'll keep changing his mom and dad's diapers until the day she dies." Makiko took a swig of her beer. "Hey, how much are you paying for rent?"

"43,000. With water and everything."

"For just one person? Well, that's Tokyo, I guess."

"That's about what it costs to live close to the station. It'd be really nice to pay a little less, though."

"Our place is 50,000, nice and even." Makiko flared her nostrils. "Rent sucks. I've been pretty good about it recently, but sometimes it's hard to stay on top. Midoriko's starting middle school next year, though. That's gonna set us back, for sure."

I looked over at Midoriko. She was in the corner, leaning on the beanbag, writing with her notebook propped up on her knees. I held out a few snacks and asked her if she wanted some. After a moment's thought, she shook her head. I turned off the TV, then grabbed the soundtrack to *Bagdad Cafe* off of the stack of CDs by my desk and put it in the CD player. Once Jevetta Steele came on after the short intro, I adjusted the volume and sat back down at the tea table.

"I think it was the worst around the time I started at the yakiniku place." Makiko fished a few orange crackers from the snack mix and sprinkled them into her mouth. "A few years before mom died, though. That was definitely the hardest. Financially."

"You remember all those red tags?"

"What tags?"

"The repo tags. These men came to the house and put them on all the stuff that looked like it had any value. The cooler, the fridge."

"What?" Makiko looked confused. "Why didn't I know that?"

"You had school during the day and work at night. Mom and Komi were out, too."

"It was the middle of the day?"

"Yeah, I was the only one home."

"Wow. Well, I know there's no end to the crap we could say about Mom, but for a woman on her own," Makiko said solemnly, "she really did everything she could."

I started to say that was why she died so young, but kept my mouth shut.

Dear Journal,

So. At recess today, everybody was talking about what they wanted to be when they grow up. No one had anything specific in mind. Not like I do. Then everyone was like hey, Yuri, Yuri, you're so cute, you should be a singer, or a model, and she was like "cut it out."

On the way home, I asked Jun what she wanted to be. She was like I'm gonna run a temple. Her dad and her grandpa are both priests. I always see them riding around on their motorcycles with their robes flapping in the wind. When I asked her what priests do, she said they read sutras at ceremonies and funerals. I haven't been to any funerals. I asked her what she had to do to become a priest, and she said there's this camp that she can go to when she's done with high school. You stay there for a while and train. I was like can women do that? She said obviously.

Jun explained that there are all these different kinds of Buddhism, and when Gautama found enlightenment, he told his disciples what to do and how to follow him, and they're still doing that to this day. According to Jun, enlightenment is when you culminate your training. Something kind of clicks, and even the idea that all is one and one is all vanishes from your mind, and you realize you're the universe, and that there is no you at all. She said that people can become Buddhas, too, but honestly I don't really get how that's different from enlightenment or whatever. Anyway, that's what Buddhism is all about. And that's why priests read sutras at funerals. So that the person who died can become a Buddha.

But there was this other thing she said that really stuck with me. Even when a woman dies, she can't become a Buddha. Because women are supposedly dirty. A long time ago, all these important people wrote about how dirty women are, and why that's bad. So, basically, to become a Buddha, you have to be reborn as a man first. What the hell is that? I didn't get it, so I was like, Jun, how do you do that? She was like 'I don't know.' I asked her how she could believe any of that. It was crazy. Things got pretty awkward after that.

—Midoriko

Sunk deep into the beanbag, Midoriko turned on her side and gazed at the bottom row of books on my bookshelf.

The lower shelves were where I kept the paperbacks I figured I'd never read again. The names on the spines, Herman Hesse, Raymond Radiguet, and Kyusaku Yumeno, had all faded in the sun. *Lord of the Flies*, *Pride and Prejudice*, and my Dostoyevsky, *The Gambler*, *Notes from Underground*, and *The Brothers Karamazov*. Chekhov, Camus, Steinbeck. *The Odyssey* and *The Earthquake in Chile*. These were the undisputed giants of literature; but from a different angle, this classic lineup was a shameful, even mortifying symbol of my willingness to truckle to the received wisdom of the canon, a stance that undeniably marked me as an amateur. Although I must admit that when I glanced over their spines, something of the sense of confrontation, or stimulation, that I felt when I first read them came wafting back to me. I could remember everything about sitting on the concrete stairs for so long that my butt got cold, and how my feet would almost fall asleep. Strange how those things made me want to read all of those books over again someday.

I'd picked most of them up at used bookstores in Osaka, but I got my copies of Faulkner's *Light in August* and Thomas Mann's *The Magic Mountain* and *Buddenbrooks* from this young guy who showed up at the bar one day. This was after Mom and Komi died, when I was in my first year of high school. I didn't remember the guy's name, much less his face. He just happened to pop in after seeing our sign glowing in the street.

He didn't want to sing karaoke or joke around or sit in one of the box seats with the hostesses. He just sat at the bar and asked for the 3000-yen-all-you-can-drink special. White Horse and water. I remember that. At some point he saw me reading, in the doorway of the kitchen, and asked me in a soft voice what the book was. Back then I wouldn't have called myself a reader, but I never went to work without a novel I had borrowed from the school library and read when there were no customers around or dishes to wash.

At the bar, I had to pass for eighteen. The boss also told me not to tell the customers it was only me and Makiko at home, saying some of these guys can't be trusted. She made sure that me and Makiko had matching stories, since at that point she was working there a little on the side. If someone asked, I lied and said that I was born in 1976, which would have made me twenty, and told them that my mother died a few years back from breast cancer (which was true), and that my father was a taxi driver.

Around that time, for reasons I never figured out, I constantly felt like I had to pee. I went to the doctor, but they told me I was fine. This thing started out of nowhere and went on for like three years. Incidentally, this overlapped with the period when Makiko, who by then was receiving a salary from the yakiniku place, working from morning to night, developed a habit of constantly gnawing on ice. She said she couldn't stop, not even when it was cold out, or when she was sleepy.

The constant urge to pee was horrible. I could spend a half-hour on the toilet, until I didn't have a single drop of pee inside of me, but once I had pulled up my underwear and left the bathroom, it felt like I had to run back in again. This went beyond simply having to pee. My urethra felt like it was full. It became impossible for me to focus. As much as I didn't want to, I had to go back to the bathroom. After several minutes on the toilet, it finally worked its way out of me, but then I felt awful—it was like being forced to wear a dirty diaper that had been soaked in a vile broth of all the anger and resignation of Osaka at its worst. When the feeling didn't go away, I started to bring books into the bathroom, and read books everywhere I went. On good days, reading could release me from this terrible feeling.

None of the customers and definitely none of the hostesses had ever asked me about books before, so when this guy asked me what I was reading, I got nervous and hid the book. His face was pale, and he was also disturbingly skinny. The hostesses tried getting his attention with stuff like "Come on, it's comfier on the couch," but he would just laugh it off, almost like he was scared of them. He barely said a word to me, either. I wonder if he even liked the place. Or maybe liking it was not the point. Either way, the guy came back, and not just once. Always sitting in the same seat and ordering the same drink, which he sipped on for an hour, then went home.

One time I asked him what he did for work. Dodging the question, he told me in a trembling voice that a few years back, he worked on Hateruma Island, down past Okinawa, doing manual labor. He quietly explained that the island had barely any lights, and after dark, you couldn't see the sea or sky or ground or anyone around you. Boats carrying all kinds of stuff stopped regularly on the island, and the second someone spotted a ship's lights in the dark expanse of the sea, they all began to whoop and cheer and ran into the waves. When I asked him (whatever his name was) if he jumped in too, he said he was too scared of the ocean—he could never move. He worked there for a while, but after a series of small misunderstandings he was outcast by the other men and had to leave the island.

The next time he came, he showed up hugging a bright-white tote bag bulging with old books. The new cotton of the tote bag made him look like someone on the way home from a funeral, carrying a wooden box of ashes. In that soft voice, almost too soft to hear, he said they were for me and left. A number of the books had tiny handwriting and underlines, but the marks were almost too faint to make out. I could see him, on a dark night, no sound but the waves, holding a book close to his face so he could underline a sentence he never wanted to forget.

Anyway, I was thrilled that all these books were mine, and as a thank-you, I bought him a mug that I had planned to give him the next time I saw him, but the guy never came back. For a while the mug sat in its packing on one of the shelves behind the bar. I wonder what happened to that thing.

"Look how faded they are. Those are my oldest books, Midoriko. The newer ones are up top. Watch the dust."

I sat down beside Midoriko, found Sartre's *The Wall* and riffled through the pages. I knew it had a story that revolved around a firing squad and remembered a scene where all the men are lined up in this wasteland. Actually, maybe that's just what springs to mind when I think firing squad, and it doesn't have a scene like that. Or does it? Now I'm not so sure. What I definitely do remember is one of the character's final lines. "I laughed and laughed, I laughed so hard I cried." When I flipped through and tried to find it, there it was, in the corner of a page I hadn't seen in over ten years. I read the line a few times before jumping back to where I was before. Then I remembered how Makiko had said Midoriko liked reading, and told her she could take some books home, that is, if she saw anything she liked. Ensconced in the beanbag, Midoriko used her feet and hips to roll her body over, to check out the books on the opposite side of the shelf.

"Midoriko, Natsu's writing a novel," Makiko declared, crushing an empty can of beer.

Midoriko shot me a look, raising her eyebrows in a way that made her interest evident. Frustrated by Makiko's unnecessary remark, I tried to drown her out.

"Whoa, whoa. No, I'm not."

"What are you talking about? Sure you are."

"I mean, I am, but I'm not. Or I'm not making any progress."

"Come on, I know how hard you're working on it." Makiko pouted her lips and gave her daughter this smug sort of look. "Pretty cool. Huh, Midoriko?"

"No it's not. It's not." I was almost angry. "There's nothing cool about it. It's just something I like to do. As a hobby."

"If you say so." Makiko kind of rolled her eyes at me and smiled. I'm sure she thought that she was only making conversation. I was worried I had sounded too defensive. But more importantly, I felt awful, even wounded, after hearing myself call my work a "hobby."

The question of whether the thing I was writing qualified as a novel was open for interpretation. That much was true. At the same time, I was sure I was writing a novel. Absolutely sure. Maybe it looked like I was wasting my time. And maybe for everyone but me, that was all it would ever amount to. An enormous waste of time. But I knew that it was wrong to dismiss my work like that. It felt like I had said something that I could never take back.

Writing makes me happy. But it goes beyond that. Writing is my life's work. I am absolutely positive that this is what I'm here to do. Even if it turns out that I don't have the ability, and no one out there wants to read a single word of it, there's nothing I can do about this feeling. I can't make it go away.

I recognize that luck, effort, and ability are often indistinguishable. And I know that, in the end, I'm just another human being, who's born only to die. I know that in reality, it makes no difference whether I write novels, and it makes no difference if anyone cares. With all the countless books already out there, the world won't notice if I fail to publish even one book with my name on it. That's no tragedy. I know that. I get that.

But that's when I always think of Makiko and Midoriko. Our old apartment, strewn with dirty clothes. The countless wrinkles in our red faux leather book bags. The stinky, worn-out sneakers in the darkness of the front door. I think of Komi, how she helped me learn my times tables. When we were out of rice, the four of us made dumplings from flour and water and spun them in the pot—from the way we laughed, you'd think that we were doing this for fun. The way the ink of the newsprint blurred under our watermelon seeds. All the days that Komi had us help her clean the building. The fragrance of the trial bottles of shampoo that we packed in plastic baggies for extra money. The icy blue shadows. How I worried that my mom was never coming home, and how she came home in her factory uniform, all smiles.

I knew these things were related to my desire to write novels. But how? The book I had in mind wasn't supposed to be autobiographical, but whenever I felt stuck, or told myself I couldn't even form a decent sentence, these thoughts and feelings started pouring in. Perhaps these memories were obstacles that I could never overcome. I still don't know. But what I do know, as much as it hurts to admit, is that ten years after leaving behind Makiko and Midoriko, and coming to Tokyo to become a writer, I have nothing to show them, and have no way of making their lives easier. It made me feel small and useless. To be honest, I was scared and unsure.

Makiko continued to address Midoriko, unresponsive as she was.

"Your aunt has always been a bookworm. You should've heard her, using all those difficult words as a little girl. She was a smart kid. I don't know the first thing about literature. Can you believe she's going to be a published author?"

I faked a big yawn. With the pads of my pointer fingers, I rubbed away the tears that had formed at the corner of my eyes and pressed my cheeks. Then I gave another yawn and tried to change the subject, saying something about how the beer was making me sleepy.

"Seriously? I'm wide awake," Makiko said, opening another can.

"I'll grab one, too," I said.

As if running away from the table, I hopped up and went over to the kitchen, muttering "beer, beer."

My fridge was less than frigid. Sometimes I wondered if it even kept things cool. All I had in there was a box of baking soda, a tub of miso, and some salad dressing, lined up in such a way that the fridge looked like a lost and found for condiments. But I had plenty of eggs. The tray inside the door was full, plus I had another carton of ten stashed on the bottom shelf.

The week before, I'd bought this extra carton without realizing I still had so many left. One or the other of them had probably gone bad. The carton I'd saved from the eggs loaded in the tray said that they had expired yesterday, while the date on the full carton said tomorrow. There was no way we were eating all these eggs by then. I'd have to separate them from the other trash and throw them out. So I rummaged through the drawer of plastic bags I'd stockpiled, but all of them were too small. When I throw eggs away, I never know if I'm supposed to crack them first, or toss them in there, or place them in the garbage like you're laying them yourself. What's the right way to do it? Is there even a right way? I had just set down the ten-pack by the kitchen sink when Makiko called me from the other room.

"Natsuko, check it out. I had Cheese Okaki in my bag. A whole pack."

"Nice."

"Hey, I'm feeling kinda hungry, though. Wanna make a stir-fry or something?" Makiko craned her neck so she could see me in the kitchen.

"Sorry, Maki. I don't have anything," I said. "Just eggs."

"Eggs?" Makiko stretched her arms and made a sound like she was lifting something heavy. "What can you make with just eggs?"

The tea table was filling up with empty cans of beer. Me and Makiko had drunk a lot already. It felt weird drinking like this in my own place. I basically don't drink—other than the occasional night out with the girls from work, once every couple of months, and I never ever drink at home alone. I'm a lightweight. Wine and sake give me headaches, which is fine since I don't really like the way they taste. Even beer, the only thing I can handle, makes me feel like a pile of crap after two tall cans. Tonight, however, I'd gone way beyond my usual limit, but for whatever reason, I felt fine. I was definitely drunk, but not crazy drunk. I felt something I wasn't used to feeling, like I could drink as much as I wanted. I asked Makiko how she was doing and she said she could keep going, too, so I ran out to the store and got us seven cans of beer along with bags of Karamucho and salted squid; and even splurged, after a lot of thought, on a wheel of camembert cheese.

When I got home and kicked my shoes off, Makiko looked

at me and held a finger to her lips, then pointed at Midoriko, who was curled up asleep on the beanbag with her journal gripped tight in her hand. I pulled the futon that I always slept on from the closet and set it up along the wall, then unrolled alongside it the old one that I'd brought from Osaka.

"Let's put Midoriko on the end," I said. "I'll sleep in the middle. I don't know about the two of you next to each other. If Midoriko wakes up and sees you right there, she's liable to flip out."

I wrested the notebook from Midoriko's grip and stowed it safely in her backpack, then gave her shoulders a gentle shake. Eyes closed so hard that she was frowning, she felt her way over to the futon and collapsed.

"How can she sleep with all the lights on?"

"She's young." Makiko laughed. "I mean, we always had the lights on, right?"

"Yeah, you're right. Until Mom came home. Then the smell of hot dogs would wake me up. Remember how we used to eat dinner together, in bed?"

"Totally," Makiko said. "I remember the times she came home drunk and woke us up, then we all had chicken ramen."

"Yeah, totally. Hot dogs and instant ramen in the middle of the night. That's why I got so fat."

"Oh, whatever. You were growing. I should've known better. I was in my twenties then." Makiko shook her head. "Mom got pretty heavy, too."

"Yeah," I said. "She was so skinny before, but she put on all that weight out of nowhere, like she was wearing a fat suit. She was always asking, 'Can you unzip me?' Haha."

"How old was mom then?"

"A little over forty?"

"No, she must have been older. She was forty-six when she died."

"Yeah, you're right," I said.

"God, she wasted away," said Makiko. "No one has any business losing that much weight."

We stopped talking, each of us taking another sip of beer. We could hear it going down our throats. Then we were quiet.

"Hey, what's this song?" Makiko dropped her jaw a little. "It's nice."

"It's Bach."

"Bach? Oh yeah?"

I don't know how many times it had played, but the *Bagdad Cafe* soundtrack was on the first prelude from Bach's *The Well-Tempered Clavier*. That cafe in the smoldering desert of the American Southwest, a place that had seen it all. One day a very fat white woman shows up, and everybody's lives get a little easier. There's this black kid who plays Bach in the last scene. He never says a word, and I'm pretty sure his back is to the camera. It's been a while. Makiko shut her eyes and let her head sway to the melody. Deep bags under her eyes. I could see the sinews of her neck. The lines to either side of her mouth ran deep, and her cheekbones were more pronounced than I remembered. For a brief moment, I could see how mom looked in the months before she died, shrinking before our eyes in her hospital bed, or in her futon back at home, between visits to the hospital. I had to look away.

Dear Journal,

Mom and I aren't really talking. Not at all, actually.

Jun's been pretty cold, too. Maybe she thought I was shooting her down the other day, but I really wasn't. I just thought it was weird. Why should I have to explain myself to her, though? All my mom ever does is research breast implants. I pretend like I'm not watching, but she's too busy thinking about boobs to notice anyway. Is she serious? I mean, why? I can't even begin to understand it. It's gross, I really don't understand. It's so, so, so, so, so, so gross. So gross. I've seen what it looks like. I've seen it on TV and online. It's surgery. They cut right into you. They slit you open so they can stuff you, literally. It hurts. What's wrong with her? What the hell is wrong with her? She's being an idiot, the biggest idiot. The other day on the phone with some clinic, she said she was going to let them put photos of the whole procedure online, so they'll do it for free. That means that her face would be in ads for them in magazines and on their website. How the hell could she do that? It's the stupidest thing I've ever heard. Idiot, idiot, idiot. My mom is an idiot. I feel like I've had this horrible pain inside my eyes since Tuesday. I can't keep them open.

—Midoriko

"Ah, it's already over," said Makiko, narrowing her eyes. "The good ones are never long enough."

The next track was an instrumental with an upbeat tempo. Makiko got up to go to the bathroom. I unwrapped myself a slice of camembert and bit into the pointy end. Here and gone, like an afternoon festival, the track was over in under a minute, giving way to the Bob Telson version of "Calling You."

"So, the bar," Makiko began, on her way back from the bathroom.

"Yeah?" I said, twisting apart a Cheese Okaki and nibbling on the part with no cheese.

"We've been having all kinds of problems."

"Hey, how's Coco doing?" I asked.

"Well, you know, the bar's just one headache after another. We have this sign outside, right out front, this really huge sign."

"How big?"

"Big. All caps, CHANEL. Yellow lights around the edges. Whichever girl arrives first plugs it in. There's an outlet right there, in the wall, you know? For the power. Well, that's where we plug it in. Then, out of nowhere, the guy who runs the cigarette stand next door was like hey that's our power."

"What?"

"He's like, you need to pay us back for all the power that you stole."

"The outlet's next door?"

"Uh-huh."

"Not covered or anything?"

"Exactly. If there's an open socket, anyone can use it, right? Who thinks about shit like that? Like, this electricity is mine, or whatever. Know what I mean? It belongs to everyone, obviously." Makiko chewed into a stick of jerky as she spoke. "Coco went crazy, though. Seriously. It became this whole big deal. At first, the guy was just like, did you know what you were doing? Then he was like no, seriously, you need to pay me back, for all of it."

"How much are we talking about?"

"Well, I guess that sign's been there forever. Fifteen years, maybe. Running for a few hours every day, for fifteen years."

"Okay . . . "

"He asked her for 200,000 yen, in cash."

"Wait, what?" I spun around and grabbed the calculator from my desk drawer. "200,000 divided by 15 . . . That's a little over 13,300 yen a year. Divide that by twelve, and it's basically 1,100 yen a month . . . Okay, it's not that much, I guess. But if someone asked me to fork over 200,000 yen right now, I'd cry."

"I know, right? I mean, it's the only outlet down there. So if we get into a fight over it, we're cut off from electricity. Then we'd really be screwed. I know it's not the end of the world or whatever, but it's not like Coco has 200,000 yen lying around to give this guy. She was furious. That wasn't the only thing going on, though. One of the girls who'd been there forever just quit because of an issue with one of the other girls . . . Anyway, let's watch some TV. That okay?"

I stopped the CD and handed the remote to Makiko. When she pressed power, the TV made this little bullfrog noise before the picture filled the screen. A variety show was on. I bought this TV used for 4,000 yen when I moved in.

"The other day, I saw a flatscreen at the store. You ever seen one of those? They're crazy thin. You know how much they cost, though? A million yen. No joke. Who the hell would spend that kind of money on a TV? Rich people, I guess. The screen, though, like I was saying at the bathhouse, it was super black." She started flicking through the channels. "What were we just talking about?"

"The girl who quit," I said, biting into a jerky stick. "What was her name? She was around for a long time, right? Longer than you?"

"Yeah, Suzuka. She was there for like five years. She's from Korea. Honestly, though, she was the best we had. She literally held the place together."

"So, why'd she quit?"

"Like two months before she left, we got this new girl. Part time. She came from China. She said she was in Japan for college, but I have no idea where she was studying. But, yeah, she's a student. Guess she needed the money. She found our listing . . . "

"Like in one of those job magazines where they print the night work section darker?"

"Exactly, exactly. Anyway, her name's Jing Li. She's pretty normal. Black hair, light skin, doesn't wear a lot of makeup. You know, a college girl. Coco liked her, though."

"Well, there aren't many girls like that in the area."

"That's true. We get a lot of Koreans, but Chinese girls are rare. But, I mean, it's not like she works for the attention. Jing Li pretty much just sits there. Her Japanese is terrible, but the guys are all over her because she's exotic or something. That's fine, though, except sometimes they'd be like, Suzuka, we don't want to drink with you, go away, putting her down to make Jing Li feel good or whatever. Suzuka's a pro, though. She didn't let it get to her. But she never liked Jing Li much anyway. I mean, the girl just sits there, right? So Coco sees Jing Li, this airhead college girl, and tells Suzuka to look after her. And Suzuka was like, yeah, okay."

"How old's Suzuka?" I asked.

"I guess she's in her thirties?" Makiko said. "I mean, she's a lot younger than me. Still, though, she's no spring chicken. She's been in the industry a long time, too. That'll take it out of you. Like, you can see the years on her. At first, I thought we were the same age.

"Anyway, yeah, it was a quiet night with no customers. It was just the three of us. I don't remember why, but Coco wasn't around. We had nothing to do, so we just started asking Jing Li about China and stuff. Or like, 'How do you write your name?' She told us 'It's the character for quiet, then the character for village,'" Makiko said, doing her best Jing Li.

"Anyway, we were like is China really as strict as everyone says? Or, you know, as poor? Do people really ride around on bikes dressed up in Mao suits? I asked her about this thing I saw once on TV, where they said everyone in China was drinking oolong tea out of empty Nescafé bottles. And Jing Li was like yeah, that's what it's like. People act like the Beijing Olympics is going to save China, but it's all lies. It'll help a small handful of people, but almost everybody is broke, so they have to scrape by. Most of the country is totally behind. When there was that earthquake in Sichuan, that school building came down and killed all those kids. She was like, bathrooms don't have doors, and in the village where I was born, it's really bad—the roads, the buildings, the animals, the people. Everyone wants China to become more like Japan, clean and rich. Then we started talking about politics. You know Hu Jintao? Not the one who's basically in charge now. That guy who put his hand on his chest and was like Deng Xiaoping will live forever in our hearts, that guy. That didn't really make sense to us, but we got the gist. Then Jing Li started telling us about her family back home and how poor they are.

"She told us that she has three little brothers, and the smallest one has a learning disability, and her grandma and grandpa live with them, too. Her family's only chance of getting out of poverty is if one of the grandkids goes to school and gets an education. But Jing Li's a woman, so her grandpa was like, college isn't for women. If we're going to spend the money on education, we should spend it on one of her brothers. They fought over that for a while, but Jing Li was the only one with a decent head on her shoulders, the only one who could really turn things around. So she thought if she could learn Japanese, she could make money here herself. She started working on it, studying Japanese on her own. She had nothing but these ridiculously old textbooks, though, so at the bar when she wants to say 'Cool!' she says stuff like, 'Remarkable.' Not like there's anything wrong with that, but yeah, then she started tearing up. Jing Li was like, 'No one from my town has ever been to college. Ever. It was so hard for Mom and Dad to get the money for me. People laughed in their faces, told them they were just throwing money away.' But she was determined to study hard and get ahead in the world and be the best daughter she could possibly be, even if tuition cost a fortune. That's why she took the job. So she could save up money and repay her parents.

"When Suzuka heard all that, she looked like she was about to break down and cry. She looked at Jing Li and said I didn't know you had it so hard. She goes, okay, listen to me, Jing Li, I'm gonna be your big sister, your sister in Osaka. Come to me with anything, okay? So the three of us poured ourselves some drinks, put our arms over each other's shoulders and sang that Yuming song, 'Midsummer Night's Dream.' It's not like we had any customers anyway. You should have seen Jing Li, though. She got really into it, like it was a competition or something. She was slapping her thighs like a tambourine and everything. The whole time she was just smiling at me. She wouldn't look away, no matter what. It was the craziest smile, though. Seriously, I have no idea what was going on in her head. Anyway, yeah, we were having fun and then we started talking about money. Then Suzuka was like, for real, Jing Li, how much are you making? And that's against the rules or whatever, we can't talk about it, but Suzuka was like I need to make sure you're not getting ripped off. You can tell me. I can talk to Coco for you. So Jing Li was like, okay, I get 2,000 an hour."

"Damn."

"Wait, though," Makiko said. "You should have heard it, the sound that came out of Suzuka when she heard that number . . . It was like a dying chicken. I honestly thought she was dying. But yeah, I never knew what Suzuka was making, until then. 1,400."

"Uh-oh."

"And that's after she fought hard for a raise, maybe a year ago."

"But she's been around so long."

"Seriously, I know."

I was tempted to ask Makiko how much she made but held back. "So that's why she quit?"

"That's right. As soon as Jing Li said 2,000, Suzuka's face turned white like the backside of a sheet of origami. Then she got all red and spotty. But Jing Li didn't get what was going on. She was crying and was like, Suzuka, let's do another song. She put on 'Survival Dance' and was tapping Suzuka on the shoulder, like come on, one more song, one more song. But Suzuka was completely out of it, barely holding it together on her stool. So Jing Li did the song alone, in literally the worst Japanese ever. She's a really bad singer, too. It'd drive you crazy, I swear. So, the next day, Suzuka confronted Coco. They got into a big fight, and then Suzuka just stopped coming.

"Coco was like 'Jing Li's from China, and she's working hard to help her family out.' So Suzuka came back with 'I'm from Korea, and I'm working to help my family, too.' She was crying and everything. Then Coco said 'Jing Li's young, though. She's worth it.' After everything Suzuka had done for the place, after all the drinks and being drunk, this shit was too much. She broke down crying."

I tried to imagine Jing Li hanging on Suzuka, beside herself with shock, pleading her to sing another song while "Survival Dance" blared in the background. Since I'd never seen either of them in my life, it was hard to say whether I got the picture right.

"Then the cops showed up."

"No way. Did Suzuka try to burn the place down or something?"

"Nothing like that," Makiko heaved a sigh. "After the whole debacle with Suzuka, we had to interview a couple of new girls. Suzuka wasn't coming in and Jing Li couldn't take her shifts. So it was pretty much just me and Coco, oh, and Tetsuko, but Tetsuko's in her fifties. Like you can only dim the lights so much, know what I mean? So in come these two girls, Nozomi and An. They show up looking for work, saying that they're friends from the same trade school. They said they could work every night, and both of them were super cute. They were always smiling and, I dunno, cheerful.

"Just looking at them, though, it was obvious. I mean, they had blonde hair and dark roots, both of them. Nasty split ends. Trade school my ass. Seriously. An was missing a tooth, and when she smiles her molars are nasty with cavities. Nozomi's hair was always a huge mess. Not to be gross, but sometimes she smelled funny. Yeah, though, just watching them sit or eat or whatever, you could tell. Nobody was looking after them. They said they had parents and everything, but I got the sense that they weren't living at home. They must have been staying with friends or boyfriends or something. I mean, sometimes they came to work with bags of dirty laundry. But we needed the help, so we kind of ignored all that. They were really into the work, too, like we'll sell tons of drinks, Coco! And they did, too. Coco really liked them. Because they really were sweet kids, both of them.

"Then, yeah, one day after like two months, the two of them stopped showing up. No warning. They'd been on top of everything until then, too. Never missed a shift. So we're all like, what's going on? You know? They didn't come the next day, either. Or the next day after that. We couldn't get ahold of them. It's not like things were tense or anything at the bar. We all got along great. We went out for yakitori after closing up. One time we even went bowling. By that time, everyone knew the whole trade school thing was bull. They didn't even try to keep that up. They just started talking about all these other dreams they had, like running a cafe together or being hair-dressers, or maybe getting married and having kids. They were really good girls, though. They worked hard. That's why we figured if they wanted out, they'd say so, to our faces. So, yeah, we were real worried. But that's when the cops came. Turns out some guy was pimping them out. And then Nozomi got the crap beat out of her, in this dirty hotel in Shobashi. By one of her customers . . . "

I looked at Makiko.

"And it was real bad." Makiko looked down at the crinkled square of foil she had peeled off of a slice of cheese, then looked back up at me. "The hotel had to call an ambulance and everything. It was a huge thing. That was like a week or so before the cops came to the bar. This all happened in Shobashi, so of course we'd already heard that something happened at the hotel, but we never thought . . . "

Makiko took a deep breath.

"It was Nozomi. The guy beat her within an inch of her life. He really did a number on her. Her jawbone was busted, and the rest of her face was bruised or worse. She lost consciousness. They arrested the guy who did it, too. They said the piece of shit was high on meth. She's lucky she didn't die."

I shook my head.

"So the cops started looking into stuff, obviously, and they figured out that the girls were working at the bar, you know." Makiko bit down on her lip. "Turns out she was fourteen."

"Seriously?"

"Nozomi, yeah. The other one, An, was thirteen. They should have been in their first year of middle school. So the cops were like did you know how old they were when you gave them the job? Is this where they picked up their customers?"

"At Chanel? That's crazy."

"I know. No way, right? I mean, we figured they were younger than they said, but not that young. It was an honest mistake. They were big girls for their age. Anyway, An disappeared. Nobody knows where she went."

"What about Nozomi?"

"I went to see her, at the hospital." Makiko picked up a can of beer, thought twice, and put it back. "She was in this room. Her face and shoulders were wrapped up in bandages and splinted. Her jaw was ruined. She couldn't eat anything. She had this metal mask over the bottom half of her face, with tubes running through it. Those tubes were keeping her alive.

"When I went in, she couldn't move or anything. Her eyes were swollen up pretty bad, but I could tell she recognized me. Her mouth was held shut, but she was trying to talk. She tried to sit up, too, and I was like don't move, honey, stay the way you are. I sat down next to her and was like, just look at you, girl. I wanted to be positive, though, and make her laugh. I stayed there for maybe an hour, telling her about Coco's latest woes and one of our regulars who made a bundle off a scratch ticket. She couldn't talk, but she was looking at me the whole time, like yeah, yeah, I'm listening. I just told her about all these stupid things, you know?

"I said I'd come back. I was like, you want anything? A yo-yo? I'll bring you one of those ones that lights up. That got her smiling. I asked her if her mom was coming, and she kinda looked away. Coco told us that Nozomi's mom was living in Kyushu. Listen to this, though. The mother's only thirty. Can you believe that? She had Nozomi when she was like sixteen. But she had two more kids with another man, after Nozomi, so she had her hands full. Nozomi said that she was gonna come, though. I said that's great and told Nozomi I would see her soon. But when I got up to go, she started pointing at this pen and paper, like she wanted to write something down. I got them for her, and real slow, she wrote me a note: 'Sorry. I'm sorry about the bar.' I was like what are you saying? Don't apologize. After everything you've been through, I said, rubbing her legs for her. It's okay, it's okay. Don't worry. You're going to get better. We're strong, stronger than this. I wanted to smile for her, but I couldn't stop crying. She was crying, too, and her bandages were getting wet. I just sat there and kept rubbing her legs, you know?"

Dear Journal,

Lately my head hurts whenever I look at something. My head is pounding all the time. All these things come in, through my eyes, but how do they get out? As words? As tears? What if those things stop coming? What if I can't talk or cry anymore? Everything connected to my eyes will grow, they'll get bigger and bigger, making it even harder to breathe. Eventually, it's going to get so bad that I can't open my eyes.

—Midoriko

I let my hand fall from my mouth, where it had been without me realizing, and looked over at Midoriko, who was fast asleep. Then me and Makiko drank our beer in silence. We'd picked all the crackers out of the mix, leaving nothing but peanuts. The TV was still on, broadcasting the Beijing Olympics. At the sound of a whistle so metallic that it sounded fake, the swimmers dove into the pool. In perfect form, the female athletes wearing racing swimsuits breached the surface with their sleek backs, digging with the left and the right, like they were carving through the water.

Makiko grabbed the remote and changed the channel. Some Japanese band I'd never heard of was screaming over wailing guitars, "My one true love / Come bask inside my heart." We spaced out for a while, watching them play, but soon we'd had enough and changed the channel again. This time to the news. Commentators were discussing how the boosted approval ratings caused by the reshuffling of the cabinet would influence the general election in the fall. Then the show ended. Next up was a special report on how to get the most out of Apple's new iPhone. We watched that for a while, saying nothing. Then Makiko changed channels again. It was a local show, and the difference in production quality was all too obvious. An imposing title in the upper right said, "TRIAL BY FIRE." The camera followed a kid as he located his ID number on the board outside a top-tier private high school, then zoomed out while his mother wrapped her arms around him and cried for joy. "It took a lot of blood, sweat, and tears to get us here," the mother sobbed. She put her handkerchief up to her nose. "I know my son has what it takes. I want him to go all the way." The cameraman asked her something. "Well, obviously, the University of Tokyo." Apparently, that sequence had been filmed a couple of years ago, because now the crew was setting off to see where the boy had wound up. They cut to a commercial for some new flavor of cup ramen, then for shochu, hemorrhoid ointment, and an energy drink, all of which we dutifully watched in silence.

"Look at all these," Makiko said. Empty cans on the table and the carpet, but there were even more in the trash can in the kitchen. I had no interest in knowing the exact number of drinks we had, but I knew it was way beyond my limit. For some reason, though, I was convinced I wasn't drunk. I wasn't even tired. I checked the clock. It was eleven.

Makiko said that she'd been up all day and it was time for her to hit the hay. She pulled a shirt and a pair of sweats from her overnight bag and got changed. I got up to brush my teeth. As soon as I was done, Makiko did the same, and I laid down beside Midoriko. Makiko stretched out to switch the light off, then got down beside me. I caught a whiff of something chemical in her hair.

Once I was reclined there in the darkness with my eyes closed, I felt like my brain was being broken down and packed away. I couldn't fall asleep. I felt my body warming up and tossed and turned in the small space between the two of them. The soles of my feet prickled. It felt like they were growing thicker. My head was clear as day, but I was definitely drunk. I writhed, trapped in my own body, breathing hard.

Behind my eyelids, I saw dancing patterns mix and break apart. Over and over. I moved down an empty hall, filled with the keen smell of disinfectant. I pushed open a door and found Nozomi, face up on her hospital bed. The bandages made it impossible to see her face. Fourteen. I remember when I was fourteen. The first year I wrote up a resume. I lied and said that I was in high school and got a job at a local factory. On my way to work I put on lipstick at the drugstore, using a sample tube that had been worn down to the plastic. My job involved inspecting little batteries for leaks. If you got the purple liquid on your fingers, it sank in like a tattoo, leaving a blue smear. And piled high in the sinks were stained ashtrays that no amount of washing could clean. The cigarette smoke, the booming echo of the microphones that would never leave my head. Carrying the empty beer crates out into the alley, Mom reaches out to lock the top lock, then crouches down to throw the deadbolt. Walking home alone, men standing in the shadows underneath the telephone poles or by the vending machines, catcalling and snickering. Filthy mouths, stained pant legs, jittery hands. I run all the way up the stairs.

Soon I couldn't see the difference between things I'd heard before and things I hadn't. Things I'd seen in dreams were tangled up in memories. I lost track of what was real. I know the veil of fog surrounding all the naked bodies has a sound. The high walls, separating the men's bath from the women's. A hollow clack cuts through the air. All the naked women in the steamy water turn to look at me. All their nipples look at me in unison. The steam churns, and I massage the soles of my own feet. The skin of my heels is always cracking, but no amount of peeling makes them pretty. My mom's feet were always flaky and white, except for her brown toenails. With lathered fingers, Komi washes the spaces between my toes. You gotta yank a little on the lever, or the stove won't light. There's a knack to it. Click click click. The gas roars into flame, Komi's naked, red dots all over her body. What are those? Blood blisters. What happens if you pop them? Will all the blood come spraying out of you? Will you bleed to death? Hey, Komi. You gotta be more careful. You can't die. What am I supposed to do without you? Don't die. Don't die. Stay with me, Komi. Stay with me. Cut it out. Come on, let's eat. Can't do anything on an empty stomach, Makiko brought home another of her yakiniku bentos, with teriyaki sauce mixed into the rice. Hey Maki, did you see those people out there, wandering around the city? They don't have homes. They're homeless. They don't have anywhere they can go. I'm always scared they're gonna talk to me. Watch out, Maki. What're you gonna do if that guy over there, that guy squatting over there is dad? Bring him home and throw him in the tub? Is that the plan? Take him home and give him something to eat? Then what? What would you say to him? Maki. Remember the way Kewpie cried at Mom's reception? He was a mess. Gave us 2000 yen. Damn it was hot that day. Kewpie bawled his eyes out. Remember how Komi used to scream when we walked under an overpass? If we heard a train coming, she'd squeeze our hands, both of us, me and Makiko, then right when it was loudest, overhead, she'd scream at the top of her lungs. Tomorrow I'll take a train ride with Midoriko. Roll on down the tracks. We'll go off, go some-where, until Maki gets back. Maybe I can braid her hair on the way. Turn in my seat and run my fingers through her hair. Look at all this hair. It's like a jungle, same as me. How come you don't have a bag with you? Those weren't your folks? Who just got off the train? We met on the train before, a long time ago. Why are you laughing? It wasn't that long ago? Just this morn-ing . . . right, that was this morning . . . but it feels like it's been forever . . . the flyers, from the paper . . . ads for houses, flyers showing floorplans, you can draw on them . . . cover them with windows, little squares, any kind of windows that you like . . . One for Mom, one for Maki, one for Komi, one for everyone, and they can open them any time they want, because once you draw it, once you draw them, the light will come in, and the wind will come in, and that was how I went to sleep.

6.
THE SAFEST PLACE IN THE WORLD

That's odd.

My thoughts were dense, like my head was stuffed with old cotton. What's the date today? I felt something wet around my tailbone. If I had my way, I would've stayed in bed, but I forced myself up to use the bathroom. I imagined my calendar, trying to remember where the circle had been for my last period. I had a general idea. But that meant that I was about ten days early.

Come to think of it, I'd been early last month, and the month before that, too. It was like the day was moving slowly forward. While the first couple of years had been a bit irregular, for over fifteen years my period had arrived every twenty-eight days like clockwork. What could have made the past two years or so this inconsistent?

Thoughts circled around my head. I peed for so long that even my sluggish mind registered surprise. As I sat there, waiting for it to end, I gazed down at the splotches of blood on my underwear. I couldn't help but see a map of Japan, with Osaka right in the middle, and the spot to the left of it was Shikoku, off the coast, and Aomori closer to the top, not like I'd ever been there. Honestly, I'd never been much of anywhere. I didn't even have a passport.

Judging from the look of the light outside, it must have not even been seven. The summer sun was still asleep, and the air had an edge. When I focused my vision, I felt a vague pain in my brow. I was hungover. It didn't seem so bad, though. I tore the wrapper off a pad, put it on, then pulled up my underwear, flushed the toilet, and went back to my room. The pad felt puffy, like a miniature futon between my legs. Thinking that, I climbed back into bed.

On the verge of sleep, I wondered how many more times I was going to get my period. How many more? How many times had it happened already? *Another month, another egg.* The words floated before my eyes like a speech bubble in a manga. I stared at the words. *Another month, another egg.* That's right. Nothing this month. And nothing next month, or the month after that, or the one after that. It's not going to happen, not in this lifetime, I told the speech bubble, setting it straight. But soon the feeble voice inside of me receded, and I fell back asleep before I realized.

When I finally woke up, I panicked for a second to see that Makiko was gone, but then I remembered, the night before when we were drinking, how she had said, "I'm meeting an old friend, then heading to Ginza from there, to the clinic, for a consultation. I should be back a little before seven or so. I guess we can figure out what we're going to eat then?"

The clock said 11:30 A.M. Midoriko was awake, reading a book in bed. I never eat breakfast, but I should have already been up and fixing something. Midoriko was still a kid, and kids gotta eat breakfast. I apologized profusely. "I'm sorry, Midoriko, I woke up with a hangover and fell back asleep. I'm so sorry, you must be starving." Midoriko looked at me, then pointed toward the kitchen and gestured like she was chomping on a piece of bread. "Oh, good." What a relief. "I know I don't have much, but help yourself to whatever you want." Midoriko nodded and picked up where she left off in her book. Summer morning. Light streaming through the windows. I stretched and my joints popped. Once I was standing, I rolled up my futon and saw a perfect circle of blood on the sheets. How many years had it been since that had happened?

I know my cycle had been wonky the last couple of years, but this was another level. I sighed to myself, unzipped the fitted sheet to free the futon, and brought all the sheets to the bathroom.

If I tried washing out the blood with hot water, the heat would only make the stain set in, so I had to wash it under cold water—where had I learned this? Not school, not from Mom or Komi. Makes you wonder. I filled a basin with soap and water, bunched up the bloody part of the sheet, and dunked it in. As I was scrubbing, I felt something behind me, and when I turned around Midoriko was there.

Crouched on the bathroom floor, I twisted my neck up to see her and said hey, how about we check out the amusement park today, then explained that I had an accident and had to wash my sheets. Midoriko didn't answer, just watched the motion of my hands scrubbing the sheets. The tiny bathroom filled with the weirdly squeaky sound of fabric against fabric and the sound of water splashing in the basin. "Blood only washes out under cold water," I said. Poking around in the suds to see how it was going, I glanced at Midoriko. We met eyes. She nodded and went back to bed.

Dear Journal,

Okay. Here's what I learned about eggs today. When egg and sperm meet, you get a fertilized egg. When that doesn't happen, the egg stays empty. O.K., I knew that much already. Fertilization doesn't happen in the womb, though. There are these tubes in the body, fallopian tubes. Then, when the egg is fertilized, it travels into the womb and settles there.

Here's what I don't get, though. In all the books and all the drawings, I can see the fallopian tubes, looking like hands, but how do the eggs get out of the ovaries and travel down the tubes? I read somewhere that the egg basically shoots out, but how? There's a space. What's going on in there? What's there to stop the eggs from falling into other places?

From that point on, it's all a mystery. Say an egg is fertilized. It's going to be a girl, and she hasn't been born yet. In the baby girl's ovaries (scary to think it, but she's already got them), she's got seven million eggs, more than she'll ever have after being born. From then on, the number only drops. When the girl's born, she's got maybe a million, and she'll never get any new ones. After that, it dips way, way down. By the time a girl is my age, she's got around three hundred thousand left, and only a small number of those fully develop. Only those eggs can get you pregnant. It's really scary to think about it, though. Before I was even born, I already had everything I needed to have a baby of my own. In some ways, I was even more prepared than I am now. Set up to give birth, before I was even born . . . This isn't just in books, though. It's happening now, as we speak, inside of me. I wish I could rip out all those parts of me, the parts already rushing to give birth. Why does it have to be like this?

—Midoriko

The amusement park was full of people. It was summer, after all. But it wasn't a mob scene or anything. The crowds at Tokyo Station the day before had been far worse. People had enough room to walk around comfortably, and everyone was smiling like they were having a good time.

There were families, high school couples who still looked like little kids. Voices so excited that they could have been confused for cries of pain. Girls shuffled around, holding hands. Dads consulted park maps with serious faces, lugging backpacks that looked so heavy you would have thought they were about to climb a mountain. Young mothers pushed strollers heavy with all kinds of bags, calling their bright-eyed, fast-legged kids, telling them not to go too far. There were a few old folks licking at their ice cream on the sidelines. The earth thrummed with the movements of people eating, people waiting. All kinds of melodies and voices intermingled, accented at intervals by the onslaught of a roller coaster rushing overhead.

I had no way of knowing how many rides Midoriko was going to do, but I came equipped with an all-day ticket for her, which we traded for a wristband at the ticket gate. "It's like a bracelet," I explained. Midoriko held up her tanned arm and I cinched it around her wrist, making sure it wasn't too tight. She flicked her wrist to check the fit, then held her hand over her squinted eyes, to block the sun.

"This sun's gonna get us," I said. "We're gonna get seriously burnt. As much as it would've sucked, it probably would've been a good idea to wear a black long-sleeve."

I hadn't checked to see what today's high was supposed to be, but it was hot enough that it must have been in the nineties. The sun was at its peak, inescapable. Its white-hot rays battered the awnings of the snack bars, the fountains where the toddlers romped, the signs of the ticket booths, the skin of people, the exoskeletons of the enormous rides. On a bench beside one of the booths, a pair of women sat in matching psychedelic halter dresses, laughing as they took turns rubbing sunscreen on each other's backs.

"If I get a lot of sun just once, I stay dark for like three years," I told Midoriko, eyeing the two women. "I like their halter dresses. Cute, right?"

Midoriko seemed to have no interest in the dresses or the sunscreen. She fixated on our map, looking up to orient herself to whatever ride we were walking past, and looking back at me occasionally to jut her chin and point me in the right direction. Sweat held stray wisps of baby hair to her round forehead. Her cheeks were faintly red.

"This one?"

Our first destination, The Viking, was shaped like a gigantic sailboat. The sign said it was a twenty-minute wait. Basically, the entire thing swings back and forth, going faster and faster. This might lead you to believe that it was not so bad, but there was more than met the eye. I'd been on it once before, thinking it was no more than an enormous swing set, but I had learned the error of my ways. When it swung you upside down and started falling, it was like the wind had been knocked out of you. I wonder if that sensation, this whole-body scream, has a name. What part of your body does it come from? What the hell is actually happening? This always makes me think about the people who jump off of buildings. They say it's only a handful of seconds before they meet the pavement, but I wonder if that scream is the last thing they ever feel. Just after we heard the choppy screams, the roller coaster barreled through the sky and shook the earth.

I bought us bottled water and orange juice at one of the snack bars and waited in the shade, resting on a bench under a tree I couldn't name. When Midoriko came back, she looked exactly the same as before she left.

"What, change your mind?" I asked.

She shook her head.

"Did you go on it?"

She nodded unenthusiastically.

"How was it? Any good?"

This time I got no response. She walked off briskly, toward our next destination. I tried my best to keep up.

Dear Journal,

Now I'm going to write about breasts. I never used to have them, but they're growing in, getting bigger, whether I like it or not. Why? Where do they come from? Why can't I stay like

I am? Some girls show theirs to each other. They jump and shake them, seeing whose is bigger. The boys definitely notice, too. What's everyone so excited about, though? Am I that weird? I hate it. I hate that this is happening, I hate it so bad, I hate it to death. But my mom's on the phone with some clinic, talking about how she wants her boobs to be bigger. I gotta know what she's saying, so I stand nearby to listen. I hear everything. Ever since I had my daughter, she says . . . It's always the same line about breastfeeding me. Idiot. So you want your body to be the way it used to be? Then why'd you even have me? Your life would have been better if you never had me. Think about how great everything would be if none of us were ever born. No happiness, no sadness. Nothing could ever happen to us then. It's not our fault that we have eggs and sperm, but we can definitely try harder to keep them from meeting.

—Midoriko

"Hey, Midoriko, let's grab some food."

We scanned the map to get a sense of all the food options the amusement park had to offer and picked the one that looked the biggest. It was well past the middle of the day, and there were lots of open seats. A waitress brought us to a table. Midoriko produced her little notebook from her fanny pack and set it down by her right hand, then rubbed her face with the oshibori that had arrived with our water. We studied every item on the menus. I decided on the veggie tempura bowl, and Midoriko chose curry rice.

"I don't know how you do it."

For the preceding two and a half hours, Midoriko had gone on ride after ride, beelining from one to the next. To make it on as many rides as possible, she checked all of the wait times and then brought us on the most efficient route. It turns out that she liked the fastest rides the most, but just watching the rollercoasters ratchet their way up to where they tipped over the edge sent shivers down my spine. I waved to Midoriko when I spotted her in line. Sometimes I took a picture with my phone, or made a visor with my hand and squinted, trying to find Midoriko, buckled up and disappearing into the sky. I jogged around, struggling to keep track of her. The sight of the ride corkscrewing through the air or rushing down the tracks at warp speed tuckered me out.

I gulped down my entire glass of water.

"You must be a natural. After all those rides, you don't look dizzy at all."

Midoriko shrugged.

"You know how lots of people get sick on these? Inside your ears, you have these tubes, right? They keep you balanced. But when you get spun around real bad, like when you're carsick, your ears get confused with what your eyes are telling them, and you feel like you're gonna throw up. Kinda like being drunk. But you're okay? Honestly?"

[Why do grown-ups get drunk?]

Midoriko held her notebook high, to make sure I could see it. Why do grown-ups get drunk? I thought about it. Why do we drink? I never drank anything but beer, and rarely enjoyed the taste of it. I'm drunk and hurting before I even know what hit me. There was a time, though. For a few years after coming to the city, I would drink so much that I'd black out and puke everything up. On the way home alone, I'd buy myself the cheapest stuff I could find—even though it tasted god awful. After that I'd have to stay in bed a couple of days, not eating, just me and my darkest thoughts. The days went on forever, like I was just stacking up these stupid blocks—all of them the same color, the same shape. Not like things have changed that much, but they're definitely better than they were. I don't much care to think about it now. I'll never put myself through that again, but at the same time, that was me. I genuinely believed that if I didn't do those things, I couldn't stand to face another day.

"I don't know. Probably because drinking makes you feel like someone else." This was the best I could come up with. When I heard myself saying this to Midoriko, I felt as if it wasn't actually me talking and cleared my throat repeatedly.

"You're always yourself, right? From the second you're born, you're you. Sometimes people get sick of that. I guess that's why." I said the words as soon as they came to me. "Life is tough, but you gotta keep living until you die, you know what I mean? Sometimes you just need to escape, from your own life."

I exhaled, letting it all out, and took a look around. The speakers in the ceiling were rattling off random numbers, and the waitstaff scampered between the tables and the carts they used for bringing out the food. At the table next to ours, a mother was scolding a little girl who seemed too young to know any better. She stared back at her mom in disbelief, frowning with her mouth clamped shut. Her hair, tied up in pigtails, dangled by the corners of her miniature lips.

"I guess that maybe people need to escape from themselves." No one had asked me to go on, but I went on. "Or from all the stuff they carry around—the past, memories, all that. For some people, though, that kind of escape isn't enough. They never want to come back to themselves, so they decide to not live anymore."

Midoriko just stared at me.

"Most people can't, though. So they drink all the time and try to make it go away. I mean, it's not just drinking, though. There are other ways to escape. People end up doing things they don't want to do, but sometimes they can't do anything to stop it. And all those things add up. It's not good for your body. All the people around you, the people who care about you, they get worried and angry. They're like come on, snap out of it. You can't keep doing this to yourself. They're right, too. But I don't know, it just gets harder."

Midoriko looked at me with narrow eyes, like she was watching something in the distance. I said no more, just stared down at my empty glass of water. Gradually, I got the sense that I had missed the mark. Midoriko just sat there, gripping her pen. Beads of sweat formed on her little temples and dribbled down her cheeks. The server showed up with our food and thanked us for waiting. Her gold hoop earrings wobbled in her ears as she set our lunches tidily before us. "Can I get you two anything else?" she asked. When I shook my head, she inserted our bill into the clear cylinder of plastic on the table and marched back to the kitchen. We each ate what we ordered in silence.

Dear Journal,

My mom has this medicine she takes before she goes to bed. Last night, when she wasn't home, I checked to see what it was. Cough syrup. The bottle was almost full, but when I looked today more than half of it was gone. Did she drink all that last night? It's not like she had a cough or anything. What's it for? She keeps getting skinnier all the time, too. She said she fell off her bike on the way home from work the other night. I wanted to ask if she was OK', but I couldn't break the silence. It makes me so sad. There are so many things I'm dying to know. Why do you have to drink that stuff? Are you in pain? Are you alright? They were saying on TV how somewhere in America, a man got his fifteen-year-old daughter a boob job for her birthday. Seriously. The world is crazy. They also said that in the U.S. women who get boob jobs are three times more likely to kill themselves. Does my mom know that? Maybe she'd change her mind if she knew. I need to find a way to talk to her, to really talk. I have to ask her why she wants to do it. Can I, though? Do I have what it takes to ask? It doesn't matter. I need to. I have to, I have to do it.

—Midoriko

"Ready to go home?"

The sun was beginning its descent into the western sky. The thick shadows all around us mellowed out and became indistinguishable. A mild breeze brushed our skin. People held hands and called after each other, drifting apart and clumping together as we all made our way slowly toward the exit.

Midoriko had the map out. She tapped her finger on the rides in the order she had done them.

"Did you get to see everything you wanted?"

She nodded repeatedly, without looking up. We fell into the outgoing tide of people, moving slowly to the gates.

On our right we passed a ferris wheel, behind which the thinning blue sky had taken on a yellow tinge. From where we were, it almost looked as if the giant wheel was perfectly still, but I knew that it was moving. I felt a pressure in my chest, watching it move that slowly, as if it hoped to leave no trace, not in the sky or in time or in the memories of the people watching it. Midoriko, standing beside me, watched the ferris wheel go, too. A minute later she was tapping on my arm, to get my attention, so I looked at her and saw that she was pointing at the wheel.

"The ferris wheel?" I asked.

She nodded yes.

A couple was waiting in line. The boy boarded the gondola at the bottom of its arc and reached his hands out for the girl, who lifted the hems of her skirt as she leapt on.

"Go ahead. I'll be over by that fence," I said and started to walk away, but Midoriko shook her head like crazy. When I asked her what was wrong, she pointed at the ferris wheel, like she wanted us to ride the thing together, and stared me down.

"What, both of us?"

Midoriko nodded with raised eyebrows.

"I'm no good at rides, Midoriko. I can't even handle a swing set," I explained. "While I'm on the subject, I'm afraid of heights, too. Never even been on a plane and that's the way it's gonna stay."

Midoriko wasn't having any of it. It didn't matter what I said. I breathed out, to ground myself, bought a ticket at the booth, and passed through the gates with Midoriko. Up on the spacious platform, it was just us and the lone uniformed attendant, whose job was to open and close the cabin doors. For reasons that I can't pretend to fathom, Midoriko let several cars pass by before darting into one that she deemed suitable. Panicking, I reached with both hands for the bar over the hatch, said "Shit," and stuffed myself into the car. Just then, it swung as if it had been pushed, and I fell into my seat. The smiling attendant waved us both goodbye, threw the bolt on the door, and locked us in.

The ferris wheel followed a fixed path over a fixed amount of time. Our car climbed slowly upward. I fixed my gaze on the horizon, trying not to look down. The sky soon occupied the greater portion of my vision. Midoriko pressed her forehead to the window and peered down on the world below, then slid herself to the other end of her seat to look out of the other window in the same way, face pressed into the glass. Her hair had been tied back in a high ponytail, but strands of it were coming loose and gathering in wisps that puffed at her neck and touched her shoulders. Her neck was skinny, and her oversized t-shirt hid her shoulders. Her legs were tanned, and the skin of her tiny knees was looking a little dry. Midoriko had one hand resting on her fanny pack and the other one pressed against the window, watching Tokyo stretch out before her.

"I bet Maki's gonna start heading back pretty soon," I said, but Midoriko remained fixated on the world outside the window.

"She went to Ginza, right? I guess Ginza would be that way . . . no, wait, over there."

I was never very good at geography, but pointed in the general direction of where I thought it was, to a place where clustered buildings loomed high above the rest of the city. That must be it.

"Hey. Today was fun," I said.

Midoriko looked at me and nodded in agreement. The tops of her cheeks and the tip of her nose were red from all the sun, but now they caught the blue of evening. This happened once—a million years ago, when I was her age . . . on a ferris wheel just like this, looking down over the city. Climbing high into the evening, blue lapsing into black. Was Makiko there, too? Had Mom brought us . . . or Komi? I tried to picture our mom waving us goodbye once we pushed off, to see the wrinkles on Komi's hands—but the more I reached for them the further away they slipped, blurring into obscurity. Little birds drew arcs in the sky, then disappeared. The tall buildings in the distance looked like columns of white smoke. Who had been there with me, as a kid, when I watched the sky and city slipping into night? Trying to remember made me doubt it ever happened. Maybe it hadn't. Maybe the mix of smells and images and feelings lined up perfectly, in such a way that they appeared to be a memory, but I had never actually been here in real life with someone, watching the sky and city slipping into night.

"It's pretty, huh?" I said. "Hey, did you know ferris wheels are one of the safest places you can be?"

Midoriko looked at me for a second before shaking her head.

"Somebody told me that when I was a kid, I forget who. Anyway, when you look at one from the side, it's almost flat, the way a firework looks two-dimensional when it explodes, like you could poke it with a stick and tip it over. Freaky, right? I always thought if something awful happened, a ferris wheel would be the first thing to come down. But it's not true. They can take all kinds of abuse. Rain, wind, even massive earthquakes. They won't budge. These things are built to withstand anything. So, when I first heard this, it gave me an idea. It just came to me, maybe we should all live on ferris wheels. I was really serious about it, too. We'd all have houses up there, and wave at each other from our windows. We could use paper-cup telephones to talk to the next cabin over, and we could set up laundry lines for hanging up our clothes. I remember drawing things like this a lot, a whole world full of ferris wheels. You know, a world where everyone was safe from earthquakes and typhoons and everything. A safer world."

We sat there, just staring out the window.

"Hey, have you ever been on one of these with Maki?"

Midoriko shrugged the question off.

"Oh. Well, I guess she's pretty busy."

Midoriko glanced at me and turned her gaze back toward the windows. Her silhouette reminded me of what my mother used to look like, when she felt good and looked good, before she got sick. Elegant nose, albeit somewhat crooked, fabulous eyelashes. Pockmarks on her cheeks. When I asked her what they were, she smiled and told me this is what you get for popping zits. I realized that Midoriko looked way more like my mom than her own mother. She'd never had a chance to meet my mom or Komi, which meant they'd never had a chance to meet her either. It was all perfectly obvious, but I'd never really thought of it that way.

"I was about your age when Mom died, so Maki was what, twenty-two?"

Who knows why I felt the need to bring this up, but there we were.

"I know I was fifteen when Komi died, making Maki twenty-four. We were broke back then, so we had both funerals at the community center. It was the cheapest service possible, seriously low-budget. We had a priest, though, a distant relative of Komi's. At some point we really need to pay him back for that."

Again, Midoriko looked at me and turned back toward the windows.

"Since our place was rent controlled, we paid less than 20,000 yen a month. We managed to scrape by. Maki was well out of school by then. That's why they let us stay together. If she had been younger, I bet they would have split us up and sent us to a children's home or something."

Midoriko was still. On the horizon, you could see a red light pulsing from the lightning rod of a distant skyscraper, like the steady breathing of a creature. I watched it go.

"I owe Maki the world," I said. "After Mom and Komi died, when it was just the two of us, Maki took care of everything. Everything. She got me a job washing dishes and brought food back from the restaurant. That food kept us alive."

Dusk was taking over. Like a cascade of lace—thousands of thin, soft layers fluttering above countless winking lights far and near. These dots of feeble light reminded me of the port town we lived in for a few years after I was born. Sailboats coming into port from the dark sea on summer evenings. People floating in the waves, little kids losing their minds when they see the white skin of a foreigner for the first time. This is how I saw the lights of home—above the faded signs, atop the concrete telephone poles, under the awnings of the stores, and by the bollards where the ships tied off to the docks—clusters of lights strung from wires and bobbing in the evening breeze.

"I forget how old I was, but it was before we went to Komi's place, so I was probably in kindergarten. We were living by the

water. My kindergarten was getting ready for this really important field trip . . . Midoriko, have you ever gone grape picking?"

She shook her head.

"That's what the trip was, picking grapes." I laughed. "I
don't remember liking anything about kindergarten, but for
some reason I was super excited. As the day approached, I got
incredibly anxious. I even made myself a schedule for the day.
I was literally counting down the days, too. It was all that I
could think about.

"Know what, though? I couldn't go. You had to pay a fee,
and as it turned out we didn't have the money. Looking back,
it was probably nothing, like 200 yen. But listen, when I woke
up that morning, Mom was like you're staying home today. I
wanted to ask why, but you can't ask that sort of thing, right?
It was because of money, obviously. Dad was always sleeping in
the morning, too, so Maki and I had to be super quiet. We
couldn't even make noises when we ate ramen.

"I was like okay, sure, I'll stay home. Pretty soon, though, I
started crying, I mean really bawling my eyes out. I was sadder
than I'd ever been in my whole life. These tears were coming
out, no matter what, but I couldn't make any noise, so I
crawled into the corner and stuffed a towel between my teeth
and cried and cried. Even though, when I was little, I was seriously thick-skinned, this thing really knocked me flat—but
what was I so sad about? It's not like I'd ever picked grapes
before. I didn't know what I was missing. I mean, I didn't even
like grapes. So why was I crying? I still wonder about that.
Who the hell cares about grapes anyway?

"Later, though, I think I figured it out. You know how it
feels to hold a handful of grapes? The way they fit into your
palm. Doesn't it feel, I dunno, special? All those grapes huddled together. Sometimes you get little ones in there, too. As
soon as you open your hand, though, they roll off, one at a

time. They aren't heavy, but they're not light, either. That's pretty special. Or not. Haha. I'm still not sure if I was crying because of the way they made me feel, or if crying was what made me feel that way.

"Later that morning, Mom went to work and Dad left the house, too, for once. I stayed there, crying in the corner with that towel in my mouth. Makiko was home. I must have made her late for school. She tried her best to cheer me up. I was a total wreck.

"So anyway, she's like, Natsuko, close your eyes a sec. Don't open them until I say so. I sat there hugging my knees and crying, and a few minutes later, Maki comes over and says keep your eyes shut and follow me. She grabs my hand, pulls me up, makes me take a couple steps and says okay, open your eyes.

"When I do, there are socks and washcloths everywhere. Tissues and mom's underwear are hanging off all the cabinets and poking out from the drawers, on top of the lampshade and over the laundry line. The whole place is like that. Then she's like, okay Natsuko, let's pick grapes now, just the two of us. You see the grapes? They're all for us.

"She puts me on her back and I reach up to grab them, all the socks and underwear and stuff. We're using a colander, like with all these holes in it, for a basket. Makiko holds my legs tight and circles around the room, saying hey there's more over here, get this one. She wants me to get them all. I don't know. It's cute but kind of sad, right? I knew they weren't even real grapes. It's not like I could eat them, but that's all that I can think about when someone mentions picking grapes."

Midoriko kept staring out the window. In no time, our car started its descent. The buildings were growing taller, and the ground was coming closer every second. Lights twinkled all around us.

"Hey, why was I telling you all that again?"

I shook my head and chuckled. After a pause, Midoriko pulled out her pen.

[Because of the color]

Midoriko looked me in the eye and gestured at the faint purple coming from her window before giving it her full attention. The sky reached into the past and into obscurity, streaked with strips of cloud like marks left by a tired finger. The light leaking between the clouds was touched with purples, gentle reds and heavy blues. If you looked far up enough, you could see the wind blowing. It almost felt as if we could touch this layer wrapped around the world, if we just stuck out our hands. It showed its colors like a melody that could never be repeated.

"That's right," I smiled, nodding. "Hey, it's kinda like we're inside a giant grape."

The day was coming to an end. Our cabin creaked as it continued its descent. As we neared the platform, the same attendant welcomed us back. When she opened the door, Midoriko hopped out of the car. The heat of the day had left, and the sweat between my shirt and skin was cold. The air was thick with the smell of summer night.

7.
ALL THAT YOU HOLD DEAR

Makiko had said that she'd be back from the clinic by seven, but then it was eight, and soon it was nine, without a word from her. I tried calling her over and over, but it kept going straight to voicemail. Either her phone was dead, or she'd turned it off. I left her a message. "Hello, Maki? You okay? I'm a little worried. Call me when you get this." I pressed END.

This was our last dinner in Tokyo together—but I guess since they were only here two nights, calling it "the last" might be a little dramatic. What should we eat though? It might be fun to take the train out to a nicer area. I figured the best bet would be to ask Makiko, once she was back, if there was anything that she was craving. Assuming that she ever came back. I thought about maybe walking to the supermarket with Midoriko and picking up a few things. That way at least the two of us could eat. But I'm all out of rice, and frankly, making a meal that time of night was the last thing I wanted. Besides, I suck at cooking. I bet once I made a mess Makiko would come home anyway. "When Maki comes back, maybe we can just go back to the same Chinese restaurant and order something else," I said. "I'm sure she'll be back, any minute." I scanned my shelves for books I wouldn't mind giving to Midoriko. Flipped through a couple of magazines. Midoriko was writing in her journal. Ten minutes went by. Then twenty. Then an hour. No sign of Makiko.

"Hey, Midoriko. Wanna go to the store?"

At that point it was 9:15. We left a note on the tea table: "AT THE STORE." Midoriko and I stepped out. I didn't like the idea of leaving the door unlocked, but I did it anyway.

The summer night was tinged with moisture. The air smelled like rain. My cheap flip-flops had worn so thin that I could feel the granulated texture of the asphalt underfoot. I imagined stepping on a piece of glass, slicing through the sole, gashing the arch of my foot, and bleeding profusely. Midoriko walked a few steps in front of me. Her legs were long and thin. The white socks pulled up to her knees made her legs look like bones. They made me think about the novel I was writing—or more precisely, the novel I'd been unable to write for who knows how many weeks. As if I needed the reminder.

Inside the store, the air was cold enough to make your skin go tight. We browsed the aisles, scanning the items on the shelves. Midoriko had seen enough. She lagged behind, not picking anything up. "Want some candy? Ice cream?"

After letting the question dangle for a while, she shook her head.

"I'll grab some bread for breakfast," I said, reaching for a loaf. "We'll figure out what to do for dinner when your mom gets back." The speaker by the automatic door rang out—*ding-dong*—and a group of kids scrambled into the store, followed by a group of adults who appeared to be responsible for them. Some of them were cackling and red in the face, probably drunk. It sounded like they were on their way to light some fireworks and stopping in to round out their supply. The dark-skinned kids circled around the bin of fireworks by the register, yipping joyfully. Midoriko stared at them from a nearby aisle.

"Let's get some, too," I said.

She didn't take the bait. Once the kids were gone, I had a look at the bin. A heap of individually wrapped fireworks and bagged larger sets. Four types of fireworks. I remembered doing fireworks when I was little. Makiko and I cupped candles in our hands to keep them from blowing out and watched as the flames lit the fuse. The air stank of gunpowder and rang with crackly explosions. Faces lit up through the growing bank of ashen smoke. I realized that Midoriko was standing next to me. "They've got a bunch of stuff in here," I said. She glanced into the bin. Lips pursed, she scrutinized the selection for a minute before picking up a pack of bottle rockets. Then I picked up a sugar snake and said, "Midoriko, check this out, have you ever seen one of these?" Her lips parted, showing her teeth. After that she picked up every single kind of firework they had and looked them over carefully. We wound up leaving with a 500-yen variety pack.

Pretty soon it was ten. No Makiko. I don't care how unfamiliar she was with Tokyo, there was no way she had gotten lost. She couldn't possibly have forgotten where to get off, and it was a straight shot back. I knew that if something had gone awry, she would have called me, and if her battery died, she would have gone to a store to buy another one. That meant she must have lost her phone, or her wallet, or it could have meant that she didn't want to contact me. That, or she had gotten in a real mess and was blacked out in an alley somewhere.

I imagined all kinds of awful things, but none of them felt plausible. Tokyo was overflowing with people. If something bad had happened, no matter what, somebody would have contacted me by now. I mean, Makiko was almost forty. Not hearing from her could only mean one thing: *she didn't want to reach me.* That was it. In that sense, it didn't matter how late Makiko came home. Of course Midoriko would have a hard time seeing things that way. She grew more nervous every minute, filling like a cup set on the floor to catch a leak. Quiet as she was, I could feel her tensing up.

If we so much as heard a person on the stairs at the end of

the hall, our eyes shot toward the door, but it was never Makiko. I turned down the TV so far that you could barely even hear it and stared down at the screen of my flip phone. Every couple of minutes, I checked my inbox, to make sure I hadn't missed something.

"Midoriko, I don't think I can take this anymore, for real. I'm starving. Want some bread?"

But she just sat there, chin resting on her knees, and shook her head—then out of nowhere, she stood up and leveled this heavy look at me, like she had something to confess . . . only to sit down, as if her mind had changed, and hug her knees again.

"What?" I asked, no clue what was happening.

Midoriko bit her lower lip and drew short breaths through her nose.

"What's the name of the place Maki went?" I asked myself. "I know it's in Ginza, but what was it called?" I replayed what Makiko had said to me about the clinic, but all I could remember was that it was in Ginza.

Had she even told me? I squinted, trying to remember something other than how popular it was—but all I got was that the pamphlet had been black with gold text, like the décor at a cheesy luxury hotel.

"Midoriko, you don't know, do you? The name of the place your mom went today."

She shook her head.

"Course you don't," I said, trying to laugh it off. "Why would you? I mean, it would be amazing if you did."

What was Makiko doing out there? Had she even gone in for the consultation? Where was she? What the hell was going on? Then it hit me. The very thought of it was crazy, too ludicrous for words. Common sense made me ashamed for even thinking it—had Makiko tried to get it over with and gone under the knife this afternoon? She wouldn't. She couldn't. No one goes straight from the consultation into surgery. No one.

This wasn't like having a tooth filled. I knew it was absurd, but now that it was on my mind, I couldn't shake it. Acting casual, to make sure Midoriko didn't get wise, I grabbed my phone and searched for "breast implants same day."

The first hit was a site called "THE BREASTS OF YOUR DREAMS—TODAY!" I clicked it, then pressed on the word "Schedule" near the top, which took me to a hot-pink page with a timetable:

Arrival:	11:00 A.M.
Consultation:	11:30 A.M.
Operation:	12:30 P.M.
Rest:	1:30 P.M.
NEW YOU:	2:00 P.M.
Time to go shopping!	

I guess I was wrong, I told myself, and flipped my phone shut.

On TV, comedians sat at the center of a candy-colored set answering some quiz. The volume was so low that I could barely hear them, but the screen bristled with activity. Midoriko sat there frowning, knees tucked up to her chin.

"Midoriko, I can't even imagine what's going through your head right now."

Midoriko looked up.

"But trust me, there's nothing to worry about," I told her, smiling as best I could. "In my experience, whenever I'm convinced that something's gonna happen, bad or otherwise, I jinx it, and it goes away. At least that's how it is for me. It's like that every time. For example . . . "

Midoriko looked unconvinced.

"How about earthquakes? Earthquakes happen all the

time, but when one comes, it's not like anyone was expecting it. No one on the planet was thinking that an earthquake was about to hit. Know what I mean? But that's exactly when an earthquake hits, when you least expect it, like it was waiting for you to look away."

Midoriko gave me a strange look, like she was unsure how to take this.

"Like right now. No earthquakes, right? That's because we're talking about them. Not like I can prove it, since you can't ask everyone after an earthquake what was on their minds a minute earlier, but sometimes the fact that we can't prove things sort of proves them, in a way . . . "

Midoriko appeared to chew on this a bit. Meanwhile, I realized that I didn't know what jinx actually meant. But when I tried to get up to check, Midoriko seized the bottom of my shirt, tugging me down.

"Don't worry," I laughed. "I'm not going anywhere."

I grabbed my electronic dictionary from my desk and sat back down. I got this thing a few years back in a raffle at the shopping arcade down the street. Third prize. It didn't have a backlit screen, but it was handy, a real gem.

I typed in "jinx" and read the definition:

jinx (ji x) *n.* 1. an enigmatic instance of bad luck 2. a curse or spell that causes bad luck. —*vt.* 1. to negatively change the course of fate.

That made me want to look up "fate." The definition was so long it nearly blacked out the small screen, but this is how it started:

fate (f t) *n.* 1. the development of events beyond a person's control. See DESTINY.

As I read her the definition, Midoriko nodded vigorously. She took the dictionary from me and searched for something else. Glued to the screen, she looked up one thing after another—then something clicked. She looked up at me, eyes bright. It was like she was finding the words for the thoughts in her head and making sure that each of them was right. Genuinely stunned at where her train of thought had led her, she stared wide-eyed at the screen again. When I asked her what was wrong, she seemed frazzled. She didn't answer. She just shook her head. I took back the dictionary and searched for something else.

"Hey, check it out. The character for 'destiny' looks a whole lot like 'green.' How about 'fatal'? Okay, it says that it originally meant 'destined by fate' and 'ominous,' but it can also mean 'causing death.' As in 'a fatal accident.' Yeah, makes sense. Happens every day. Next up: 'murder.' Happens all the time. Every day. I mean, somewhere out there, someone was just murdered. Hey, you know how lots of murderers use kitchen knives? Did you know they always check how they were holding it? I mean like if the blade was pointing up or down. That's how they determine whether it was first- or second-degree murder. Judges get really serious about that kind of stuff. I'm serious. Someone I know . . . " I realized things were spinning out of control. To reel us in a bit, I proposed we look up something horrifying, the kind of word that gives you the chills.

Slaughter. Damnation. Hellfire. Abomination. We stared so closely at the little liquid crystal screen we practically bumped heads.

"Okay, next . . . It's crazy, though, if you think about it. I'm not talking about people dying or being murdered or anything, but right now there are people out there going through all kinds of hell. Like, I don't know, torture. There are people being ripped apart or having their eyes gouged out. All of that's actually happening, somewhere. You know what I mean? Not just in the movies. I'm saying that right now, on this planet, people are going through the worst kinds of pain imaginable. Like, what would it feel like to be on fire? Or to have your teeth pulled out? These things actually happen. Or what about, I don't know, getting tickled to death? Okay, maybe not. But what about those poisonous mushrooms that make you laugh so hard you drop dead? That would be the worst, I swear. To laugh until you die? What a nightmare. Or like—"

I was free-associating, but Midoriko didn't share in my enthusiasm. She shook her head to signal me to stop. "Sorry," I said, and turned my focus back to the screen—when it happened. An enormous crash, like something the size of my apartment building had just plowed through the wall. We hadn't been more frightened the whole night. We literally flew into the air. Holding hands as tight as we could, we turned to see what the matter was. Through the darkness of the kitchen, we saw Makiko—standing by the open door. The lunar glow of the front hall light outlined her figure.

Since the light was mostly coming from behind her, it was hard to see her face, but it was all too clear that she was hammered. It's not like she was mumbling, or staggering, or like she reeked of booze. But she was drunk, really drunk. That much was palpable.

Makiko announced, "I'm back," and tried taking off her shoes, only to realize that she already had. In her brief struggle with the phantom footwear, she stepped on her own feet and looked down, confused.

"They're already off, Maki," I said.

"I know, I was just scratching an itch," she said, finding her way into the room.

"Why didn't you call?"

Annoyed by my question, Makiko frowned and stared me

down with raised her eyebrows. Her forehead was all wrinkles. I could see now that her eyes were bloodshot.

"My phone died. I mean, the battery."

"They sell batteries at the store."

"Those things cost too much." Makiko tossed her handbag on the carpet. "Do I look like a chump?"

She dropped her bag on the carpet and walked across the room to the beanbag.

I felt like screaming "Where the hell were you?" but managed to suppress the urge. Instead, I cleared my throat, but it was a lot louder than expected, like how you clear your throat before you ask a serious question. So I cleared my throat again, to signal that the first one signaled nothing in particular, except this time something got caught, and I ended up hiccupping. When I finally stopped, Makiko turned just enough to see me from her burrow in the beanbag. Her eyebrows were gone, and her bottom eyelashes were messy with black eyeliner. The bags under her eyes seemed to have darkened and spread. Traces of mascara flecked her cheekbones. Sweat was ruining her foundation, creating splotchy patterns.

"Maybe you should wash your face," I found myself saying.

"Who gives a shit about my face," said Makiko.

Midoriko, dictionary still in hand, watched us from across the room. *Oh no*—I thought. *What if Makiko had met up with her ex-husband, Midoriko's father?* That morning, when she left the house, she said something about meeting up with an old friend, but since when did she have any friends in Tokyo? Even if she had an acquaintance in the city, they would have come up at least once. But no one ever had. She didn't have a single friend in Tokyo.

So who had she been drinking with? It wasn't like her to get this drunk alone. Neither of us could stomach anything but beer. Makiko could hold it a bit better than me, but it wasn't something she enjoyed. Besides, she hadn't seen her sister in forever, and she knew that I was waiting up for her, minding her daughter. She said she would be home at seven.

Things must have gotten away from her. Some kind of an unexpected rendezvous, leading to an unexpected turn of events . . . Next thing she knew, she was drunk. But who with? Makiko may have spent her nights at the bar, chatting with customers, but she was shy deep down. If some guy had struck up a conversation with her, I can't imagine her ever grabbing a drink with him. In other words, there could only be one explanation—her ex-husband. He was the only person in Tokyo she could have been with.

But what was I supposed to ask her? "Looks like someone had a lot to drink. Who's the lucky guy?"

There's no way I could've made it sound casual, like I was joking. She could go out drinking with anyone she wanted. That was up to her. It wasn't any of my business, but that doesn't mean I had to like it. If she'd have said that she was out with some girls she used to know, I could see myself taking an interest and asking what they talked about, or what they ate, or what's going on with her friends these days. But I didn't want to hear about her ex. I couldn't care less what they talked about, or how it made them feel, or what each of them had said, what they regretted about the past and what concerned them about the present. But why? I didn't hold any sort of grudge against him. No lingering resentments. I'd forgotten almost everything about him. I could barely even picture the guy's face. I'm sure that Makiko was struggling with some complicated emotions. As her sister, I wanted to be there for her—but I was not about to get involved in any bullshit started by her ex, or any man. I didn't want to hear it. So I held my tongue.

"Take a shower. You'll feel better," I assured her. "Oh, yeah. We got some fireworks from the store. I was thinking that, you know, since you two are heading home tomorrow, we could do some fireworks tonight, the three of us."

Makiko's face remained buried in the beanbag. She nodded, just enough to show that she was listening.

Her legs were rail-thin, like a pair of disposable chopsticks. She had a tear in the foot of her pantyhose, running from her big toe to her ankle. The skin at the back of her heels was cracked and dry like old mochi. Nothing to her calves but skin and bones, like the taut stomach of a sundried fish.

Midoriko set the dictionary on the table and ran out into the kitchen. Standing in the dark, she set herself up by the sink and glowered over the room. I went into the kitchen to stand next to her and see what she was seeing.

Same room as always. Bookshelves along the wall. Small desk in the back-right corner. Window in the middle. The cream-colored curtains that I'd had since the day that I moved in, which were still in good shape despite constant exposure to the sun. And below them, balled up on the beanbag and motionless, was my older sister. The images on the TV were the only things moving.

After a while, Makiko pressed her palms into the carpet and worked her way onto her hands and knees. From there, she rotated her head slowly to the left and right, like she was doing some kind of a physical therapy routine. Then she let out a deep sigh, more of a groan, really, and took her time standing up.

Our eyes met. I could see her face much better than before. She squinted and looked back at me, before taking slow steps toward us, the soles of her feet pressing hard into the carpet. She stopped at the boundary of the kitchen, where she leaned against the doorway. After scratching at her scalp for a second or two, she addressed Midoriko.

"Well, look at you."

When Makiko spoke, it was clear just how drunk she was. Never—not in all the years we'd lived together—had I ever seen my sister as hammered as this. What if she was like this all the time in Osaka? Was Midoriko used to this by now? I imagined her seeing her mother like this, drunk beyond recognition. Considering her condition, this was hardly the best time to bring it up.

There was a bucket on the floor that I'd put out for doing the fireworks. Just a blue plastic bucket. Nothing special, although I guess it was strange that I owned a bucket at all. I'd bought it on an impulse at a 100-yen store or someplace like that, but never actually put the thing to use. It looked brand new. But as I watched the bucket, it stopped being a bucket, transforming into something else entirely. It was like that thing that happens when you say a word so many times it loses meaning, only this time, it was happening with an object. I glanced at the fireworks beside it. Still fireworks. What a relief. Fireworks—okay. I was having a look around the kitchen, checking off all of the other silly things I knew, when Makiko spoke again.

"Don't wanna talk to me, huh?" She was walking over to Midoriko. "Fine. Doesn't matter to me."

Her voice was stern.

"Acting like you came into this world alone, like you're the only person in the whole wide world."

She sounded like the dramas that were on TV when we were kids.

"You think I care? Does it look like I care? I'm fine."

She didn't sound fine. Midoriko turned away, staring at the dry metal of the sink. I felt for her. I really did. Makiko got closer, leaning in so she could see her daughter's face, since she was dead set on not looking at her mother.

"You never listen to me," she said. "You just think I'm an idiot. That's fine, too."

Midoriko squirmed to get away from her, but Makiko doubled down.

"Fine! If you don't want to talk, or can't, then keep on

writing in your stupid notebook. If you have something to say, by all means, write it down. I guess that's how it's gonna be. Until we're dead, the both of us."

Makiko's tone was growing wilder by the minute. Midoriko was cowering, cheek turned into her shoulder.

"How long do you think you can keep this up? Because I can—"

Just then, Makiko grabbed Midoriko by the elbow, but Midoriko shook herself free. The next moment, she slapped her mother right in the face, her fingers hitting her in the eye. Makiko whelped and covered her face with her hands. Tears were spilling from her eyes, but it was like she couldn't open them again. No matter how she pressed the pads of her fingers over her eyes and wiped the tears away, her eyelids refused to cooperate. The tracks of her tears caught the light from the other room. Midoriko pursed her lips so tight it had to hurt. She dropped her hands, balling them into fists at her sides. She stared at her mother, watching her pressing her eyes through an onslaught of tears.

Now even Makiko was out of words. That much was clear to me; and watching them exploding in my face, I found myself speechless as well. I had no words. There was nothing I could say. Nothing for me to say. The kitchen was dark. The vague smell of trash. I kept my eyes on Midoriko. Her jaw was tense, tight at the molars. She was staring at something, but I had no idea what. Makiko buried her head in her hands, crying out in pain. As I watched the two of them like this—I felt myself reach for the wall and turn on the kitchen light, as if my hand was moving on its own.

The fluorescent bulb clicked on and blinked to life. Once it was fully on, we could finally see each other as we were, huddled in the kitchen.

This kitchen was beyond familiar—it was almost an extension of my body. But now it looked older than ever, no more than a shell. The white glow of the fluorescent lights spilled evenly into every corner of the room. Makiko opened her reddened eyes. Midoriko held her fists tight against her thighs and set her eyes on her mother's neck. Then, after taking a sharp breath, she spoke.

"Mom."

A cluster of the word and everything it meant fell from her mouth.

"Mom," she said again, even louder this time, although Makiko was right beside her. Makiko was stunned. Midoriko's fists were shaking. She looked like the slightest tap would make her crumble.

"Mom," she said, practically coughing on her words. "Tell me the truth."

Just saying that took everything Midoriko had, her shoulders rising and falling with every breath. Her parted lips were shaking. I could hear her swallowing her spit, like she was holding something back. The nervous energy mounting inside of her was searching for a way out. Then she said it again, in a voice so faint it almost wasn't there.

"Tell me."

Hearing this, Makiko sighed and started cracking up.

"Huh? Hahaha. What's that supposed to mean? Tell you what?"

Makiko looked at Midoriko and laughed, shaking her head dramatically.

"You hear that, Natsuko? The truth? What's she want me to say? Can you translate?"

Makiko tried to laugh it off, but this was no laughing matter. She was making a mistake—but I couldn't bring myself to say so. Midoriko stood there, staring at the floor. She was breathing heavier now. I figured she was on the verge of tears, but Midoriko looked up and grabbed the carton of eggs that I had left by the sink earlier—and ripped it open so fast that I barely saw it happen. She took an egg in her hand and raised it high over her head.

Here it comes, I thought. In that moment, Midoriko started crying, her tears flying, gushing like they do in comics, as she cracked the egg over her own head.

Splack. Yolk was all over the place. The egg was broken, but she kept smacking her hand against her head, making her hair frothy with egg. Bits of eggshell dug into her scalp, yolky liquid dripping from her ears. She rubbed her palm across her forehead. Crying harder now, she grabbed another egg.

"Why . . . " she started, "do that to yourself . . . " she spat out, breaking the second egg over her head, same as the last one. Yolk and white oozed down her forehead. Without hesitation, she grabbed another egg. "You're the one who had me," she told Makiko. "And it's too late to do anything about that now, but why do you have to . . . " Midoriko slapped the egg hard against her forehead.

"I don't know what to do, and you don't tell me anything. I love you, but I never want to be like you. No . . . " She took a breath. "I want to start working, so I can help. I want to help so bad. With money, with everything. Do you have any idea . . . how scared I am? I don't get it, any of it. My eyes hurt. They hurt. Why does everything change? Why? It hurts. Why was I born? Why did any of us have to be born? If we were never born, none of these things would have happened, none of it would—"

Bawling her eyes out, Midoriko grabbed two more eggs, and broke them both over her head. Pieces of shell flew through the air, and goopy chunks of egg white stuck to the collar of her shirt. Yellow gobbets clung to her shoulders and chest. Midoriko doubled over, crying louder than anyone I had heard cry in my entire life.

Makiko didn't move. For a few seconds, she just stared at Midoriko, crying on the floor. Then finally, it hit her.

"Midoriko," she said, grabbing her daughter's egg-sodden shoulders.

But Midoriko whipped, pulling herself away from her mother. Makiko froze with both hands in the air. Unable to approach her crying daughter, let alone make contact with her sticky, quivering body, Makiko just stared, taking slow, deep breaths. Turning to the open carton, she reached for an egg and knocked it against on her head, but hit it just the wrong way, so that it tumbled down and rolled across the floor. Makiko hurried to chase it down, got down on all fours and bashed it against her forehead. Face smeared with yolk and shell, she stood and went back to Midoriko, grabbed another egg, and cracked it right between her eyes. Midoriko was still in tears but paying close attention, watching everything. She grabbed another egg for herself and rammed it into her temple. Its insides ran down her cheek, followed by bits of shell. Makiko grabbed the last two eggs, then broke them on her face, one after the other, then turned to me.

"No more?" she asked.

"There's some in the fridge," I said.

Makiko reached for the fridge door and took them out. They took turns, working their way through the carton. Their heads glistened from the eggs. Shells crackled underfoot. The floor puddled with yolk and blobby egg white.

Once all the eggs were broken, the two of them sat there a while in silence. Then Makiko spoke up.

"Midoriko?" she asked in a hoarse voice. "What did you want to know the truth about?"

Midoriko didn't answer. She shook her head and cried. Egg traveled down their necks and arms, but it was starting to coagulate in their hair and on their clothes.

The truth. Saying those words had taken everything Midoriko had. She shook through the tears.

"Midoriko, Midoriko . . . You wanna know the truth? You

think there's always gonna be some truth, right? Who doesn't want to believe there's some kind of a truth to life? But know what? Not everything works like that. Some things don't work like that at all."

Makiko went on, but I couldn't hear what she said. Midoriko looked at her mother and said, "You're wrong. You're wrong," shaking her head. "What about all . . . all . . . all," she said, three times, then collapsed onto the kitchen floor, wailing loud as before. Makiko tried combing the egg out of Midoriko's hair with her fingers, tucking her eggy hair behind her ears. She patted her back for what felt like an eternity, saying nothing at all.

Dear Journal,

Mom said that she can take a little time off in August so we can visit Natsuko. I've never been to Tokyo before, so I guess I'm a little excited. Just kidding. I'm super excited. I've never been on the Shinkansen, and it's been forever since I've seen Natsuko. I can't wait!

—Midoriko

Dear Journal,

Okay, so last night, in the middle of the night, Mom woke me up. She was talking in her sleep again. I sat up to listen, expecting her to say something funny, some random thing. But then out of nowhere, she shouted, BEER PLEASE. I didn't know what to do. I couldn't stop crying. I couldn't fall back asleep the rest of the night. I wish we didn't have to suffer. Any of us. Why can't it all just go away? I feel so bad for Mom. I always have.

—Midoriko

*

Once Makiko and Midoriko fell asleep, I peeked into Midoriko's backpack and found her journal and read it under the light by the kitchen sink. The pages were full of writing and these drawings she'd made from countless little squares. Under the dim gray light, her handwriting looked like it was trembling. But the more I looked at it, the more I wondered if it was my eyes that were trembling, or maybe the light between my eyes and the page. I spent twenty minutes reading through the entries, and when I was done, I read them all again, then went back to the room and slipped the journal back inside her backpack.

We never got to do the fireworks. The next morning, Makiko and Midoriko went back to Osaka.

"Can't you stay another night?" I asked, but knew there was no way.

"Sorry," Makiko said. "I have to work tonight."

So I turned and asked Midoriko.

"What about you? Do you want to stay a little longer? It's summer, right? You can stay as long as you want."

Midoriko said she was going with her mom.

While they were packing up their things, I looked outside the window. I knew every car parked in the parking lot. The street was the same color as always. Straight shot. I remembered what Midoriko had looked like the other day, when she came back from her walk. She walked with her hand on her fanny pack. I watched her from this window. Legs like sticks, coming up the road. The scene was nothing special, but I had a feeling it was an image that I would keep returning to. Midoriko and Makiko and me were still there, in the same room, but it felt like all of this was already a memory. I turned around. Midoriko was putting her hair up but making no real progress. I said that she should ask her mom for help, but she told me she could do it and clamped down on the black elastic between her lips.

We took the stairs down to the street. I carried Makiko's bag and Midoriko carried her own backpack. The heat and humidity were exactly the same as two days earlier, when the three of us walked back here from the station. Maneuvering the sidewalks and slipping past all kinds of sounds, we sweated like crazy and made it to the train that carried us all the way to Tokyo Station.

Makiko was wearing the same thick makeup she'd been wearing when I found them on the platform. There was some time before their train arrived. We ducked into the gift shops, checked out the magazines piled on the carts outside the stores, and sat down on a bench near the timetable and the ticket gates, where we let the endless waves of people come crashing over us. Nothing had changed in these two days.

I asked Makiko if she wanted to get some soy milk.

"Soy milk?"

"Yeah, soy milk. It's supposed to be really good for women. Let's get some."

"I've never tried it," Makiko said and laughed.

"Me neither. Come on. You too, Midoriko. Let's try some." Soon we had five minutes left.

"Hey, Midoriko. Get yourself something with this." I handed her 5,000 yen. She looked at me, stunned beyond belief.

"Please," Makiko said, shaking her head. "You don't have to do that. Come on."

"It's fine." I said. "Everything's gonna be okay. We'll get there."

"Sure we will." Makiko scrunched up her lips, then cracked a smile as she made a gesture like she was writing something with a fountain pen. "Sure, it'll be fine, definitely." Komi was in her smile. So was Mom. The face was familiar. Smiling at me. It was every face of Makiko I'd ever known—the one who laughed and cried with me, who ran up to greet me the second she saw me, who sat in the park in her uniform and rode off on her bike, who shut her eyes tight and cried through the entire wake, who took money straight out of her pay envelope to buy me new indoor shoes for school, who sat there, all alone, in her hospital bed after giving birth to her daughter, who was always there for me—every side of her was smiling now. I blinked a few times and pretended to yawn.

Makiko checked her watch.

"It's almost time."

"Safe trip," I said, handing her the bag.

Midoriko stood up and did a little hop, to make her back-pack fit right on her back.

"Hey, we never got to do the fireworks last night. I'll keep them for you, okay? Somewhere safe and dry. We'll do them next summer. Actually, it doesn't have to be summer. It could be winter, or any time. Whenever you want."

"Okay," said Midoriko. "Let's do them this winter, when it's cold out."

They were out of time and rushed through the ticket gates, heading for the platform. Midoriko kept turning back and waving at me. Every time I thought that they were gone, she'd poke her face out of the crowd, waving to me. I waved back until I was absolutely sure that they were out of sight.

The second I got home, I felt compelled to sleep. Walking had pulled the heat into my skin and lungs. I had wanted to take a cold shower, but after five minutes in the AC all the sweat had dried away, as if nothing had ever happened. Makiko had left her imprint in the beanbag, and Midoriko had left some books stacked in the corner. After I had shelved the books, I let myself drop face first into the beanbag, same as Makiko the night before. Makiko and Midoriko. Covered with eggs. The three of us wiped down the floor a dozen times and tossed the soggy paper towels in a heap. Midoriko waving. Makiko smiling. They disappeared into the distance. My eyes were getting heavier by the second. My arms and legs were warm. Watching the thoughts float around in the darkness, I fell asleep.

I dreamt that I was on the train, swaying as we went.

I couldn't tell where we were going. There weren't that many people, and the nap of the seat fabric scratched at the backs of my thighs. I was wearing shorts. I had nothing with me. I looked down at the dark skin of my arms. The creased skin on the inside of my elbows looked black as night. My turquoise tank top was a little baggy. If I leaned forward or raised my arms, I was afraid my chest might show. But I told myself there was no reason to obsess over that kind of thing.

People got on and off at every stop, but the train was slowly filling up. A woman took the seat across from me. The skin under her eyes was sagging. Her cheeks were kind of dark. She wasn't old, but she wasn't that young, either. Her hair was dark and stiff, just like mine. She had it tucked behind her ears. Now and then she turned around to have a look outside the windows. It was me, on my way to pick up Midoriko and Makiko. I was thirty. Huddled in my seat to make sure that I didn't touch the people sitting next to me. Sitting quietly with my hands folded on top of my busted tote bag. Legs crossed painfully tight. My knobby knees looked so familiar—that's right, I got them from Komi. The me sitting across from me looked like a smiling Komi. I'd seen her smiling like that in a photo.

The doors opened. My father came on the train, wearing gray work clothes. He sat down next to me and whispered we were almost there. We were out for the day. Mom and Makiko had stayed home. Today it was just me and dad. I wouldn't let myself ask him where we were going. I just sat there, saying nothing. People pushed onto the train. Standing men pressed their legs between our knees. People were piling up. It felt like everybody's bodies were expanding. We were there. My father hoisted me up onto his shoulders. He was only an inch or two taller than me, but he put me on his shoulders. It was the first time that I touched him. Dad pushed his way through the enormous strangers, gripping my wrists. I was riding on his short, little shoulders. He pushed through a wall of people who had no idea that we were there. They pushed him away and stepped on his feet. We had to stop and start again. The door shut. Somebody was smiling and waving at us. Without letting me down, Dad ran straight for the next car, and we hopped onto the ferris wheel. We rose in silence through the deepening blue of the sky. People, trees and the lights of night were glinting from the dusky earth that stretched away below us. I was there on dad's shoulders, counting every single one of them, not blinking once.

I woke in the static coolness of the air-conditioned room.

The AC unit said that it was 70 degrees. I sat up and switched it off. I knew that I had just been dreaming, but after blinking several times it slipped away without a trace. I heard the ventilation fan hum to a groggy halt, and out of nowhere warm air seeped into the room. The summer sun burned through the curtains. I heard laughter, the voices of children, the sound of cars passing in the street.

I went into the bathroom and took off my clothes. My pad stuck to my underwear. I pulled it off and looked at it. Barely any blood. I balled it up in tissues and put it in the trash, then found another pad and stuck it in my underwear, which I set on my towel for later. I got in the shower and turned the shower on hot.

I turned the shower on all the way. Water sprayed from the holes of the showerhead, enfolding me in steam and heat. The tips of my toes screamed from the difference in temperature.

My shoulders went numb, like they were being burned from the inside. I looked at myself in the mirror. My thighs and arms were covered in giant goosebumps. The hot water striking my skin got even hotter, dissolving any difference between me and the room. The steam was blinding white, but the mirror had a coating that prevented it from fogging, so that I never lost sight of my own body.

I stood up straight and tucked my chin. With a few adjustments, I could see basically every part of myself in the mirror, except for my face. I stared at my own body.

My breasts were in the middle of the mirror. Little, just like Makiko's. Brown and bumpy nipples. My hips had barely any shape, but there was flesh around my belly button, stretch marks curving around my sides. Through the little bathroom window, unopened as ever, what remained of the summer day mixed gently with the fluorescent light from overhead. I had no idea where it had come from or where it was going, but it felt as if this thing that held my shape, this form before my eyes, would be stuck floating there forever.

BOOK TWO

8.
WHERE'S YOUR AMBITION?

Okay, what about this—what if your husband has a problem with his kidneys? Both of them. Things are really bad, and he needs a new one. Say you're the only one in a position to help, by giving him one of your own, and he's definitely going to die if you don't, what would you do? Would you do it?"

Aya posed her question long after we had finished our dessert. The ice in our glasses had melted. It was getting to be time to go.

A bunch of us from my old job were out for lunch. We weren't exactly friends, but when we met up again for Yuko's wedding a couple of years ago, Aya proposed we get together a couple of times a year, and she'd organized these meetings ever since. All of us were basically the same age, give or take a year. It felt like it was only a little while ago that we were all working at the bookstore. How was that ten years ago? I say that, but every one of us had changed, especially in the last few years, and since we only rarely saw each other, we were all on different wavelengths. To an outsider, we probably didn't even come off as a group of friends. I'm sure that every one of us had better things to do, but none of the five of us had ever missed a get-together.

The question was whether or not you would give a kidney to your dying husband.

For everyone but me, Aya's question was extremely relevant. All of them were married, most even had kids. The conversation showed no sign of letting up.

"Honestly!"

"I dunno . . . "

"Seriously?"

They shared their take on things, acting stunned or nodding sympathetically at what the others had to say. When Yuko noticed that our drinks were empty, she asked "Want another one?" Everyone said sure and ordered another of whatever they were having, but when Yuko looked at me and asked, "What about you, Natsuko?" I said, "I'm good with water."

I was listening to them, but I couldn't get my mind off what we had to eat for lunch. I don't know who picked this place, and I'd never even heard of galettes before, but it was obviously not going to cut it as a main course. Imagine the saddest pie on earth, unsure if it's a snack or a dessert. And, being a specialty shop, the place served nothing but galettes. I could've eaten a whole stack and still been hungry. Besides, in my book, nothing topped off with whipped cream could ever qualify as lunch.

"Yeah, well, I'd do it." Yoshikawa said, from the end of the table. She was thirty-eight, same age as me, and had a younger husband who I think worked as an osteopath. They had a little kid together. Yoshikawa was into the whole "natural living" thing. She never wore makeup and was always dressed in loose-fitting earth tones. Ever since she discovered homeopathy, she'd been telling me to take these funny lozenges she said would cure literally anything, no matter the symptoms. She must have walked me through the way it works a hundred times, but it was in one ear and out the other. She says that if kids only took these magic pills we could forget about vaccinations, or even visits to the doctor. That gives you an idea of Yoshikawa. And here she tells us that she'd give a kidney to save her dying husband. As soon as she said it, everybody said back, "Yeah, of course," at practically the same time.

"Not for the same reason Yuko would, though. I know

we're family and all, but—for me —it's a lot simpler than that. I need him to keep working. How could I maintain my current lifestyle if he died on me?"

"I hear you," Aya said, backing her up.

Out of all of us, Aya had spent the least time working at the bookstore, and I'm pretty sure our time there overlapped by no more than a year. She was gorgeous, and at one point got involved with one of the "up-and-coming" novelists who stopped by our store. When his next book came out, she told us the love interest was based on her. When her next boyfriend got her pregnant, they got married, and Aya quit the bookstore to focus on her family. Her daughter's two now. Her husband runs the family real-estate business, so they live in this absurd apartment building along with the rest of his relatives. Sure they pay their way, but her in-laws find no shortage of things to complain about, and it sounds like the feeling was mutual.

"Well, yeah. Giving up a kidney would be rough, but how rough would it be if your husband died? Doing everything on your own? I guess I could get by with one kidney, if I had to. But seriously, if my husband died, I'd be gone so fast. I forget what it's called . . . a post-mortem divorce? I'd take everything I could, then make a clean break from my in-laws. They'd never hear from me again, I swear."

"Damn, Aya. Listen to you." Yuko said with a laugh. "I dunno, maybe it's just me, but my husband pisses me off, all the time. Sometimes I seriously wish he'd die. Except, well, he is my son's dad. I guess it's better if he's alive."

"There is that," Yoshikawa said. "I guess it makes you ask yourself what kind of man you've had a child with. I mean, what a miserable life, right? Still, though, our kids. We need to do the right thing, for them."

Once the conversation started to wrap up, Aya took it upon herself, as usual, to look over the bill. Everyone who got an extra drink paid 1800 yen, but I paid 1400.

Meandering our way toward Shibuya, we chatted about how much the area had changed or wondered what the hype was when we saw a place with a long line. When we reached the Shibuya Scramble, we said we'd be in touch and waved goodbye and parted ways. Aya, Yuko and Yoshikawa headed for the Inokashira Line, while me and Rie Konno—the fifth member of our group, who never did anything but giggle in the corner (today being no exception)—were both taking the Den'en Toshi Line, so we walked together to the station.

August. Two-thirty in the afternoon. Everything before our eyes burned white, and the sky was a perfect blue over the buildings, the total blue of a computer screen. Everything was shining in the heat. When you breathed, it came in through your nose and when you didn't it came in through your skin.

Every time the lights turned green, enormous groups of people crossed the street and passed each other, trading places. The young girls were pasty white. They wore flared skirts in gentle hues and clomped along in Mary Janes that looked like stilts. It had to be the latest thing. Lots of them had bright red eyeshadow. It seemed like all of them were wearing color contacts.

"Rie, where are you headed?" I said, wiping my temples with the little towel I had with me.

"Me? Mizonokuchi," she answered in a little voice.

"Oh yeah? How long have you been living there?"

"Maybe two years. Because of my husband's work."

I'm pretty sure Rie had a kid, too. Three years ago, she started working part-time at a different bookstore. I had no idea what her husband did. Rie was tiny, at least a head shorter than me. Her skinny eyebrows pointed downward, and her canines jutted out so much her top lip couldn't cover them. This made it look like she was always on the verge of cracking up, even when she was just sitting there. It was only a few min-utes to the station, but this was already the most time I'd ever spent alone with Rie. We'd seen each other plenty of times, but I honestly couldn't say if we'd ever had a conversation. To save us from the awkward silence, I went ahead and asked her about giving a kidney to save her husband.

"You were with Yuko, right?"

"Actually," Rie said, glancing my way. "I'd keep it."

"Seriously?" I looked back at her.

"Yeah," she said.

"Wow," I said. "Even if you knew he was gonna die?"

"I'd keep it." she repeated. "Personally, I'd throw mine in the street before giving it to him."

At a loss for what to say, I tried my best to fill the silence. "Well, I guess he's basically a stranger, right?"

"I'd rather give it to a stranger." Rie said.

We crossed the street and took the staircase underground, where we followed the signs for the train. Sweat dripped from my every pore. I felt it streaking down my back and sides.

"You're headed to Mizonokuchi?" I asked. "I'm going to Jimbocho. Looks like we're going opposite ways. See you next time. Winter, right?"

"Winter, yeah. I don't think I'll come, though."

"You won't?"

"Nope." Rie smiled. "Everybody's just so stupid."

When I was silent, Rie laughed and went on.

"They're a bunch of hopeless idiots."

With that, she waved goodbye and slipped through the turnstiles, disappearing into the station.

In Jimbocho, I opened the door to the hole-in-the-wall coffee shop and saw Ryoko Sengawa sitting by the window. She turned to wave hello.

"It's hot, huh?" Sengawa said cheerfully. "Did you come from home?"

"No, I was in Shibuya. Lunch with friends." I sat down

opposite her and wiped the sweat from my temples and neck with my little towel.

"Lunch with friends! I feel like I don't even know you anymore," Sengawa said, teasing me. She grinned, showing her big teeth. "How long has it been? Last time we met up, it wasn't nearly this hot, was it?"

Ryoko Sengawa was an editor with one of the big publishers. We met for the first time two summers earlier and checked in periodically so she could ask about the novel I was working on and keep herself informed about the plot. Sengawa was ten years older than me, so almost fifty. She had worked on magazines, then switched over to children's books for a while, before moving to fiction four years back. She looked after a handful of well-known contemporary authors, and several of the books that they had done had won important prizes. Her short hair gave her ears nowhere to hide, and when she laughed her face went wrinkly, which for whatever reason made me smile. She lived alone in an apartment in Komazawa.

"I keep writing and writing. I just can't see an end to this."

She hadn't even asked about my novel yet, but I voluntarily changed the subject and drank the entire glass of water sitting on the table. Sengawa smiled with her eyes and opened the menu so that I could read it too. I ordered an iced tea and Sengawa did the same.

I moved to Tokyo to become a writer when I was twenty. Thirteen years later, when I was thirty-three, I won first prize in a contest run by a minor publisher. I could now say I was a writer—but the piece I wrote went unpublished, making it impossible for anyone to read my work. I spent two years working over what I'd written with this male editor, who forced me to practically rewrite the thing more than once. Those were not the best years of my life.

Whether I was working on my own fiction or a short essay for a magazine, I gave it everything I had, summoning all the confidence that I could muster, but it seemed as though this guy was already convinced my work lacked any merit whatsoever.

His favorite dispensations included "I can't see the reader's face," "This isn't how people act," and "I need you to convince me." That should give you a taste of our sessions. At first, I assumed he was right, that his opinions were important, but once I gave myself permission to be skeptical, I realized he was full of crap. We weren't talking about my work at all. It was just so tiring. Over time, I stopped showing him my work and stopped answering his emails—we grew apart. The last time that we talked was on the phone. He called me up in the middle of the night. When I picked up the phone, I could tell that he was drunk. After telling me every last thing he thought was wrong about my stories, he added this:

"I think it's the right time, so I'll come out and say it. I think you're missing something, something a writer needs. It just isn't there. I guess it's ambition, genuine ambition. That's what's keeping you from writing something that matters. That's why you'll never be a great writer. I've always thought so, and somebody has to tell you. It's never going to happen for you. Never. Let me put it this way—how old are you? I know age has nothing to do with writing. Well, except it does. Say you're going on forty, right? Are you really about to turn around and produce something incredible? I sincerely doubt it, at least in your case. That's how I see it. And I'm telling you I'm right. I mean, it's my job to know these things. I can see it coming, I can see it."

I barely slept that night. For the next week, his voice played over and over in my head, making it hard for me to focus. *What if after all these years, when I finally started writing, everything just fell apart like this?*—The thought of it was infinitely depressing.

The next few months were awful. I brooded endlessly, and only left the house to go to work. Then one day—while I was ruminating on the harshest moments of our last phone call, I heard my anger—I actually heard it bubbling inside of me, rising up from the bottom of my throat.

"Who the fuck does he think he is?" I thought.

I'd been lying face down on the beanbag, but now I raised my head and sat straight up. I opened my eyes wide. They were filling up with blood, like any second they would pop out of their sockets and take a ride somewhere.

"Who the fuck does he think he is?" I said, this time aloud.

I pressed my face into the beanbag and screamed at the top of my lungs. I felt it vibrating the pills inside the beanbag, which helped to gobble up the sound. I screamed a few more times, then let it all go and lay face down, unable to move.

After some time, I went to the kitchen for a glass of mugicha and drank it in one gulp. Then I went back to the room and took a deep breath, sending my eyes from the bookshelves to the desk and to the beanbag. It felt like everything was brighter. I thought about how much my editor liked to say "the real deal." If I told him "I don't know what you mean," he'd say, "Just listen," like he was positively thrilled. What a complete waste of time. Every interaction, all of it. But when I set my glass down on the table, it landed like a thunderbolt; in an instant, I could see that all of it was nonsense. I decided to forget the asshole ever existed.

A year later, my luck finally changed.

My book, a short story collection, was profiled by a few well-known TV personalities, who couldn't say enough good things about my writing. It wound up selling over 60,000 copies. It was a hit.

One celebrity known for her literary taste got particularly worked up and said, "This book upended my conception of the afterlife." A fashion model said, "I couldn't keep myself from crying. I kept thinking about people close to me, people I'd lost." Someone else had described it as devastating, but added that it was not without a certain optimism.

The book, which included my prizewinning story, was a collection of newer and older work that I'd reworked so that they shared a common theme. I had called in all the favors that I could to get it published. It had no snappy elevator pitch. The first print run was under 3,000 copies—it goes without saying that no one at my tiny publisher thought it would take off. It was a bubble rising to the surface, created on the premise it would disappear. My new editor and I had barely interacted, much less discussed the finer details of the content. All they told me when they read it was that they could get it out that very month and published like it was only there to pad their catalog. Suffice it to say that no one—myself included—ever thought that the book would wind up in the hands of tens of thousands of readers.

I came away from the experience happy, but disconcerted all the same. The book sold well because it found its way onto TV. We'd like to think that the books that merit attention find a readership—but after what happened with my collection, it felt safe to say that merit had nothing to do with it.

I got a call from Ryoko Sengawa soon after it came out. This was two years ago, on a muggy day in August just like this one. She met me at the coffee shop down the street from me, and after quickly introducing herself, she gave it to me straight, in that quiet but commanding voice of hers.

"It really works. All the characters in all the stories are dead, in another world, dying over and over. In this world, death isn't the end to everything, but it's not exactly a new beginning, either. After the earthquake, a lot of readers were able to find consolation in that kind of a story. But now I want you to forget all that."

Sengawa took a quick sip of water. I fixated on her fingers, where they gripped the glass, and waited for her to say more.

"What made that work special? What made it yours? It wasn't the setting or the theme or even the idea. It wasn't any of that. It's your voice, the writing, the rhythm. It has incredible personality, and that matters more than anything if you're going to keep writing. You need to hold onto that, your rhythm."

"My rhythm?" I asked.

"I'm glad the book was a success," Sengawa said, "But you can't count on celebrities who hardly read a book every five years to help you find your base. I'm not saying sales don't matter. It's just that readers matter more. You need to find real readers, the kind who will seriously stick with you, readers who will stick with you after the hype dies down. I'm talking about readers who want nothing more than the unknown, the mysterious."

"You mean," I said, "real readers, who read real literature . . . "

The server topped off both our glasses. Sengawa paused for a moment before going on.

"Well, we use words to communicate, right? Still, most of our words don't actually get across. You know what I mean? Well, our words might, but not what we're actually trying to say. That's what we're always dealing with. We live in this place, in this world, where we can share our words but not our thoughts.

"They say 'good friends are hard to find.' It's true. It's so hard to find people who actually listen, who try to understand your words, who try to understand you. It's basically luck. At least that's how I see it. It's like trying to find water in the middle of the desert—it's vital, if you're going to stay alive. Of course, if people on TV start talking about your book and you end up selling tens of thousands of copies, that's its own form of luck. I guess there's another form, too, when someone gets one stroke of luck, just one moment. But that first kind of luck is something different, right? It's the kind you can count on— it's strong, it lasts. That sort of luck will always be there for you and your work. And I can help you make that happen. We can produce better work, together. That's why I wanted to meet you."

For a minute neither of us spoke. The ice inside our glasses melted just enough to settle. Sengawa rested her hand on the edge of her coaster. I noticed the veins standing from the skin on the back of her hand.

"Sorry to just launch into things like that," Sengawa said. "I just had to make sure I said it, so I wouldn't regret anything later."

"No," I said. "I'm really glad you did."

Sengawa looked relieved. I watched her nod and scrunch her lips like she was having a conversation with herself—it made me wonder whether someone as confident and forthcoming as her could actually be as nervous as me.

"No one's ever talked with me about my work like that."

"Hey, you're from Osaka, right?" Sengawa asked, betraying an Osaka accent. "There's no place like Osaka."

"You're from Osaka too?"

"Not exactly. I was born and raised in Tokyo, but my mom's from Osaka, so I guess you could say it's where I came from. She set the tone for the whole house. The accent comes out when I'm with people from Osaka. I guess I'm basically bilingual," she laughed.

"I never would have guessed."

We talked about our favorite words and expressions people use only in Osaka, and about the STAP cell controversy that had been Osaka's claim to infamy since winter. The scientist responsible had taken his own life only ten days before. They say his papers were a work of art.

"So tell me," Sengawa said. "Natsuko Natsume . . . that's a pen name, right?"

"No, that's my real name."

"No way," she said. "Is Natsume your husband's name or something?"

"Never married. Some things happened between my parents, and I went back to my mother's maiden name when I was maybe ten."

"I see," Sengawa nodded. "So your mom named you Natsuko to keep part of her family name going?"

"Part of her family name?" I asked. "You mean Natsu?"

"Yeah," she said. "It just seemed like that was probably it."

"I guess I hadn't thought of that before," I stammered.

"I'm not married either," said Sengawa, "but I can understand how it would sting to give your name up. I don't know. Maybe that has nothing to do with it. Maybe your mom just really liked the sound of it."

We chatted for a solid hour and talked about the books that we were reading. Then we exchanged phone numbers. From then on, we met up from time to time to talk about my work and all kinds of other things.

"What's wrong?" Sengawa asked, staring at me.

"Nothing. I just realized. It's already been two years since we met."

"I guess you're right. When you think about it, life isn't very long, is it?" she laughed and started coughing. "God, this cough. I've been in and out of the hospital lately. It's terrible. No matter how much I sleep, I never feel rested. I had them check it out, but they said it was anemia . . . "

"You need to make sure you get enough iron."

"Yeah. Well, I didn't know this before, but apparently what you really need is ferritin. Things have been a little better recently, but it's only going to get worse as time goes on, right?" Sengawa took a sip of water. "Time goes by so quickly."

"No kidding," I laughed. "How is it 2016? I've been in Tokyo what, almost twenty years now? That's insane."

"Tell me about it. Hey, how's the story coming?"

Now that Sengawa had so deftly nudged us in that direction,

we started talking about the novel. Not like I had anything concrete to run by her. I wasn't going to show it to her until I was done anyway. We barely ever talked about specifics. Sometimes I wonder if it even makes sense meeting up with editors like this, but they have a way of teasing stories out of you. You start off talking about what you're writing, like you're talking to yourself, but pretty soon what started as a tangled mess feels neat and tidy, which clears the way and helps you play with options that you may have overlooked. It's such a help. After an hour and a half or so, we ended just like last time, without making any plans, and waved goodbye.

It was evening, but the daylight refused to let up, and the steaming asphalt looked like it was melting. I thought of my unfinished novel and felt a tarry liquid fill the space behind my eyes, threatening to swallow everything in darkness. With heavy breaths, I made my way back to my apartment.

After fifteen years in the Minowa apartment I had lived in since I moved to Tokyo, the building was demolished, so I moved to another spot in Sangenjaya. My old landlord had died of a heart attack, and because of issues with inheritance tax, his family took the building down and sold it as an empty lot. I felt a little uneasy leaving the only home in Tokyo I'd ever had, but once I moved my apprehension disappeared. I brought all my stuff from Minowa—from the curtains and the beanbag to the dishes and the floor mats—and my new place was on the second floor of a small building, like the last one, and had essentially the same floorplan. It didn't really feel like much had changed (except my rent, which went up 20,000 yen).

With eyes heavy from the heat, I squinted at my wristwatch. A little after five. I went and took a shower that was about as cold as I could bear, just standing there. Pretty soon I got cold and toweled off. I thought I smelled a swimming pool.

Chlorine? Or maybe drying off triggered the smell. The concrete floor that badly needed fixing. Warm underfoot. Screaming and splashing. The call of a whistle. The last few minutes set aside for free time. The time of afternoon when your body stops cooperating and your eyes start getting heavy. What I would give to fall asleep feeling like that. Those summer days felt worlds away, as if they happened in another life. But they happened to me, and to my body. The thought gave me the chills.

For the first time in two days, I opened the file—the novel. Lately I'd been trying hard to get a good night's sleep, but I could never seem to get enough. I woke feeling lethargic, and my head was foggy the entire day. Still, it was only five in the afternoon. Way too early to go to sleep. I sort of wished that I could waste away the evening cooking myself something tasty, but there was no chance on a day like this. The heat had killed my interest in food. The file opened in the middle of my screen. Seeing the sentence I'd left unfinished made me want to close the file right away. I took a breath and opened a new window. I had a column due next week, so I decided to get that out of the way first.

Three pages one day for the morning edition of a local newspaper. A four-page column I'd been writing about various everyday topics for a women's magazine. A spot on a webzine run by a little publisher who asked me to write about the books I've enjoyed reading. My pay was set and there was a minimum word limit I had to meet, but it was fine if I went over. I also sent short stories out to literary magazines, although this year I had stepped away from that a bit to focus on the novel. Once in a while, someone would come along and ask me to write a one-off essay.

That was basically my life. The temp agency I had worked at for a number of years after quitting the bookstore had kept me in the system, so I could go back if I ever needed to, but I was at a point where I could make a living from my writing.

Sometimes I thought I must be dreaming. How did I wind up getting paid to read and write? To spend my time no other way. To fill my head with this and nothing else. When I think about the way things used to be, it seems unreal. It's shocking, in the best way possible. Just thinking about it makes my heart race. But still—

Still. For the past year, or maybe a bit longer, whenever I sit down at the computer, or walk to the convenience store at night, or climb in bed, or realize the cup sitting on the table will just sit there for eternity unless I pick it up—on any given day, I hear it. *Still.*

This word spawns all sorts of thoughts. They like to sit off to the side and stare at me. I know that being stared at makes me anxious, angry, and depressed, but I can't bring myself to look straight back at them. It's just too scary. I know that if I give *them* my attention, I'll come to the conclusion that *those things will never happen, not to me.* So I look away and try to rid them from my mind. But that only makes it hard to tell if I've escaped my demons or invited them to stay.

I sighed and took a notebook from my desk drawer. Leafing through the pages, I found some stuff I'd written down six months ago, after I'd had many beers alone at home. Short lines, I guess sort of like a poem. The next day, when I found it on the table, I felt ashamed, idiotic, and tired, in all senses of the word. I was tempted to toss it in the garbage right then and there but couldn't bring myself to do it. I felt even stupider for having kept it, and for looking at it now and then, like I was now.

Is this my life?
I'm glad that I can write
I'm thankful for this life

And all the good it's given me
But can I live like this forever?
Alone
Can I really be alone like this? Forever?
I can't take it—actually, that's not true, that's a lie
I'm fine on my own

It's fine, but what about you
Am I really okay
Not knowing you? What if I regret it?
My child, unlike any other,
Can I really say I'm okay
Never knowing you?

"Wow," I said softly, all the more discouraged by how low and hoarse my voice was.

I closed the notebook and stuffed it in my desk. Then I went over to my computer and clicked on the various infertility blogs I had bookmarked and read through the latest posts. For a few months, I had struggled to keep up with what they said, but I was finally getting the big picture. While there were always technical terms I didn't understand, I was able to figure most things out from context.

The details and the anguish of a thorough round of testing. Talking with your mother-in-law and meeting your husband for dinner on your way home from the hospital. Does his sister have to ask for help planning her wedding on a day like this? Some blogs were brightened up with precious illustrations; one had a photo of a blue sky at the footer. It's so hard to watch another woman push her baby down the street. So many thoughtless remarks. The scoop on a Thai restaurant where you could eat your lunch in peace without seeing kids or babies.

I had forgotten about Naruse's Facebook page. I'd held off

checking for the past ten days, and after going back and forth, decided not to take a look today.

I checked the window. It was still bright out. Just shy of 7:00.

I put my computer to sleep and went out into the kitchen to fix myself a bowl of rice and natto, which I picked away at slowly. What's the rush. I wasn't in the mood to do a thing. If I slowed my movements down enough, I could probably make it through the day until I was tired enough to sleep; but the slower I chewed, the more I paid attention to the way that I was eating, and the longer every moment lasted. Time skidded to a halt, no thanks to my bowl of rice. You can eat as slowly as your body will allow, but a bowl of rice is gone in a few minutes. Once I had washed the dishes, I had nothing left to do again. Seeing no other option, I sprawled out on the beanbag and lay there without moving a muscle.

Sitting completely still can sometimes make me feel like I'm a kid again. I know I'm in a different space and time, and seeing different things, but I'm seeing them the way I used to see them. Lately I've been thinking about Mom and Komi. When Mom was my age, she had two kids, fourteen and five. I never would've thought back then that I had only eight years left with her, and how could Mom have known that she only had eight years remaining?

If Mom had only had us ten years earlier, we would have had an extra ten years as a family. Though then she would have given birth to Makiko at fourteen. And that's too much to ask. I laughed as I thought about the day. Galettes. So I did eat something today. I couldn't remember how that crusty vehicle for whipped cream actually tasted. Maybe because it didn't taste like anything. I imagined what Yuko would be saying. "Now that we all have kids, I never get to eat like this. It's always noodles and rice." Poor you. I don't have kids, *but I'd rather die than eat this shit.*

The last thing Rie said to me popped into my head.

"They're a bunch of hopeless idiots."

I thought about giving her a call. When I pictured her slipping through the turnstiles into the station, I saw a little girl beside her. Right . . . because even Rie had a kid. Then I remembered that I had my kidneys. *At least I had my kidneys.* Not like that qualified me to take part in their conversation. Whatever. I thought about Ryoko Sengawa. How's the novel going? What would happen if I came right out and told her that I wasn't sure if I could finish it? What did her question even mean? Things were hard when I had no one watching out for me, but at least I'd been free to do as I pleased. But what right did I have to complain? I was sick of hearing my own thoughts. I couldn't help but think about Sengawa's way of pushing the conversation—she claimed to have a total grasp of the creative process, but all her gestures, sighs and pauses, left me feeling like I was being interrogated—just thinking about it got me so worked up I tensed all over. I was tired, but the voice inside my head asked what I had to show for it. *Where's your ambition?* Thanks, Mr. Editor, but could you please define ambition? What the hell does your idea of ambition have to do with me? I wish I could have told him off. Words and emotions vied for my attention, but a couple of years too late. I was tired. Get out of my sight, all of you. I'm fine, on my own. I was so tired. Even though I'd gotten nothing done. I wound up lying in my bed with my eyes open, deep into the night.

9.
ALL THE LITTLE FLOWERS

N atsu, how's everything? Wait, I mean, congrats!"
Getting nowhere with the manuscript, I was spending
some time rearranging books when Makiko called.

"Huh? For what?"

"Your student loans!" she cheered. "You're all paid off."

"Wait, seriously?"

"Yeah, the notice came this morning in the mail. And the
other one finished up a little while ago, right? What was that
one called? Wait, I have it right here . . . JASSO? And the
notice that came today is from the Osaka Scholarship Society.
I can't believe it's actually over. Hold on, listen to this."

On the other end of the line, I could hear Makiko sorting
through some papers and clearing her throat.

"Thank you for your final payment. As of August 2016, the
account above has been settled. Please keep this letter for your
records. The following is a detailed breakdown: Total dis-
bursed: 620,000 yen, returned in full . . . "

"Crazy." I went out to the kitchen and poured myself a glass
of mugicha. "How many years did that take? Twenty?"

"Yeah, a loan like that would take forever, both of them,"
reported Makiko.

"Well, I'm just glad it's finally over." I said. "All those
months where I thought it was gonna kill me to scrounge up
5,000 yen to pay the bill, and had to miss a payment to survive . . . You remember those letters they sent me? I can't
believe this is a state-run organization, the way they treat kids.

They can be real bastards, shaking people down like that. They did a real number on me. I never want to see one of those notices again as long as I live."

"I totally get it. But I think you're gonna wanna get a load of this one. It almost looks like a diploma, like they want you to frame it and hang it on your wall. It's real ornate, like a fancy birthday card. I guess they want you to celebrate . . . "

"I'll celebrate never having to think about that crap again."

I exhaled through my nose in anger, although I had to admit a part of me was thrilled that I had paid off all my debt.

"The things we put kids through when all they want to do is learn. I mean, this is real debt we're talking about. It doesn't go away. By the way, Maki, what are you doing about Midoriko? What's she doing about money?"

"She got a scholarship that covers some of it," Makiko said. "She took out a loan, too, so she'll have to pay that one off. She still has a bit of time until graduating, but I wonder what she's gonna do. She likes studying, I guess . . . "

Midoriko was twenty, in her second year of college. She commuted from their apartment in Osaka to her university in Kyoto. Makiko was turning forty-eight this year, but she still worked at Chanel in Shobashi. Coco was well into her sixties. Her bad knees made it hard for her to make it to the bar more than a couple of times a week, and it was up to Makiko to keep it afloat. She had to interview the new girls, make sure everyone was taken care of, stock the bar and manage everybody's sales. Her responsibilities were growing, but the bottom line was only getting worse, and her pay had barely increased. While she was ostensibly in charge of the place, she was right there on the payroll with the other girls, even though she was pushing fifty. How much longer could she make even a meager living keeping drunk guys company all night?— Makiko said so herself a little while back, when she was wasted and feeling low.

"How's the bar been?"

"You know, no real change."

Makiko was talking about the uncertainty of working as a hostess, but looking on the brighter side, things weren't all bad. Midoriko had made it into college, even if she had to take out student loans, and I was making headway with my work, but above all, above everything else, me and Makiko and of course Midoriko had our health. We had nothing to complain about. For a while there, Makiko had been downright skeletal, but in the past few years she'd picked up all the pounds she'd lost, and at this point looked like any normal woman in her fifties. Nothing like the Makiko she was that summer, when she looked like a chicken wing someone had picked clean. It's amazing, really—how the human body never stops changing. Back then, I couldn't shake the feeling that she wasn't going to last much longer. Maybe no real change wasn't such a bad thing.

"Hey, though, I'm gonna work real hard. I won't drag Midoriko down in my old age. Natsuko, you there?"

"Yeah, I'm here."

Makiko was always asking me if I was there, not that I'd ever gone anywhere.

"Hey, you feeling okay? I feel like you've been a little out of it lately."

"Me?" I was flustered. "Seriously?"

"Well, yeah. I know summer can be kinda draining, but you sound real spacey."

"Maki. No one says 'spacey' anymore. But I'm good. I promise. Work's good, and I'm stoked to face every day."

"Natsu, no one says 'stoked' anymore."

"Hey," I was getting visibly annoyed, so I changed the subject. "What's Midoriko up to?"

"Vacation. She's on a trip with Haruyama right now. What's that place called again? You know that island with all the art and sculptures? That's where they went. They saved up money from their jobs for it and everything."

"Those two have been close for a while, huh?"

"Yeah, he's a good kid." Makiko said thoughtfully. "Haruyama's been through a lot. They really get each other. It's a little early still, but they're planning on moving in together after they graduate."

"That's great," I laughed. "I hope it works out."

I hung up and went back to the room—everything was just as I left it. Of course it was. There were a few stacks of books, small cardboard boxes filled with documents, the slumped beanbag on the floor, the eyedrops sitting on my desk, the starchy curtains, and the tissues poking from the tissue box were all in the same places they had been. It made my heart sink.

It was the end of August. The brutal sunlight seemed determined to expend every drop of summer that was left. I was ready to believe the summer had been going on for years, like it was stuck on repeat.

I couldn't give the novel the attention it deserved. Gazing idly at the white light shining through the curtains, I thought about what Makiko had said. Midoriko was on vacation. She was on an island, visiting museums. That must mean that they were on Naoshima, or one of the other islands around there. Midoriko and Haruyama had been together for two years now. I'd never met the guy myself, but I was happy that she found someone her mother thought was a good kid, a man who she could see herself sharing a place with after graduation. Good for her.

Right now, that relationship defined their world—I thought that was a tidy way of putting it. That doesn't mean that it was puppy love. I mean it really changed the way they saw things, as if the strength of how they felt for one another had produced a sturdy faith in how the world would operate. When

BREASTS AND EGGS · 173

they gazed into each other's eyes, they saw a world replete with promise, strong and soft. The world was there to make their dreams come true, and they could trust without a shred of doubt that it would make good on its promises.

While I hadn't had the chance to see Midoriko around her beau, we talked about him once over the phone. Like Makiko had said, she sounded like somebody telling you about her best friend. Her voice had such a happy cadence to it that I couldn't help but smile. She was so full of life. Midoriko was cute, but she didn't care much for makeup or fashion. She was not your average girl, as if that wasn't clear enough from her strong personality. I had no doubt she contributed a lot to the dynamic of sincerity that she shared with Haruyama.

I imagined Midoriko and Haruyama walking down some quiet road, spending an hour together, speaking a language only they could understand. Over that image, I came to see myself around their age, at nineteen, twenty-one, or twenty-three—but with Naruse, who was always there to lend an ear and walk with me. No one knew about us, but the intimacy and conviction of the time we spent together made us both sure there was nothing more important in our lives. We met in high school, when we were just kids, and from seventeen until the end of my third year in Tokyo, we were lovers.

I knew that if I was going to get married, it would be to him. But even if we never got married, I was certain then, without the tiniest misgiving, that the two of us would always be together. I couldn't even tell you how many letters we wrote each other. We talked about the things we loved and confessed the things that scared us. After school, we hung out until I had to go wash dishes at the bar. Saying goodbye nearly drove me to tears. If I had been a normal kid and had a normal family, we would have had more time together every day. I must have said this to myself a million times. Naruse tried to cheer me up by saying once he graduated, he would get a real job and before long everything would be okay. He was the one who got me interested in books. He wanted to be a novelist and read all kinds of fiction. Every time he showed me something he had written, I got goosebumps, and felt positive that a person who could write like that was made to be a writer. We never ran out of things to talk about. It didn't matter where we were or what we did. I was convinced that it would be that way forever.

But things changed. Three years after coming to Tokyo, I found out he was sleeping with another woman. They were doing it like crazy. I lost it, but when I asked him if he loved her, he said no. He said it wasn't about love, and that it had nothing to do with how he felt about me. He just wanted to have sex with someone. I didn't know how to respond. It was a perfect silence. At that point, things weren't physical between us anymore. It had been a couple of years.

Naruse meant everything to me. I wanted us to be together. I could see us decades down the road, talking about all kinds of things and going all kinds of places. I wanted us to build a life together. But sex with him was not something I needed— not something I wanted.

I wanted him to feel good, but I didn't understand myself. I thought it was on me to make it better, that I had to make some effort. I tried, too, but somehow it never felt right. It wasn't physically painful. It just made me so uneasy, and I couldn't make the feeling go away. Lying naked on the mattress, I felt like I could see black spirals coming from the ceiling and the corners of the room. When Naruse moved his body, the spirals grew larger and edged closer, until they swallowed me, like somebody had slipped a black bag over my head. The sex was never enjoyable or comforting or fulfilling. Once Naruse was naked on top of me, I was alone.

I could never bring myself to tell him. We could talk about anything else, and if I had something to say, I knew that he would listen. He was basically my best friend, but something stopped me short of being honest about sex with him. I wasn't scared that he would hate me. It wasn't like that. I just assumed I had to go along with him—because it was on me, as a woman, to fulfill his sexual desires. This wasn't something anyone had said to me, or that I thought was right. But at some point, I picked up the idea that when you're in that situation with a man—your man—it's your job as the woman to go along.

I couldn't do it. Whenever we got naked and I let him start, the world went dark. It felt so wrong that I wanted to cry. Sometimes I wished I could just die. Other times I felt like something had to be seriously wrong with me—how could I not enjoy doing this with someone I love? I tried to broach the topic with friends, but none of them had any problem having sex multiple times a day; they even seemed to like it. I had a hard time understanding their positive feelings about sex and their libidos. As I listened to them talk about wanting to do it and wanting to be touched and wanting to have somebody inside of them—I realized that I lacked the appetite they took for granted.

I understood wanting somebody beside you, wanting to hold somebody's hand. I'd felt those bursts of passion after saying something major, or when it hit me just how strong my feelings were. I wanted to share this sensation, but once things started getting physical, my shoulders tightened, and I tensed up all over. Passion and sex were incompatible for me. They didn't connect.

I logged on to Facebook and clicked on Naruse's name. I didn't love him anymore. I had let go of him entirely. I didn't have any regrets about the way things went. Until he called me out of the blue five years ago—two months after the disaster in Fukushima—I had no clue where he was or what he was up to.

When the phone rang and his name popped up on the display, it took me a second to realize what was happening. Naruse? That Naruse? At first, I was positive he died. My heart raced as I took the call.

"It's Naruse," his voice said on the other end. "It's been a while. How've you been?"

"Fine, I guess. Naruse? Is that really you?"

"It's me. I thought for sure you'd change your number . . . "

"Nah," I said, trying to calm myself. "I kept it."

"Huh."

I hadn't heard Naruse's voice since we broke up when we were twenty-three, but there it was, coming from my cell phone, exactly the way that I remembered it. No noise, no static. The call was clear, as if the last ten years had never happened. He spoke as if we were close—like he was picking up where we'd left off the day before.

"When I saw your name on my phone, I thought maybe you died or something."

"What do you mean? If I had died, how would I call you?" He let out a quick laugh.

"No, not you. I thought maybe someone else was using your phone to call people, letting them know what happened."

After that, we caught each other up, in the way you do when it's been ages since you've heard from someone. Naruse had heard about my novel but confessed that he'd lost interest in literature and hadn't read it yet. I told him I didn't mind at all. We talked about Fukushima and the earthquake. Naruse was married. He'd been in Tokyo for the past five years, but ten days after the nuclear meltdown, he brought his pregnant wife down to Miyazaki, hoping to keep her and the baby safe.

Naruse talked at length about how dangerous the nuclear disaster had really been. About how the government had no idea what it was doing. About which articles could be trusted, which information was correct, which reporters were in the government's pocket, and who was telling the truth. About the coverup to come, and the thousands and thousands of people who would end up with thyroid cancer. How decontamination was never going to happen. Naruse was starting to sound upset.

"Are you there?" he asked, openly perturbed. "Do you even understand what I'm saying?"

"No, yeah, of course," I said.

"What's gonna happen when the ocean gets messed up beyond repair? We won't have anything to eat. Think about how important the ocean is to Japan. It's so much of what we eat, so much of our culture."

I wasn't sure what to say. I had my own opinions about the earthquake and the meltdown, and I understood what he was saying, but I had a hard time linking these outbursts with my idea of Naruse, which was disturbing to say the least. Hearing this voice I knew so well go after the government and energy industry for their incompetence made me feel like I was talking to a stranger.

"Hey, though, weren't you writing a column in some magazine?" he asked. "About whatever you've been reading, crap like that . . . "

Naruse cleared his throat.

"Why are you wasting time on stuff like that? I mean— you're supposed to be a writer now. Is that really the best way for you to use your platform? In times like these, isn't there something more meaningful for you to write? People are looking for information, online and everywhere. Do you know what I mean?"

He was referring to a short series of essays that a print magazine had hired me to do, but he didn't realize that the one he had read came after several I had written on the earthquake. I explained that he had stumbled on a lighter piece that I'd written to give readers a little room to breathe, but Naruse wasn't buying it. He said I wasn't trying hard enough and assured me even he was doing more to get the word out, through his Facebook page and blog. He asked me if I'd taken part in any protests. Signed any petitions. Told me that whatever I was doing, it wasn't enough. I had to do more.

I can't remember exactly how we finished the call. What I do remember is the conversation growing tense. Naruse took a deep breath and said: "You've always been this way. If you're not into something, you act like it's impossible. Well, you can't make yourself like something if you don't. That's why you're single, right? Honestly, I think you're better off alone."

Days later, I couldn't rid that comment from my mind. I started checking out his Facebook and his blog. They were full of all the things he had been talking about on the phone—links to the same kinds of articles, over and over, ad nauseam. A few months after that, I learned that his baby boy had been born, happy and healthy.

When I saw photos of the newborn, who looked like Naruse, a strange feeling came over me. I knew this child had nothing to do with me, but the fact that half of him had come from Naruse really got under my skin. I didn't know the first thing about Naruse's wife, this baby's mother. What I did know, however, is exactly how they'd made this baby, and imagining that made me dizzy.

I wasn't thinking that I could've been the one who had this baby—that wasn't it at all. But for a while, I was at a loss to understand why I had gotten so worked up about this anyway. Maybe I was stunned that sex could have such radically different outcomes, depending on who you slept with. I'm sure the fact that I had never slept with anyone but Naruse had lots to do with my reaction. He played the lead in all my mental images of pregnancy and babies. I had never done it with anybody else.

Does that mean there was a time when we had a chance of having a kid together? No. Not a chance. I'm sure of that. Considering how young and broke we were, and how I felt about things, it never would have worked. Sex was so painful for me that I never wanted to do it again. Sex was the reason we broke up, even though I loved him as much as I did. If the love was there, though, could we have gotten back together and had a kid? These days there were all kinds of ways to have a kid without actually having sex. Was that a possibility for me?

I never heard from him again. Every time I went to his page, his child was bigger than before. He'd be in elementary school in a couple of years. These days, Naruse mostly shared photos and posts about life at home. No more earthquakes or radioactive waste. He hadn't touched his blog in over two years. I no longer had feelings for Naruse, but seeing all these pictures of his growing son made me feel even more alone.

Would I ever have a child? If so, when? I didn't have a partner, and I wasn't looking for one. Could I really have a baby if I couldn't handle sex? What was I supposed to do? Visit a sperm bank? I'd looked around a little online, but I almost laughed at how unreal it all sounded. It felt like something from a movie. Married couples could only register if they met certain criteria, but there was no room for unmarried women. It might be different in a freer country, but I couldn't speak a word of English. I got up from my desk, hugged my beanbag and let my eyes close.

When people say they want kids, what is it they actually want? Lots of folks would say they want to have a baby with their partner, but what's the difference between wanting that and wanting your own baby? It felt like people with kids knew something at the onset that I still couldn't understand. It's like they were all members of a club that I could never join. I buried my face deeper in my beanbag. Cicadas rattled in the distance. As I tried counting them, my phone vibrated. I took my time picking it up and saw it was a text from Midoriko.

"Hiii, Natsu. I came to check out the Monets. They're amazing. They're huge."

She followed up with several photographs. After Makiko and I got off the phone, she probably texted Midoriko about dropping me a line.

The first photo was of flowers.

Little flowers dotted a bed of sumptuous green. I couldn't identify them, but all the flowers reminded me of a dress I used to have. When I was maybe ten, me and Mom and Makiko and Komi all bought different versions of the same one. The dress was sleeveless, scooped out at the neck and shoulders, and made from gauzy cotton. We were at the store and found a display heaped with dresses in the same floral design but different colors. It must have been obvious that we were hung up on the price, because a woman from the store came up and said that normally they're three for 3,500 yen, but she could give us four for 3,000. After going back and forth, we finally caved. We must have smiled the whole way home. The second we walked in the door, we all got changed and had a good laugh at seeing how we looked. I remember feeling happy, tickled and embarrassed, all at once. That was a nice, long belly laugh. We loved those dresses. We wore them all the time.

When Mom and Komi died, we really should have tucked their dresses into their caskets, seeing as they basically lived in them all summer, but Makiko and I just couldn't bring ourselves to do it. At some point, when I was with Naruse, he saw me wearing mine and said it looked great on me. The dress was cheap, and I'd honestly thought he would laugh at me for wearing it, which made it feel so good to hear him say that.

The flowers in that first photo really matched our dresses. The second photo was of Midoriko poking her face out of one of Yayoi Kusama's polka-dotted pumpkins. The third photo was Midoriko again, her hair blowing in the ocean breeze. The blue sky looked like it could shatter any second. I hadn't seen Midoriko in forever. She looked like she was having loads of fun.

"Yeah, Maki told me. Are you having a good time? Those flowers are so Monet, aren't they?"

"Totally. Yes. Right on the Monet."

"I've never been out there. Tell me all about it later!"

"Totes. There's a lot to see here. I don't think I can get it all in this trip. Tomorrow's our last day here. Talk to you later!"

She sent one final photo of her and Haruyama. They were smiling in front of a big white tower or something. Haruyama was wearing glasses and gripping the straps of his backpack. His eyes pointed downward when he smiled. He really did seem like a good guy. Midoriko was wearing a tank top and shorts and a floppy red hat, like she was heading to the beach.

I put my phone down and sat up to look out the window. It was getting late. Evening again. I went to the kitchen and made myself some spaghetti. It was 7:00; when I turned on the TV, the news was just starting. The announcer was listing off the events of the day. They had identified a body found days earlier along a hiking trail in Shiga. An eighty-five-year-old man had lost control behind the wheel and driven his car into an appliance store, but luckily had not been injured. A look back on the Rio Olympics. Exploring the possibility of the Emperor abdicating before he dies. The world had more than its share of problems for the day, just like the day before. Next up, weather. Watch out for sudden downpours tomorrow. Heatstroke warning remains in effect. Now for a special feature.

"There's a problem single women face today—" said the woman on screen, speaking calmly. "Is it possible, without a partner, to get pregnant and raise a child on your own? One option for women considering doing so can be found online: sperm donation sites. Yet, in the following report, we ask: What do donors hope to get out of these arrangements? And what potential risks await the women who seek out their services?"

A caption appeared at the bottom of the screen.

Sperm Donation: An In-Depth Report

I placed my fork in my spaghetti and stared at the TV.

I must have sat there, not moving a muscle, for about an hour, but once the special report was over, I went straight for my computer and looked up all the things that I had learned. Before I knew it, hours had gone by. My throat was dry, and my head was aching. I drank several glasses of mugicha and took another shower. Then I got ready for bed and slipped between the covers, but my mind was somewhere else. I couldn't fall asleep. I got up several times to go to the bathroom. The uneaten spaghetti hardened on the plate.

10.
CHOOSE FROM THE FOLLOWING OPTIONS

I was scared at first," the woman said. "Of course I was. I didn't know what was going to happen. I didn't know what they were going to do."

Her face had been blurred out. Her hair was shoulder length and dark brown. She wore a white cardigan over a gingham shirt. She put her words together carefully, as if she were making a collage.

"I wasn't that serious about it, not at first. I guess part of me didn't even think it was possible, to get pregnant like that. With some man I didn't even know. Someone I'd never even met. I'm honestly still shocked I went through with it. Shocked . . . " The woman paused and nodded slightly, as if confirming something. "But I didn't have any other options. I was out of time. No matter what I had to do to make it happen, I wanted my own baby."

They cut to an interview with a man—a donor. His face had been blurred out, too. His hair was clipped short, and he wore a plaid shirt over a pair of khakis. The whole time he was talking he was picking at his fingernails. His voice and silhouette suggested that he wasn't very old. Late twenties, maybe early thirties.

"Why do it? To help out. It's as simple as that. Here's this woman, and she's in need, right? I want to help, and if there's something I can do, why wouldn't I? . . . Oh, you mean do I see the child as mine? Well, in a way, I guess I do. It's strange, of course. We've never even met . . . Anyway, first and foremost,

I wanted to help, to do whatever I could to make that woman happy."

I paused the video and stretched without standing up.

It had been ten days since I first saw the special report on TV. The next day I found the video on the internet and watched it again and again.

Here's the gist:

Infertility treatment using third-party sperm had been happening in Japan for over sixty years, resulting in over 10,000 births, but the hospitals only treated married couples who had undergone conventional infertility procedures and discovered that the husband was sterile. Unmarried women who wanted kids were not allowed access to treatment, and same-sex couples were obviously out of luck. None of this was news to me.

But things changed a few years back with the appearance of websites where men offered their sperm directly. Requests from single women and same-sex couples had been on the rise. The men were volunteers: they would allow for you to cover travel expenses or buy them a cup of coffee but drew the line there. Afterwards, they assumed no responsibility and played no role whatsoever in the child's life.

One day, a woman in her late thirties who wants to have a child meets a man at a cafe to pick up sperm. Back home, she injects the sperm into her uterus herself, using the sort of plastic syringe that you can buy at Tokyu Hands. She gets pregnant on the second try, and gives birth, as a single mother.

Half of the special centered on interviews with this woman and her donor. During the remainder, experts talked about how self-injection puts women at risk to infectious diseases and outlined a slew of philosophical dilemmas.

I had to see what these sperm donor sites were all about.

Like the show had said, a large portion of the forty-odd hits were either so obviously fake it was hilarious, or clearly made by some guy on a whim. I had signed up for Twitter after

Fukushima, but hardly ever used my account. I went on and searched for "sperm donation," which led to dozens of accounts, but they all seemed bogus—with handles like "sperm.co.jp" and "we ♡ sperm"—in all likelihood redirecting you to porn sites.

This being the situation, I was surprised to find a sperm bank that operated as a non-profit. Their website was well-organized and looked like it had cost a pretty penny. The paperwork that you received together with your sperm gave you the blood type of your donor, as well as the results of a gauntlet of tests for infectious diseases, a genetic profile demonstrating that their genes were not at risk of cancer, and even proof that they had graduated university. If what they said online was true, then they'd already proven their ability to yield positive results.

I bought all the books on the subject I could find, but most turned out to be memoirs or extended interviews with women who had gone about it the *proper way*, with the aid of doctors. There were histories of artificial insemination, or books introducing the latest technological innovations and public debates over the right to reproduction, but no one had published anything on the experiences of a single mother who had used sperm from a volunteer.

There was the world of the woman on the special, and the world set forth in the available literature.

Which of these worlds did I belong to?

Did either of them overlap with my reality?

The night I watched the special, I was too keyed up to sleep. I felt like all the things that had been bobbing around in the back of my head had floated into view. Not like I had an answer or a solution, but I felt like I was finally on the right track. All the same, once I had cooled down a bit, I couldn't help but notice that the waves of excitement were diminishing.

Meet some total stranger at a cafe and go home with a vial

of sperm he's just filled in the bathroom, or otherwise have sperm overnighted, in a refrigerated truck, from a donor who was no more than a clean bill of health and a college degree . . . then do the job myself with a syringe I pick up at a drugstore, get pregnant and give birth to my own baby? No thanks. Not for me. Is this really what the woman on the special went through? If every word she said was true, then she was really willing to go to extremes. I could say this much for sure. Just the idea of a strange man's sperm inside my body was too much to imagine.

The whole thing was basically fiction to me. There *really were* women in the western world who used sperm banks like it was nothing. Even in Japan, plenty of people had come into the world in this way, and all of them had mothers who had pulled this off. Seeing the process as unthinkable had to be some kind of prejudice on my part.

Still, if I was honest, something was holding me back. Maybe I was hung up on where the sperm was coming from— either reputable hospitals or random guys off the internet. They sounded different, I suppose, but insofar as both involved the sperm of a stranger, they were really more or less the same. There had to be some meaningful difference between the two of them. What was it? At a university hospital, most of the sperm on hand was coming from med students, which meant that it had at least been subject to some sort of administrative oversight. The donors may be anonymous, but there was a paper trail of sorts. Somebody out there knew whose sperm it was.

Then there were the websites. Something was fishy. Was it the idea of meeting up at a cafe? Or possibly the offhand references to everyday stores like Tokyu Hands? Maybe I had trouble accepting childbirth as some sort of do-it-yourself project. DIY insemination. And what to make of all this attention to the donor's education? That wasn't part of how I saw the world, or how I got a sense of who a person was. Start judging people by their genetic profiles, and pretty soon you're seeing them like handbags, ranking them like brands.

Either way, I had a problem with not really knowing who this other person was, but when you get right down to it, what does it mean to *really know* somebody? Think of all the husbands and wives trying to have kids, and all the couples having sex who could wind up having a baby. Could all of them look each other in the eye and say they really, truly knew each other?

Going back and forth on everything, I eventually lost track of who or what it was that I was trying to figure out. It all seemed so dumb to me. It had nothing to do with reality, nothing to do with me. Taking sperm from a strange man to have a baby on my own? Yeah, right. Having a baby would only be the beginning. I've got my hands full just trying to keep my own act together. My only sister is in Osaka, stuck working as a hostess well beyond her prime, with no hope of retirement, and a daughter who still needs to be provided for. And I'm not getting any younger. At this stage of the game, I need to plan ahead, for myself and for my family. Why add a child to the picture? The idea was absurd, no matter how you slice it. More than impossible. In every way imaginable—I went from excitement to dismay, going back and forth.

The one thing that I couldn't shake was what the woman said at the end of the special. She clasped her hands in her lap, then brought them up to her chest, enunciating every word:

"I'm glad I did it. Truly. My child means the world to me. I'm so happy I went through with it—that much I never questioned. I can't even imagine what my life would be like . . . If I hadn't done this."

The voice of someone who has finally found happiness. I'm not sure exactly what to call it, but whatever it was, it was so radiant, so blinding that I had to shut my eyes. Letting them close, I meditated on her gestures and her choice of words. The sniffles, the frog in her throat. I was certain that behind the pixilation she was crying. I'm glad I did it. Truly—for a second, I could have sworn I saw my mom's face where the blur had been. Her face when she was young. She smiled and shook a head of hair so dense it could have carried a black kitten and you never would have known. Her smile was so wide it probably made her face hurt. I'm so happy I went through with it— *that much I never questioned.* I can't even imagine what my life would be like . . . If I hadn't—next thing I knew, I was the one with my hands over my chest and saying I'm glad I did it. My child means the world to me—cradling a little baby, blissfully unaware that I was alone in my room, imagining these things.

* * *

One day, like every summer that had come and gone, the heat abated, and the breeze took on a tinge of autumn. You could smell it on its way. The sky towered overhead, and the clouds spread into thin strands, lingering before vanishing entirely. It was the time of year when long-sleeved shirts no longer sufficed, and if you stayed home, you were wearing socks.

Day in day out, I waded my way through the novel I was writing. On top of being dense, the book was getting long. When people asked me what it was about, I found it hard to answer, but in broad strokes, it was sort of a portrait of the day laborers in a fictional part of Osaka. The main characters were a teenage girl whose father belonged to a gang of yakuza, who in this rundown town were mostly old guys, and another girl the same age who was raised nearby, in a cult led by a group of women. Ever since the crackdown on organized crime, life got hard for members of the yakuza, on account of which the gangster's daughter had been discriminated against from an early age, especially in her first few years of school. Meanwhile, the girl in the cult hadn't been registered at birth, because of her family's religious beliefs, and as a result she didn't have citizenship. When these two finally meet, they flee the ruins of their town and end up in Tokyo, where they get caught up in a sticky situation.

At present, I was racking my brains to flesh out my depiction of the yakuza. I had so many things to research, from protection money, the blades they used, and weapons trafficking to the particulars of real-life revenge killings and the code of ethics that informed them, not to mention the intricate system of ranks and compensation. There was too much to look up. I lost so much time watching videos and reading up on things. Every time I had to stop to check something out, it killed my rhythm. But sometimes, when I was watching interviews with the bosses of the past or footage of conflicts between rival gangs, I'd get so absorbed that I lost track of time completely. I wanted to do justice to the complicated situation, but there didn't seem to be any end in sight.

I was working on a scene where a guy "takes a finger," or when a gang member cuts off his own finger in a gesture of remorse, to take the heat for somebody below him, or to reconcile with an adversary. Almost no one does this anymore, but what I'm writing takes place in a different era, when this was all too common. Normally, you chill your pinky finger with ice until it loses feeling, then put it on a cutting board and chop clean through it with a tanto. I was writing a part where a guy with no tolerance for pain is trying to get a general anesthetic from his doctor, but predictably, there were so many things I had to look up. For example, where does the finger go once it's been cut off? Is there a cap on how many fingers one person can lose? Once I started digging deep, the writing slowed to a crawl. I had planned to spend the next day working on a part about the cult, about a drug that the founder had created at a lab years earlier, but I wasn't making any headway. Hell, I was backsliding. Taking a deep breath, I picked up where I'd left off in *Mercy Killing and the Yakuza*, my most recent piece of research material.

Propped up by the beanbag, I had given the book a good two hours of my focus when I checked my phone and saw a missed call from Sengawa. She'd sent me a bunch of emails, too. How many days had it been since the last one? Had it already been a week? Even longer? I thought about sending her an email but decided to call her back instead.

"Hey there, Natsuko." Sengawa picked up after three rings. She sounded like she was in a good mood, even a little jokey. "Glad I got a hold of you. How've you been?"

"Oh, you know, I'm writing. I mean, it's going pretty slowly, but I keep on plugging away at it."

"Good, good."

"Sorry I didn't get back to you sooner. I guess it slipped my mind . . . "

"Don't worry about it."

She was calling with an update on the information I had asked for. I wanted to know if she could find anything on people living in the countryside who had declared themselves to be religious visionaries and committed crimes that landed them in court. Evidently, she had found some promising resources and said that she would bring them by whenever worked for me. After that, we started talking about the book I was in the middle of reading.

"So he manages to get out, but there's still no way back to society for him after that. His body is falling apart along with everything else. In the end, it's just like, how is he gonna die? It's a real heartbreaker, I swear."

"I believe it. Hey, it'd be great if you could find a good way to work that into the story."

Our conversation took a few turns before Sengawa told me

about what happened at the afterparty, or after the afterparty, at some literary award ceremony. It sounded like Sengawa must have had too much to drink, because an older woman writer slapped her across the face.

"Like hard?" I asked. "And this is an author? An author you work with?"

"Yeah." For some reason Sengawa sounded bashful. "Well, I was pretty drunk, too. It wasn't really an argument, but I guess I said something that upset her."

"No no no no." I said. "There's no excuse for something like that. I mean, hitting someone you work with? At this age?"

"It's really not a big deal," Sengawa said. From her tone, you'd think it was somebody else's problem. "She's been around a long, long time, and she's been good to me, too, the whole time I've worked here. More than twenty years now . . . we know each other pretty well, too. We were both out of our minds drunk, though. This sort of thing happens."

"What did that look like for everyone around you?"

"I have no idea. They definitely noticed though."

I hadn't read any of this author's work, but she was famous enough that anyone who read books would have recognized her name. I knew nothing about her as a person, and had obviously never met her, but this whole episode was a definite departure from the mental image I'd got from seeing her at some point in a magazine. She was small, with feminine features. Her writing straddled the line between children's literature and fantasy. On top of her fiction, she'd even had a few hit picture books.

"So what do you do after something like that, the next time you meet?"

"Nothing," Sengawa cleared her throat. "Act like nothing happened, I guess."

"No sorry? No nothing?"

"Well, I don't think we'd have to say anything. We both

know what happened, you know what I mean? Plus, it had to do with her work. There's nothing more sensitive to a writer than that."

I tried to ask another question but Sengawa laughed it off and changed the topic.

"But enough about me. How are things on your end?"

"Well," I said, but stopped short. What was I supposed to tell her? I did the same thing every single day. I had nothing to report, except for what I'd been reading. For a second, I considered telling her about what had intermittently monopolized my mental bandwidth for the past few months—*that thing* I couldn't get my mind off, the idea of getting pregnant from donated sperm. The notion came and went, but it was always somewhere in my brain.

I kept my mouth shut. It was too much information, and it would've sounded crazy. Besides, even if I wanted to give this thing a try, I had no clue where to start.

As I gazed around the room, chiming in just enough for Sengawa to feel like I was giving her my full attention, my eyes drifted from the books about gangs and cults to the neighboring stack of books on sperm donation and fertility treatment. The last one I had read, *Half a Dream: Hearing from the Children of Donors*, centered around interviews with people who were conceived from the sperm of volunteers.

The interviewees had two things in common: no knowledge of their biological fathers and growing up without their parents giving them the facts. These treatments have always been conducted under a shroud of secrecy; the parents weren't supposed to tell their relatives or friends. Why would they tell their children? Thing is, though, this meant that there were practically 10,000 people born like this in Japan who were in the dark about the circumstances of their birth.

Some of them stumbled on the truth, discovering that the person who they grew up calling dad was not their dad at all, and their parents had been lying to them all along. The book gave me some sense of just how great a shock this revelation must have been, and of the deep and painful void it left.

The last man they interviewed said he was still searching for his father, to this day. According to the hospital that administered the procedure, the related records had long since been destroyed, and the doctor in charge had passed away. All he knew was that his biological father was probably a medical student at the university around the time he was conceived. Toward the end, the man listed some of the features that didn't seem to come from his genetic mother, on the reasoning that these were perhaps traces of his father.

"My mother is petite, but I'm on the tall side. Just about 5'10". My mother has clearly defined double eyelids. I don't. I've been a decent distance runner from the time I was little. The man I'm looking for is likely on the tall side, a good runner with single eyelids, between 57 and 65 now. At the time, he was a medical student at the university. If anyone can help, if any of this rings a bell . . . "

These words hit home for me.

Can you imagine searching for someone special, someone irreplaceable, a parent or someone else—with nothing to rely on but a few *features* that were little more than incidental details? The thought of it made my chest go tight. A tall man with single eyelids and a knack for long-distance running. If any of this rings a bell—a cry for help, but to who? I envisioned a figure, standing in the middle of a boundless wasteland, emptiness all around him. For a while, I was unable to take my eyes off of that final sentence.

"So what do you think? You could go to Sendai . . . "

When I realized that Sengawa was still talking, I switched my phone to the other hand.

"To Sendai?"

"It'd be fun, just listening to the stories. And it's Sendai, so a day trip isn't out of the question, but why not just spend the night, right?"

"Uh, is that okay?"

"Well, it's work, right?" Sengawa said. "If you wanted to hole up in some high-end hot spring for an entire month, that'd be another story. But I'm happy to treat you to a night in Sendai. You're writing the cult part, right? Those people can be a little cautious, but it sounds like the so-called 'devotees' up there will actually talk to you. Well, I suppose it depends on the person. Anyway, the foliage is beautiful right now. It'll be good for you to eat well, recharge, and close out the year strong. What do you think?"

"Well, closing out the year strong, sure, but I don't know about Sendai." I searched for a way out. "I think the books will be enough."

"It's just like you to stay inside, but sometimes you need to mix things up." I could hear Sengawa take a deep breath through her nose. "Oh, right. There was another thing I wanted to tell you. There's going to be a reading early next month. Think you can come?"

"A reading?"

"You know, a reading—" Sengawa coughed into the receiver. "Sorry. With poets and novelists, reading from their work. There have been a whole lot of readings around, maybe the last ten years or so. They're usually timed to happen as the book releases and things like that. People come, listen to the reading, buy books, have them signed . . . Sometimes we go out for a little get-together after."

"Oh yeah?"

"The one next month should be pretty big. There are maybe a hundred seats in the space. I think we have three people reading. One of the writers works with me. It should be fun. You should come. There are some people I want you to meet."

"Listen, though," I laughed. "I better not get slapped."

"Please, Natsu. I'd take a bullet for you." Sengawa made it sound like we were back in Osaka.

Once we hung up, I turned on the computer and checked my mail. Just ads. No word back.

It had been maybe three weeks since I'd sent out a couple of emails. The first was to the site that offered the most information and appeared to have the best "results"—and also seemed the most legit.

Using a gmail address I had just registered, I filled the blank white box with a candid cry for help: "I'm 38 years old and single, so finding a sperm donor through a medical institution is off the table. But I would like to have a child on my own. That's what brought me to Sperm Bank Japan. I'm considering all of my options. If I chose to use your services, how would I proceed?"

It had been nearly a month, but they hadn't responded. Ten days later, I created another account and emailed them from that address. The same thing happened.

I also wrote to a blogger who said he did direct donations. He hadn't responded either, but I wasn't too surprised. When I clicked send, I was nervous as hell, but I doubt I would have actually gone through with it if he responded. It was an empty gesture, unaccompanied by curiosity or consolation.

I pulled my notebook from my desk drawer and drew a line through "Sperm Bank Japan" and "direct donation." There were only two options left:

• Denmark Sperm Bank VELKOMMEN
• Life without children

I stared at my despicable handwriting and sighed yet another sigh.

Velkommen was a Danish sperm bank I found on the

internet. They had been in business for a number of decades and were known throughout the world. They had a proven track record, up-to-date facilities, and regularly screened collected sperm for disease. They even conducted chromosomal testing and genetic screening to identify any major genetic disorders. Not overlooking even the tiniest concern, they made every effort to ensure that only healthy, viable sperm was frozen and added to the bank. As a result, only one in ten donor applications were accepted. Their clients, on the other hand, were numerous. The bank had provided sperm to over seventy different countries, opening their doors to infertile couples, lesbian couples, and even single women like me— they had a system in place so that anyone could order sperm over the internet.

The site also had a database of donor profiles that you could search by checking boxes off for things like blood type, eye color, hair color, and height. If you found a donor that you liked, you could take a look at the rest of their profile. Each vial of sperm cost about 200,000 yen. Once it arrives, you inject it yourself. There was obviously no guarantee that you'd get pregnant. What really set Velkommen apart, though, was that you could opt for either anonymous or non-anonymous sperm, which allowed for children to find out who their fathers were once they grew up. The non-anonymous sperm was popular with lesbian couples, whereas infertile couples, already having a father figure, tended to prefer anonymous sperm.

Once I had familiarized myself with Velkommen, I wondered what had made me ever bother with Sperm Bank Japan or that sperm blogger, but the answer was all too clear: the Japanese language limited my options. I didn't know a single word of Danish, and my English skills had peaked in the eighth grade. I had no memory of anything beyond the present perfect. If I couldn't write anything of substance, how could I convey the complicated nature of my situation? But maybe there was no need. All I had to do was check the boxes. Once I'd paid, the frozen sperm would ship from Copenhagen, arriving anywhere in the world in as little as four days.

I got up from the computer and laid out on the rug. It was a little chilly, so I grabbed the cotton blanket balled up by my feet and draped it over my chest, making a comfy place to rest my hands. I had been thinking nonstop about sperm, but what about my eggs? For the most part I had a regular twenty-eight-day cycle, and I got my period every month, but at my age, there were plenty of other things to worry about.

I turned on the TV. The weatherman was pointing at a giant weather map, saying how tomorrow the weather would change for the worse. The light behind the closed curtains was growing dim. Almost night. How many more times in my life would I sit back like this and find myself transfixed by the blue of the evening? Is this what it means to live and die alone? That you'll always be in the same place, no matter where you are?

"Is that so bad?" I asked myself out loud.

I don't need to tell you that no one answered.

11.
I'm So Happy Cause Today . . .

Maybe I should've stayed home. This was my first time hearing authors read their own work, so I had no idea if anyone was any good. I honestly had no idea what they were trying to achieve up there. I obviously knew that they were reading, but why, I couldn't say. The first reader, a supposedly famous poet well into his eighties, sounded like his face was buried in a pillow, but every minute or two he'd launch into a coughing fit so violent he had to grab his chair. It was painful to watch.

The next guy was supposedly a novelist. He wore a chocolate-colored cardigan and had a moustache and conspicuously long hair tied in a ponytail. I'd guess he was in his forties. His reading voice was so monotonous that I could only make out the occasional word. His reading ran so long I was afraid that it would never stop. I started to feel like I was listening to a tape of a sutra on loop. I caught myself keeping time on an imaginary temple block, trying like hell to divine some kind of a rhythm. I tried playing on the upbeat, I tried triplets, I tried everything, but nothing I did got us closer to the end. I'm not sure if he was actually shy or putting on some kind of show, but he looked down as he read, and as a result his mouth drifted from the mic. The first few times someone tried to fix it for him, but before long he was out of range again, so they just let him be.

Since the start of November, it had been cold every single day, like we were already in winter, on account of which I'd worn a heavy sweater. Big mistake. The space was hotter than I thought possible. I was so spaced out that I felt like I was high. As the sutra played on, sweat trickled ominously down my back. I always carry a towel with me for moments like this—except for that day. I had not been more pissed off for the entire year, but when I looked around the room, to my dismay, everybody was perfectly still, eyes focused on the stage. The women to my left and right were practically devouring the sutra-chanting novelist with their gaze; they didn't even blink. What really blew me away, though, is what these two women were wearing. One of them had a cable knit cap pulled down over her forehead, and the other one had a mohair muffler wrapped around her neck. I was boiling. Still no clue what this guy was reading. I was about to blow a fuse. Someone more punk rock would've shot up out of their seat and screamed hard enough to drown out the stupidity of it all. I made an effort to quiet my breath and fidgeted in my seat. Then suddenly it stopped. I knew there was one more reader, but the instant the sutra ended, I got up and ducked out, taking advantage of the low lighting, and sought shelter in the stairwell by the bathroom.

"You made it."

After it was over, Ryoko Sengawa found me standing by the exit.

"What did you think? I had them set aside a good seat for you—not too close, not too far."

"Yeah," I said. "It was kind of strange. I felt myself losing track of who I was, where I was. It was almost like I was melting . . . Hey, was it really hot where you were sitting?"

"Yeah, now that you mention it."

"I was sweating so bad." I shook the collar of my sweater, to get some air in there. "Bullets. I was sweating bullets. Where were you? I didn't see you."

"I wasn't in the audience. They had me watching from the wings."

"Oh, that makes sense." So she hadn't noticed that I snuck out early. What a relief. "I've never been to a reading before. They're really something, huh?"

"Aren't they? The prose part was good, but I thought the poetry was absolutely wonderful. So powerful. What a great event."

I wanted to head home, but at Sengawa's insistence, I showed my face at the afterparty. I checked my watch. Eight thirty. It was a brisk fall night, and when you breathed in you could feel it spreading through your lungs. The party was at an izakaya ten minutes on foot from the bookstore in Aoyama that had hosted the reading. Sengawa and I walked past the decorated shops of Omotesando, storefronts twinkling for as far as the eye could see.

"Christmas already . . . " Sengawa gazed down the street. "Is it just me or is this stuff appearing earlier every year?"

"A few years back, I remember things getting started toward the end of November. The past couple of years, though, once Halloween is over, it's like all the Christmas lights are strung up by the next day."

"It's pretty, though." Her face relaxed. "I think I like the yellows better than the blues. Hey, Natsuko, don't the blue or I guess white ones feel a little cold to you? What are those called? LEDs? The yellow ones are a whole lot warmer."

We stopped at a pharmacy so I could buy some eye drops, but afterwards we got spun around and took some time getting our bearings. When we made it to the party, things were already underway. About a dozen people were chatting at a lengthy table. Nodding hello, Sengawa and I took seats at the end and ordered drinks. The poet who had gone first was slouching in the corner. He wasn't talking to anyone, but he was grinning like a madman. At the middle of the table was the novelist who had gone second. He couldn't have had more than a drink by that point, but his face was visibly red. I didn't know if the others were editors or from the venue. It seemed like they were having a decent time. Obviously, Sengawa was the only person there I knew.

The two of us drank beer and chatted over cubes of yakitori slipped off of their skewers. Sengawa introduced me to a number of the people there. We exchanged names and mentioned what we did. Other parties arrived, filling up the seats. As the place got rowdier, our table got louder, too.

About two hours in, everybody had a nice buzz going and started laughing even louder, although I guess there were a few people trying earnestly to talk about business. One of the female editors sat down next to me and told me about how well these coloring books for adults had been selling. The old poet sitting by the wall, though gripping his cup, had shut his eyes, like he was sleeping or possibly even meditating, despite the din around him. I couldn't figure him out. I made eye contact with the bald guy beside him, presumably his editor, who only nodded reassuringly, as if to say "business as usual."

Everybody just wanted to hear themselves talk, which made it hard to tell what anyone was talking about, but I could easily pick out the voice of the male novelist, who had cranked things up a notch. His face was flushed and splotchy. The guy was a regular chatterbox. Nothing like the way he'd been onstage, delivering that endless sutra. From the few words I was able to make out, he was talking about the conflict in the Middle East. I was missing lots of context, but it sounded like he was sharing his perspective with the older female editor sitting beside him.

"Like I said, it's all there in the report. It's about time that the world called out America for its arrogance. Oh, I know it's still America, even if it's going to shit. That's true. There are different ways of going to shit, though. We can certainly think about *how* and *why* something is going to shit. In fact, that's our responsibility. You know what I mean?"

The male novelist shook his head like an irritable horse, then lifted his glass of wine and kicked the whole thing back like it was some kind of a ritual. The female editor promptly poured him more, which he tasted with a grimace. "This is how I see it." Emboldened by the folks around him, the male novelist was going off the rails, indulging in a glut of generalizations and minutiae. What can literature do about politics? About terrorism? Sengawa and I were still at the end of the table, carrying on a separate conversation and not particularly listening to him. We had just ordered our fourth round of beers when we heard the guy gloating about how he saw everything coming—he claimed to have predicted it and told the world as much on Twitter.

"Too bad no one truly understands my work. Just look at what happened in Syria. That report I was talking about is basically a rehash of stuff I wrote at least ten years ago."

For a second, everyone stopped talking, but then the female editor saved him. "You're right. Novelists always see things coming . . . " Someone else backed her up while the male novelist threw back another glass of wine and sat up straight. "It's more than that, though," he said, ready to continue, before someone finally cut him off.

"What the hell are you talking about," a woman said, loud and clear. "Listen to you. I mean, how many years has it been since you wrote anything worth reading?"

It got painfully quiet. I turned to see who had been speaking.

"Look, I don't know what you wrote, or what you predicted, but whoever wrote that report, the one you're talking about, actually went to Syria, right? Then there's you. Sitting in your apartment, all comfy in your PJs while you skim it over. So you go on Twitter, and start bragging, like, I saw this coming years ago? Do us a favor and give it a rest. Unless you want to hop on the next flight to Syria and discover, with your own eyes, just how well your prediction is holding up. What's the point of going on like that anyway? You looking for attention? Then stop ripping off other people's work to inflate your own ego."

This sudden outburst, or difference of opinion, or what have you, made me panic that I'd missed some kind of a performance when I slipped out of the space—and that this was a continuation of the show. Or maybe this was a good friend of his, just giving him a hard time. But no. The woman speaking was the writer Rika Yusa, who Sengawa had introduced me to a little earlier. This was neither performance piece nor friendly joust.

After a few seconds of silence, during which the rousing voices of the other bargoers took on the distant timbre of a memory, someone said, "That reminds me . . . " in an attempt to change the subject. Then someone else jumped in with "Tell me about it," which made a bunch of people laugh. The male novelist nursed his wine. The rancor lingered in the air, and the discomfort inside me was screaming, but then I remembered Sengawa getting slapped by someone on what sounded like a similar night out. Evidently, in the literary world, this sort of thing was a common occurrence. This wasn't the backstreets of Shobashi—I drank my beer and scanned the room, half-expecting another flare up, but in a matter of minutes everything was back to normal. Sengawa ordered another beer. As soon as it came, she gestured to the woman next to Rika Yusa and switched seats with her. The two of them were cracking up in no time. I grabbed a largely untouched bowl of motsuni and picked at it with my chopsticks. At some point, I checked on the old poet. His mouth was open, and he looked totally asleep, lifeless as a figure in an Egyptian wall painting. When I met eyes with the bald editor beside him, he nodded reassuringly, *business as usual*, just like before. I nodded back.

Eventually, things started wrapping up. Before I knew it, the male novelist and the female editor beside him disappeared, and everyone else started saying their goodbyes. Sengawa said we were going the same way and should get a car together. Rika Yusa said she'd join us, since she was in Midorigaoka in Meguro.

The three of us shared a taxi. Sengawa sat up front. I was going to Sangenjaya, so I let Rika Yusa get in first.

Once Sengawa told the driver where the three of us were going, she turned around toward Rika Yusa.

"Listen, Rika," she said. "I get where you're coming from. I really do."

"Hard not to get!" Rika laughed. "He's always been that way. Always saying the same shit. Hell, for most of these guys, it's the only line they know. *I saw it coming, I predicted the whole thing* . . . I've heard that line a million times this year. Just hear me out, though. If someone else read his stuff and said, 'He saw this coming,' that'd be another thing entirely, but to sit in front of everybody blowing your own horn like that? Come on! Anyway, what was going on with today's line-up? Who wants to listen to these guys? I guess this asshole is all over the place these days, on Twitter and on TV, acting like he's got a crystal ball, but he's pure evil. You know what happened with him and that editor, right? Did you hear about that?"

"Oh, that girl?" Sengawa said. "I heard about that."

"Yeah. The second he found out there was a pretty new girl in the office, he asked to be reassigned, then came up with all kinds of excuses to call her up and have her do stuff for him . . . He even made her pick up his manuscripts at his apartment, in person . . . Send her an email, for fuck's sake. He was harassing the shit out of this poor girl. I'm sure he thought he was in love, but he was really being a self-absorbed maniac. I mean, the publisher should have done something. Like, cancel the bastard's contract already!"

"I know, I know. But Rika," Sengawa sighed. "I think you might be drunk."

I'd never read any of Rika Yusa's work, but I'd heard plenty about her. She had to be a couple of years older than me. A few of her books had been made into films. Sometimes I'd walk into a bookstore and find her latest novel piled high for everyone to see. She was what you call a literary star. When she went home with the Naoki prize a few years back, she caused a sensation by arriving at a press conference with a shaved head, carrying a baby. I remember seeing her on the news. Her slit eyes and lunette eyelids were striking enough, but she showed up to the ceremony in a sweatshirt and jeans. What really stood out was her head. If she were younger, it might have come across as some kind of fashion statement, but that was not the case. Whoever she was, she wasn't giving any helpful cues. Seeing her onscreen, I felt mildly disturbed trying to make sense of her. At the same time, I had to admit that the look really suited her.

How can she pull that off?—Watching her on TV, I rolled the question over in my head and realized what it was: her head was absolutely perfect. It crested toward the back, adding a sense of depth, and while her face was thin, her round forehead took up space. The bridge of her nose was well-defined, suggesting a sense of purpose. Not the sort of woman that people would label drop-dead gorgeous, but everything about her danced. She had a memorable face. I remember being taken by the way her facial structure, reminiscent of a squirrel, managed to make such a grand impression. As far as I could gather from the way she spoke during the clip, her personality could not have matched her image any better. When a reporter noted the baby she was carrying and asked, "Are you trying to send some sort of message? Is this a statement about women's rights?" she answered with a smile. "Message? No, no. I'm a single mother. It was just the two of us at home. There wasn't anyone around, so what else could I do?" When another reporter followed up with "The shaved head looks great, by the way, but I was wondering if there was something behind it. Something you wanted to say?" she countered with "Your curls look great, too, but is there something behind that? Anything you want to say?" which won a big laugh from the crowd. "Also, not to get too picky, but my head's not shaved. This is a buzz cut. Maybe it doesn't matter to you, but words mean a lot to me," she added with a devilish grin.

It felt strange to share the backseat of a cab with that woman, with Rika Yusa, but I wasn't the least bit uncomfortable. She was leaning against her door, so that she sort of turned my way, sometimes gazing idly out the window as she bantered with Sengawa. Her hair was past her shoulders, and her hands were folded in a shimmery black blouse. I wasn't sure whether it would be okay to jump in, and couldn't find a good break in the conversation, so I just sat there and listened to the two of them talk.

"So you and Sengawa go pretty far back?"

We had hopped on Route 246 out of Shibuya and were passing through the Dogenzaka-ue intersection when Rika Yusa asked me this.

"Not really. Well, I guess it's been a couple of years."

"Sengawa's really not the type to hold back, is she?" Rika joked.

Coughing in the front seat, Sengawa turned around enough to see her, feigning outrage.

Rika laughed.

Sengawa shook her head, exasperated. "Rika loves calling people out on how insensitive they are."

"So what happens now?" I asked Rika. "Was that the end of it?"

"The end of what?" Rika looked me in the eye for the first time. The signs and streetlights shining through the window cast strange shadows on her forehead, making patterns that immediately spun away. My arms and legs felt heavy. Maybe I was drunker than I thought.

"You and that guy. He didn't say anything back. Is that just how it goes?"

"Maybe," Rika nodded. "We'd pretty much never met before, so I bet he was surprised. I'm sure he'll look back on it later and grit his teeth. Telling everyone I'm crazy or whatever."

"You think you'll ever see him again?"

"I don't know," Rika didn't seem to care much either way. "I doubt it. It's not like authors are always getting together. Readings are a total waste of time. Hey, it's Natsuko—Natsuko Natsume, right?"

"Uh-huh."

"That's a pen name?"

"No, that's my real name."

"No way," she laughed. "Anyway, sorry you had to be there tonight. Our good friend Sengawa here dragged you along, didn't she?"

"Yeah, she asked me to come."

"And how was it?" Rika snickered.

"Completely lost on me," I answered honestly. "But the place was packed. Everyone seemed really into it."

"Right?" Rika laughed. "They ate it up. A crew of amateurs with no real skill, myself included. If that's how it's gonna be, I'm done. Never again, no matter what."

"How can you say that with a smile?" Sengawa laughed derisively.

"I know this was my first time and all . . . " I laughed too. "But shouldn't it be easier to make out what they're saying? Unless the audience sits perfectly still, you're gonna miss something important. Everyone's there to hear the story, right? If they can't follow along, what's the point? Why go?"

"Out of a sense of duty?" Rika revealed an enviable set of teeth.

"What duty?" I asked.

"No clue. A duty to literature or something?"

"What good does that do anybody?"

"Well" Rika cracked up. "I don't know if it's good, but some people find comfort in telling themselves, hey, everybody around me who's breezing through life is a total idiot. And look at me, never catching a break, no recognition, no nothing. But that's not because I'm short on luck or talent. The reason my life sucks is because I get it, because I understand what's going on. Know what I mean? Forget about that, though. There's only one thing everyone in the audience is dying to hear at one of these readings. Know what it is?"

"No idea. I feel like they're too busy trying to sit still and look like they're paying attention to worry about what anyone is saying . . . What?"

"And now for our last reader of the night."

Rika and I howled. Up front, Sengawa did her best to laugh along.

The taxi pulled over alongside Route 246 in Sangenjaya. I said goodnight and hopped out. The door slammed shut and the car sped out of sight. I fished my phone out of my purse and checked the time. Just after midnight. I had a message from a name I didn't recognize. Rie Konno . . . Rie Konno?— Oh, Rie. Right. I never heard from any of my bookstore friends unless we were planning a get-together. Odd as it sounds, this was the first time any one of them had texted me directly.

"How are you doing? Last time we met it was still summer! Life is crazy. It looks like I'm going to move early next year."

Rie went on to explain that her family had to relocate to the town in Wakayama where her husband had grown up. She wanted to know if we could get lunch before she left.

"It would be great to see you before the end of the year. I can meet you in Sangenjaya, if that works for you. Let me know if you have time. Also, I know this might sound weird, but it'd really help if you could keep the move a secret! I haven't told anyone yet."

Why was I the only one she texted, and why did I have to keep it secret?—Why me? After reading through her texts a few times, I had more questions than answers, but decided I'd better let it go. I couldn't remember what we said when we met in the summer, but then I remembered the galettes we had for lunch. It was all coming back to me. I knew that afterwards I had gone to Jimbocho . . . Sengawa wore something breezy, a natural cotton blouse. She was sitting on a dark red antique sofa. What had we talked about?—Did we really talk about anything? The novel I was writing popped into my head. I felt like somebody was standing on my chest. Things got dark. I dropped the phone into my bag and counted the steps back to my apartment.

I unlocked the door and entered the familiar assortment of shadows. It was uncomfortably cool, almost like winter. The carpeting felt damp. It actually smelled like winter. Which was funny, since I hadn't noticed it outside. Does that mean the smell was inside my apartment? When the temperature and intensity of the sunlight and the quality of night all met certain criteria, did that smell issue from the books and clothes and curtains and the other nooks and crannies all at once? Remembering something.

Like a row of white boxes, all lined up, the same shape and the same weight, the days of November came and went. I woke at eight-thirty in the morning, ate a slice of bread, and sat at my computer. For lunch I heated up a packet of sauce and poured it over some spaghetti. Then back to work. In the evenings I stretched for a bit, then ate a bowl of rice with pickled vegetables and natto. After my bath, I checked the infertility blogs I followed. Things were always touch-and-go. If people started mentioning a new blog, I'd check that too. These women were hellbent on trying, even if their chances were slim. As for me, I hadn't even made it to the starting line. Sometimes, I'd remember Naruse's Facebook page and have a look.

Rika Yusa emailed me the week after the reading. She said she'd rather talk over the phone than write a big long thing. If I didn't feel like talking, I could let it go to voicemail. Ten minutes after I sent her my number, my phone rang.

"I'm glad we could connect this way," she said. "Hey, I read something of yours."

"The book?" I wasn't expecting this.

"Yeah, your book. It was so good. It got billed as a short story collection, but it's basically a novel, isn't it?"

"Thank you, I appreciate you saying that."

"Don't be so polite. We're the same age."

"No way," I was taken aback. "I thought you were older."

"I was a grade above you, but we were born the same year."

"Hey, Yusa, I ordered three of your books," I said.

"Oh, thanks, Natsume." I was having trouble reading her tone. "Hey, you can call me Rika. What should I call you?"

I told her I was fine with Natsuko. She sort of hummed.

"Sure. Otherwise it's almost like we're on a volleyball team together."

"I know what you mean. Not that I ever played sports."

"Can we go back to your book, though? I seriously enjoyed it. It reminded me a lot of *The River Fuefuki*. I bet you love that book, don't you?"

"I've never read it, actually," I said.

"Seriously?" Rika sounded appalled. "It's great. This village saga. Generation after generation, one life story after the next. The story covers this obscenely long stretch of time, but the novel itself is pretty short."

Then we started talking about dialect in fiction. Rika asked me if I'd ever thought about writing a whole book in Osaka dialect. When I said I'd never even toyed with the idea, Rika told me what she thought about the way that people talked in Kansai, and Osaka in particular.

"That was seriously amazing," she said. "When I went to Osaka, I saw, or really heard, these three women just talking, a million miles an hour, getting everything in there. There was so much going on. Multiple perspectives, mixed tenses, the whole shebang. They were cracking up, but they were having a real conversation. Nothing like on TV. Everything on TV is tailored for TV. The real thing, the real Osaka dialect, isn't even about communicating. It's a contest. Somehow, you're both in the audience and on the stage . . . How can I put it? It's an art."

"An art?" I asked.

"Yeah, you know. The Kansai dialect represents the evolution of language into a verbal art . . . No, that's not right. Evolution doesn't cut it. Language is always art, but in order to achieve its highest form, the language itself—intonation, grammar, speed, everything—had to mutate over time. And as the form of the language changes, so does the content. It mutates."

I had never given my own dialect much thought. Curious to hear more, I let her go on.

"Anyway, it blew my mind. I have a lot of friends who speak in dialects. I guess I used to think dialects weren't all that different. It's not the same as a foreign language or anything. I didn't really get it, but it's not like that at all. Have you ever noticed what I'm talking about?"

I told her no, not really.

"Know what, though? What really gets me is how writing always fails to capture it. Like, the way those three women were talking. I mean, you couldn't reproduce that performance on the page and get the same dynamic. A lot of people from Osaka have written things in Osaka dialect. I've read a bunch of them, just to see how they'd handle it. But it really, truly doesn't work. Like it's impossible. I guess what really struck me, though, was how it didn't make any real difference if the writer was from Osaka. It didn't really matter if the writer grew up speaking that way. I guess it's pretty obvious, but every writer ends up creating their own language. Your style is an invention. It doesn't matter where you come from. All that matters is having a good ear."

"A good ear?" I asked.

"Exactly." Rika was getting excited. "Think about it. Rhythm, or maybe even biorhythm. It's physical. Sonic. In your face. You take that and turn it into something else. That's what it takes. I guess what I'm saying is you need a good ear. Take Tanizaki."

"Junichiro?" I asked.

"Exactly, Tanizaki." Rika enunciated each syllable like she was reading off a blackboard. "I'm talking about *Shunkin*. Forget *Makioka*, forget *Nettles* . . . It's all about *The Story of Shunkin*. Of course Tanizaki's no Kansai native. He's all Tokyo, all the way down."

"Hold on, though," I said. "It's not like the whole thing was written in Osaka, or, uh, Kansai dialect. Just the dialogue, right?" I hadn't read *The Story of Shunkin* since I was in my twenties, and barely remembered any of the details—but my memory of Shunkin hatcheting away at Sasuke with a plectrum was so vivid that it definitely felt physical, like I had done the act myself. I wondered if this is what Rika meant by "in your face."

"Yeah," laughed Rika. "That's what I mean, though. It has nothing to do with whether or not you're writing in dialect. It could be standard Japanese, or even another language, but you could still capture the spirit of the thing I'm talking about. I guess that's what I meant about the language mutating."

"So that's how it is," I said in dialect.

"It is what it is," Rika asserted, not sounding like anyone I'd known in Osaka.

After that, Rika started calling about once a week. She had a way of calling just when I was thinking I would give myself a break. One time, at night, I heard a kid's voice in the background. She told me that she had a daughter, Kura, who was turning four this year. I said I didn't think I'd heard that name before. Rika said that she was named after her grandmother. Rika and I had a lot in common. She grew up without a father in the house. Her mother sold insurance door to door, which meant that she was home alone much of the time growing up. Her grandmother practically raised her. When Rika was twenty, her mother remarried and moved out to live with her new husband. For the next ten years, until her grandmother passed away, it was just the two of them at home. When I told her I had grown up living with my grandmother, we realized that both of our grandmothers had been born in 1922. She asked me what my grandmother's name was, and I told her it was Komi. Rika loved it. "God, that's so 1922."

On the last Sunday in November, Sengawa invited me and Rika over for dinner. Her building had a refined elegance, decorative gateways at the entrance and over the veranda. Her den was way bigger than necessary and boasted an expensive-looking rug. Her bedroom had a walk-in closet. The style and smell and quality of her furniture had no connection to the universe of my apartment. I recalled the flowery copy I had read in ads for other luxury buildings. Sengawa ladled borscht into our soup bowls, saying that the recipe was a recent addition to her repertoire. She cut thick slices from a boule that she had purchased at some famous bakery, and sliced into a stick of butter, a foreign brand, serving us each a golden pat on its own plate. There was a tureen of something I was never able to identify, some creamy thing that had a strangely sour flavor, and a salad made from beans of different colors and shapes. These weren't the sort of things I normally ate. In fact, I'd never eaten any of them. We ate and ate and talked and talked. Rika said her mother had come by to spend the night with Kura, so she was free to drink. The way she tasted her wine said it all.

Sipping at my glass of beer, I tried to make sense of a number of things. Did Sengawa really live in this enormous place alone? How high is the rent for this kind of an apartment? And how much does an editor make anyway? We'd never talked about our love lives. Was Sengawa dating anyone? Or did she used to? Also, how did Rika become a single mom? What was Kura's father like? How was her experience with pregnancy and childbirth? What about Sengawa? At almost fifty, what were her thoughts on never having children of her own? Had she considered it, and if not, why?—I listened to the two of them talk, adding just enough to stay involved, but all the while hoping for the topic to drift naturally toward any of the above. To my dismay, they only talked about the sorry state of publishing, or whatever they'd been reading. Work, work, work. No one touched upon their private lives. Sengawa had been coughing all the night, so Rika asked her if she had a cold or something. She explained that she had chronic asthma, but that it wasn't anything serious. That it had caused her a lot of problems as a kid, but as an adult it was mostly under control, except for when it flared up during stressful periods of work. Then the conversation shifted to juice cleanses and alternative medicine. Rika said she'd downloaded a "life expectancy calculator" for her smartphone and showed us how it worked. Each of us tried it out. Rika and I both got ninety-six. We had a good laugh when Sengawa came up with sixty. "Next time listen when your editor tells you that you're going to be the death of them," she teased and took a sip of wine.

Makiko called sometimes, too.

Early in the afternoon, she'd call and in her usual spunky way ask if I was busy, then tell me all about the new girl at the bar, or some fad diet she had heard about on the TV, or an old hostess friend that she had run into at the mall, who was in a wheelchair now because of complications with her diabetes, or how one of the ladies down the block was walking around the neighborhood the other day and found the body of an old guy who had hanged himself—Makiko spoke with tremendous energy, like she was watching scenes unfold before her eyes. Whew, all bad news these days, Natsuko. This guy who hanged himself, he didn't use a tree. He did it on a fence. Just a normal fence, not even a tall one. And with a towel. Who hangs himself using a towel? Towels are for wiping your face, not for stringing up your neck. Where did he learn to do it that way? Natsu, sometimes I wonder why we're even born, she said, letting her anxiety show. Then, just before she hung up, she rallied and said, "Oh, right, Natsuko. I got this month's transfer. Thanks again."

With my first book on the market, I was getting work more regularly, and started wiring Makiko 15,000 yen each month. At first she refused. "Keep it, you keep it. Don't be ridiculous." Then she changed her mind. "I'll just leave it in there for now, I won't touch it, so that it's there for Midoriko." I wasn't sure whether Midoriko knew, but I sort of thought it would be better if she didn't find out.

In December, I began to wear a coat over my sweater when I went outside. The bark had almost turned black on the gingko trees planted at even intervals along the sidewalk, and the wind was getting chillier by the day. It was hotpot weather, and the supermarkets displayed the soup stock and the ponzu just inside the door. Gazing at the eerily white pyramid of cabbage, I lost track of what I was even looking at. The store was overrun with people shopping for dinner. I passed by a mother pushing a baby in a stroller and leading a girl in a kindergarten uniform. The daughter was trying hard to tell her something, and the mother answered her with smiles. The baby appeared to be asleep, under the sunshade of the stroller, but the toes of its little white sneakers were poking out from a cozy-looking blanket. I imagined myself pushing a stroller all around the store. I tried to picture myself holding a child's hand and talking about the different kinds of vegetables and meats. Meanwhile I bought natto, green onion, garlic and bacon and left the store. I didn't want to go home yet, so I wandered around the station, carrying my plastic bag of groceries. Stepping off the main drag, I found myself inside a network of narrow streets lined with neon signs for bars, izakayas and used clothing stores.

Heading in no particular direction, I caught the unmistakable aroma of a laundromat, a mix of hot air and the smell of drying clothes. I looked up and saw a bathhouse down the street, just after the laundromat. When I got there, I stopped in front of the entrance for a second. I wasn't very far from my apartment. I had no idea there was a bathhouse here. Back in Minowa I got to the baths once in a while, but I hadn't been once since I moved. The thought hadn't even crossed my mind.

It didn't seem like anybody was around. The building was obviously old and could have used some love here and there, but it had to be in business, because the smell of bubbling water rode the air. I ducked under the faded noren and went inside. Two wooden doors, one for the men's side and another for the women's side. A flip calendar hung from the post between them. Paint flaked in patches from the low ceiling. Almost all the yellow fobs on the shoe cubbies were available, and there were no shoes on the concrete step. I stepped out of my sneakers and went inside. There was an old woman with a bad back sitting on the perch between the changing rooms. She glanced at me and said in a wavering voice, "460 yen."

Nobody else was in the changing room. The electric fan probably started its life white, but it had turned cream over the years. The platform of the iron scale was rusted. There was a hair dryer shaped like a space helmet, and the seat cushion below was cracked all over. The straw mats spread over the floor were fraying. Beside the sink for washing your face was a rattan chair that must have been there forever, and on the clouded glass table beside it was a bud vase, looking like an heirloom no one wanted.

I was standing in a typical bath house changing room. Beyond the glass doors were the baths, where the hot water would be bubbling over the tiles. I must have shown up before anybody else, but people would start coming in before too long. That's how it worked—but this wasn't like the bathhouse that I used to visit almost every day. It was different, and it had nothing to do with the lack of people or the age of the space. Things had changed. Standing with my coat on in the middle of the empty changing room, I felt like I'd been left behind, trapped inside the weathered skeleton of an enormous creature that had shed its flesh and skin. Then I started to feel as though it was me, that my body had become the empty husk. The feeling was more desolate than anything I'd ever felt, like I was watching myself dying, helpless to fight back, at the hands of someone who was making some kind of a big mistake.

Way back when, although it didn't feel so long ago, we used to visit the bathhouse all the time. But did we? I mean when Komi and mom were alive, and Makiko and me were little. We loaded our washbowls with our shampoo, soap, and towels and laughed our way through the night. Water so piping hot it made our cheeks red. We had no money. We had nothing. But we had each other. We had our words, and all the feelings that we never even thought of putting into words. There were always women in the space beyond the steamy air. Babies, girls, and older women. Naked as they sudsed up their hair, sank into the water, heated their bodies. Countless wrinkles, straight backs, sagging breasts, gleaming skin. Stubby little arms and legs, age spots dark and light, articulated shoulder blades— bodies laughed and chattered about the silliest things, airing their frustrations or bottling them up but most importantly surviving, day by day. Where had all those women gone? What had happened to their bodies? Maybe all of them were gone by now. Like Mom and Komi.

On my way out the old woman nodded goodbye. I put on my shoes and stepped outside. I'd had these sneakers now forever. They were embarrassingly filthy, the dense gray of a thunderhead. I walked around and around, nowhere to go. The smell of cooking meat wove through the sleepy winter air. Daggering lights flashed on and off all around me. The laughter of men passing by. I pulled my collar up and swung my bag of groceries to the other hand. People were walking at all kinds of different paces. Wearing different faces, different clothes, speaking in different keys, like they were thinking, or maybe not thinking, about all kinds of things. The streets were inundated with text. Words were everywhere, no matter where you looked. Signposts, for-lease signs, storefronts, streetside menus, logos flanking the vending machines. Prices, hours, medicinal properties. The words leapt out, whether you tried reading them or not. A dull pain radiated from my temples. I realized I was freezing. I somehow hadn't felt the cold when I left home or left the bathhouse. I slipped the bag over the crook of my arm and squeezed my fingers. They were cold as ice. The air passed through the fibers of my coat and the sweater I wore underneath. It ravaged my skin and melted into my blood, turning my whole body cold.

I looked up and a little ways ahead—some people were crouching in a smoking area.

They crowded around an ashtray, huddled in a cloud of their own making. Nearby, in an alley between the buildings, I saw another person squatting by a stash of bicycles in the shadows. The smokers didn't seem to notice they were there, in spite of their proximity. They puffed away, laughing, staring down into their smartphones. What was going on here? They couldn't be children. I approached them, as if drawn in by their presence.

Upon closer examination, they were grown men, though they were small as elementary schoolers. The ashen hair they probably hadn't washed in months or years was stiff with sweat and grime. They wore work clothes that were about as dirty as it gets, and equally dirty canvas shoes, the cheap inside shoes that kids wear in class. Slumped over, the men looked like they were poking something on the ground. When I got closer, I could see what they were doing. Picking cigarette butts from the flooded ashtray, they smooshed them against the iron waffle of the street drain to squeeze out the moisture. Their bare hands shone in the low light like an oil slick, black with dissolved nicotine and tar. They put their weight into it, until each butt was relatively dry, and placed whatever scraps were left into plastic bags, which they tied off once they were full to bursting.

I have no idea how long I stood and watched them. It could have been as little as two minutes. One of the men noticed me and turned around. We met eyes. His face was as grimy as his clothes and hair, and his cheeks were sunken, like they were being sucked away. His eyes were cavernous. His lips were parted, so you could see his crooked teeth. *Natsuko*—I thought I could hear him call my name. Natsuko. My heart was pounding. I had this awful feeling in the pit of my stomach. Natsuko. I took a step back. He was staring at me with his beady eyes. I couldn't look away. Softly, he said my name again. *Natsuko*. Whose voice was this? I searched my memory to no avail. Next thing I knew, I was swept up in the past. Salty air. The stone of the seawall. Waves rising like a dismal inhalation and crashing endlessly. The narrow stairwell of our building. The rusty mail slot. The stack of magazines beside his pillow. The heaps of laundry on the floor. The shouts of drunks. Where's Mom, the man asked in a hoarse voice. I took another step back. Where's Mom, he said again, even more quietly. Dead, I said as if forcing out the word. The man didn't seem to understand. He gazed at me, dark face and inky eyes. He was small and frail, as if all his energy had left him. He looked like he could barely stand up to a kindergartener. But I was terrified. My breathing hastened, and my heart beat against my chest. *She's dead*, he muttered, eyes hollow. He continued talking in a voice like gravel. At first, I couldn't make out what he said. I blinked and blinked and tried hard to calm down. He spoke again. *What were you doing?* Pain clamped my throat. My pulse drummed in my ears. *What were you doing?* My blood was thumping through my body so violently I rocked back and forth. An irrepressible anger swarmed around my collarbone. It was like my blood was boiling, running backwards, and I was being swept off in the process. I wanted to shout *What about you?* and come at him from behind. I wanted to grab him by the shoulders and drag him down the street. But I couldn't do anything. I couldn't even speak. This man terrified me. I was scared of this man, despite him being so emaciated that he probably couldn't lift his hands over his head or even shout. All I could do was stare at him in silence. Yet my hands were throbbing for some reason, as if I'd grabbed him by the collar and thrown him to the ground. I could feel myself pummeling him, in tears, shoving him in the chest. My fists were tight now and I couldn't let them go. I didn't want this. I didn't. I'm not doing anything to him—I told myself over and over, shaking my head. The man parted his lips again. Squinting hard, I heard him speak—*Why didn't you do anything?* He sounded even weaker than before. His voice was so wizened and low it couldn't possibly have reached me, but in my head it hummed like he was speaking right into my ear. *Why didn't you do anything?* He said it again. *Why didn't you help her? Why didn't you save her?* His words transformed, branching off inside of me. Something black started oozing from his eyes. Lines of liquid trickled down his cheeks, until they covered his whole face like a fatal stain. Just then, a shaft of light swung at us from the left, accompanied by a metallic screech. A bike stopped inches short of running into me. The startled woman behind the handlebars shouted, telling me to watch out, then rode away. When I turned around, the man had looked away, returning to his task. Plumes of smoke swirled around him. The men were smoking again, as if they had never stopped.

I closed my eyes and swallowed the spit that had been collecting in my mouth. My lips were dry. They stung. Licking them only made the pain worse. I got out of there and fast. Weaving my way around the pedestrians, I turned right at the corner and went until I hit another intersection, then turned again. I barged into the first cafe I found, practically breaking down the door.

I sat there with my coat on but felt like I was never going to be warm again. Still, I swallowed the glass of ice water in front of me and asked for another. The shop was long and narrow. The front was a cafe, but the back was stocked with clothes and trinkets. The walls were decorated in band shirts, all of them black. The whole place had that dusty, cloying smell you only get inside of thrift stores. Nirvana was playing from speakers buried somewhere in the decor. I couldn't remember the name of the song, but I knew it was the third track on *Nevermind*. A girl in an old gray hoodie whose ears were full of piercings came over and took my order. Just coffee. The stars tattooed on the backs of her hands were so crooked you'd have thought a kindergartener had drawn them. Then I remembered someone telling me that, in tropical climates, everything they eat and drink is made to cool the body down, even if it's warm. I didn't want a cup of coffee but didn't know what else to order.

My lips were burning. When I touched them, I realized the

skin was peeling. I wished I had some lip balm. I would've smeared it over my lips, then rubbed it over the rest of my face. That's how much my lips hurt. I was tempted to flag down the server with the star tattoos and ask her if she had any chapstick I could borrow. Too bad vintage stores don't sell things like that. It's the sort of thing people don't typically want to share anyway. Listening to the tortured voice of Kurt Cobain made them sting even worse. But I was fine with that. I started to think. When your lips hurt, what's actually hurting? Then I thought of Naruse. Neither of us was all that into punk or grunge, but in our late teens, *Nevermind* was all we listened to. We knew that Kurt Cobain had died a little before we started listening to it, but the reality of that was lost on us. Most of the musicians we liked were dead. I realized "Lithium" was playing. Kurt sang the same way he did twenty years ago. "I'm so happy, cause today I've found my friends." No, *the same way* wasn't quite right. It was *perfectly identical.* Dead people and the words they leave behind can't change. Those guys would sound the same, screaming the same things from the same space, until not one person was left listening. Kurt's daughter was an infant when he died. I think I read somewhere that her parents never taught her how to read or write. What would it feel like to have a father who had blown his head off, who would be young and melancholy for eternity?

The coffee was still as hot as when it came. I took little sips and let them trickle down my throat, but I didn't feel like I was calming down. At least I was finally a little warmer. I took off my coat, bunched it up and set it down next to me. A sigh worked its way out of me. My lips were screaming, throbbing like crazy. As my thoughts repeatedly returned to the encounter at the smoking area, I shook my head and shut my eyes. I pictured a brilliant white cloth. An imaginary hand wrapped the cloth around its fingers and wiped out the inside of an imaginary skull, reaching every nook and cranny, all the divots and cracks and bumps inside. To really shine things up in there. I swallowed my saliva and kept working my fingers. There was no end to the residue the cloth picked up. It didn't look like I would ever wipe it clean. I grabbed one of the sugar cubes and took a bite. Before I had a chance to chew, its sweetness spread over my tongue. It almost tasted like papier-mâché.

I felt like giving Makiko a call. I had nothing to say, but that was never an issue with us. I just wanted to hear her voice. It was a weeknight, though. Makiko was probably at work by now. I wondered how Midoriko was doing. How long had it been since we texted? Was she out with Haruyama, or was she working too? I pulled out my phone to text her, but I stopped myself.

I checked my email. Mixed in with a number of daily digests from newspapers was a message from Rie. I'd answered her the week before and said let's try and see each other before New Year's, but we had yet to come up with a concrete plan. I opened up one of the news digests and scrolled through, like my fingers were trying in vain to catch up with something. I read through all the glowing headlines without a thought. Another messy day for planet earth. It had been a month since Trump had been elected, but people were still up in arms all around the world, and the pundits in Japan were analyzing what had happened from various angles, with no shortage of articles to choose from. There was a story on the Nobel Prize ceremony in Stockholm. Now and then I'd hit an ad encouraging me to subscribe, followed by more recommended reading. Things like "Anger Control—How to Stay Mad Without Ruining Your Life" and "The DIY Approach to Combating Noroviruses." Next came the events. Seminars on asset management. Some famous essayist holding a master class for women. Photo exhibitions. But when I got to the next item, my finger stopped. I opened my eyes wide. "The Future of Life and Parenting—Artificial Insemination by Donor."

The event details were listed below the header.

"Artificial Insemination by Donor (AID) has been practiced in Japan for over sixty years, catalyzing the miracle of life 10,000 times over, but the laws and policies surrounding treatment have not received the attention they deserve. Technology is advancing, and so are our values. A whole range of questions deserve consideration. Who benefits from third-party reproductive treatments? How can we make sense of the various implications? Drawing from personal experience with these and other questions, Jun Aizawa will lead us through a conversation on the future of life and parenting."

Jun Aizawa—I knew I'd seen that name before, but where? I couldn't place it. I set my phone down on the table and examined the nibbled sugar cube. I closed my eyes. The name "Jun Aizawa" flickered like a neon light in my mind. Artificial insemination . . . Jun Aizawa—then I saw the figure of a man, standing straight up with his back toward me. "My mother is petite, but I'm on the tall side. Just about 5'10". My mother has clearly defined double eyelids. I don't. I've been a decent distance runner from the time I was little." It was him. "The man I'm looking for is probably a good runner with single eyelids, somewhere between 57 and 65. If any of this rings a bell . . . "

Now I remembered. A few months back, I had seen his name inside that book I'd read: *Half a Dream*. I could see it perfectly. The man who had been searching for his dad forever, equipped with nothing but the most miniscule fragments of information. I clicked the "Read More" link and took a screenshot. Not like I was going to forget.

12.
MERRY CHRISTMAS

The event was held on the third floor of a compact building a few minutes away from Jiyugaoka Station. The room itself was minimalist. Picture a conference room, a little on the larger side. A chair sat before the whiteboard at the back of the room, and a microphone was ready on a little wooden table set beside it. Folding chairs fanned out in a semicircle from the whiteboard. When I showed up fifteen minutes before start time, fifty of the sixty or so seats were taken. I left my tote bag on a free seat at the end of the back row and went to find the bathroom.

When I came back, there was a woman sitting in the seat next to my bag. We met eyes and nodded hello. I quickly scanned the room, then read over the program I had picked up by the door. The plan was for Jun Aizawa to spend the first half of the event giving us his story, then open up the floor during the second half to give the audience a chance to share their thoughts.

A moment later, Aizawa came in. I knew him right away. He was tall, wearing beige chinos and a black crewneck sweater. He bowed slightly, took his seat, ran his fingers through his hair to part his bangs, and rubbed his eyelids. There they were: the single eyelids that linked him to his father.

He picked up the mic.

"Hello, thanks for coming."

Something about his haircut reminded me of a tennis player. Parted down the middle and trimmed around the ears.

Perfectly normal. What it had to do with tennis, I can't say, but that was how I felt. Maybe it was the way his bangs sort of stood up at the roots. Aizawa seemed distracted by the volume of the mic. His voice wasn't particularly high or low, but something about his manner of speaking left a strong impression. He knew how to enunciate; his voice carried well, but the main thing was the way he took his time, pausing when you weren't expecting it, which made it feel like you were listening to someone talking to themselves. Like he was sitting alone in the corner, working on a coloring book. That's how it sounded to me.

Aizawa started by telling us about his background.

He was born in 1978 in Tochigi Prefecture. When he was fifteen, after his father passed away, he and his mother continued to live with his grandmother, on his father's side. The three of them lived together until he went away to college. One day, not long after he turned thirty, his grandmother told him, "You're not my grandson. Not by blood." When he confronted his mother, she revealed that she had gotten pregnant with the help of a university hospital in Tokyo. Since then, Aizawa had done everything he could to find his biological father, but to this day he was still searching.

Next, he started talking about the state of donor conception today.

In the United States, they were developing a system that would allow for donor-conceived children to learn about their fathers, if they wanted to, but in Japan, even the existence of donor conception wasn't common knowledge. And while there may have been as many as 15,000 or 20,000 children born this way, almost none of them, statistically speaking, ever found out. He told us how very few parents were willing to sit their children down and state the facts. It was much more common for donor-conceived children to find out accidentally. The act of conveying and explaining this essential information was called "telling." In an ideal world, telling would take place when the family was together, during happy times, when everything is going well. Unfortunately, in most cases, people found out when a parent was on their deathbed, or soon after losing a parent, which could have a severe impact on the child, grown or otherwise. Then there's the suspicion of—or anger over—being lied to, which only builds after finding out this way. He spoke about the sense, or the feeling, of not really being the offspring of two people, so much as the result of a procedure. For most donor-conceived children who find out where they came from, this burden is carried everywhere they go.

"Neither the medical community, nor the parents who go through with this type of treatment, have adequately considered how the children—and this is about children—will eventually see themselves," Aizawa said, in summary. "As for donors, most haven't given much thought to these issues, either. For them, it's something akin to giving blood. Legal reform has a long, long way to go, but recent attention to the child's right to know has caused more and more hospitals to suspend treatment entirely. As such, quite a few parties have asked advocates such as myself to stop making a big fuss. They say that a threat to donor conception is a threat to infertility treatment as a whole. These people think we're making waves . . . But shouldn't we be putting children first, above all else? Donor conception goes beyond pregnancy and childbirth. It impacts the child for their entire life. And a time may come when that child wants to know exactly where they came from. When that time comes, they need answers. As I've said, quite simply, they *deserve* answers."

When Aizawa was finished, we took a short break before jumping into the discussion. At first nobody wanted to break the ice, but after a period of silence, a woman tentatively raised her hand. The event assistant, a small woman seated by the door, came over with the mic, which she accepted with a little bow. Rather than spark a discussion, she took the opportunity to share her story. She spoke of the agonizing years of infertility treatment she had been through, adding that because her husband wouldn't be cooperative, she had no way of knowing if her husband was infertile, and had no idea what to do next. When she made it sound like she was done, the audience gave her a nice round of applause.

Another woman raised her hand and told a similar story. She suspected that her husband was to blame, but wanted more than anything to have a child of her own flesh and blood, which brought her to donor conception, but she had not yet mentioned any of that to her husband. Yet another woman in a wrinkly gray jacket raised her hand. She had a thick black ponytail and a large wooden barrette keeping her hair out of her eyes. When the event assistant circled around with the mic, the ponytailed woman tapped twice on the windscreen covering the microphone to make sure it was on.

"Being a parent . . . " She coughed like she was trying to clear something stuck in her throat. "Being a parent means placing your child's wellbeing, your child's happiness, above your own. That's what it takes. But donor conception is all about the parents, about their egos. Having a child has always been determined by forces beyond our control, by nature. But with donor conception, it's all about ego. Foremost, the egos of the parents, but also the egos of the doctors, who view the life they bring into the world as an end that glorifies the means. For them, this is simply about showing off. No more than a test of their abilities. That's why I'm adamantly opposed. Just look at the state of surrogacy today. As long as you have the money, you can have some underprivileged woman carry your baby in your stead. It's exploitation, pure and simple. It's wrong, and it's about time somebody said so."

The woman was so worked up she slammed herself down in her chair. The audience applauded, but their uncertainty was audible. I wanted to speak up and ask the woman whether she thought there was any form of childbirth that did not involve the egos of the parents, but I decided against it. Up at the front of the room, Aizawa sat still with his hands folded in his lap. He nodded at the woman's story, but it seemed as if his heart wasn't really in it, or like he wasn't actually listening. He looked like he was thinking about something else entirely.

"So," another woman said, raising her hand. She had a round face and a cornflower blue dress, a yellow sweater draped over her shoulders. Her hair was neatly curled. She looked like she was probably my age, but I could've been convinced that she was ten years older. Her wrists clacked with an assortment of power stone bracelets.

"I think imagination is extremely important here."

The woman smiled. She spoke like she was reading from a poem she had written just for us.

"What if a donor-conceived individual is born with a disability? Or what if, as the child grows, he or she doesn't fit in with the rest of the family? Who can say whether that couple, the child's parents, will stay together or not? If they separate, what happens to the child? To what extent will the parents act like parents or see themselves in a parental role? That's what I want people to think about when they consider donor conception. I want them to give it some real thought. Think about how the life you're bringing into the world creates connections, both to you and to the greater world. Nobody is truly born alone. I believe there really is a god out there, somewhere, watching and providing children to the couples who are ready to be parents. Family matters, it matters more than anything. Children need to be raised by real families, in real homes, in an atmosphere full of love and responsibility. Every child brought into this world, by artificial insemination or otherwise, is an example of the gift of life, and I believe their life deserves to be cherished. Thank you."

She met her hands in prayer and bowed her head to us, smiling beneficently. The crowd offered her more of the same applause. Then I raised my hand—I instantly regretted it, but it was too late. The woman with the mic was making her way toward me.

"With regards to the perspective that you've shared," I said, "these issues aren't necessarily limited to those who are considering donor conception. Any child with a disability could have difficulty connecting with their family. Who can ever guarantee if any couple is going to stay together? Aren't these questions relevant to anyone considering parenthood? I believe you also mentioned god, but how does that matter? Do you really think that there's someone or something that can determine which families are ready for a child? What, exactly, qualifies as a 'real' family? Or a 'real' home? If the world is full of these 'real' families, why all the abuse? Why do some parents murder their own children?"

I realized I was basically shouting.

Everybody turned around to look at me. I couldn't believe that I had gone and said this kind of thing at an event like this. It felt like the whole room was throbbing to the beating of my heart. My face went hot. I stared at my knees, trying to calm down. The woman came back to retrieve the mic. I was used to being angry and complaining to myself, but I never thought that I would make a speech like this to a bunch of people I had never met. I mean, I knew I had it in me, but I hadn't done something like that in maybe ten or twenty years. My heartbeat was so violent that it almost hurt. I could feel my earlobes heating up. My fingertips were twitching.

Seated not too far away, the woman in the cornflower dress stared me down and said, "Abuse is, in a way, a trial . . . " under her breath. Her use of the word "trial" made me cock my head, but I kept myself from responding. Aizawa nodded openly at this exchange but didn't weigh in.

Once he had the mic again, he simply said: "Anyone else?"

Our discussion, if you could call it that, drew to a close, and with it the event. About half of the attendees left the room, but the remainder drifted into little groups and started chatting. My face was pulsating. In a desperate attempt to cool down, I stayed seated and pretended to check my email, but my head was occupied with what I just experienced.

No matter what, I had no business going off like that on people who were only sharing their world view and how they felt. I knew I had gone too far, and I regretted it, but every word I said came from a place of truth, and even now I couldn't conceal my resentment for what that woman had said. Try as I might to rid it from my mind, our little spat kept playing in my head, and when I focused on the details of her argument, my irritation mounted to a new high.

When I glanced in her direction, I saw that she was gabbing in a circle of other women. Now and then there was a swell of laughter. It seemed like she had brushed off our exchange. Why had any of us come here? Sure, only a handful of people had actually spoken up. Who knows how the rest of the audience saw things, but the event felt less like a discussion of donor conception than a chance for airing prejudices against the idea. Aizawa, who had started off the event by offering his real-life experience, clearly had a strong opinion on the matter, which naturally set the tone for the entire evening. Having read his interview beforehand, I knew where he was coming from. All the same, I couldn't help but feel like there was something major missing from his argument.

When I was waiting for the elevator, I heard somebody coming, and sure enough it was Aizawa. Now that he was beside me, he looked impossibly tall. Naruse was 5'4", barely any taller than me. I wondered if I'd ever seen a man this height up close and personal.

Aizawa was carrying a black cotton tote bag. It was a little surprising to see the event's headliner leaving before the room had even cleared. We met eyes, so I nodded. He nodded back. I was worried he was going to bring up my exchange with the woman, but he didn't say a word. The elevator was up on the ninth floor, no sign of coming down. I decided to say something.

"I've never been to one of these before."

"Thanks for coming," Aizawa said. "And for your comments."

"I'm sorry, it probably sounded out of line."

"No, not at all."

The conversation sputtered out. The elevator was still up on the ninth floor.

"Do you do events like this often?" I asked.

"Personally, no . . . "

Aizawa pulled a flyer from his bag and offered it to me. A generic business card was attached to the upper-right-hand corner with a little paperclip. Under his name it said: "Children of Donors." No phone number, just an email address and their website.

"The group that puts these on gives donor-conceived individuals a place to come together. That flyer has all the information for a symposium we're doing early next year. We'll have experts giving presentations, and people speaking from our group, too. If you're interested, you should come by."

Aizawa spoke flatly, like someone reading the back cover of a book they probably wouldn't read themselves.

"Will you be speaking?" I asked.

"No, my role is generally more administrative."

"I read *Half a Dream*, by the way."

"I appreciate it." Aizawa thanked me automatically, bowing his head, then stared up at the light-up numbers above the elevator and switched his tote bag from his left hand to his right. The elevator finally moved down to the eighth floor. Watching it descending through the numbers made me feel like I was being chased. I heard my heartbeat speeding up again. When the number four, the floor above us, lit up on the panel, I knew that it was now or never.

"The truth is, I'm considering donor conception," I said. "I'm not married, not involved. I'd be going into it alone, like as a single mother, but I'm considering it anyway."

The elevator arrived empty. We stepped inside. Aizawa pressed the button for the first floor. Seconds later, we were there. The doors opened. Aizawa held the button down and gestured for me to exit first.

"Sorry to come out of nowhere like that, by the way," I said.

"No, that's what these meetings are for." Aizawa nodded. After a beat, he asked, "If you're going to do it on your own, I assume you're looking overseas?"

Something I'd read on the Velkommen website popped into my head, but I couldn't bring myself to say it. I was unsure how I should respond, so I said nothing. Aizawa grabbed his phone out of his pocket, like he had received a text, and gave it a quick look before dropping it in the tote bag.

"Best of luck," he said. "Thanks again for coming."

With that, Aizawa walked away and disappeared around the corner.

I headed toward the station under the clear December sky. I checked my watch. A little past three-thirty. Dead leaves gathered at the edges of the street, in a mixture of red, yellow and brown, and when the wind picked up it sent them swirling. The chill in the air made sense for winter, but the sun was warm.

This was my first time in Jiyugaoka. Since it was Sunday, the sidewalks were mobbed. People were snacking on the benches, watching their kids play, walking big dogs that I'd only seen in movies, and popping in and out of all the shops along the street. Tons of strollers. At first, I kept a tally of how many I had passed, but I gave up after seven. The sugary fragrance of crepes was on the breeze. People were laughing, mothers were calling their children.

Pretty soon I came across a giant Christmas tree, surrounded by people taking pictures with their phones, and a few people using professional-looking cameras. The tree dazzled with Christmas lights and gave off an amber halo, even though it was the middle of the day. Then it hit me: today was Christmas. I heard a shriek and turned around to find a pack of little girls, probably still in elementary school, playing around. They were wearing white tights and had their hair done up like ballerinas. Guess they have ballet all the way through Christmas.

Crossing the tracks, I made it to the station plaza and sat down on the first bench that I found. Buses and taxis were slowly circling the roundabout, while outside the shops across the way, men and women dressed in Santa outfits welcomed customers to check out their selection of Christmas cakes. I pulled out the flyer Aizawa had given me and looked at the business card, then slipped it into my wallet. Then I read over the flyer. The symposium was on January 29th, at some conference center in Shinjuku. Just like Aizawa had said, the presenters were experts—university professors and doctors specializing in infertility treatment. Admission was free but limited to 200 participants. At the bottom, the flyer named the organizer, gave an address and phone number for the venue, and listed the various ways that you could register.

I folded the flyer in half and slipped it into my tote bag. For a while I watched the people coming and going through the station turnstiles. Then I pulled out my copy of *Half a Dream* and flipped through it. I'd read it twice, cover to cover, and picked up from a random page a handful of times since. This may sound obvious, but the interviews never failed to call to mind the real-life experiences and struggles of donor-conceived individuals. Every time I read them, they cut through me as deeply as the first.

Wake up, Natsuko, I told myself. What I wanted to do, what I was thinking about, was *wrong.* The biggest reason it was *wrong*, what donor-conceived individuals had cited as the hardest part of their experience, was the fact that the children were always left in the dark, tricked by the people closest to them. One day things would change forever. Come to find out, their whole life had been a lie. Everything they'd ever known. The earth would fall beneath their feet.

But I don't know. I'd do things differently. If I use a sperm donor to have a kid, I'll tell them everything there is to know. First things first, though, I had a hard time picturing myself putting a strange man's sperm inside my body. Part of me couldn't believe that you could even have a kid that way. I was pretty sure I couldn't actually go through with it. But as I sat with the idea, I came to realize it wasn't so unusual.

These days, it's not uncommon to have sex with someone you barely know. Casual sex means letting strange men put themselves inside you. There are plenty of men out there who don't use protection, and protection isn't foolproof anyway. Lots of women end up pregnant with the baby of a man they'll never see again and don't know the first thing about. I'm not saying this is good or bad or smart or stupid. I'm just saying it's not out of the ordinary.

Picking up girls. One-night stands. Friends with benefits. To lots of men out there, all sex is casual. And how many of those guys can say for certain that *they aren't the father of some kid somewhere they've never met?*

Damn straight. There are plenty of ways a kid can wind up never knowing their real father. Donated sperm isn't the problem. Plenty of people grow up not knowing where they came from. What about adoption? Or baby safe havens? Besides, I refuse to believe 100% of people born from donated sperm have horrible lives. In this American book of interviews with kids whose parents took that route, I read about a girl who says she's proud that her moms had her that way, and about a boy who said he didn't ever see it as a big deal, since it just seemed natural to him. But things are totally different in Europe and America, where they're actively creating networks for donor-conceived kids and providing ways for them to track their donors down, if they so choose. There must be children out there who think positively about where they came from.

The problem, I decided, was the lying and the coverup. If I asked Velkommen for a "non-anonymous donor," my child would have an opportunity to contact him, if that was what they wanted. If they asked about their dad when they were little, I could simply say, "I decided to have you on my own, so I got help from a nice man in Denmark." Then once they were old enough, I could explain my reasoning for choosing this specific process. Or was that wrong too?

What if I found out that my dad wasn't my real dad? What if my mom had told me that I was the result of a procedure, and that she didn't know my father? And what if she had told me everything from the get-go—that was a whole lot of ifs, but speaking for myself, because I can't pretend to speak for anyone else—could I really say that wouldn't give me peace of mind? Then again, who knows. It's hard to say.

So, I thought. At the end of the day, it's pointless speculating what a kid might think. There's no way to know ahead of time. I'll do everything I can so that my kid is happy they were born. What more can you do? At the moment, I had 7,250,000 yen in my fixed deposit bank account. The sum total of my royalties. I hadn't dipped into it once. I grew up in a house where there was no such thing as wiggle room. We were barely scraping by. Saving absolutely nothing. Zero. Sometimes we had to take on debt. It wasn't uncommon for us to live without heat or gas for a while. Compared with that,

I had more of a cushion than I knew what to do with. There probably aren't too many parents in their late thirties who had saved as much as me. Since it would be just the two of us, me and my baby, I was confident that if I tracked all of our expenses, we would have enough to lead a decent life. Sure, I might get sick, or get into an accident, and sure, we would be basically alone—there was no shortage of potential problems, but the same goes for most married couples, or parents left single after a divorce, or for parents who are single from the start. Life is hard, no matter the circumstances.

A young smiling couple passed me, hand in hand. They were wearing matching leather jackets and pushed a stroller as they sipped their coffee. They looked like they were having fun.

Right, Christmas . . . I'd been sitting almost the whole day, but my arms and legs were spent. I tried cheering myself on, mobilizing all my mental resources, but my body wouldn't stand up from the bench, so I continued staring at these happy people. I thought of what Aizawa said to me before he walked away—*Best of luck.* I tried remembering the little things about the way his eyes looked and his tone of voice. *Best of luck.* I knew he wasn't being sarcastic. This was a throwaway line offered to a person that he didn't know or care to know. But for whatever reason, I couldn't rid it from my mind.

I could see people all around me, but I almost felt like nobody could see me. I heard a train go by, rumbling down the tracks, drawing a thick line between the world and my experience. I was getting cold again.

After changing trains, I finally arrived in Sangenjaya. The lights that had been strung up outside the station for a month or so were blinking, same as ever. It didn't really feel like Christmas there. Cars drove along the busy street honking their horns, and people walked like they were in a hurry.

I walked home wondering how many years had passed since I had done anything on Christmas. Way back when, Naruse and I spent all our Christmases together, but I couldn't remember if we'd ever shared a Christmas cake. Did we give each other presents? I couldn't recall.

When I hear the word Christmas, the first thing that comes to mind, or what comes to mind most easily, are the balloons that used to fill the ceiling of the bar where I used to work. The holidays are the busiest time of year for any bar. The whole staff would come in for the three days leading up to Christmas to spruce up the shop. We'd been using the same decorations forever, so they were gross with dust and grease, but nobody cared. We even set up a little Christmas tree. Every customer got three free karaoke songs, and as a kind of an hors d'oeuvre, we served cold chicken on silver paper plates. It cost an extra 2,500 yen for the whole night (and I made all the tickets from construction paper).

Admission got you one free pass at a game called "Harpoon the Balloon." The hostesses all came in at lunch and spent the afternoon blowing up balloons with paper prizes slipped inside and tacked them to the ceiling until it was covered. I'm not sure how many balloons there actually were, but every Christmas each of us must have inflated as many as the average person inflates in their whole life. At first, we chatted as we went, but about two hours into the process our cheeks were so tired that they started going numb, which effectively shut everybody up. The prizes were things like a ten-song pass for karaoke or a bottomless cup coupon, or a number that won you some useless tchotchke. The grand prize was a one-night trip for two to the Arima Hot Springs. Once all the customers had a good buzz on, we pulled out this stick with a needle on the tip. You stabbed at the balloons on the ceiling until one popped. Even though this was almost thirty years ago, I still remember having a hard time understanding how a bunch of grownups got such a kick out of popping balloons. Every time someone nailed one, all the hostesses and customers would clap and shout like a bunch of little kids. Sooner or later a couple of customers would come to blows, one guy busting the balloon another guy was after, but I'm amazed at how joyous I remember it being overall.

The next day, we blew up more balloons to replace the ones that had been popped. Once we were done, we had a break until we opened, which gave the hostesses a chance to do their makeup, have a smoke, step out to a cafe, or grab a bento box for dinner. I sprawled out on the sofa and gazed up at the balloons crowding the ceiling, a space that usually held nothing but darkness. There was something deranged about filling this dank realm of smoke and drunken men full of balloons of every color, but it made me happy all the same. Until someone told me to go in and get started, I would just stare up at the ceiling, endlessly fascinated by the balloons.

I felt my phone buzz at the bottom of my tote bag. It was Makiko.

"Merry Christmas! I'm on my way to work. Hope you're doing good!"

The text was chock-full of emojis. Then came a selfie of Makiko wearing thick makeup and a Santa hat, cheek to cheek with a bleach-blonde woman, presumably a coworker, who also wore a Santa hat and had even thicker makeup. They were making peace signs, touching fingertips.

"This is Yui! She's new."

I started walking with my phone out, staring at that picture. A minute later I stopped for a second, to tell her she looked great, but I had only gotten as far as "You look" when a call came in and the name "Rie Konno" took over the screen. In the midst of my confusion, I picked up.

"Hello? Natsuko? It's Rie."

"Oh, hey, how are you?" I pressed my ear to the speaker.

"Sorry, I know it's totally out of the blue," she said apologetically. "Is this an okay time?"

"Yeah, it's fine."

"I figured I should check in. The year's almost over, and we never settled on a date."

"Oh," I said. "You're right, you're absolutely right. It's almost the end of the year. Time flies, huh."

"Yeah, and I'm moving in January. I actually have something I wanted to give you. Just something small."

"Really?"

"Yeah, it's—"

I heard the frantic beeping of a train behind me, followed by the sound of locomotion. This made it hard to hear what Rie was saying.

"What was that?" I asked.

"Sorry," Rie said. "Can you hear me?"

"Yeah, now I can."

"Great. Hey, this may sound crazy, but is there any way you could meet up today?"

"Today? You mean right now?"

"Well, maybe. If you could. You can't, though, right? Sorry, just forget about it. It's fine."

"No, no," I said. "I can meet up. I was just about to head home anyway."

"Really?" Rie practically screamed into the phone. "Great. Let's get something to eat."

She said that she would see me in half an hour. I had some time to kill, so I took the escalator to the second floor of Carrot Tower and perused the DVDs at Tsutaya. There was a bookstore across the way, but I wasn't in the mood to face the new releases. Tsutaya was playing the sort of treacly music peculiar to this time of year. Cutouts of musical artists and signs announcing their latest hits surrounded me. I didn't recognize a single thing I saw.

After making a lap around the store I ran out of things to look at, so I went down to the first floor, looked around the clothing shops and ogled the bountiful displays of the food kiosks. The chicken gleamed like hunks of amber. Cake boxes tied off with red and gold ribbon stood in tiers. Crowds of people carrying shopping bags foraged for the last few things they needed for the night. I decided to go outside to wait for Rie. The sun was down. The sky was dark, with the exception of a fading swath of color to the west. In the winter sunset, the traffic signal glowed like ruby liquid. Little black birds tumbled through the strips of sky between the buildings. A little while later, I heard a voice calling my name.

"Natsuko!"

When I spun around, those protruding canines caught my eye. "Rie," I replied. Her hair was short when we met in the summer, but now it was long enough to tie back. Her black scarf made her skin look much whiter than I remembered. The skin around her eyes almost looked gray.

"I already quit my job, but I've been busy all day dealing with loose ends and stuff. So much for Christmas," Rie said. "I can't believe we got seats today. I guess it's a little early for dinner?"

"You sure you're okay meeting up today?" I asked. "Don't you need to spend Christmas with your family?"

Rie looked up from the menu and shook her head.

"Really, it's fine. They're with my husband's family."

We were at an izakaya known for its sake collection. It was pretty much full, but quiet nonetheless. Handwritten signs pinned to the walls announced the various specials. The servers were wearing festive happi coats. It felt like the sort of place where they'd take your order with a show of enthusiasm, like at a chain restaurant. The room was oddly serene, but then I realized why: all the other customers were couples. Leaning close and talking about things only the two of them could understand, no reason to speak any louder.

"Well, congrats about quitting your job and everything."

"Thanks! Cheers."

We clinked mugs. Rie drank most of her beer in a single gulp.

"God, you're fast," I said, after swallowing a mouthful. "Do you always drink like that?"

"You could say that," Rie laughed. "I get drunk quick, too, but I can keep going all night. If I'm in the mood, I can go for like two liters of sake. With wine, I'm usually good for two bottles."

"I can't handle anything but beer," I said. "I don't even drink much of that."

Rie finished her beer and asked for another. Picking at the fried tofu that was served as a matter of course, we looked through the menu and ordered a sashimi platter and the bacon and spinach salad. This was our first time drinking together, or even going out just the two of us. We had only just sat down, but Rie had already cut loose, and I couldn't help but do the same. It may have been because she was small, but watching Rie mutter her way through the menu, or open her eyes wide after every single thing I said, or laugh at her own jokes—I could have sworn that I was back in middle school after a day of class, wasting time in a deserted homeroom or in the halls. She was no longer a friend from work I'd barely got to know, but a dear friend I had known forever.

"I haven't seen you since the summer," I said. "I can't believe we haven't all met up since then."

"Yeah," Rie nodded. "Well, the others got together, without us."

When I noticed that she looked a little tense, I put two and two together. By "without us," she meant I hadn't been invited, and I was sure it was because I didn't have a kid. If they wanted to go on and on about their kids, having someone like me around would only spoil the fun. Rie changed the subject and opened up her menu, like she might order something else.

"Didn't I say so before?" she asked. "I stopped hanging out with them."

"Yeah, I think you said something like that last time."

"Yeah. It's just a waste of time. Can't believe I took so long to realize."

"Oh I remember now. You said they were a bunch of idiots."

"Did I?"

"Yeah, you did. You called them a bunch of hopeless idiots."

"Good. I mean, it's true." Rie took a big gulp of beer. "You think so, too, right? They act like friends, but it's just a competition. They need to make sure that everyone else's life is at least as shitty as theirs. It's always clothes, shoes, money, piano lessons. They're like a bunch of schoolgirls, but in their thirties."

"They love that stuff."

"Of course they do. They're devoted housewives. What else do they have to look forward to? I was the only one of us still working, even if it was part-time, now that I was a mother. They were always mocking me for it, too, like I was a real champ."

Rie drew little circles with her chopsticks.

"Why are you moving again?" I asked. "Where was it? Ehime?"

"Wakayama," she answered, raising her eyebrows. "Not like there's much difference, really. But yeah, I'm going to be in Wakayama. The middle of nowhere."

"What's taking you there?"

"That's where my husband's from," she said. "He's clinically depressed. He had to stop working, so we're moving to his hometown."

"What was it he did again?"

"An ordinary office job. But things started getting bad. It started a couple of years ago, really. He couldn't take the train anymore, he couldn't sleep. So we moved to be closer to his office, in Mizonokuchi. That way he could walk or bike to work. But even that was too much for him. It's textbook depression." Rie moved our empty plates to the edge of the table. "I think you're the first person I've told."

"You're going to be living with his family?"

"You got it. The family business is construction—contract work—and he's the only son, an only child. Things have been hard. My mother-in-law has some real fire in her. She's always been way too involved in her son's life. She'll call him every other day, send him frozen tupperware of oden. And she can't accept that he's depressed. She's always like hey, what are you crying for, snap out of it already . . . She's so sure that he couldn't possibly be that weak of his own accord, so she's ready to blame me for everything. That's her narrative, at least. Anyway, they'll give him a post at the office and put him on payroll."

"You're from Tokyo, right?"

"Chiba. But after me and my sister left, my parents moved back to Natori, where my dad's from. To look after my dad's parents and everything. My dad died a while back now. My mom was up there, on her own, but that's up by Sendai, so the house was basically destroyed in the quake. These things happen, right? My sister got married years ago, and she's been in Saitama, so my mom's living there with her now. I can only imagine how my mom feels. All I get is these texts from my sister, all these complaints, and these endless letters from my mother. As far as my brother-in-law is concerned, three's a crowd, you know? Even if she is his wife's mom. She's still a weird old lady, collecting a measly pension, in her own little world . . . My sister's got kids, too. They keep telling me I gotta pitch in, too, I mean financially. But I'm just like, no thanks. To make matters worse, my mom barely ever talks. When she does, she never says anything except how she wished she died in the quake. The whole situation is driving my sister batty, too. But that's what it's like."

I saw that Rie's beer was empty and asked her if she wanted something else. She said she'd have some sake. I got another beer.

"You can't really talk about stuff like this with people, you know what I mean? Family and money and all that, even if it's on everybody's minds. It feels a bit weird, right? To talk like this." Rie looked embarrassed. "It's the kind of stuff people only say online."

"Online?" I asked. "Like social media?"

"Yeah, exactly. Children, husbands—everything. It's not just me. There's a whole community of people, following each other. They're not just venting, either. It's a real community."

"And you post things?"

"Ha! Do I ever," Rie said, pouring herself a cup of sake. "Anonymously, of course. It might be a real community, but it's also its own version of hell, with all these asshole men writing mind-numbingly shitty replies. Still, sometimes I'll write something and it'll get retweeted a hundred times or more, which always feels good. Right now, I have a little over 1,000 followers . . . but I guess I shouldn't brag about that to a real writer, huh?"

"It's not like that," I said. "It's been a couple of years since I put out my one and only book."

They brought out the sashimi, and we got our soy sauce ready. It was a lot more food than we had been expecting, light and dark fish carefully arrayed into a spiral. We hummed, agreeing that it looked delicious. Rie had finished her sake, so she ordered another round. When the server brought a new carafe, Rie poured herself a generous cup and threw it back.

"So your daughter's in Wakayama now?"

"Yeah," Rie said, after a pause. "My husband's completely useless. It's just faster if I handle everything on this end without him. All the paperwork and the move, you know? My daughter's been staying in Wakayama for the past week. Living there, I guess. Going back and forth would cost a fortune. We'll spend New Year's apart. I'll finish taking care of the move at the start of the year. And then I'll move down there myself."

"How old is your husband?"

"Three years older than me. 37? Wait, 38? I always forget."

"His mom has got to be part of his depression, don't you think?"

"Probably. Who knows. There's no coming back from depression, right?" laughed Rie. "It's made him useless as an employee. It got to the point where he couldn't leave the house or take a bath. We got him on some medicine, and that made things a little better, but who knows what's going to happen here on out."

"What about his mother? Does she treat your daughter right?"

"Well, it's her only son's only child, so she's good to her and all that. She was really against the two of us, my daughter and me, staying in Tokyo alone. It's like she thought we'd run away. She put up a real fight—saying that the two of them better come together, and that's exactly what happened. For her, it was okay to have her son show up with his family, but I guess it would have looked bad to have him come home on his own. He said as much himself . . . "

"What do you mean?"

"People are always saying that. Men aren't supposed to visit home alone. Wives are always taking their kids home, right? But you never really hear about husbands taking their kids home, I mean without their wives, now do you? Know why? Because it doesn't happen. Things need to look a certain way.

You need to show everyone you're happily married and all that. Besides, most men can't even talk to their own families without a woman around. It's pathetic, really. They'll just sit around the room all day and leave everything around the house up to the women."

"Aren't you sad being separated from your daughter?" I asked her.

Rie thought about this for a second.

"You know, I'm surprisingly okay with it. I thought I'd be lonelier than I am. Dads do this all the time, though, right? Go away on business trips or whatever—I think it's fine."

She stared into the sake brimming from her cup.

"I love her. I really do, but sometimes I just don't think our bond is very strong."

"Bond?" I asked.

"I mean, the pregnancy was pretty smooth. She was an easy birth. After that, though, I just fell apart. Looking back, it was definitely postpartum. I should have seen someone about it, but I didn't. My husband didn't do anything about it. At least, not anything to help. He was, like, *What's wrong with you? Having a child is a totally natural part of being a woman—How could it possibly take that much out of you? My mom did it. Every woman does it. Get over it*—he said, just laughing."

"Unbelievable." I drank the last of my beer.

"That was when I made up my mind. If this guy gets sick at some point, if he gets cancer, and he's in real pain, I'll be there when he's dying, standing over him, looking down, and I'm gonna say the same things he said to me. *Dying is totally natural. Get over it.*"

Rie snorted and grinned at me.

"My daughter wasn't a difficult baby. She didn't need much, so I was able to get some sleep and turn things around, little by little. By that time, though, things were already cold between my husband and me. We didn't say anything to each

other unless we had to. He was almost never home to begin
with. It felt like we were separated, even though we were living in the same house and everything. I think, for most people,
when that sort of thing happens, you turn to your baby. She
becomes your everything, you know? It wasn't like that for me.
At some point, I realized that when I'm alone with her, something isn't right."

"Not right?"

Rie nodded as she sipped her sake.

"Don't get me wrong, I love my daughter. I really do. I'd do
anything for her. But at the same time, I just have this feeling,
like we won't have that much time together, like we'll never be
that close. It won't be long before she starts to hate me. She'll
leave, and that's fine. I think about that a lot, though. It's normal, right? It's the same for parents and children everywhere.
I mean, I hate my mother. I genuinely despise her. I used to
think all kinds of things, too. Maybe it'll pass. It could be a
phase. Maybe I'm just cold-hearted. Things like that. Because
people say you'll always love your mother, no matter what she
puts you through. My mom never hit me or anything. She
raised me well enough, and I still hated her."

"For no reason?"

"For every reason." Rie emptied her sake cup. "Let's start
off with how she viewed my dad. He was your typical king of
the hill. We couldn't say anything growing up. I was a kid, and
a girl on top of that, so he never saw me as a real person. I
never even heard the guy call my mother by her name. It was
always *Hey you*. We were constantly on red alert because my
dad would beat the shit out of us or break things for no reason. Of course, outside the home, he was a pillar of the community. He ran the neighborhood council, and all that. My
mom was my mom, always laughing it off, running the bath
for him, cleaning up after him, feeding him. She looked after
both of his parents all the way to the end, too. There was no

inheritance, either. Yeah, my mom was free labor—free labor with a pussy."

"Whoa," I said. "What a phrase."

"You heard me. That's what she was. Free labor with a pussy."

"Damn. I've heard people call women baby-making machines and all, but that's like ten times worse."

"Seriously. I know that's the way things were back then, but if that's your life, how could you ever be happy? Here's this guy, walking all over you, slapping you around, and you can't go anywhere or do anything without his explicit permission. You can't even leave the house. That's slavery. Why should you have to put up with some random dude's bullshit? Just because you're married? Anyway, I always thought she was putting up with it for us. I assumed she hated my father every bit as much as I did, but tolerated him, because she had to. She never complained, just laughed. I was so sure that she was just protecting us, sacrificing herself. I was young, but I remember thinking about how badly I wanted to grow up and rescue her from that shithole place and that shithead of a man. I seriously thought I could rescue her, from him and from his world. Then something happened. I was still really young, and it was just the three of us at home. Me, my sister and my mom. We were just talking and, I don't know how it came up or why, but me and my sister were like *Who do you love more—us or Dad?* You know what she said? *Your dad, of course.* No hesitation. She didn't even think about it. Can you believe it? We were shocked. We thought she'd get mad at us for even asking and say *Of course it's the two of you—how could you even ask me something like that?* Neither of us saw her answer coming. She kept on going, too. *I could always have more kids—but there's no replacing your father.* She literally said that. I felt like my heart stopped. I felt like my whole world stopped. My sister and I haven't talked about that since, not once. That's how bad it was. I couldn't understand it, how a man like that could mean more to her than her own children. Sometimes I still think about that. I wish she'd said, *I know he's your father, but I hate him, I hate him so bad I want him to die. For now we can't do anything but live with it, but at some point, we'll run away just the three of us. We'll start over.* If that's what she thought, we could have fought, we could have done something. I was just a kid, but I really thought I was protecting my mom from my dad. I was so wrong. She wasn't putting up with him at all. She never wanted to leave. She never wanted to fight. Leaving him had never even occurred to her. She just smiled at us, her kids, and said: *He's the only one for me.*"

I set my empty beer mug down on the table edge and asked our server for another bottle of sake and an extra cup for me.

"After that," Rie said, "I realized I had no idea who my mother was. Nothing changed—she'd get beat up, laugh it off. Around me and my sister, she acted the same as always, but I couldn't understand her. I knew she was my mom, but I just couldn't see her as my mother after that. We talked, same as always, and we went on living together, but I was just baffled, you know? Who was she? Who was this woman?"

When our bottle came, we filled our cups and drank. I could feel the hot sake passing down my throat and entering my stomach. Rie was talking like she was fine, but from the splotches on her ears and cheeks and all around her eyes, it was obvious that she was plastered. I was feeling wobbly myself. The server came over to ask if they could get us something else to eat. I opened the menu and turned it so that Rie could see. She got closer and squinted her bloodshot eyes.

"What the hell," she said. "Let's get some pickled vegetables."

"Sounds good," I laughed.

"I thought you could only drink beer," said Rie.

"I guess tonight is an exception."

"Yeah?"

We pressed our lips against our cups and emptied them again, then topped each other off.

"I wonder what would happen," Rie said after a while. "Like, if I didn't go to Wakayama."

"You mean, like if you stayed in Tokyo?"

"Stayed," she said, looking down at her oshibori, "or disappeared."

I brought my cup to my lips.

"I'm obviously going," Rie snorted, then tried to smile. "It's crazy, though, to think about stuff like that, at this age. It's like I was saying. At home, my parents were fighting constantly. Life was always put on hold. But they were always at each other's throats. I just couldn't take it anymore. I wanted to get out, I needed to get out. All I could do was stay in my room, with my hands covering my ears. I really don't have any good memories from back then. I was always thinking: *Why am I alive? Why do I have to go on living?* I hated my parents, hated my family. I really hated all of it. I remember clearly thinking this is it, *family is the root of all suffering.* I told myself I'd live my whole life without a family, dying single and alone. I seriously thought I'd do it, too. But look at me. I got married, had a kid. Got all wrapped up in other people's lives. Haha. I'm attached to this person who never really had anything to do with me, and now he's all depressed, not that we ever had anything in common, and I have to look after him, take all of his family's crap while living off their money, until the bitter end, biding my time in fucking Wakayama. Before long I'll be looking after my mother-in-law, taking care of the house instead of her. Just look at me now, free labor with a pussy, same as my mom."

Rie gazed down at her fingertips and smiled softly.

"So," she said, after a long silence. "Why wouldn't my daughter end up hating me? Runs in the family."

There was a chorus of thank-yous as one couple exited and another came in, wearing Santa hats.

"What if you got a divorce and lived alone with your daughter?" I asked.

Rie eyed me momentarily before returning to her fingers.

"No way. How could I afford to pay rent? Go back to working part-time at a bookstore?"

"It would be tough, but you should really think about it."

"It's literally impossible." Rie looked at me. "Things were hard enough when both of us were working. There's no way I could do it on my own, no way."

"It'd be really hard, but you could get help. Child support and all that. Plenty of people—"

"Those people have jobs," she interrupted. "Real jobs. If you have a career, you have some degree of security. But you need to have a jobs, or family money, or someplace you can always run back home to. I've got none of that. I don't have any qualifications or skills . . . I quit my job. And good riddance. Working that hard for 1000 yen an hour. They'd rather give those shifts to some eighteen-year-old kid anyway. There's nothing out there for a good-for-nothing single mother, going on forty, with no real work experience. You can't raise a child like that. It isn't possible."

"I dunno, though."

"No, Natsuko. I don't think you do."

The server brought the pickles, a bowl piled high with vinegary cucumber and turnip, and some other kind of vegetable cured in shiso. Another server came by holding a big box and said it was a Christmas present giveaway. Taking turns, we each reached into the hole and pulled out a piece of paper. All we came up with was a couple of 10% off coupons, good for our next visit. We got started with the pickles.

It was time to change the subject. We ordered another round of sake, choosing the cheapest option, at only 480 yen for a carafe. I shared some curious facts that I had learned about the yakuza in my research or did impressions of the guys in some of the gang wars I had watched on YouTube. Rie talked about the absurdly vague estimates the moving companies had given her, using lots of body language as she joked her way along. We laughed hard and winced audibly, exaggerating our reactions in an attempt to clear the air. We gossiped about our bookstore friends and mutual acquaintances and shared in our befuddlement at why celebrities who have cancer or some other serious illness try to make the problem go away by donating to temples or using pseudoscientific gadgets, instead of undergoing conventional treatment. Every time I shouted or clapped my hands, I felt the alcohol coursing through my veins.

Before I knew it, they had cleared the table. No more pickles, no more sake. I checked my watch. Somehow it was ten-fifteen. We asked for water and drank it on the spot. We each paid 4,500 yen and went outside.

The night was cold. Lights were strewn all over the station, and a peculiar energy filled the air, as if a parade might be starting any minute. Me and Rie were both toasted, staggering toward the stairs down to the train, when Rie spun around and looked at me. Her eyes were bloodshot, and her upper lip, pushed back by her canines, was totally chapped.

"I'm glad we could do this, on such short notice. Whoa, I'm drunk."

"Are you okay taking the train?"

"I'm fine." Rie squeezed her eyes shut, like she was eating something sour. "It's a straight shot."

"What about the walk home from the station?"

"Straight shot, all the way."

"Come on, there's gotta be at least one turn."

"It's straight enough, trust me. Oh, almost forgot." Rie rummaged through her purse. "Here. I wanted to give this to you."

She pulled out a shiny pair of scissors.

"You probably don't remember, since it was years ago. Back when we worked together, you always used to say how much you liked them."

"No, I remember," I said.

While the rest of us walked around with pens or boxcutters, Rie carried these scissors, safely holstered in the pocket of her apron. I remember the first time I saw the pretty lily-of-the-valley engraved on the part between the handle and the blade, and how Rie slipped them in a leather sheath for safekeeping. Seeing Rie working with her personal pair of scissors when the rest of us made do with whatever plastic-handled junk we found laying around, I knew I had encountered something special.

"I remember how you always had them with you."

"I sure did. You can tell I got a lot of use out of them. Just look at the blade." Rie laughed, gazing off into the street. "Anyway, I won't need them in Wakayama."

"Come on, you should keep them."

"No." She shook her head. "You always said you liked them. Take them. Please."

The silver scissors caught the lights and glimmered in her hands. It was then that I realized just how small her hands were. I glanced up and took a good look at the rest of her. I knew she was a head shorter than me, but seeing her like this, up close, she seemed way smaller than I had thought. Her legs stuck out from her coat like poles, practically nothing to them, conjuring images of what Rie looked like as a girl, before I ever knew her. I saw her lean into the wind, gripping the straps of her giant bookbag as she shuffled off, head hanging low. Neck bent, so thin it looked like it would snap. Lugging around that bright red bookbag, big enough for her to fit inside, heading somewhere, maybe home—Rie walked the empty asphalt, all alone.

"Hey," I said. "Wanna grab another drink?"

"Not tonight," Rie said, shaking her head. "I'm wasted."

Rie waved goodbye and took the stairs down to the train. As I watched her going down the steps, this voice kept telling me to chase her, catch up with her, insist we grab another drink. But all that I could do was watch her go.

Back home I collapsed on my beanbag. I had a splitting headache. If I closed my eyes, amorphous waves came at me through the darkness. Like I had turned into spaghetti, spinning round and round inside a boiling pot of water.

I kept my eyes shut anyway and waited to fall asleep, but as the minutes passed, I lost track of whether I was still awake. Next thing I knew, I startled from a vision that could just as easily have been a dream. I tossed and turned, unable to relax. So this is what they mean by *sleeping with your eyes open.* When I felt cold, I tugged the comforter up over my face, but pretty soon that made it hard to breathe, so I tossed it to the side until I felt cold again. My hand landed on something chilly, and when I looked, I saw it was the scissors Rie had given me. When had I pulled them from my bag? The metal sucked up the cold air and shone like something ghastly in the night. I grabbed them and sat up. A medley of colorful balloons crowded out the ceiling. I got up on my stool, stood on my tiptoes and started popping balloons, but there were no prizes inside. Stabbing upward, I heard a voice cry: "Merry Christmas!" Whose voice was this? Every time I popped a balloon, another one took its place, like they were coming out of a bubble machine. My chest hurt, I couldn't breathe, but the balloons were moving like a bank of clouds and growing. The sight was almost too much for me to bear. Standing on my toes, I reached as high as I could, trying to pop all the balloons. *Merry Christmas!* Rie waved to me in the middle of the night, saying goodbye forever. I stabbed again, popped another, watching it disappear without a sound, but they were multiplying so quickly that I almost lost my balance and fell off of the stool. Just then someone grabbed me by the elbow. I looked and saw that it was Jun Aizawa. He helped me back onto my stool and pointed his finger toward my next balloon. I adjusted my grip on the scissors and jabbed away. *Merry Christmas!* One, and another, then onto the next. *Best of luck.* His hair had a flow all its own, parted down the middle and snipped just above the ears. It whispered to me, expanding like a ripple, ready to spread like wings or fall into a pattern like eroded stone. What will you do, which will it be. Soon it became impossible to tell his flowing hair from the rumbling echo of the karaoke machine. *Best of luck*—I dropped the scissors and fell asleep.

13.
A Tall Order

New Year's came and went the same way that it always had. It was 2017. Unless you count my Happy New Year text from Makiko and Midoriko, I only got four greetings: one from a chiropractor that I only visited once last year, and three from magazines that ran my work.

Once the holidays were over, I got a call from Sengawa. I braced myself, expecting her to ask about the novel, but she didn't say a word about it. She just mentioned she was going to be in Sangenjaya the next night and wanted to know if I'd like to grab some dinner. We met up in front of the station for tonkatsu. Sengawa had gotten a perm just before New Year's. I told her it looked great on her (because it did), but she just blushed and touched her hair and said, "I'm still not sure about it."

After dinner, we went into a cafe and chatted for a while. I'd been worried she was trying to warm me up with lighter topics before bringing up the book, but that didn't seem to be the case. Despite giving the impression of a person who avoided sweets, she ordered tiramisu with her coffee and really savored it.

I'd talked with Rika a few times over the phone. She said that she and Kura had been down with the flu over the holidays, living in their own private hell. At the moment Rika was going over galleys for a novel that was coming out in spring while working on another novel she was serializing. By her account, she barely had the time to breathe.

"Didn't you just put a book out last summer?" I asked her, kind of stunned. "A pretty long one?"

"Yeah," she laughed. "But there's no time to rest. I've got another serial in the pipeline, too. This one for a newspaper. Who does this?"

"Seriously, it's unbelievable."

It was a new year, but the first month was the same old thing.

I was losing confidence and making almost zero progress with the novel. While I had a few different columns going and had a book that had sold pretty well a couple of years earlier, I was basically a nobody. Sometimes I wondered whether anyone remembered me. It was nice that Sengawa wasn't bugging me about the book, but maybe it meant that she had simply lost her faith in me.

Feeling guilty, I did my research and took notes or rewrote the same lines over and over. Dozens of novels hit the bookstores every month, launching the careers of younger writers. And while the number of infertility blogs I followed ebbed and flowed, more babies were born every single day. There was always someone somewhere discovering a different life, a different experience than the day before, stepping off into uncharted territory. But I wasn't getting anywhere. I couldn't move; in fact, I was being pulled away, slipping further every second from the blinding light of that reality.

I got in the habit of rereading the interview with Jun Aizawa between work sessions or before bed. After some searching, I found the site for Children of Donors, their social media, and an interview with the organization's founder, but not a trace of Jun Aizawa. I didn't even know if that was his real name. The best I could uncover was a photo from an old symposium—off in the corner, you could see a man, turned away from the camera, who had the same haircut and stature as him. The website offered an assortment of writing by donor-conceived individuals, but there was nothing credited to Aizawa in any of the posts.

I opened up the calendar on my phone and tapped the twenty-ninth, the only date that I had marked. This was the day of the symposium that Aizawa had mentioned in the elevator. I was planning on attending, but when I imagined how the day might go, I got discouraged. I had so much more to learn from the children born this way, from other people like me who saw sperm donation as a way out, and even from the people who wholeheartedly opposed the idea, but my experience on Christmas made me wonder whether I should even go.

Then again, I had questions for Aizawa. After studying his interview and listening to his talk, I was pretty sure I understood his stance on sperm donation, but there were things I felt the need to ask him. Clearly it was deeply damaging to grow up not knowing the truth. In that case, what if everything had been laid bare from the start? Would he support donor conception if everyone were guaranteed the right to access personal information on their donors? There were lots of people who didn't know their family history—what set donor conception apart?

The ideas came and went. I asked myself which questions were appropriate to ask a person in his position, and which were not, and the more I thought about it, the less sure I became. In the end, I wound up going anyway.

The symposium was a zoo, on a whole other level from the seminar in December. The venue itself wasn't so big, but it could seat about 200. Over half of the seats were taken. I found an empty seat at one end of the back row and waited for the event to start.

The first presentation was entitled "Unmarried Women and the State of Artificial Insemination in Japan Today." Using

PowerPoint, the presenter unpacked the reproductive treatment legislation drafted by the Liberal Democratic Party in Fall 2013 and walked us through the findings of a number of investigative bodies, hammering home the extent to which Japan was lagging in the policy debate surrounding reproductive ethics. In his opinion, the only answer was to start a revolution.

The second presenter took the stage. Examining artificial insemination from a legal perspective, he explored questions of fatherhood with respect to children born from frozen sperm and investigated how the Japanese government has historically dealt with children born from donated eggs or surrogate mothers, drawing from past court cases to glean some overall trends. His conclusion, in both cases, was that the welfare of the children must be paramount, and that human beings should not be treated as a means for reproduction. To save our dignity, he said, we must ban the commercialization of reproductive treatments.

After the first two talks there was a ten-minute intermission, to give the audience a chance to stretch their legs. The stage crew adjusted the mic cables and rearranged the tables and chairs. No sign of Aizawa. Not in the auditorium, not out by the registration table. He said his work was generally behind the scenes, and if that meant he was working on the PR side of things or social media, he may not show. I pulled a bottle of tea from my tote bag and drank it slowly, so I could feel the liquid passing down my throat. My temples had started throbbing halfway through the first talk, and by the time the second talk began I was having difficulty sitting still. Lately I'd been having trouble sleeping.

Looking around the room, I watched people returning to their seats. They dimmed the lights and a voice announced the third talk was now starting, a conversation between a researcher, a donor-conceived individual, and a medical professional. You would have thought this would have been the most important talk of the day for me, but fifteen minutes in, the researcher was still going on, like this was some kind of a keynote speech. My head was pounding. I knew that everyone had valuable things to say, but I'd reached my limit, so I got up and left.

I headed to the bathroom, gave my hands a thorough scrubbing and then looked at my face in the mirror. I looked awful. My poor neglected hair was dull and scraggly, and my eyebrows were perfectly crooked. I was wearing foundation, but it was streaky and patchy, which defeated the point of wearing foundation at all. I'd bought it years ago, so maybe it had gone bad. My complexion was horrendous, and my face was lifeless. I reminded myself of pickled eggplant. Not the skin, but the greenish flesh inside. How could the dried-up, worn-out woman staring back at me be the source of a new life? The thought of it left me feeling empty. I gripped the sink and devoted several minutes to stretching my neck, rolling my head around in circles. Dry crack after dry crack. I scrubbed my hands one more time and left the bathroom. At the end of the hallway, by the registration table in the lobby, a man was sitting on a bench. It was Jun Aizawa.

The bench was on the path between me and the escalator down. I gripped my tote bag tight and started walking. I was debating whether to say something, but when we met eyes, I nodded automatically, and after a moment, so did Aizawa. I figured I'd better keep on walking, but then he said something to me.

"Glad you could make it. Leaving already?"

His tone was notably more relaxed than the last time that we talked, together in the elevator. He had nothing with him other than a paper cup of coffee, and he was wearing what appeared to be the same black sweater, paired with dark-brown cotton pants and black tennis shoes.

"I wish I could stay until the end . . . "

"I know, it's long."

"How about you, Aizawa? You're not going in?"

Aizawa paused, surprised to hear somebody he barely recognized say his name.

"Not today. I'm stationed elsewhere."

"Um, my name is Natsuko Natsume," I said. "I don't have a card . . . "

I pulled a copy of my book out of my bag.

"This is my novel."

Aizawa raised his eyebrows.

"You're an author?"

"Well, this is my only book so far." I offered the copy to Aizawa.

"Wow." He examined the cover, then turned the book over in his hands, reading the spine and all the back matter. "I can't even imagine what it would be like to write a book."

He was about to hand the book back to me, but I insisted that he keep it.

"Are you sure?"

"Of course," I nodded.

Taking his coffee and the book, Aizawa slid over to the right, to make a space for me to sit. I nodded a few times and sat down on the bench. For a while, we both gazed at the copy of my book that he was holding. I was so nervous. When he cracked it open and started flipping through, I turned to look at him. His parted hair had the same even flow as last time. Up close, it was much straighter and silkier than I thought. I remembered how my own hair had appeared in the bathroom mirror.

"Are you in a good mood today?"

"Huh?" Aizawa was taken aback. I'd felt the need to break the silence, and only meant to say that something felt different about his demeanor, but what came out was very strange indeed. Now I was blushing. I wanted to explain myself but held back, scared of what I might say. Aizawa was quiet, too. Before long, a woman in her sixties wearing a knit hat with ear flaps appeared at the top of the escalator, like a piece of luggage emerging from the baggage claim.

"You probably don't remember this," I said, "but when we were in the elevator, after the last event, I told you how I was considering donor conception as an option."

Aizawa didn't respond, except for a single nod a moment later. His confusion was palpable. Either he was wondering why I would share something so personal with a stranger, or why I had to burden him with my life story. And who could blame him? I mused that I would've felt the same thing in his position, but took a deep breath and continued.

"If you'd rather not hear about this, I'll understand . . . "

"No, no," said Aizawa. "I spend most of my time in the back office, but when I'm working at events like this, I have conversations like this all the time—by the way, are you from Kansai?"

"Yeah, Osaka."

"I didn't notice earlier. Do you go back and forth? When you speak."

"I've never really thought about it, but I guess I don't use dialect in more formal situations."

"That makes a lot of sense," he nodded. "I probably do the same kind of thing."

"In what way?"

"What you said a minute ago. I must look like I'm in a good mood. We're going to have a reception after this. I'll be talking to people for a while, so I think I'm a bit nervous."

"And getting nervous puts you in a good mood?"

"Well, I put on a good face," he laughed. "When we met last time, on Christmas, right? I was definitely out of it that day."

"No, not at all," I said. "I just had the feeling like you had something else on your mind."

"Born in 1978, too, huh," Aizawa said, reading the inside flap of my book. "I guess that makes us the same age. It's amazing. Writing, I mean writing fiction, creating whole worlds on your own. Maybe it's all in a day's work for you. It's just I've never met a real novelist before . . . "

"I'm not sure I'm a real novelist, to be honest," I shrugged. Then came another silence. I knew I had to say something and started to ask "Do you do this full—" but stopped myself. It was one thing if he volunteered the information, but it was rude to put him on the spot. That's why I had given him the book. After studying his interview and listening to his story, I knew some very personal information about Aizawa, but he knew nothing about me. It didn't seem fair, though I was sure I was the only one who thought so. Aizawa couldn't care less about me. All the same, he knew what I was about to ask, and told me that he was a physician.

"You're a doctor?"

"That's right," he said. "Though I'm not affiliated with an institution."

"So you're not actively working?" I asked.

"That's one way to look at it. I have to work sometimes, though, to make ends meet," he laughed. "I used to work at a hospital. Now I work at a number of different places. I'll do routine checkups at schools. Sometimes I'll teach classes at cram schools, too, for national exams . . . "

"Different hospitals, you mean?"

"Exactly. If I get called up, I go where they need me. It's like being a temp, but as a doctor."

"I thought all doctors were affiliated with specific hospitals," I said.

"Most are. It's not so bad, though." Aizawa chuckled. "Sometimes I see other doctors in their sixties, even seventies, doing the same thing. That's reassuring."

"So, wait, does that mean you're paid by the hour?" I asked the question as soon as it came to mind, but instantly regretted it. "Sorry, why am I asking you about money like that?"

"I don't mind," Aizawa laughed it off. "It's probably a stereotype, but they say people from Osaka are really open about money."

"Could be," I said. "But I guess we're not shy about asking, like, 'Hey, what'd you pay for that'?"

"Sure, I get that. Well, in terms of pay, it varies, but it's usually around 20,000 yen. When a hospital's in a real pinch, it can be closer to 30,000."

"Per day?"

"No, hourly."

"No way," I was so stunned I jumped back. I was yelling. "So, like 100,000 yen for five hours of work?"

"Well, it's not something I do every day. Sometimes I work shorter shifts. And sometimes there are dry spells."

"Doctors sure make decent money."

It got quiet. I knew that I had said too much and asked too many questions, but I kept telling myself that Aizawa was the one who had volunteered a concrete figure. He sipped his coffee, which had to have been cold by now. I drank some tea.

"So," I said. This was it. I was resolved to speak my mind, after a month of brooding. "Reading *Half a Dream* has really got me thinking. If it's not too much trouble, I'd love to ask you a couple of questions."

"About my experience?"

"Right," I nodded. "I know this has nothing to do with you, but I'm trying to figure out my future. Not like I have my whole life ahead of me."

"I assume you've read some books on the topic?"

"Not many, but a few."

"At the risk of repeating myself," Aizawa said, "our main

objective is to get people thinking about donor conception, regardless of their position. Let's be in touch."

"Thank you," I bowed my head.

"And thank you for the book," Aizawa eyed the book in his hands. "Natsuko Natsume. It's a good pen name."

"That's my real name," I said.

"Seriously?"

"Seriously."

The auditorium doors swung open, sending a flood of people into the lobby. One woman in particular caught my eye. She wore a black dress that came to her knees and had her hair tied back in a ponytail. She scanned the lobby, like she was looking for somebody. When she spotted Aizawa, she walked over to where we sat. She was short and exceedingly thin, and her collarbones were so pronounced you could've hooked your finger on them. A spray of freckles, densest on her nose, spread across the pale skin of her cheeks. Its shape and smoldering hue reminded me of a picture of a galaxy I'd seen once in a science book. Something about her was strangely familiar. We nodded at each other.

"This is Natsuko," Aizawa explained. "She came to the last meeting in Jiyugaoka, the one we had in December."

"Right. The one who spoke at the end?" the woman asked, looking me over.

"That's right." Aizawa nodded. "You had the mic that day, so I guess you've already met. Natsuko, this is Yuriko. She's with Children of Donors, as well."

I stood up. "Nice to meet you."

"Likewise."

She handed me a card. Yuriko Zen.

"Natsuko is a writer."

Aizawa waved the book for her to see.

"Is that right?" Yuriko narrowed her eyes and looked over the cover of my book. Something made her grin.

"Well, this is my only book so far." I shook my head,

uncomfortable with how I had been introduced. "But I was hoping to talk to Aizawa about donor conception . . . "

"For a project?" Yuriko cocked her head ever so slightly.

"No, for myself. I'm considering donor conception."

Yuriko blinked slowly. Staring at me. Then she nodded once, narrowed her eyes and smiled. There was something oddly high-handed about the expression. I felt like I was suddenly a kid again, waiting for instructions from my teacher. Except Yuriko didn't speak.

"You should probably get going. It's about time."

Yuriko nodded briskly in my direction and walked away. Aizawa checked his watch, stood up, and bowed. "I guess I'd better get back."

"Can I email you?" I said. "The card you gave me last month had an address on it. Do you mind if I send my questions there?"

"Sure, that'll be fine," Aizawa said. Then he was off. The lobby was packed. Soon I'd lost track of both of them.

It was a warm February. The novel wasn't going any better, but something in the winter sunlight streaming through the windows gave me peace. Now and then I talked on the phone with Makiko, just shooting the breeze, or texted with Midoriko, who told me all about her new job at a restaurant or sent me pictures of the books that she'd been reading, all stacked up.

Aizawa and I were exchanging emails. In his first response, he mentioned that he'd started reading my novel and would let me know when he was finished. I responded by saying thanks. Compared to how he sounded on the day of the symposium, his emails were brief, the way he sounded when we first met. This made it hard for me to gauge the proper tone to take when writing to him.

I decided that the receptivity, or the approachability I felt the day we chatted in the lobby could be chalked up to his bedside manner, the rapport that he affected to put a patient's mind at ease. Then Yuriko's face came to mind. Freckles like stars. Another child of a donor. How old was she? Pondering these questions as I watched a pool of sunlight on the carpet, something hit me: if the sperm donor Aizawa had been unable to find—his biological father—had been a student at the university hospital, there was a good chance that his father was now working as a doctor, like his son.

On the second Tuesday of the month, after my evening bath, I found my cell phone buzzing on the tea table and saw that it was Sengawa. It was after ten, but I picked up. Sengawa said that she was in the neighborhood for work but just wrapped up and wanted to know if I would meet her by the station for a drink. Judging from her voice, she'd had a number of drinks already. I had half a mind to say I'd just hopped out of the bath, my hair was wet, goodnight—but for once Sengawa didn't care what I was up to. She had already taken for granted I was coming, so I gave in.

"I have to dry my hair first. Text me when you get a seat somewhere."

She found a basement-level bar outside the station. I walked past this building all the time during the day, on the way to the grocery store, but had no idea there was a bar down there. At the bottom of the steep stairs was a heavy iron door. Pushing it open, I entered a bar so dark I almost thought it was a joke. Flames twitched from candlesticks on the tables. At this time of night, you would expect most bars to be doing decent business, but there were only a few other customers in the place. I was about to tell the server I was meeting someone when I saw Sengawa sitting in the corner.

The second we met eyes she shook her head apologetically and smiled.

"Sorry to ask you to come out so late. I have no idea what I was thinking, but I'm glad you came."

"It's totally fine," I said.

In the dim light, Sengawa's face was layered with shadows. They jostled as the candles flickered. On the table were a thick rocks glass of whisky and some water. I ordered myself a beer.

"This place is really dark, isn't it?"

"I don't know. It seems right, considering the time."

"It's like being in a cave. It feels, I don't know, clandestine."

"I see what you mean. Not that I can see much of anything else."

"Hey, I'm all for it. Under this coat, I'm wearing gym clothes, so . . . "

"Haha, in this light, it's like is that Jil Sander? That's what they call normcore." Sengawa laughed and took a sip of whisky. "At least, that's what my friend at a fashion magazine told me."

Sengawa said she spent the first half of the evening dining with a different author in Futako Tamagawa. Most authors and their editors meet over a meal around seven, but this one was evidently the early to bed early to rise type, and loved to drink, especially with company, which meant Sengawa got started at four in the afternoon. As a result, she had already been drinking for several hours. When I asked her how much she had had to drink, she said she didn't know, or couldn't remember. She spoke clearly enough, but her eyes were bleary, and her gestures overemphasized the contours of our conversation—in other words, she was hammered. I laughed and said, "Maybe you should call it a night," but she was having none of it.

"Who, me?" she teased. "Don't be silly."

Her eyes were vacant. I sipped my beer in silence.

Even though she was the one who asked me to come out, Sengawa didn't seem to have anything particular to say. We didn't talk about the novel—which, to be honest, hurt a little. But it was probably for the best. I was at an impasse, and nothing we could say was going to change that. It was better left untouched altogether.

Sengawa talked about her family. Before long, it was clear that these were the sort of problems you can only have when you come from money. I heard her out on everything, affirming her frustration with sympathetic groans. She spent her early years in and out of hospitals, assisted in her studies by a team of private tutors. They went over her work at her bedside, there in the hospital. Her family had a yard so big they hired three gardeners during certain seasons. The bath at home was made of marble, and one time she slipped and hit her head and had to get five stitches. The scar still bothered her on rainy days. Her parents used to have an unlocked moneybox in their bedroom, stuffed with banded bills. She and her cousin used to play with them like Legos, stacking them up and knocking them down. But that was years ago, she said. Some of that was gone now, but not everything.

"And all of that's going to be yours?"

"Well, being an only child and all." She smiled sadly and took a snort of whisky. This brought on a coughing spell. I waited for it to pass.

"You alright?"

"Fine. Where were we? Oh, right. When my parents die . . . " She nodded as she took a drink of water. "I suppose I'll wind up with something, but think about it. Between now and then, I need to take care of them, maybe get them into a home, all those things . . . In the end, it's probably going to be a wash. It's a big house, yeah, but it's so ugly I can't imagine anyone living there. Maybe if it were in Tokyo proper, but this is outside Hachioji."

"I don't know," I said. "The idea of not paying rent is pretty appealing."

"Yeah, I guess so. I'd probably see things differently if I had kids."

As soon as I heard Sengawa utter the word "kids," I made my move.

"Kids, right?" I steered our conversation in that general direction, trying my best to sound indifferent. "Have you ever thought about having any?"

"Kids?" Sengawa peered into her empty tumbler. Then, as if in a burst of inspiration, she called over the server and asked for another whisky. Stroking the back of her lightly permed hair, she snickered and said it again.

"Kids. Hah. It's not like I've ever been strongly against having kids or anything. Not really. It's more like I was living life. I never really saw an opening. No time ever came when I could imagine adding children to the mix. There was too much going on."

"Right?" I said and drank some beer.

"Isn't that the way life is? There's always something there, demanding all of your attention. Once you start going, the work never ends, especially when you work for a company. Life doesn't change much except in those pivotal moments, right? If you get sick or, yeah, end up getting pregnant. You know what I mean?" Sengawa massaged the skin under her eyes. "I don't feel like I ever really made a conscious choice . . . "

I nodded and drank some more beer.

"Honestly, though," Sengawa said. "I feel like that was natural. I guess some people still think women instinctively want to have babies, like we're just doing what our genes demand of us. But I never really felt that way myself. At every stage in my life, I feel like I did what I had to do, and that was enough. But maybe it depends on how you think about it. For me, not having children was perfectly natural. Really, all I've done is live my life, taking each day as it comes."

"I get that," I said.

"Yeah, right?" said Sengawa. "But sometimes . . . "

"What?"

"Sometimes I get these thoughts." Closing her eyes tight, Sengawa shook her head. "What if something big happens, tomorrow, and everything changes? What if I got pregnant? Thoughts like that. Maybe they're too vague to call thoughts. I don't know. That sort of thing can just happen to you, right, the way it has to everyone else. But I don't know. For me, that someday never came."

Sengawa let this simmer, examining her fingernails. When she looked up again, she was smiling.

"It's the same for you, right?"

Both of us attended to our drinks. I ordered another beer. Sengawa looked over at a poster on the wall. After a minute, she broke the silence.

"I guess I think about it sometimes, how I'm glad I never had kids of my own."

"Like when?"

"Well, it never happened, so it's hard to even imagine. It's not a fair comparison. But looking around me, I guess I'm glad I never got caught up in all of that. I know it's not the sort of thing you should go around saying. Of course some women are genuinely happy with their families, but between that and getting sick and work they're literally falling apart. It's bad enough when you have financial security like me. For most women, there's no way they could keep on working. So much pressure. And everything becomes their husband's fault. There's a million articles and books about it. Look at all the novels women writers publish once they're mothers. They're all about how hard it is to have kids and to raise them. Then they're weirdly grateful about it all, too. All that miracle of life crap. Authors can't afford to have middle-class values. If you ask me, once a writer starts going in that direction, their career's pretty much over."

I nodded through a sip of beer.

"Still, though." Sengawa swallowed a mouthful of whisky, then chuckled. "Whenever I read that sort of thing, or every time an exhausted coworker complains to me—and of course this is between you and me—I'm shocked by how shallow and how selfish they are. Really. You can see it coming, too. It's just like, you wanted this, you did this. How can you complain about it now? It's not like I don't understand. It's a long time, years, spent working and raising their children. They've done it all themselves—school, sick days, awkward teenage years, finding work—and the second they finally get a grip on things they have to go back and start all over with their kids. Like, why would anyone want to go through all that again? Anyway, there was never a moment for me when I decided I wasn't going to have kids, nothing like that. But I guess I'm glad I never did."

Our conversation moved to other topics on its own. We each ordered a few more of the same drinks and talked about whatever, joking and laughing out loud. We talked about Rika, bemoaning the time her brand-new electric bicycle had been impounded twice in the same day. Some luck. My eyes eventually adjusted to the darkness of the bar. Soon I could see the outlines of the menu items posted on the wall, the different sake bottles, the posters from a bygone era. Sengawa got up and excused herself with a quick wave, heading for the bathroom. As she stood up, some men in suits marched into the bar, followed by another group of men and women. The place had come alive in no time.

I waited, but Sengawa didn't come back. People called the server. The glow of smartphone screens dotted the bar. Worried that Sengawa might be throwing up, I went to check on her and found her leaning over the bathroom sink.

When I said her name, our eyes met in the reflection of the mirror. Despite the low light, I could tell that they were bloodshot. I asked if she was okay. She didn't answer, staring back at me through the mirror. I offered to get her some water, but she shook her head no, then slowly turned, reached out her arms, and wrapped herself around me. At first, I didn't realize what was happening. As she hugged me, I kept seeing her arms reaching out towards me, and I felt her breathing in my ear. I couldn't move a muscle. Her shoulders were unbelievably frail, as were the arms wrapped around my back. How can being held explain so much about the other person's body? I still wasn't sure of what was happening, but I could almost hear my heartbeat. It was all so strange.

I'm not sure how long we were there like that, but eventually Sengawa stepped away and looked at me. She was herself again. I could have sworn I saw her lips move, like she had said something, but if she did, it was too soft for me to hear.

Before I could ask what she had said, we were heading back to our seats, talking about being too drunk to know how drunk we were.

We drank what was left of our drinks and paid the bill. Outside, I offered to wait with her until she got a cab but Sengawa wouldn't hear of it.

"It's cold, go on, I'll be fine."

I took her arm to steady her and cracked a joke or two as we proceeded to the taxi stand. After her car pulled away, I stood and watched the passage of the cars. Something was missing. I wasn't sure if it was what I needed, but I figured I could stand to have another drink, so I stopped at the store. I had a hard time deciding, but settled on the second smallest bottle of whisky, something that I barely ever drank. I would've gotten a beer, but when I went to grab one, the cans were way too cold.

I'd left the heater running. My place was warm. I hung up my coat and touched my hair. I'd dried it earlier, but it felt like it was damp, so I hit it with the blow-dryer and thought about what happened in the bathroom at the bar. Sengawa had been really drunk. I wondered whether something had been going on at work. Maybe she had more to say, or maybe she just needed to cry, to let it out. All I could be sure of was the thinness of her shoulders, the look of her eyes through the mirror, the color of the light. If I tried to delve below the surface, my thoughts dispersed.

I poured myself a glass of whisky. When I took a sip, it burned my throat. This stuff wasn't even remotely good. Nevertheless, in twenty minutes I had worked through more than half the bottle. I flicked off the lights and climbed into bed. No part of me was sleepy. My cheeks and my extremities pulsed with restless heat. I scrolled through some articles on my phone, all the while knowing it would only make things worse. On one of the infertility blogs I was used to reading, I clicked a link that they had posted and discovered a new blog, whose message board was full of fruitless exchanges, which didn't stop me from devouring it all. Women who were undergoing treatment, who had given up, or who had no personal experience to speak of. Quite the crowd. Written anonymously, their indelicate messages were stricken with lament, misery, ridicule, belligerence, commiseration, and self-pity. I was awake now, and my head was pounding. A mud black feeling swarmed my heart.

I knew these women were only venting their frustration and their anguish, but so long as they had someone, they were blessed. Technology was on their side. They had options. There was a way. They were accepted. That's even true for same-sex couples who wanted kids. They were couples, sharing a dream with someone who could share the load. They had community, and people who would lend a helping hand. But what if sex was out of the equation? What if you were alone? All the books and blogs catered to couples. What about the rest of us, who were alone and planned to stay that way? Who has the right to have a child? Does not having a partner or not wanting to have sex nullify this right?

I didn't care if any of them made it. I didn't care if nothing came from spending all their time and hard-earned money. Let them fail. They'd give up once they'd blown through all their options. I didn't care if it made them bitter or resentful, or if they screwed up the remainder of their lives. At least they had the option. At least they had a chance. They had no clue how lucky they were.

I ground my fists into my cheeks and sat up to finish off the whisky. Back to bed, and to my phone. This message board. Gazing at the sharp, flat brightness of the screen, I felt hot tears run down my cheeks, but I couldn't stop myself from reading. My mind was like an empty kettle, fired from below. My heart was throbbing in my eardrums. My chest was tight, my body fuming. I gave up and let the tears fall from my eyes and down my face. My phone pinged. An icon appeared telling me I had an email, and when I checked, it was Aizawa.

He was answering the email I had sent the week before. It was a simple message saying there would be a small gathering in early April, and I was welcome to attend. There was also a PS: "I'll finish the book soon."

I pressed reply and started typing in the empty window. I was completely drunk. I kept misspelling things in ways no one could hope to decipher, but when I caught myself and went back to set things straight, I felt even more drunk. I tried reading what I wrote, but my head was spinning. I told myself I wasn't so drunk I couldn't write an email, but the end result was absolutely miserable.

"Hello, sorry for the April meeting, but I won't be gone. I know how it works already. It's just a one-way street. I'll never know how you feel, but I think I can see the parallels. What I want you to answer is what would happen if there were never any lies? What if the mother says it all without a shred of guilt? And doesn't a woman without a partner have the right to meet her child? Or is it her fault? This isn't the same about everyone's critical families or looks. It's not that I want a child. I don't want them, I don't want to have them. I want to meet them. My child. I want to meet my child and live with them. But who is it I want to meet? We've never met before. I won't go in April. I can answer my own questions for you, thank you very much. Nice knowing you."

I clicked send without reading it again and threw my phone into the darkest portion of the darkness that surrounded me, then pulled the comforter over my face and shut my eyes. Sleek black waves enveloped me, an upswell of evasive patterns. When they settled, Komi was hugging her knees on the floor. I sat beside her, drinking mugicha. We were in our old house by the harbor, leaning against the discolored wooden post, talking and laughing. Komi your knees are huge! Look who's talking, Natsuko. You're right, they're huge! Cause I look more like you than Mom. Mom's always saying so, how I was always just like you. Whatever, it's cool. Hey Komi. Know how everybody has to die sometime? Does that mean you'll die too? Well yeah, I suppose I will . . . Hey, Natsuko, you crying? Come on, there's nothing to cry about. That won't happen for a long time. Cheer up. Everything's fine. Cause when I die, I'll give you signs. Really? What kind of signs? Too soon for me to say, but I promise I'll come visit you. I'll call your name. That's how you'll know. You'll become a ghost? You could say that. Okay. Just don't be the scary kind of ghost. And don't forget to visit. No matter what happens. Okay? Sure. I might come as a bird, or a leaf, or the wind, or electricity, but I'll make sure you can't miss me.

Okay, just promise that you'll visit, alright? No matter what. Alright, alright. I promise. Okay, you promised—I'll be waiting, I'll be waiting. Forever.

* * *

"I'm so sorry."

"It's fine," Aizawa nodded.

"I was really, really drunk."

"I wondered what that was about. That email was a real surprise."

"I was pretty shocked, too, when I read it again later." It had been over a week, but it felt like alcohol had puddled in a corner of my head.

"Did you throw up at all?" he asked.

"No, somehow. But I had some trouble standing the next morning."

"Next time you drink, make sure you have something to eat beforehand. Maybe some dairy."

"Will do," I said, embarrassed.

Aizawa had done his best to respond to the message that I'd sent to him in a drunken fit. In the days that followed, we sent some messages back and forth and eventually decided to meet up. He brought me copies of a few articles on reproductive ethics that had been published in magazines but had yet to appear in book form. I thanked him and put them in my bag. It was Sunday, and the coffee shop where we had met in Sangenjaya was packed.

"By the way," Aizawa said. "I read your novel. I really enjoyed it."

"I'm glad to hear it."

"I haven't read that much fiction before, so I don't know how to put this . . . "

I know that I had asked for this, since I had given him my

book and all, but now that he had brought it up in person, I had no idea how to respond. When Aizawa started talking about my book, I stared down and began to mumble.

"You can read it all these different ways." Aizawa gazed at his coffee cup. "I guess it's about rebirth, in a way . . . Everyone dies, then they die again, and everything around them keeps changing. The world changes, the language changes, but they're the same people, with the same souls. It keeps repeating forever . . . "

I nodded apprehensively.

"Maybe repeating isn't the right way to put it . . . " Aizawa paused, as if to ponder this a moment, then looked at me, eyes wide, like he had thought of something big.

"I guess I meant that you could see it as rebirth, because it keeps on happening, but things are definitely progressing, in a straight line."

When I was silent, unsure of what to say, Aizawa shrugged and took it back. "Sorry, I can't find the words. Anyway, I really enjoyed it."

"You said you hadn't read a lot of novels. I'm surprised."

"I'm very interested. I just don't know a lot about them. I wonder, though, what it would be like to write a story . . . "

"You mean for you to write your own?"

"Me?" he laughed. "No thanks. My father used to write, though. All the time."

"Your father?"

"Yeah. The one who raised me. He didn't do it for a living or anything. I think he just did it for fun. He died years ago."

"How old was he?"

"He was fifty-four. Too young to die. It was a myocardial infarction. I was fifteen at the time and didn't know yet that he wasn't my biological father. There are a couple of prominent patterns, ways that donor-conceived individuals learn what happened. It's usually after their parents get divorced, or when one of them dies. In my case, though, it took another fifteen years. No one told me anything until I was thirty."

"Nothing at all?"

"Nope," Aizawa said. "I might have already told you this, but my extended family's in Tochigi. They're a real handful. I guess they're what you might call an old family. We all lived out there together. My grandfather died when I was just a kid. After that, my grandmother ran things. She was the one who told me that my father wasn't actually my father."

"All of a sudden?" I asked. "When you were thirty?"

"Right," he sighed. "For a few years, after my dad died, but before I went to Tokyo for school, it was the three of us living in Tochigi together. My grandmother, my mother and me. When I left home, it was just the two of them. My grandmother had always been really strong-willed, incredibly so. I guess I knew that arrangement wasn't going to be easy on my mother, but it seemed unavoidable. Then, around the time I finished up with school and got my license, my mother said she couldn't do it anymore. She couldn't keep living with my grandmother. She started saying how she wanted to get away from Tochigi and move to Tokyo."

"Move to Tokyo and live with you?"

"Well, not really. She just needed to get away from my grandmother. She told me what my grandmother was putting her through on a daily basis. She really couldn't take it. She said if things kept up, she thought she'd lose her mind and die. She went to my grandmother and said she wanted to leave. When she did, my grandmother lost it. Half of my grandfather's estate already belonged to my mother, as would the rest, eventually. My grandmother thought that it was only right for my mother to stay put, look after the house, and take care of her in her old age. As a matter of course."

"Right, right."

"That money was also why I was able to go to a private

medical school in Tokyo." Aizawa said. "Still, I figured that my mother's mental wellbeing was more important than anything, so I suggested that she consider forfeiting the remainder of her inheritance. But my mother had her own views on that. As she saw it, she'd done everything for that family, for fifteen years after her husband died. She thought the money was her due. This sort of thing is never easy."

Aizawa finished off the coffee and looked out the window. I asked him if he'd like to have another. He nodded yes. When the server checked in on us, she refilled both our cups.

"I'm sure your mom had her reasons," I said.

He nodded several times.

"My grandmother really had a bad temper. She basically threw tantrums. It was never easy for the people around her . . . As far back as I can remember, I didn't know how to act around her, either."

"Were you scared of her?"

"I don't know if I was scared. As a child, I suppose I was. She could be frightening. Whenever it was just the two of us, I always got nervous. She never once let her guard down. She never acted like a grandmother. I guess it all makes a little more sense now . . . We weren't blood relatives, after all."

"And she told you that when you were thirty?" I asked.

"Yeah. My mother had already reached her limit. We got her a room in Tokyo where she could stay for the time being. One of those places where you pay by the week. Then I went up to Tochigi to talk things over with my grandmother."

"Yeah."

"When I got to the house, there were a few other people there, people I don't think I'd ever met before. Maybe they were relatives. My dad was an only child, but his father had a few other siblings. They must have been related somehow . . . "

"Oh, I think I can see it," I said, squinting. "All these men in suits standing in a grand hall, in front of a giant gaudy altar, and in the middle of it all is an elderly woman in a beautiful kimono . . . "

"Well, it was a pretty normal room, and I'm pretty sure my grandmother was wearing a tanzen over a sweatshirt. Everyone else was probably wearing work clothes . . . " Aizawa said, scratching his nose with his index finger. "Disappointing, right?"

"No, not at all."

"Then again, the house itself is pretty big," he laughed. "This is way out in the country, after all."

"How big are we talking here?"

"Well, it's a single story, but way bigger than we ever needed. Between the gate and the main house, there's a little orchard and an ornamental garden."

"What."

"It's out in Tochigi. We never used a large portion of the house. The room we were in that day was basically a living room, the room we used for everything."

I tried to imagine this giant home out in Tochigi, replete with its own orchard and ornamental garden, but needless to say I came up short.

"Anyway, we talked. I did my best to explain how my mother was feeling and recommended that they get a little distance from each other, for both their sakes. I asked her to let my mother stay in Tokyo. I assured her that she wasn't going to disappear completely. She'd still come back on weekends to take care of the house and prepare a week's worth of meals. She'd do everything my grandmother needed. And if that wasn't enough, I was ready to hire a housekeeper to come in and pick up the slack. I'd handle the costs for that."

"Nice one." I snapped my fingers. "Then what happened?"

"She shot it down, of course. She was never going to let my mother walk away. The way my grandmother saw it, her family had taken good care of my mother, for years. She'd gotten a whole lot of money from them . . . Her staying in the house, looking after my grandmother, wasn't up for discussion."

"Was it that much money?" I asked without much thought.

"Well, this is all coming from my grandmother, so it's hard to say, but I'm sure it was a lot."

"Are we talking, like, a hundred million yen?"

"At least," Aizawa frowned. "Maybe twice that, actually."

I drank my water in silence.

"Including land and everything. Not in cash. Most of it was tied up in assets. After taxes, I don't imagine there being much left. You see, my mother had never had a job. She had used her share to pay for everything, including raising me. I'm sure it's pretty much gone by now."

"But if your grandmother still has money, why not hire a pro? Someone who could take care of things impartially? Factoring in future care and all that's happened. You'd think your grandmother would go along with that."

"That's what I thought, too, but my mother knew it was out of the question. My grandmother would never allow it."

"Why?"

"My grandmother had been forced to do the same sort of things by her own mother-in-law, and she saw it through. It's a matter of pride. She had sacrificed herself for the sake of the family. She couldn't just let my mother go scot-free, not after everything she'd been through herself."

"Hmm."

"After that, we started talking about money, about how my mother had never done right by the family . . . It started as an attack on my mother, then ended up directed at me. I had never taken to my grandmother. Something was always off with us. I felt bad for her, watching her son die with so much life ahead of him. I guess I figured there was this pain in her, this sadness she was keeping to herself. While we never got along, I never doubted that we meant something to one another. I mean, we were family. I was her grandson."

Aizawa heaved a sigh.

"When I said as much, she shot back: 'You're no grandson of mine.' It rolled off her tongue so easily. At first, I assumed she was just lashing out. That's how it sounded. So I said: 'I understand how you may feel, but let's not let our emotions get in the way.' But she just doubled down. 'You're not my grandson. My son wasn't your father. You're no part of this family.'"

I nodded.

"She basically said I had no reason to be there at all, that I was nothing to her. As she spoke, it gradually sank in. I'd never heard my grandmother tell a joke in all my life. I asked her to explain, but she refused. She simply said go ask your mother, then sent me away. And that was that. I have no idea how I got back to Tokyo. I honestly can't remember."

Aizawa looked outside again, then stroked his eyelids with his hands. The sunlight of the winter afternoon was falling gently on his neatly parted hair.

"What did your mom say?" I asked.

"Well, when I got back to Tokyo, I went to my place first, just for a bit. Once I had calmed down as much as possible, I went to where my mother was staying. When I opened the door, she was lying in the middle of the room, on her side, back toward me."

"She was like that when you went in?"

"Yeah. She didn't move when I opened the door, didn't turn around. She was on the floor, this cream-colored flooring. I figured she must be asleep, so I called to her over and over. The fourth or fifth time, she responded. I didn't know where to begin, so I just said, 'I'm back.' She didn't say anything. She didn't move. Then before I knew it, I heard myself ask her. 'Grandma said dad wasn't my real dad.'"

"Where were you? Standing in the doorway?"

"I think so," Aizawa nodded. "Thinking about it now, I wish I'd done things differently. I should have at least been looking her in the face."

"So what did she say?" I asked.

"Nothing. She didn't say anything. I stood there, staring at her back, for who knows how long. Eventually, she sat up, slowly. She just said, 'Yeah,' as if it wasn't even worth discussing. 'That's ancient history, Jun.'"

Aizawa grew quiet. We looked into our cups of coffee.

"Then what?"

"Then my mind went blank. I must have closed the door and walked out. I guess I knew something had changed, something big, but I had no idea what I was supposed to do. I knew I had to think but didn't know what to think. I didn't know how. I felt something inside me, physically. This lump I'd swallowed. With every blink, that thing got harder and heavier in the pit of my stomach. That's how it felt. There was this pressure, in my chest. It was hard to breathe. It was strange, though. I couldn't even tell if it was really me there, struggling to catch my breath.

"I just kept walking. When I came to a corner, I'd go right. At the next corner, I'd turn right again. I just kept going. At some point, I stopped to buy a bottle of water. I came to this park, so I sat down on a bench and started staring at my palms under the lights."

"Your palms?" I asked.

"I know. It doesn't matter how long you stare at your palms, all you'll see is your two hands. Nothing will come of it. It's just that at the time, I don't think I could have done anything else. I kept coming back to what my grandmother had said, about me being no part of her family. Back then, I didn't know anything about donor conception. So I guess I kind of assumed that my mom had me with someone else, in a previous relationship. Either that, or maybe I was adopted. I didn't know what to think, really. I just sat there, doing nothing, staring at my hands. I looked at all the creases, the lines in my fingers. I looked at the knuckles, the pads of skin. The more I stared, the more I started to think, hands are so bizarre, the way they're shaped and all. Then my thoughts started to drift, to my dad . . . "

I nodded.

"Knowing what I know now, I'm amazed my dad loved me the way he did. He really cared. When he was young, he had a hernia. They had to operate on it, but this was a long time ago. They didn't have laparoscopes back then. They went in from the back. Cut their way in. And in this case, with my dad, it didn't go very well. Luckily, his family had money, so he didn't have to work. This was my grandmother's only son, so she really doted on him. She had him clean the garden, do simple repairs around the house, things like that. So, when I was a kid, my dad was always at home, waiting for me to get home from school. Really waiting for me. Every day, he'd ask me all about what happened and listen to me talk about anything, about everything. I forget when it was, but at some point he told me that he was writing a story. My dad had all these bookshelves in his room. He had so many books, all over the place. He was always reading books or writing. I have this image of him in my head, at his desk, writing late into the night. Sometimes I'd look up at the books on the shelves and read the names on the spines. My dad would come stand beside me, pull books down, one at a time, and explain what each one was about in a way that even I could understand. This book will tell you more about whales than any other book on earth. This one goes on for days about family, God and judgment, but it's actually pretty funny. I remembered the way his hands and fingers looked as he flipped through those books. It was probably just the lack of sun, but he was always pale, even his hands. He had splotches of red on his palms, flaky skin on the backs. Fan-shaped fingernails. I have no idea if his hands were as big as I remember, but I always thought they were thick and kind of doughy. Sitting on that bench in the park, looking down at my own hands, I got to thinking. About how those hands and my hands had nothing in common."

Aizawa looked out the window, then looked back at me, as if something had just occurred to him, and shook his head.

"I really shouldn't be talking about myself like this. I came here to hear your story. Why did I end up going into all of this?"

"It just happened naturally, talking about fiction," I smiled, nodding reassuringly.

"That's right," Aizawa smiled too. "I never figured out what he was writing all those years."

"You never got to read it?"

"I never found the notebooks. He showed them to me once, said this is the novel I'm writing. I can't tell you how hard I tried to find them after he died. They never turned up. I still don't know if he was really writing a novel, but I know he loved reading and writing stories. I guess on some level, that's why I'm so curious about what it's like, to write a novel. Anyway, I know that you're a novelist, but I shouldn't be going on about my dad like this . . . I'm sorry."

"No, I don't mind at all," I shook my head. "So did you go back to your mom's room when you left the park?"

"I did," he said after a pause. "I couldn't just sit on that bench forever. I didn't know what to do, but I guess I wanted to hear her out. When I got there, she was watching TV. I sat down against the wall and did the same. We watched TV, neither of us saying anything. After a while, I started talking about Tochigi. About how the persimmon trees were dying, about my grandmother, about all the relatives there, the people I'd never seen before. At first, my mom was quiet, just listening, then she said, 'Your grandma made me do it.'"

"Use a sperm donor?" I asked.

"Yeah," he nodded. "I guess my folks had been married for years, with no children. My grandmother was always tormenting my mother about it. This was a long time ago, but I guess these things haven't really changed. Still, back then, there was no such thing as male infertility. When a couple couldn't have a child, it was always the woman's fault, no matter what. That's the way everybody thought. For years, my mother had to put up with all kinds of things. Everyone said she was barren. Then, at some point, my grandmother came to her and said, 'Before it's too late, you should go to Tokyo and see a specialist. If you really can't have children, then the only option left is going to be divorce.' So my mother called the hospital, and they told her to bring her husband, so they could examine both of them. And that's what they did. What the hospital found was that my dad, or my grandmother's son, had no sperm whatsoever."

"So what'd your grandmother say?" I asked.

"What could she say? I guess she was speechless at first. Then she started screaming about how they must have got it wrong. She made them get a second opinion. And they did. But the results were the same. She told my mom not to tell anyone about any of this. My family had all kinds of connections, with businesses and politicians, from offering their financial support, so my grandmother must have pulled some strings to get them into to the university hospital where there was research being done on donor conception. My parents frequented that hospital for maybe a year or so, and at some point my mom got pregnant. After that, they transferred to the local maternity clinic. Pretty soon, my grandmother was leading my mother around the neighborhood, to visit relatives and make sure that they saw her belly. A few months later, my mom gave birth to me.

"That was the first time I heard anything about donor conception. When I was at the park, all I could imagine was that I was from another relationship or adopted. In other words, I assumed that my father was out there somewhere, and my mom knew who he was. If I wanted to meet him, I figured that I probably could," Aizawa said. "But that wasn't the case. No one knew who my father was. It was like he didn't exist. I don't know how to put it. I started thinking that half of me was . . . not human. I know I was born from egg and sperm, same as anyone else, but half of me was . . . "

Aizawa grasped his coffee cup and realized it was empty. Mine was too. Looking a little nervous, he asked if I was okay with this conversation. I told him it was fine and suggested that we have some cake. The server brought over dessert menus. Aizawa sat up straight and peered into the menu, like it contained some kind of curiosity, and after considerable deliberation, ordered the flan. I asked for shortcake.

"But what really surprised me," Aizawa said with a lonesome smile, "was the way that, after she had explained the whole process so nonchalantly, my mother gave me this look, like she really didn't know why I was asking. Honestly, I didn't know what to say to her. It felt like a punch in the gut, but what surprised me most was my mom's attitude. To put it very lightly, this news was a big deal to me. I mean, as a writer, what do you think? What could be more significant than that?"

"I agree," I nodded. "Completely."

"Right? When you see this sort of thing on TV, or in the movies, and they're explaining to the child where they came from, they always do it the same way, you know? They take it very seriously. I guess that's what I thought would happen. My mother would explain everything in detail, say how sorry she was that she had kept it hidden for so long, and tear up while asking for forgiveness. I guess I thought that would be normal.

"But she just acted like she didn't even know why we were

having this conversation. I can't tell you how that felt. My world was spinning. I was angry. I asked her: 'Do you have any idea what you're saying? Do you realize what you're doing to me?' She told me: 'You were born in perfect health, with everything you ever needed. What more could you want?' I was dumbfounded. 'What do you want?'

"After some time, I managed to say: 'Who my father is, that's what.' My voice was shaking. She looked as though she truly couldn't grasp what I was saying. It was making me anxious. It was like she was a shell of herself. Or like a mirage. I thought I heard her voice, like it was trembling. Then she turned to me, at a loss, and spoke. 'What's a father, anyway?' I didn't know how to answer her, so I said nothing. She didn't say anything either. Someone was singing on TV. That was the only sound in the room, pouring from the screen onto the floor. Watching the screen, I almost forgot where I was. My mom's lousy rented room.

"How long were we there—watching the TV? At some point, my mother said quietly: 'Who cares who your father is.' I didn't say anything. Some time passed, then she turned, looked me in the eye and doubled down.

'You're mine. I carried you for nine months. That's where you came from. That's all there is to it. What else matters?'"

Aizawa grew quiet. I was quiet too, and cast my eyes over the coffee cups, the paper towelettes, the nearly empty water glasses. The coffee shop was as crowded as when we'd arrived. At the table beside us, a woman in a red sweater was absorbed in studying, electronic dictionary in hand. I figured she was studying some foreign language, but it was hard to tell which one. Her ceramic cup sat at the edge of the table, the only space not taken up by reference books, as if the slightest nudge would send it crashing to the floor, except she didn't seem to care.

Finally, the server brought our dessert and fresh cups of

coffee. We ate what we had ordered without saying anything. The second the whipped cream hit my tongue, the sweetness mixed with my saliva, sending the sugar straight to my brain. I almost moaned.

"This is so sweet," Aizawa said. The flan must have had the same effect on him. He kept nodding.

"I can really feel it, in every wrinkle in my brain, in every little ridge."

Aizawa laughed. "I bet imagining it that way only heightens the effect."

"So what happened with your mom after that?" I asked him. "Did she stay in Tokyo?"

"No." He shook his head. "She decided to go back to Tochigi."

"No way."

"I have no idea how that conversation went, or if there even was one. But she told me she was moving back into the house, to see things through."

"Wow."

"She said, 'It's mine to suffer through, until the end.' And now she's back in Tochigi."

"Did she ever tell you more? About the treatment?"

"We've never talked about it, other than that night in Tokyo."

We fell silent again. The server came by with a pitcher of water. We watched the brilliant liquid catch the sunlight as it filled the glasses.

"I'm sorry," Aizawa said after a while. "I never talk about myself like this."

"No, not at all," I said. "I'm happy you shared that with me."

"You're very kind," he said quietly.

"No one's ever said that to me before."

"Really?"

"Really," I said, thinking it over. "Yeah, I'm sure of it. Not even once."

"How's that possible?" Aizawa laughed.

"What do you mean?"

"I wonder if maybe you're so kind that no one's ever noticed."

"What do you mean?"

"This happens with all kinds of things, not just kindness. It's like people only pick up on things when they're somewhere in the middle, not too strong, not too weak."

"But you caught on?" I smiled.

"Exactly," Aizawa laughed. "Maybe this is a very special day. The day that someone finally understood how kind you truly are."

We drank our coffee and ate our desserts. I couldn't even remember the last time I'd had shortcake. It was soft and light. The whipped cream was sweet, but not too sweet. It was so good I almost wished that I could go on eating it forever.

Aizawa was kind of smirking, like something was up.

"Everything alright?" I asked.

"Yeah. It's just strange," he said. "I've never talked about any of this before, even with anyone at the organization."

"Never?" I was a bit taken aback.

"Never." Aizawa examined the remains of his flan. "I'm not much of a talker. I've barely even spoken in public, except that time in Jiyugaoka, and maybe one time before that."

"I never would have guessed," I said, and meant it, too. "It didn't look that way at all."

"You think? I mean, everyone involved talks about themselves to some extent, but I tend to think of myself as more of a listener."

I nodded.

"I manage our Facebook page, make flyers for events,

things like that. I also send out all the memoranda to medical associations and universities."

"Right, I saw the post about the 'right to know' becoming law."

"Well, that hasn't really gone anywhere yet," Aizawa laughed. "I've also been working on a database of students who donated sperm at that specific university back then."

"And everyone's cooperating?"

"It feels like things are slowly moving in the right direction, but I wouldn't say that people are cooperating. They're convinced that if we gain the right to know, the donors will disappear. And that's a problem for them. The country's population is declining across the board. Why make things worse? Sometimes it makes me wonder what I'm trying to achieve."

Aizawa looked out the window and took a second to think things over.

"Life became so complicated for me once I found out. Of course, it's not like everything was simple before. But things changed. That's when I quit my job . . . "

"Oh."

"It doesn't matter what I do. It never feels real," Aizawa said. "It just feels . . . like I'm only half there . . . I don't really know how to put it," he said. "I guess it's a cliché, but honestly it feels like I'm stuck, living in a nightmare. That's really how it feels. Part of me feels like the only way to get back on track would be meeting my biological father. I don't even know if he's still alive, though. I did everything I could to find him, but I know now that I probably never will."

"Has anyone in Children of Donors ever found someone?"

"Not that I know of, actually," Aizawa said. "The procedure was absolutely anonymous. The university claims that it destroyed the records. And even if they didn't, I doubt they'd hold the answer."

We drank what was left of our coffee. Aizawa turned

toward the window, narrowing his eyes. Looking at the side of his face, I felt as though I was being judged. I knew this wasn't about me, but I couldn't help but feel like I was being blamed for what I wanted.

I remembered reading Aizawa's interview. About 5'10", on the tall side. Single eyelids. A decent distant runner from the time that he was little. If anyone can help, if any of this rings a bell—that call for help had really stuck with me. Every time I thought of it, I felt overwhelmed. The fact that I was sitting there with the person who wrote those words felt so strange to me.

Aizawa paid for both of us. I thanked him for the cake and coffee, which made him smile. On the walk back to the station, we kept talking about all kinds of things. When I asked him what it felt like to have hair so straight, he acted surprised. He confessed that there were times he worried that it might be thinning, but the quality of his hair had never crossed his mind. I asked him if he'd ever seen a human brain up close. He said of course he had. It was years ago, in med school, but he remembered everything.

At the stairs down to the station, Aizawa thanked me.

"This has reminded me how much I used to like to talk," he said. "I used to talk so much."

"It was fun—I hope that doesn't sound too weird. I had a lot of fun, though."

"It's so easy to talk to you. Maybe it's because we're the same age," he said. "Or maybe it's something else."

"Everyone in my family has worked in bars, me included. Maybe that has something to do with it."

"In bars?"

"Yeah. In Osaka. Listening to all kinds of people drink and talk, familiar folks and strangers. That was a big part of the job. It used to be my life."

"You were a hostess?" Aizawa looked a little stunned.

"Me? No. I was just a kid. I washed the dishes. My mom died when I was thirteen. I worked in bars for years, but in the kitchen. I've had all kinds of jobs."

Aizawa's eyes were open wide.

"You started working as a kid?"

"Uh-huh."

He looked at me, really looked at me, and shook his head.

"Here I am, giving you my whole life story, when I wish I'd asked for yours."

When I told him we could talk about me next time, Aizawa said that he was looking forward to it. He looked like he really meant it, too.

"I'll be in touch," he said. "I'm going to do a little shopping before going home."

Aizawa pointed in the opposite direction from the station. From how he said it, you would have thought he lived nearby. This made me wonder if he did live close to here, or at least not very far away, along the Den'en Toshi Line, so I asked.

"I live by Gakugeidai," Aizawa said, "but Yuriko's place is just a fifteen-minute walk."

"Yuriko from the symposium?"

"Right, Yuriko Zen."

Aizawa said that she was the one who introduced him to Children of Donors, and that they'd been seeing each other for about three years.

"Next time we meet," he said, "you'll have to tell me more about yourself."

He waved goodbye and walked across the intersection.

14.
A Stiff Upper Lip

Yuriko Zen was born in Tokyo in 1980, but she didn't learn she was the child of a donor until the age of twenty-five. As it turns out, she was interviewed in *Half a Dream* as well, but under a pseudonym. Aizawa told me who she was.

Her parents never got along. For as long as she could remember, home was a place where she had to walk on eggshells. Her mother constantly griped about her father, who eventually found somewhere else to stay. Yuriko's mother worked the night shift at a restaurant. On most of those nights, her grandmother looked after her. Some nights, her father would decide to come home. He sexually abused her, but Yuriko told no one. The interview did not go into details.

When she was twelve, her parents got divorced. Yuriko went into her mother's custody and stopped seeing her father entirely, but around the time that she turned twenty-five, she found out he was dying, after a long battle with cancer. Relatives she never knew she had reached out to offer their opinion. "Your parents may be separated, but you're his only daughter. Go see him before he passes." Yuriko had no desire to reunite with her father. She had never been particularly close to her mother, either—and moved into her own apartment as soon as she graduated from high school—but she still felt like it was her duty to tell her mother about her father's dire condition.

"Don't worry about it," her mother snorted. "That man's

got nothing to do with us. I never wanted kids, but when that prick found out he couldn't make it happen, he lost his mind and said we had to figure out a way, so that no one would know. The sperm came from the hospital. I have no idea who your father is."

Like so many other children of donors, Yuriko was gutted by the news, flung into a bottomless abyss. All at once, a slew of questionable events from her past fell into place. She watched her modest foothold on life collapse beneath her feet. Nevertheless, Yuriko said, at least she had the consolation of knowing that the man who had abused her was not her actual father.

I closed the book and set it on my chest. Gazing up at the stains on the ceiling, I thought of Yuriko. Thin and fair. Freckles dotting her nose and the skin below her eyes. Her interview didn't elaborate, and I had no business filling in the gaps, but it made my skin crawl to imagine how much Yuriko, a kid with nowhere else to turn, had suffered, in the hands of her abuser. The man she had been told to be her father. I envisioned her the way I saw her in the lobby. The way she stared at me when I said I was considering donor conception, how she said nothing in reply. I sat up, put the book away, and leaned into my beanbag.

March was coming to an end. Aizawa and I were exchanging emails all the time now. The previous Saturday, we got dinner and drinks. I said we should get fish and he said he knew just the spot, which turned out to be the izakaya that Rie had brought me to on Christmas. When I said I'd been there before, he told me that he and Yuriko had been a few times, too.

We talked about our lives. Aizawa had all kinds of questions about my work, but I confessed to him the novel I'd been working on for two years was a mess. The style and the structure were all wrong. I'd lost sight of what had made me want to write it in the first place. I felt stuck and thought that maybe I should quit while I was ahead and write an entirely different book.

"Focusing on the same thing like that," Aizawa said, "for so long."

"Don't doctors do that all the time?" I asked. "Don't you have patients who are hospitalized for years?"

"I suppose," he said. "Some doctors even say that those are the relationships that really keep them going. Personally, I don't think I was cut out for it."

"Well, I suppose if you don't work at one place, you don't really see the same set of patients, do you?"

"A long time ago, when I started out as a GP, I was so nervous. I felt this sort of responsibility I'd never felt before. When someone got better, though, I can't tell you how happy it made me."

"Do you remember your first patient?"

"Of course. He had Parkinson's. He was already living in a facility, and they brought him to the hospital for aspiration pneumonia. He was strong, though. He did everything he could to pull through. It's strange to look back on it so fondly, but it made me feel like I'd made the right decision by becoming a doctor."

"What does Yuriko do?"

"She works for an insurance company. But as a private contractor. We're both basically freelance."

Aizawa added that regardless of where they took their relationship, they had already decided they weren't having kids.

"I read an interview she did for a newspaper. That's how we met."

"An interview about donor conception?"

"Exactly. It was anonymous, since at that point she was already appearing in person at meetings and seminars. But just when I was feeling lost, I found that article. I had never heard of donor conception and somehow didn't know that artificial insemination was a thing. So I made up my mind and reached out to the paper. We wound up getting together, which is when she told me about Children of Donors."

He said that Yuriko had helped him through one of the hardest periods of his life. I had to read between the lines, but it sounded like he was still seeing someone else the first time he met up with Yuriko.

I mentioned that I'd been with someone throughout high school and for a number of years after—and that he was the only guy I'd ever been with. For a moment I hesitated, unsure of whether this was too much information, but I went ahead and told him why we broke up. I told Aizawa that having sex had been intolerable for me. How it had made me sad and made me want to die. How it had never worked, no matter how I tried. How I had never felt desire since, or felt like I was missing out, though I admitted there were times I thought I must be crazy. Aizawa listened patiently. I told him how I realized that I wanted to have a child, and that for the past two years, the thought had never left my mind, despite not having a partner, being incapable of having sex, and feeling less than qualified, financially or otherwise, to be a parent.

"When you say you want to have a child," Aizawa said, "what is it you're after? Do you mean you want to raise a child? Give birth? Get pregnant?"

"I've asked myself that same thing," I admitted. "I've given it a lot of thought. I guess it's all of the above. The best way I can put it is I want to *know* them, this child, whoever they are . . ."

"Know them . . ."

Aizawa solemnly repeated my choice of words.

I thought about what I had said, but couldn't explain what I meant. What made me want to know this person? What did

I think it meant to have a kid, or for this kid to have me as a mother? Who, or what, exactly, was I expecting? I knew I wasn't making any sense, but I was doing all I could to string the words together and convey that meeting this person, whoever they may wind up being, was absolutely crucial to me.

I told Aizawa that I'd tried to sign up with Velkommen, the Danish sperm bank, but that I must have made some kind of a mistake when registering, since I hadn't heard a word from them, in spite of multiple attempts. Considering my age, I wondered if it may be time to think about freezing my eggs. My head was full of questions about the future that I was dangerously unprepared to answer. I can't imagine what I looked like, rambling about my situation as I covered my mouth with my oshibori—but Aizawa heard me out, nodding as I spoke.

"The first time I was there when a patient died," he said, "I was in hematology. Still training. Her name was Noriko. She had leukemia. Only twenty. She was an animated kid, a real fighter. She loved her mom. When she was doing well, we talked about all kinds of things. She'd been in drama club since middle school. When she was in high school, they won second place at nationals. Someday she wanted to write plays. I remember her smiling and telling me: 'I have so many ideas bouncing around in my brain that I figure it's going to take me a good thirty years to bring them all into the world.' She was a smart girl, a whole lot of personality. When she went in for a bone marrow transplant, she had a severe negative reaction, so we had to put her on a respirator. We gave her a sedative to help her fall asleep and intubated her. Right before I administered the sedative, I said: 'You're going to sleep for a little while now. See you soon, okay?' She said: 'Yeah, see you soon.' And that was it."

"Just like that?"

"Yeah," said Aizawa. "Later on, I saw her mother. At the hospital. She said she knew it was coming, and she was strong, but then she asked me this. 'What am I going to do about her eggs?'"

"Her eggs?"

"Sometimes when young men and women are about to go through radiotherapy or chemo, they freeze their sperm or eggs so they can use them later. To give them the option of having kids, once they're better. Noriko had done that. But then she died, leaving just her eggs. I can't imagine how hard it was for her mother. That woman was an extremely thoughtful person. She thanked all the doctors and nurses, but when it was just the two of us, she started crying and told me: 'Maybe if I used those eggs, I could have Noriko again.'"

I was speechless.

"She told me that she knew Noriko was dead, that she had suffered so much, vomiting until there was nothing left, and that as much as she had wanted to do something, anything, to lighten her load, she knew that there was absolutely nothing she could have done. But that was over, no more suffering, which was a good thing, since it had been absolute hell for the poor girl," Aizawa said, "Still, she found it hard to believe that she was never going to see Noriko again. Through her tears, she asked me, 'What can I do to get Noriko back? Maybe if I use her eggs, I could have another Noriko.' There wasn't anything I could say, anything I could do."

Aizawa exhaled gently.

"I'm not sure why, but what you said reminded me of that, of Noriko."

Trading emails with Aizawa and meeting up from time to time became an important part of my life.

He told me all about the clinics where he worked, and how he always brought a death certificate packet when he left the house at night. How the father who had raised him played piano beautifully, and tried his best to teach him, but that he never got the hang of it. He told me all about the two times that he'd been in accidents in taxis, and how as far as he was concerned, being tall could either be a blessing or a curse, for him probably the latter. I told him more about myself. About Komi and Makiko, telling all kinds of stories about the town we used to live in. The two of us ate yakitori and drank beer. Sometimes we met for coffee. One time we met up near Tokyo Station, to check out an art exhibit on the Nabis, after Aizawa finished working a night shift. I remember how we asked each other afterwards which of the paintings we liked best and laughed when we both said *The Ball* by Felix Vallotton.

Spring worked its magic. The cherries blossomed overnight, opening to the blue darkness of the city. They shed petals for days, as if the earth was pulling them down. I learned more and more about Aizawa. I thought about him when I was working, when I was walking to the supermarket, when I lost myself in all the shapes I saw before my eyes, into the night.

Over time, I realized how I felt about him. Hearing from him turned my day around. If I read something or saw some cute animal video, I wanted him to see it, too. I imagined us listening to my favorite songs together. I wanted us to talk about our favorite books and really delve into our thoughts about the world. But once I'd gotten myself worked up with all these happy thoughts, I saw the figure of a man, turned away from me, facing a world that may as well be empty.

Aizawa confessed he wasn't even sure himself what made him want to meet his biological father. Maybe because he knew he never could? What did it even mean to "meet" someone? I wasn't sure what I could do to put his worried mind at ease, but I wanted to be there for him, in any way I could.

Yet I could never forget how inappropriate this feeling was. Aizawa was with Yuriko, and they had bonded over their complicated histories and trauma in a way that I could never fathom. Just the thought of all the pain and suffering they'd been through was too much for me to bear. It left me feeling helpless, overwhelmed.

How I felt about Aizawa didn't change things. My feelings were private, an indulgence, a charade. I was alone, and well aware that I would stay alone—but when I pushed myself to do my best and get things done, I wound up feeling like I was standing in a limitless expanse, forsaken and alone, no dream to chase.

As much as I loved to hear from Aizawa, I always felt a little lonelier after we spoke. My novel wasn't going anywhere. I was still doing my serials, and occasionally got asked to do one-offs, but I started logging into my old temp agency account every now and then. Spring came and went, like someone opening the door to an empty room only to slam it shut again.

At the end of April, I realized I had a couple of emails from a man calling himself Onda.

"Thank you very much for your interest in direct donation. I responded to your query by email several months ago, but have yet to receive a reply. Please let me know if there is anything I can do to assist you."

It took me a few seconds to realize what I was reading, but then it hit me all at once. I'd forgotten all about the email that I'd sent the year before to a blogger who did what he called direct donations. I hadn't been expecting a reply, and I wasn't even sure that I was really interested, which is why I hadn't been checking the dedicated email address I'd set up.

As it turned out, this guy Onda had responded once in late December and tried again around the end of February. The second message was basically the same as the first, but not identical. He had obviously spent a fair amount of time composing both. Beginning with a tidy declaration on what made him decide to donate his sperm in the first place, Onda went on to summarize, in clear prose, what he had learned from his time volunteering at a sperm bank.

He explained the various donation methods, along with their respective success rates, and noted his personal restrictions—for example, he refused to work with women who smoked, and said that we would need to do an interview, so he could make sure I was physically and emotionally prepared to give the child the upbringing they deserved. He added that while, as a baseline, his donations were anonymous, he would provide hardcopies of his results for a full panel of infectious disease tests, and if I needed samples for an STD screening, he could furnish blood and urine on the spot, as long as I made all of the arrangements. Furthermore, if both parties found it mutually agreeable, at a later date we could exchange as little or as much of our private contact information as I desired. For the time being, he shared that he was in his forties, lived in Tokyo, and had a child himself. He was 5'7" and weighed 130 pounds. His blood was Type A Positive. For my personal reference, he attached copies of his latest test results. To close, he expressed his commitment to a deeper understanding of women opting for this path to motherhood, offered his profound respect for all the women who had made this choice, and reiterated his commitment to helping those who wanted children find their happiness as soon as possible.

I pored over the message three more times. Since this was a response, it should have been self-evident that he was writing it for me, but I was absolutely stunned. *This email is for me and no one else.* I couldn't believe it. There were lots of other things to be surprised about. His lucid prose style, for example. I had chosen him out of the countless other sites because he seemed to be the safest bet—but he made the process sound so simple. What surprised me most of all, however, was finding myself warming up to the idea.

Over the next several days, I imagined meeting up with

Onda. I didn't try to picture his appearance or demeanor, so much as where we'd meet and what we'd talk about. Every time I saw that meeting in my head, it was accompanied by the words *me and no one else*. But I always wound up thinking about Aizawa. Nodding, smiling, listening to what I had to say. I'd see Yuriko sitting beside him, not saying anything. She just stared at me. When she looked at me like that, I could feel my chest tighten. I shook my head, trying to rid them from my mind. *Me and no one else*. I was doing this alone.

* * *

Rika called me after the string of holidays in May.

She had left Kura with her grandma for the week so she could focus on work. By the end of it all, she said she couldn't tell if she was staring at her screen or if her screen was staring at her.

She asked me if I'd done anything special, and I told her that my week was a lot like hers. Then we started talking about how it had been too long since we met up. She said I should come by for dinner, so we quickly settled on a date. Since neither of us had seen Sengawa in a while, Rika said let's make a night of it, the three of us. "I'm a horrendous cook, but I'll come up with something. Leave that to me. Just bring whatever you want to drink." We talked another ten minutes before hanging up.

So—we got together for dinner on a Sunday in May. It was so hot you would've thought that it was already summer. Sweating in the kitchen, I whipped up some dashimaki tamago and harusame salad and packed them in tupperware from the 100-yen store. Once I made it to Midorigaoka, where Rika lived, I stopped at the FamilyMart outside the station and picked up a six-pack of beer and three bags of jerky sticks.

Her apartment was on the third floor of an old five-story building. I guess Sengawa's gorgeous home had skewed my expectations. I was imagining Rika's place to be another of those sleek jet-black affairs you see in real-estate advertisements, or maybe even a standalone house, but I knew I was wrong as soon as I saw it. It was made of old brown brick, with window frames and concrete ledges that had seen better days. Your typical apartment complex. Inside, by the mailboxes, there was a giant steel mesh trash can more than half full of junk mail thrown out by the tenants. I found the keypad by the automatic door and punched in Rika's unit number. Seconds later, I heard her voice say, "Come on in!" The door slid open, and I went inside.

"There it is!" Rika was thrilled when I showed her what I had brought. "Dashimaki tamago. Classic Osaka. It's gotta be dashi. The older I get, the clearer it is. Savory is the way to go. I don't think my body can handle sweet things anymore."

"I know what you mean," I laughed. "Sugar goes straight to my head."

We went into the kitchen and put the beer into the fridge. The round table was decked out with a pot brimming with green curry, a bowl of chicken salad, a platter of ham and cheese, and a plate of tuna sashimi. I transferred the harusame salad to a plate and set it among the other dishes. Rika grabbed some beer from the fridge and we sat down at the table with a couple of glasses for a toast.

"Wait. You made all this?"

"No way. It's all from the Tokyu Store. Except for the naan and the curry. Those came from the Indian place down the street. There's more on the way, too. It'll be out soon."

Rika's apartment wasn't cramped, but it wasn't exactly spacious either. Like I said, your typical apartment. Other than the kitchen table, which was just the food, every flat surface, from the TV stand to the shelves beside the stove, was covered with papers, little toys, picture books, rogue socks and colored pencils. Half of the sofa in the living room was piled high with laundry waiting to be folded. From the looks of things, Rika was either bad at cleaning up or simply didn't care. Either way, she wasn't the type of person to get worked up over interior design. In that sense, her apartment was more like my place than Sengawa's. I'd only just walked in the door, but I felt right at home, like I could let myself relax. The walls were decorated with crafts and drawings only a kid could have made and a note that said, "I LOVE YOU MOM."

"It's a mess, I know," Rika laughed. "My office is the worst. When I'm working, I'm always worried all the piles are going to collapse around me."

"I think it's nice," I said.

"Messes like this don't happen overnight. It's always a gradual descent into chaos. You don't see it coming, even though you're there, and it's happening right before your eyes. Kind of like aging. In other words, it probably looks a lot worse than I think it does. But you're okay, right?"

"Totally."

"It's just, the other day, Kura had a play date with a friend from preschool. This five-year-old kid, a total cutie. Kura likes her a lot, so we had her over. Still, I know I can't have any of the other mothers see my place in this condition. You can't stop rumors like that from spreading. I'd never be able to show my face at the school again, know what I mean? The moms around here don't mess around."

"Here specifically?"

"God yes," she laughed. "So I told her mom to drop her daughter off for dinner, on her own. I just figured, I don't know, kids don't care how messy a house is. They just want to play, right? If the place is messy, they might actually be into it. So this girl came by. The first thing we did was eat, right here.

I slaved over a couple of bentos and was like here you go, sweetie. Guess what, though. This kid takes a real long look around the place, gives me this super serious look and says: 'At my house, we always clean up before friends come over.' Natsu, I thought I was going to die. I apologized over and over. You're so right, you're so right. I'm so sorry."

I had to laugh.

"This kid has a real way with words, not that I mind that. Anyway, when I said, 'Different families do things in different ways,' she said: 'I know you tried. Don't worry about me.'"

"By the way, where's Kura?" I asked.

"Sleeping in the other room. It's nap time. I'll wake her up in a little bit."

We poured more beer and served ourselves the different foods on little plates. Sengawa had some work to finish up, but she promised to show up by the time the sun went down.

"Well! Here's to the end of another week." Rika said and took a swig of beer.

"Have you had Sengawa over here before?" I asked.

"Sure. A couple of times, at least. At first, when she saw how messy it was, she was like: 'You're a real author, aren't you?' The next time, or maybe the time after that, she asked me, 'How can you live like this?'"

"There's nothing wrong with a little mess, in my opinion," I said. "But before I came, I was sure you'd be living in a completely different kind of space, something more like Sengawa's house."

"No way. That's not for me. I grew up in a dumpy fourplex. I couldn't care less about where I live. I have everything I need right here, a place to work, a place for Kura and me to sleep, a couch and a kitchen. What else could I want? It's an older building, but it's quake-proof. Besides, most of my neighbors are pretty nice. Then there's the view I have from my desk. I can see this giant tree outside. I love that thing."

"Hey, were you married?"

"Not for long."

"Who was he?"

"He taught at a college."

"Really?" I said. "Don't tell me he taught literature."

"You guessed it."

"That must have been a lot," I laughed.

"Oh, it was." She shook her head. "But that wasn't the problem. As a partner, he was completely useless. Our lifestyles were incompatible."

"You still have to deal with him, right? As Kura's dad?"

"No, actually," said Rika. "He doesn't care about Kura. I never write to him, he never writes to me. I don't even know where he is these days. I'm pretty sure that he left Tokyo."

"No problem on that front, then."

"Right. Anyway, the two of us were no good as a married couple. It's not like one of us really messed up. It just imploded, on its own. It was so smooth, like when you hit nothing but green lights and get where you're going way earlier than expected." Rika nibbled at the tip of a piece of camembert cheese. "I make enough money on my own, so I don't need a partner, not in that sense. My mom lives around here, too, so that makes life a little easier. There was no reason for us to stay together."

"Maybe that's true for the two of you, as far as not needing to see each other anymore and all, but what about his daughter? I bet he misses her."

"I doubt it," she said. "But we both know there are parents out there, men and women alike, who go and have a kid, then split up like it's no big deal. Weird as it is, I guess some parents manage to separate themselves from their kids. It blows my mind. That was the opposite of my experience."

"The opposite?"

"Yeah," she said pensively. "Maybe it sounds strange, but I

can't even imagine being separated from her. It's like I was born for this, for Kura. That's what my whole life was leading up to. Hah. I know, stupid, right? I mean it, though."

I took a sip of beer. Rika continued.

"She's definitely the best part of me, and my ultimate weakness. She's part of me, but she's also out there in the world. Anything could happen, she could get sick or die in some freak accident. Thinking about that, even for a second, scares me so bad I can't breathe. Having a kid around is terrifying."

She served me some green curry.

"Since we're drinking beer, let's skip the rice for now." She said I should take little bites of the curry and handed me a tiny kid's spoon. "It's good this way, I promise."

As we ate, Rika caught me up on things. We talked about the other moms from the preschool, this actor she met during an interview who turned out to be a total scumbag, and the ridiculously cute otter she and Kura saw at the zoo. Then Rika got a phone call, from Sengawa. She said that she was wrapping things up ahead of schedule and would be over within the hour.

We drank our beer and picked away at all the different plates. I thought everything was great, but Rika kept going on about my dashimaki tamago. She grabbed a jumbo pad of sticky notes and asked for me to give her the recipe, so I wrote down all there was to know: four eggs, half a tablespoon of shirodashi, a sprinkle of salt, three drops of shoyu, and green onion, if you have any on hand. Rika slapped it on the refrigerator door and stared at it for a minute with a look of total satisfaction. Then she turned to me and nodded.

"Look who it is."

I turned around. There was a girl standing by the sliding door to the next room.

"Kura, come say hi."

The girl tottered over to her mother and reached out her hands. Rika hoisted her up and held Kura in her arms. She wore a little turquoise tank top. Her fluffy hair, tied back at the top of her head with an elastic, fell a little bit off center. Kura looked like she was much younger than four. Her rosy lips were full of color and her cheeks were round and puffy. I couldn't take my eyes off her. I'd spent a good amount of time with Midoriko when she was this age, but this somehow felt like my first close encounter with a child. For a while, Kura spaced out in her mother's arms, but eventually she said "Water," wriggled her way down, and walked over to the counter. Using both her tiny hands, she brought her mom a yellow plastic cup, which Rika filled at the sink and handed back to her. We sat back and watched Kura as she drank it all, tilting her chin up more and more until the water was gone. Then, with a serious look on her face, she let out a huff of air. Rika and I couldn't help but smile at how cute she was.

"Kura, this is my friend Natsu."

"Hi, Kura," I said, holding up a spoonful of egg. "Want some?"

She was hardly shy. Kura ate the egg off the spoon as if we did this all the time. She hopped up on my knee and said she wanted some cheese, so I unwrapped a piece for her, and she opened her little mouth wide. Then she grabbed my hand and led me to the bedroom, where she had spread her toys out on the futon and told me a little story about every single one. Rika came in, carrying my glass of beer. We spent a little time playing with her Licca dolls, some Calico Critters and a few Pretty Cure outfits and accessories.

Kura's hands and fingers were so unbelievably small. Her fingernails were tiny. Clear and fragile, like little sea creatures just brought into existence. I couldn't help but stare. This made Kura giggle. She got up and gave me a great big hug. I felt so good I thought I might faint. Her body was so small and soft. A mixture of memories, the smell of clothes dried in the open air, spring sun, the warm belly of a sleeping puppy, the sheen of asphalt following summer rain, and the feel of cool mud wafted from her neck. I gave her a big squeeze and breathed in through my nostrils, over and over. Each breath filled me with calm. My scalp tingled.

We hugged until Kura decided it was time to do some coloring. Together we flipped through a photo album of when Kura was a baby. As an infant she was plump and round, adorable in every picture. Rika, sporting her postpartum buzz cut, appeared in a few of the shots. I mentioned seeing her on TV.

"Quite the look, wasn't it?" she said, stroking her head.

"I want a kid so bad."

While I hadn't planned to share this, it sort of slipped out.

"Yeah?" Rika looked me in the eye. "I didn't realize."

"Yeah," I said. "Not with anyone specific, though. I'm not with anybody."

"I see."

"And I can't have sex . . . "

"That's rough," Rika said, nodding seriously. "As in physically? Or emotionally?"

"Emotionally, I think. I don't know, I'm not sure. I just don't want to do it. I've done it before, when I was younger. I was with this guy for a while, I forget how long. It was bad. I couldn't take it. I just wanted to die." I shook my head. "He was a good guy. I liked him, I trusted him. I tried, I really tried, but it wasn't working."

"I think I get that."

"Sometimes I wonder if I'm really a woman," I said. "I know I have the body of a woman. I have breasts like a woman, I get my period like a woman. When I was with that guy, there were times when I wanted to touch him, and I wanted to be with him. But sex . . . opening my legs and having him inside me . . . was the worst."

"Seriously, I get that," she said. "Personally, I find all men repulsive."

"Repulsive?"

"Yeah. Everything men do repulses me. I can't tell you how good it felt when we got divorced and my ex left the house. It was like I could breathe again. Who knows, maybe it was mutual. It's just, men can be such idiots. They can't do anything around the house without making a ton of noise, not even close the fridge or turn the lights on. They can't take care of anyone else. They can't even take care of themselves. They won't do anything for their kids or their families if it means sacrificing their own comfort, but they go out in the world and act all big, like I'm such a good dad, such a provider. Idiots. This guy was unable to take any kind of criticism. It's something I guess he never had to do. He'd get so bent out of shape over the smallest little comment, then wait around for someone to inflate his stupid, flabby ego. God, that pissed me off. At some point, it finally hit me. Why am I wasting my precious time getting angry over all his stupid shit? So I put an end to it."

"That sounds awful. I've never lived with a man."

"When you start listing stuff off like this, it probably sounds a little petty, but it's not. For better or worse, living with someone is nothing but friction, the collision of incompatible ideals. It takes trust to make it viable. I mean, love is basically a drug, right? Without love and trust, resentment is the only thing that's left. And that's where we found ourselves, real fast."

"How do you build trust with a man?" I asked her.

"If I could tell you that," she laughed, "I wouldn't be divorced, now would I? Don't listen to me, though . . . I would have ended up alone regardless. That life isn't for me. I mean, a man can never understand what really matters to a woman. Ever. When you say this sort of thing, people are quick to call you narrow-minded, or say you've never known true love or whatever. They say you can't lump all men together like that, but sadly it's just the truth. No man will ever understand the things that really matter to a woman. If you think about it, it's just obvious."

"But what do you mean about 'what matters to a woman'?"

"I mean the pain," said Rika. "How much it hurts to be a woman. If you say that, though, people look at you like you're throwing yourself a pity party. They'll tell you how men have a lot of pain to deal with, too . . . but sure. Who said they didn't? They're alive, now, aren't they? Of course they live with pain. The difference is, who's putting them through that pain? How can they make it better? Who's to blame for hurting all these men?"

She exhaled through her nose.

"Just think about it. They're on a pedestal from the second they're born, only they don't realize it. Whenever they need something, their moms come running. They're taught to believe that their penises make them superior, and that women are just there for them to use as they see fit. Then they go out into the world, where everything centers around them and their dicks. And it's women who have to make it work. At the end of the day, where is this pain that men feel coming from? In their opinion: us. It's all our fault—whether they're unpopular, broke, jobless. Whatever it is, they blame women for all of their failures, all their problems. Now think about women. No matter how you see it, who's actually responsible for the majority of the pain women feel? If you think about it that way, how could a man and a woman ever see eye to eye? It's structurally impossible."

Rika laughed, exasperated.

"Then there are the real bastards, like my ex," she shook her head. "He went around, patting himself on the back, like he's so much better than all those men. 'I know the pain that women feel, I respect women. I've written papers about it, I know where all the landmines are. My favorite author is Virginia Woolf' and all that . . . So fucking what, though, right?

How many times did you clean the house last month? How many times did you cook? How many times did you go grocery shopping?"

I laughed.

"But trust me," Rika said, laughing too. "There will come a time when women stop having babies. Or, I don't know, we'll reach a point where the whole process can be separated from women's bodies, and we can look back at this time, when women and men tried to live together and raise families, as some unfortunate episode in human history."

Kura came over with her coloring book. Rika threw her head back, like she was totally blown away. "Another masterpiece! A work of genius! Natsu, don't even look. It's so beautiful it'll kill you." Then pressing her hand to her heart, she fell over on her side. Kura laughed, overjoyed by this reaction, then dashed back to the corner of the room.

"I saw something on TV the other day," said Rika, sitting up. "They were interviewing this old woman from some other country. She was 109 or 110. Really up there. And the reporter asked her: 'What's the secret to long life?' You know what she said? 'Stay away from men.' I mean, she's right, you know?"

Rika was too funny.

"It's just the two of us living here, and I feel like that's the way to do it. Maybe I'm biased, but so what? I'm through with men. They don't do a damn thing for me. It's not like I couldn't stand having sex or anything, but to be honest, I've never been too crazy about it. I guess we're not so different, you and me."

"If you think about it," I said, "that's what it was like when we were younger. Sex wasn't a thing, it had no real role in our lives, you know? It didn't matter if you were a woman or not. It's just, for me, things stayed that way. It's like that part of me never grew up. I don't think there's anything strange or unusual about it, though. That's why sometimes I have to ask myself: *Am I really a woman?* Like I said, I have the body of a woman, I know that. But do I have the mind of a woman? Do I feel like a woman? I can't say either way with any confidence. I mean, what does feeling like a woman actually entail? I'm not sure how that relates to how I feel about sex, but it must."

"Hmm."

"When I was younger, I'd talk to my friends, about sex and everything. About how I felt. About how it makes me want to die. They said all kinds of things to me. How they felt bad for me. How maybe there was something wrong with me. Or maybe I'd feel different if I had good sex. I never listened to them, though. That's got nothing to do with it."

"Well, it's the same with growing older, right? Maybe some women are still doing it at seventy or eighty, but not most, right? I dunno. At a certain point it must become impossible. In the future, as medicine advances and our lives get longer, we'll be old for an even greater portion of our lives. Which translates into more time on earth without sex. Less time spent fucking—all the panting and the gasping, in and out, sweating your miserable fucking face off, fucking your brains out, the temporary insanity of our lives."

We moved into the kitchen, opened another beer and filled each other's glasses. Rika drank hers in one go, then grinned and held her glass out for more. I drank mine too and had her top me off.

Rika wiped the sweat off of her forehead with the back of her hand.

"It's hot in here, huh? Let me lower the temperature on the AC."

Kura was in the tatami room, absorbed in whatever she was drawing.

"So," I said. "There are these sperm banks."

"Whoa," Rika's eyes went wide, almost shimmering. "In Japan? I thought they were all overseas."

"The legit ones are. Anyway, I applied to one, but I guess I didn't make the cut."

"What's it called?"

"Velkommen. It's Danish."

Rika did a quick search on her phone and hummed at what she found. "Okay. Looks like a pretty major outfit. So this is what you're thinking."

Then I gave Rika a crash course on donor conception, how single women couldn't receive treatment, and how lots of children had been born this way, but in a shroud of secrecy, so that the vast majority of them still didn't know who their real fathers were, resulting in a lot of pain. Rika listened, looking genuinely intrigued. Then the intercom buzzed. It was Sengawa. We dropped the conversation and focused on our beers. The doorbell rang, and Rika went over to the door to let her in.

"God, it's hot out."

Sengawa stepped in carrying paper bags in both hands. "It's gotta be at least 85 degrees. Natsu, how have you been? Have you guys been drinking?"

"Sure have," I said. "How have you been?"

I hadn't seen Sengawa since our evening at the basement bar in Sangenjaya. To be honest, I felt a little nervous, but she didn't seem the least bit fazed. She spoke like nothing had happened. "Truth is, I've been drinking some, too. Haha."

"Wait, I thought you were working . . . " Rika said. She read the label on the wine Sengawa handed her.

"I was. It was an event, with wine. They call it Drunk Lit. We were drinking, talking about literature . . . "

"What the hell!" Rika frowned. "And that's work, huh?"

"Hey, it's Sunday, right? Why not?"

After we had a toast, Sengawa caught sight of Kura in the back room. Waving her hands in a cutesy manner, Sengawa chirped her name.

"Kura!"

This launched a coughing spell. Once it settled, Sengawa tried to reassure the child, still using her baby voice. "I'm fine, don't worry. It's just asthma. Stress is scary, scary stuff."

We made room on the table for the food Sengawa brought and popped open the wine, which Sengawa and Rika savored. I stuck with beer. We talked about politicians, the latest best-sellers, and whatever else crossed our minds. Before long, they had made it through the first bottle of wine and promptly opened up another. Kura decided she was done with coloring and said she wanted to watch PreCure. I asked Rika how to navigate the recorded episodes and went over to the couch to watch it with her for a while. I could hear Rika and Sengawa talking at the table, getting really animated, so I went back to rejoin the conversation and have some more beer. Kura would come to visit me at the table now and then, climbing up on my knee for a minute before sliding off to go back to the sofa.

"I think she likes you," Sengawa said with a smile.

"She does," Rika said. "You really have a way with kids."

She nodded, clearly drunk by now—then gave me this look like she was asking if it was okay to pick up where we'd left off before Sengawa arrived. For a second, I panicked, but when I realized that Sengawa noticed something going on, I nodded as if to say I guessed we had no choice.

"I think you should do it," Rika asserted. "Have a kid."

"A what?" Sengawa asked.

"Natsu wants a baby. She's been looking into sperm banks . . . "

Sengawa looked at me. "Sperm banks?"

"It's not really working out, though," I said.

I decided against mentioning how I'd been in contact with an independent donor and was thinking about meeting up with him.

"I've been thinking about it for a couple of years now."

"I don't see the connection." Sengawa looked puzzled.

"You're not seeing anyone, so you're going to go to a sperm bank? We're talking about getting sperm from some random guy, right?"

"You don't need a partner," Rika said. "If you have a baby, that baby is yours. It doesn't matter who the dad is. Even if you don't give birth, the child can be yours. But Natsu can't adopt. She wants to get pregnant, and she can, so she should. Just because she's not with anybody doesn't mean she has to give up on having her own baby."

"I dunno," Sengawa said, shaking her head and sort of laughing. "Sounds crazy to me."

"It's not, though. Why would you even say that? How is it any different from infertility treatment? That's really normal these days."

"Well, because in that case, it involves two parents, as a couple, and you know who both the parents are."

"There are plenty of kids who don't know who their biolog-ical parents are," said Rika. "I've never met my dad. I have no idea who he is. And I don't care. It'll be the same for Kura, too."

"But, how can I put this . . . " Sengawa said. "Even if your parents break up, it's important to know they loved each other, when they were together. It's important to know that's where you came from."

"Oh, spare me," Rika waved her hand like she was brush-ing Sengawa's words off. "Think about all the couples in Japan getting infertility treatment. You think they're having sex? You think they really love each other? How many children are born like that? How do you think they make their babies? The guy jerks off in some room to another woman's naked body, and they mix that together with eggs from the mother. If you're okay with that, then why can't Natsu get pregnant this way? What's the problem?"

Sengawa and I sat there, waiting for Rika to continue.

"There's this college professor I've met a few times," Rika said. "He acts all high and mighty, but he's secretly into little girls, what's commonly known as 'Under Twelve' stuff . . . "

"Wait," I said. "Is that what I think it is?"

"Yep, sure is. He can't get it up except for girls who are twelve or younger. What a sicko." Rika practically spat the word out. "Anyway, I don't know how he tricked her into it, but he married this woman. His wife doesn't have a clue. She got an injection of his sperm, so that they could have a kid, and it worked out. I mean, if they raided this guy's stash, he'd be ruined, know what I mean? Where's the love in that? Where's the connection? But what does any of that have to do with children? Are you telling me that if you register with city hall as husband and wife and have the money to get treatment, that makes you worthy of being a parent? Here's hoping he doesn't have a girl, that asshole—"

I looked at Rika, not even blinking. My chest was getting hot. My hands were shaking. Sengawa sipped her wine. Rika filled her wine glass halfway, then swallowed it slowly.

"If you want a kid, there's no need to get wrapped up in a man's desire," Rika declared. "There's no need to involve women's desire, either. There's no need to get physical. All you need is the will, the will of a woman. If Natsu makes up her mind to take that child in her arms, to always be there for them, thick and thin, that's all that matters. Really, it's a good time to be alive."

"It is," I said, trying to quell my nervousness. "It really is."

Rika looked at me. "Natsu, what if you wrote about it?"

"Wrote about it?"

"Yeah. If it were me, I'd write a book on it. Get the publisher to pay for everything you need. Travel costs, hotels, interpreters. Everyone else gets their parents or their husbands to fork over the money for infertility treatment. I mean, authors are always making money writing about childbirth and parenting. Why shouldn't you get paid to write about your path to motherhood too?"

I looked at Rika.

"Although I guess if you used your real name," she said, "it could make things hard for your kid down the line. You might need a pen name for this one. Have you come across any other books like this out there?"

"There's a blog, but it's probably fiction. And there are plenty of testimonials about how couples have experienced donor conception. One woman wrote a short piece recently about doing it alone," I said, "but no one's written a whole book. There's really nothing out there based on actual experience. Only gossip."

"It'll work," Rika said. "And you'd make enough money to put the kid through college, I'm telling you. I can introduce you to publishers. But Natsu . . . As great as it would be to make some money, this would be so much more. If you can write about yourself like that, about your sexuality, your finances, your emotions . . . if you can get pregnant on your own and become a mother—or even if you can't—but if you write about everything that happens in the process, do you have any idea how much that would mean to so many women?"

Her eyes were full of urgency.

"It would mean a whole lot more than another stupid novel, not like your last novel was stupid. You could give women something real. Real hope. Precedent. Empowerment. You don't need a partner. A woman can make the decision to have a child and go through with it alone."

I realized I was nodding. Sengawa was nodding, too.

Rika urged me on, making her case from every possible angle. She told us about her experience with pregnancy and childbirth. Morning sickness. Labor pains. How the pressures of motherhood were almost too immense for her to bear, even for someone with her steely nerves. Having a child in your life was such a beautiful thing. She said that she could never say as much in public, but until she had a kid of her own, she didn't know the first thing about love. Like half the world had been just out of reach. The thought of missing out on motherhood gave her the chills. It terrified her to think how close she came. She nearly went through life oblivious to how miraculous it was. She wouldn't change a single day of it. Becoming a mother was the most important thing that ever happened to her. Talking about it nearly reduced her to tears. It was that beautiful.

Rika had my undivided attention.

We ate more curry. Rika made Kura a trio of onigiri and sat her down to eat. Then me and Kura went back to the tatami room and played with her toy piano while Sengawa and Rika talked about work.

"Maybe it's time to call it a night," Sengawa said. I looked at the clock. It was a little past eight. "After all, it is a week-night. Doesn't Kura have preschool? I bet it's someone's bath time."

As much as I didn't want to say goodbye to Kura, hearing the word "preschool" made me feel like it was time to go. I'd had a lot of beer; and while I admit I was a little drunk, I was feeling good for an entirely different reason. I don't think I'd been that happy in the past ten years.

"Thank you, thanks for tonight," I told Rika, closing the door. "I had a great time."

The night air was warm and pleasant. I was in a great mood. An unfamiliar power sprung up from my stomach, as if a balloon was working its way up my throat. It was like my heart was going to leap out of my chest. I remembered a scene like this from a Garcia Marquez story, where this guy, I guess the family patriarch, has such a horrible case of gout, like in his feet, he can't stop moaning, but as he cries into the Caribbean night, his screams become an aria. That was exactly how I felt.

Except instead of having gout, I was bursting with a feeling that can only be described as bliss. *I can do this*. What's stopping me? Who cares who the father is—as long as I'm the one who has the baby? For the first time in my life, I felt as though I had the power to do anything.

"I feel like Garcia Marquez," I said to Sengawa on our walk back to the station.

After a long pause, she asked me flatly: "Garcia Marquez? I don't follow."

Something was off. I wondered whether Sengawa felt like Rika had negated her perspective. I decided not to let it bother me. An azure Caribbean sky surrounded me in all directions. My heart was bursting, freeing giant wings of white, and I prepared myself to fly over the mighty deep.

We were saying goodbye right in front of the turnstiles when Sengawa stopped me.

"Hey, Natsuko . . . "

I turned around.

"I know you already know this," she said, "but don't take her seriously. Rika, I mean. She was really drunk. She's just trying to fan the flames."

"You mean about having children?" I asked. "She made perfect sense to me."

"Quit joking around." Sengawa sighed condescendingly. "Sperm banks? Seriously? What is this, some old-school sci-fi movie?"

My cheeks were burning from the inside.

"It's disgusting," she scoffed. "But hey, if you wanna have a kid that way, by all means."

I swallowed a wad of spit, then said:

"You're right. It's up to me."

"How's the novel, Natsuko?" Sengawa snorted. "What makes you think you can have a child on your own? You can't even stay on top of your work."

I didn't say anything.

"You could never handle motherhood," Sengawa laughed. "Take a look at yourself. Think about money. Think about work . . . Do you know how hard it is for two working parents to raise a child these days? Even if there's some truth to what Rika was saying, you're not Rika. She's got a lot of readers, she doesn't need to worry about money. She says she has no interest in men, but if she ever changed her mind, she'd have her pick. It's not like that for you. No one knows you, and who knows what's going to happen to you tomorrow. You're lazy, and you're irresponsible. You're nothing like Rika."

"I don't believe this." It was all I could get out. "You don't know the first thing about me."

We stood there for a while, saying nothing.

"Maybe you're right. Maybe I don't." Sengawa shook her head. "But I know that you have talent. I know that much, Natsu. Don't you have more important things to think about? That's all I want to say. You've got bigger fish to fry. I'm only pushing you like this to get you moving."

Sengawa took a step in my direction. I took a step back.

"I'm trying to help you. You've got what it takes to be a great novelist. Don't squander your gift. Everyone goes through times when they can't write. The important thing is that you keep on going. If you want to write, you have to make it your whole life. I mean, you knew that when you started, right?"

I stared down at the round tips of her shoes. Nothing to say.

"How is having a kid going to help you? Get a grip. Kids. Do you know how boring you sound? Great writers, men and women alike, never have kids. When you write, there's no room in your life for that. You have to go where your stories take you. You owe it to your writing. Don't listen to Rika. What she does isn't literature anyway. It's pop. It's trash. What she writes anyone could write. Sure they're readable and make people feel cozy, but her prose is hackneyed and derivative. She churns them out like nothing for a reason. That isn't literature. You can do better than that. If your story is putting up a fight, that means it has a heart. That's all that matters. What's the point of writing some novel you could breeze through in a month or two? The struggle means something. It means everything. I'm here for you. I'm with you. I'm working on this with you. The story's going to be great. I believe in you. You can write something that nobody else can, I'm sure of it."

Sengawa reached out her hand and tried to grab my arm. I dodged her, swatting it away, and hurried through the turnstiles. Sengawa called after me, but I didn't look back. When she said my name again, I was already halfway up the staircase to the tracks. On the platform, a spurt of music told me that the train was coming. Before long, it roared into the station. I stepped inside as soon as the doors opened and found a seat and crossed my arms to make myself as small as possible. Following an announcement, the doors slid shut. When the train pushed off, I could see Sengawa through the windows. Looking everywhere, trying to find me. Our eyes met for a split second, but I turned away and closed mine, squeezing them tight.

I had to transfer twice to make it back to Sangenjaya. I didn't feel like going home, but I had nowhere else to go. I felt awful. Anger and adrenaline coursed through my veins as my body got hotter and hotter. I realized that my phone was vibrating. Assuming it was Sengawa, I didn't even look; but when it buzzed again a couple of minutes later, and twice more after that, I made myself look at the screen and saw that it was Makiko. Thinking something must have happened, I called her right back. Makiko should've been working. She never called me at this time of night. Especially not multiple times. My heart was racing. Had there been an accident? Did something happen at the bar? Various scenarios flashed through my mind. But wait. If Makiko had called me, she must be fine. Had something happened to Midoriko? Or maybe someone else was using her phone to call me? As I listened to the phone ring, my heart pounded so hard it hurt. It rang six times before the call went through.

"Maki?" I said, when I heard the call go through. "Everything okay?"

"Hey Natsu." It was Makiko. She sounded tired. "What's up?"

I breathed a sigh of relief. Frozen, standing with the phone pressed against my ear. Within seconds, my worry morphed into anger.

"Maki, why aren't you at the bar? I thought something was wrong."

"It's Sunday. I'm off."

She was right. Today was Sunday. The bar was closed.

"Still, you surprised me. What's going on?"

"Nothing. You're coming at the end of August, right? I was wondering where you wanted to go out to eat when you visit. There's this really popular samgyeopsal place in Tsuruhashi. What do you think? It's supposed to be amazing."

"Uh, do we need to decide that now?"

"Well, no. Not really, but it's fun to talk about . . . So, you keeping yourself busy? How's work? Finish the book?"

"Book? I'm not really thinking about that right now." I was having a hard time keeping my cool.

"Then what are you thinking about?" Makiko asked, teasing me.

"Kids," I said.

"Whose kids?"

"My own."

"Natsu!" Makiko screamed into the phone. "Are you pregnant?"

I almost told her I that was but stopped myself.

"No, I mean, not yet, but I'm gonna be."

"You're seeing somebody?"

"Nope."

"Then who are you having a kid with?"

"They have these sperm banks now, for single women like me who want kids. I guess you haven't heard, but it's a normal thing in Tokyo."

"Natsuko," Makiko said. "Is this something from your novel?"

"No, this is real." Losing my patience, I gave her a quick and dirty summary of donor conception, but before I could finish Makiko started yelling so excitedly I couldn't hear myself think.

"No! No. That's not for you to decide—that's for some higher power to . . . "

"What higher power? You don't believe in god. If the option's out there, why not take it? It's totally normal."

"Natsuko, listen to you. You're wasted, aren't you?"

"I'm actually not, though."

"Whatever. You're out though, right? Just go home and work. Instead of babbling about—"

"Who's babbling?" I growled. That one had set me off. "It's going to happen. All I have to do is confirm a couple of things."

"Natsuko," Makiko exhaled into the receiver. "Do you know how hard it is to have a kid? I mean really raise a kid? Do you honestly want to go through that without a father? Think about the child."

"What about Midoriko?" I snapped. "You're raising her alone."

"Don't be dumb," Makiko said. "That's just how things worked out."

"Why is it okay for you, but not for me?" I asked. "Why are you so against it? What gives you the right? I'm not asking for your blessing, but why you gotta try and stop me? Not like it's your life. Do you know how many women raise children on their own? How many children don't know their parents? It's not like I can't afford it. Our family got by on less, right? If we can make it, anyone can."

"Then why not find somebody to raise a kid with," Makiko said soothingly. "It's the right thing to do. You gotta try."

"Makiko," I said. "Do you really want me to be alone forever?"

"What are you talking about?"

"You don't want me to have kids, do you? You want me to be alone. You think that if I have the money to have a child, I should just fork it over to you and Midoriko? You don't have to say it. I know that's what you're thinking. You're worried that if I have a kid, I'll send less money home. If I have a kid, all that goes away. It's bad for you, bad for Midoriko. I get it . . . "

Makiko was speechless. A moment later she let out a massive breath.

"Natsu, listen to me—"

"I'm hanging up. Bye."

I dropped my phone into the bottom of my bag and started walking. I still felt awful. It made me want to scream. I walked faster and faster, my thoughts ripped to smithereens before they had the chance to fully form. Some guy bumped into me and clicked his tongue. I clicked my tongue back and kept walking. I stopped at a crosswalk, waiting for the signal, but when it turned green I couldn't for the life of me decide which way to go. Home was straight. The store was to the right. The station and its crowds behind me. Nothing felt right. I thought about Aizawa. I thought about calling him, but before I could even picture his face, Yuriko got in the way. Maybe Aizawa was in the neighborhood. Maybe they'd gone out together. Yuriko stared at me, blank faced and silent. I wondered if she joked around and laughed and stuff with him. What did she do the nights she was alone? I could see the freckles on her pale face. A hazy nebula of dust and gas and countless planets spreading over her cheeks. I pulled out my phone and opened Gmail. I clicked Onda's message again, as I'd done several times before, but this time I clicked reply.

When I finally hit send, I felt all the energy leave me. A tiny old woman with a clear umbrella and a pair of toy poodles came over to ask if I was okay. I realized I was leaning against a sign. I wondered why she was walking her dogs at this hour, but then realized there wasn't actually anything odd about it. I told her I was fine. I don't know how long I stayed there before going home.

15.
TAKE IT OR LEAVE IT

I wound up meeting Onda in a restaurant called Miami Garden, just by the Shibuya Scramble, below street level. I'd seen their sign, but never gone downstairs. By then it was late June. Charcoal clouds had been hanging just over the city since the morning, and you could hear thunder rumble like the grumbling of a giant beast. We'd been in the rainy season for a while now, but apart from a quick drizzle the week before, most days had been overcast.

Our meeting was for 7:30 in the evening. I'd wanted us to meet during the day, but Onda couldn't make it work. Since I'd picked the area and the date, I compromised and went along with it.

Befitting an establishment with Miami in the name, the interior had fake palm trees here and there. Way tackier than your average family restaurant. The clientele was all across the board. Students, salarymen, teenage girls, ladies out for dinner. Everyone but kids. Playing with their phones, laughing loudly, enjoying their coffee, slurping spaghetti. No one cared who else was sitting near them, and some of the couples didn't seem aware of their own dates. Everyone was conscious, or at least their eyes were open, but they didn't seem remotely aware of their surroundings. That much was a relief.

I'd told Onda that my name was Yamada, that I'd be wearing a plain navy blouse, and that my hair was bobbed and reached my shoulders. He said he had a medium build and a regular haircut, trimmed high above the ears, but not to worry about trying to find him. He'd find me.

It had been a month exactly since I answered him.

As we were going back and forth and working out the details, there were multiple times I almost called the whole thing off. But I talked myself into it, reasoning that Shibuya was full of people, so if things got weird, I'd simply call for help, and besides, there was nothing odd about two strangers, in a city of strangers, meeting up for tea.

I was fifteen minutes early. An unfamiliar variety of anxiety made all my muscles tight. My molars clenched so tight they ground together. My cheeks and temples throbbed. Each minute was interminably long. I had no idea where I should sit or what to do with myself. I did my best to come back down to earth, trying to relax. Everything's okay. What do I have to lose? It may go nowhere, but it doesn't hurt to try. I did my best to blend in, but I couldn't take my eyes off of the entrance, so I pulled out my phone and checked my email. Aizawa had emailed me or texted me a bunch of times that month. I'd sent him some emojis but no actual response. Rika had been texting me too, just light stuff, but I only sent emojis to her too. No word from Sengawa.

"Yamada?"

I looked up like someone had just punched me. There was a man standing in front of me. Onda was the only one who would have been calling me Yamada, and the only person who was likely to address me, but for whatever reason, the fact that this was Onda didn't click. He wore a baggy navy pinstriped suit that made him look like a small-time chief of police, and his forehead was flecked with sweat as if he'd run here. While definitely trimmed above the ears, his hair had been combed back and held in place with sticky pomade, hardly a regular hairstyle. Not medium build, so much as portly. For a second I thought, or hoped, that there had been some kind of a mistake, but this was him. This man was Onda.

His eyes were plain and unexpressive, double lidded. A

giant wart clung to the corner of a droopy eyebrow. That wart must have been growing there for years, discoloring over time. Even from across the table, I could make out the collection of individual elongated pores. That thing was like a little rotten strawberry, gray with age. I had to look away.

Under his pinstriped suit jacket he wore a shimmery white t-shirt emblazoned with the FILA logo, which he made amply visible by generously parting his lapels. He pulled out his chair and took a seat, taking a second to wipe his forehead with his pinstriped cuff.

"I'm Onda."

His voice was on the lower side and muffled.

Neither of us spoke until the server came to take our orders. Miami Garden was full of chatter, but no words made it to my brain. I asked for an iced tea and Onda said "I'll have one of those," pointing at the coffee special on the menu on the table.

"So, let's talk about direct donation." Onda wasn't wasting any time. "Yamada's an alias, isn't it?"

"Um, yes," I said, my voice a little too loud. His opener had caught me by surprise.

"Of course. Privacy is important. You say that you're a free-lancer, but you're in decent shape financially. No issues there. You don't smoke and don't drink either. That correct?"

"Yes," I nodded, unsure about the question I was answering.

"As I said in our earlier communication, I can't be held responsible down the line for any form of financial support." Onda covered his mouth and eyed me cautiously, like a fortune teller who can see the future in your face. "Is that clear?"

"Yes."

"Okay. Well, that covers the interview," Onda said. "You passed."

"Sorry?"

"I've been doing this a long time. I can tell with one look, really."

The server brought our beverages. Onda raised the steaming cup of black coffee to his lips and took a drink before it had the chance to cool.

"Now, there are multiple ways to go about this. Ultimately, the choice is yours," he reassured me. "But first I'd like to have you take a look at this."

Onda produced a few sheets of paper from his jacket pocket.

"As you likely saw in the email attachment, I have no health issues. But there's something else I want you to see. This is important. My semen analysis results. These are the five most recent. Every time I get tested, I use a different place. Here's the English, here's the Japanese. Following? They're the same, but hey, check this out. Here's the density, per milliliter. These numbers are very important here. See? You've got total concentration, motility. This here is rapid sperm . . . "

He handed me the papers to let me see for myself. I accepted the pages and placed them on the table to look them over.

"So here are my results. Let's start with density. When it says 143.1 million, that means sperm per milliliter . . . *per milliliter*," Onda opened his eyes wide, for emphasis. "Next is motility. My most recent score was 88%. The time before that was 89%. Before that, it was 97.5%. See that there? Do you realize what these numbers mean? I bet you do. It's simple. This is basically a report card for my sperm. Over here we have the MI. That's the motility index. It's over 200 million. Now, let's look at morphology. Nearly 70% normal. The average is 4%, by the way. For me, it's *seventy percent*. Moving on, let's check out the totals. An average total would be around 80, maybe a little over 100. Now take a look at mine, the number all the way at the bottom. You see that? 392. One time, I got a score over 400. I'm sure you can do the math in your head, but that means my semen is five, maybe six times stronger than your average man. I've even received certification from the testing agency noting that this is the highest possible level."

He took another mouthful of coffee, then looked at me and at the forms and back at me, as if expecting a reaction.

"In other words," he said, blinking repeatedly, "I have the very highest quality of semen. As potent as it gets."

"Um," I pressed my napkin to my mouth and chose my words carefully, taking pains not to reveal my accent. "How many women have you . . . gotten pregnant?"

"That information isn't public, but I can tell you that the oldest woman was 45 at the time. The youngest was 30. In both of those cases, they used store-bought syringes. Of course, I've had all kinds. Sometimes it's a woman on her own, sometimes it's a couple. Recently, I've seen a lot more lesbians. Everybody finds a way to make it work for them."

I watched the ice cubes shifting in my glass of tea. Was this guy for real? Was this legit or what? After that preamble, had any women actually taken home his sperm and used it to get pregnant?

It was hard for me to believe, but what was even harder to believe was that I'd shown up, and was sitting there across from him, giving this guy a chance. But there I was. I'm the one who wrote him back and showed up to hear him out. I guess there could be women out there who were so desperate they took his motile sperm and had a baby. I looked at Onda without exactly facing him. I was searching for something, anything that was okay about any of this. I desperately needed something to justify my being there with him. I got nothing. My mind was empty, but the FILA logo and the giant wart readily filled the void. My heart was palpitating. I entirely forgot about my iced tea.

"Of course, I was an adult when I started donating."

I had been quiet for so long that Onda started up again.

"But I was probably about ten when I realized that this was my calling . . . "

"Ten?"

"I was in the fourth grade when I ejaculated for the first time. Like most boys, the first time it happened, I had no clue what was going on. But over the next couple of years, I became obsessed with my own semen," Onda grinned, eyes wide. "You know how schools have labs, right? For science class. Filled with microscopes. Well, about the time I started middle school, I decided to use one of those microscopes to get a good look at my own semen, after class, when no one was around. I couldn't believe what I discovered. They were alive, darting around. I could've watched them swim forever. So I had my parents buy me a microscope. It was a pretty nice one, too. I'd masturbate every day, to get a fresh sample for my microscope.

"They're incredible, those little guys. Not to toot my own horn, but it's the honest truth. I've seen the numbers. Pros have told me they've never seen anything like it. Even as a kid, I could tell from the volume, the thickness, the color. This was something special. Of course, the main reason I do this is to help out those in need. But I have to admit, it feels like I was meant to do this. This semen. So strong, so vital. I want them to live on, to grab ahold of eggs and exercise their full potential. To prove their worth. Man. It thrills me just imagining my sperm making their way into the womb . . . It's got nothing to do with carrying on my genes or having children, but it gives me this sense of fulfillment.

"Maybe that's how all men feel. You know how men go to places where they can pay to cozy up with women? Or, you know, call girls over to their house? Of course you're supposed to use a condom, but some guys do this thing, when they're going at it from behind, where they slip the condom off at the last moment, like that's what you get for doing this kind of work, then come inside. I have a friend—well, maybe not a friend—but I know someone who does this all the time. So I asked him why he does it. He said, yeah, of course it feels better, but it's not just that. It gives him this sense of fulfillment. But he's also into how the girl he's shacking up with doesn't even know what's going on. He says there's nothing like the thrill of it. While I understand what he means, you really shouldn't do that sort of thing. First off, it's against the rules. I'm not like that. I'm here to help, but only when my services are requested.

"Anyway, like I said, there are a few different ways to go about things. In your email, you said you're interested in using a syringe. That can work. You look a little younger than your age, and you seem pretty healthy to me. That said, there's no time to waste, as I'm sure you're well aware. Which brings us here today, right? That being the case, you should give some serious thought to how to achieve optimal results. Of course, the most reliable method would be *skin to skin*. During female climax, the vagina and the uterus swell, sucking up the semen—there's a change in alkalinity, too. Maybe you know this, but semen can't handle acidity. I'm sure mine would be fine, though, they'd rise to the challenge. Jump into the fray. Whatever the case, you'll want to time things around when you ovulate. I'm sure you have all of this under control, but I have a few handy forms with all the information you're going to need that I can give you later. Well, anyway, what I mean is, if you're really serious about this, you'll want to give some thought to using the ovulation method. For the best odds, you'll want to follow the path of least resistance. I've received a lot of positive feedback when it comes to my penis, by the way. In terms of size, shape, everything. To be honest, I think that we should try it out, to get the full experience. That way you can see it for yourself—the amount of semen, how if you try to hold it in your hand it just spills over. If you look closely, you can probably see the sperm moving, too. Well, maybe not.

Sometimes it seems that way, though. Oh, I have videos, too, if you're interested . . .

"Correct me if I'm wrong, but you seem a little apprehensive. You wouldn't want to do something like that with a stranger. I understand, believe me. You just want to get pregnant, right? And, if that's how you feel, we can always keep our clothes on. That's one option for sure. We would just take off our underwear, of course. Or we could get naked from the waist down. That would be virtually the same as being naked. I've also thought of a solution if you'd like to keep your clothes on. I had someone I know put this together for me. I've used it lots of times already, and it's been a hit so far. See? Well, it's bagged up, so it's a little hard to see, but there's an opening just the right size for the penis to come out . . . and here's the same thing, but for a woman, a slight opening in the crotch. It's just like wearing tights. If you need to wear something else over them, a skirt maybe, that's fine, too. Everyone who's tried it out so far has been very satisfied. Whatever the case, there's no substitute for what nature intended. Beats a syringe any day. That way it's the warmest and the freshest. Like I said, though, increasing the alkalinity of the vagina is essential. Hearing that sort of thing is bound to make most women nervous, but with my penis and sperm, it's as good as guaranteed. You're in good hands. The best there is. Just figure out the day you're going to ovulate, and we'll start two days before."

After leaving Miami Garden, I eventually made it to the station, but I couldn't let myself go down the stairs, so I dragged myself over to the bus terminal, the only other option. People flew around me, passing by at furious speed. Shibuya was bursting with light. Traffic signals, billboards, headlights, window displays, streetlights, the glow of cell phones. I got in line and leaned against the guardrail, waiting for the bus.

Packed with quiet passengers who sat still in their dark blue seats, the bus took off like it was cutting through the belly of the night. Lights spilled over us, like blood and organs gushing from a wound. I crossed my arms and slouched down, burying myself into the corner of my seat, wanting to hide. I couldn't think at all. I was beyond exhausted. I closed my eyes and didn't open them again for the remainder of the ride. Curled up in a ball, I took stock of all the sounds as the driver called out stops, stepped on the gas, worked the doors, and lowered the bus with a pneumatic hiss, horns blowing down the street.

It was 9:30 when I made it back to Sangenjaya.

When the bus spat me out, I found myself once more surrounded by lights. I wanted to lay down. I didn't want to sit down, or lean on something, or sleep. I wanted to lay flat and be still. Except I couldn't take another step. I wasn't sure if I could make the fifteen-minute walk. I wasn't injured and I didn't have a fever, but my body was dull and heavy, like I was on some kind of drug. My eyes smarted, like they'd been smeared with something hot. My arms and legs were tingling. I told myself there was no way I would make it home. I crossed the intersection, heading for a karaoke center. The well-lit lobby blazed like a snow-covered mountain under spotlights. Like a survivor reaching safety, I dragged my body toward the light.

The guy behind the counter led me to a room on the first floor, more like a closet, really, all the way down the hall. Once I was alone, I flicked off the lights and turned off the microphone, but I couldn't find a way to switch off the monitor. I tossed my bag onto the rock-hard sofa, but the second I sat down I heard a rapping on the door. The door opened. It was the guy from the front. He had the oolong tea—no ice—I'd ordered at the counter. He told me to have a nice time, then left.

I had one sip of tea, took off my sneakers and lay down on the sofa. The vinyl upholstery stank of saliva, cigarettes and sweat. The deep voice of a singing man, thick with echo, shook the walls, blending with other music playing down the hall. I sighed and closed my eyes.

I had a hard time believing what had happened back in Shibuya, but I knew that it was all too real. After he had said his piece, Onda asked me how I wanted to proceed. Not coercively, but like the choice was up to me. What did I even say? I couldn't remember. Maybe I didn't say anything at all. Maybe I couldn't. If I so much as opened up my mouth, everything would spew forth from my lips like molten tar and I would lose control. On the inside I was chanting "so disgusting" and watching for a chance to make a run for it. What kind of face had I been making? Onda's face popped into my head, awaiting my reaction. Eyes opened wide. The wart. That waxy, bulging, unbecoming wart. This guy was trash. A real scumbag. But who was I to judge? I'm the one who voluntarily contacted a strange man from the internet and agreed to meet up in person. And to discuss him giving me some sperm—*his sperm*—so I could have a kid! The thought of it made my hair stand on end. That shit-eating grin. When I told him I'd think it over and get back to him, he picked at something in his teeth and said "Look, you can take it or leave it." Then he just looked at me and started shifting in his seat, squirming. His hands were under the table, out of view. At first, I didn't know what he was doing, hunched over in this awkward way. But soon that grin shifted into a grave expression. His eyes were terrifying. Something was off about his focus, so that I couldn't tell where he was looking, but soon the grin returned to stay. "Here's another option," he muttered. "Girls like you don't have what it takes to ask. You need somebody to show you the way. Well you're in luck. I'm just the man you need." He prodded his jaw downward, under the table, giggling at his crotch. Feigning composure, I blinked a few times, grabbed my wallet, left 1,000 yen on the table, and headed for the exit, trying to act normal. Once I made it through the door, I ran up the staircase and sped off in the opposite direction from the station. I went into the first drugstore I saw, then made a beeline for the back, where I hid behind the shelves.

The man in the room next to me was in it for the long haul, crooning but always a little behind his energetic choice of music. I heard a woman's squeaky voice in one of the other rooms. The songs were all familiar, and yet somehow not. Sometimes laughter cut through the songs. It'd been years since I'd been to karaoke. We had a going away party for someone at the bookstore, but that was so far back I couldn't remember who. When I was younger, back in Osaka, once in a while me and Naruse went to a karaoke parlor in Shobashi. We were kids, nowhere to go. We used to walk all over the city and come home with sore feet. Karaoke was the only place we felt at home. We got hot drinks and fried chicken and talked about all kinds of things. Both of us were awful singers, so we almost never sang, but sometimes Naruse would sing for me, red with embarrassment. He only ever did one song: "Wouldn't It Be Nice" by the Beach Boys. When we were in our late teens, music from the sixties and seventies made a comeback. I wonder how many albums we listened to together. Naruse loved the Beach Boys, and sang that song as best he could, but his English made it hard for him to get the lyrics, and overall the key was way too high, so most of the time he sang it out of tune, except when he broke into falsetto. That part sounded just right. Lots of times we'd start cracking up before he finished. Naruse made this silly face, hamming it up to cover his embarrassment, and told me "Brian may have written that one, but I make it come alive."

I sat up, grabbed the remote, found "Wouldn't It Be Nice," and pressed play.

When I heard those familiar opening bars, and that single snare hit—everything came back to me. It felt like I was in an

empty room alone and witnessing a drop cloth fly away, reveal-
ing furniture and paintings and old memories I thought I'd lost
forever. Nobody sang the melody, but I could hear a faint chorus of voices in the background. The lyrics changed colors on
the screen. I read every single word.

Wouldn't it be nice if we were older
Then we wouldn't have to wait so long . . .

You know it's gonna make it that much better
When we can say goodnight and stay together*

I watched the words come and go. I couldn't even blink. I
felt unbelievably sad. My throat quivered. I placed my palm
against my chest. I knew that me and Naruse were still alive
and everything, but the people we were then, back when he
sang to me, were gone forever. It hurt so bad I thought my
heart was going to pop. It pained me to remember Naruse, the
teenage Naruse who was gone now, and the way he'd felt about
me back then. He really cared about me, even though I was a
lost cause with nowhere to go. Wouldn't it be nice if we were
older. We could say goodnight and stay together. Wouldn't it
be nice. Wouldn't it be nice—but that was a long, long time
ago. Now I was in Tokyo, in Sangenjaya—all alone.

When I paid the bill and went outside, it smelled like rain.
The June sky was covered with clouds, but it was hard to say if
they were rain clouds. The evening air was warm and thick.
Seconds after I was on the street, I felt sweat trickling down my
neck and back. I slung my bag over my shoulder and crossed
the intersection. Each step was a struggle.

Seeing all the cars reminded me of sitting on the curb when

* "Wouldn't It Be Nice," The Beach Boys, lyrics by Brian Wilson / Tony
Asher / Mike Love

I was little, watching the traffic. My mom worked constantly, leaving early and coming home exhausted every night. Sometimes I felt like it would help things if I died. I just watched the cars go by, thinking how with one less mouth to feed, Mom wouldn't have to work so hard. But I could never do it. What would have happened if I got hit by a car and died? Komi would have been sad. Mom would have been sad, too, but maybe she could have stopped working so hard. If she had less on her mind, and had had a chance to live her life, maybe she wouldn't have gotten cancer . . . Who knows. Hard to say. But now, but now—I made it across the intersection, went down the alley next to Carrot Tower, and slowly made my way across the brick-paved plaza.

Outside the Starbucks on the other side, I could see tons of people through the windows. A mother walked by me holding hands with her little son. It looked like fun. The boy was wearing a green baseball hat. His mother stopped and looked him in the eye, smiled and said "Great job! We made it." The supermarket seethed with light. People coming, people going. I could smell fried food on the wind and realized that I hadn't had a proper meal all day. Just some yogurt in the morning. I was too nervous to even consider eating lunch. Onda's wart came to mind. I shook my head, trying to make the image go away, but it only made it grow before my mind's eye. The elongated pores puckered, drooling out a yellow, creamy pus. The pores were multiplying. They twitched like little black insects, fluttering their wings and checking to see if the coast was clear, ready to fly away and find a place to lay their eggs. Stopping short, I pressed my clumsy fingers to my eyelids and felt my eyeballs move beneath my pointer fingers, then transferred my fingertips to my eyebrows, just above my nose. No warts. Nothing there—I heaved a sigh and filled my lungs, like I was testing them for leaks, and exhaled slowly, letting all the air out of my chest. When I looked up, I met eyes with a woman who was walking straight toward me. I stared right at her as she approached. She stopped and stared back. For several seconds, we just stood there, staring at each other. It was Yuriko.

Nodding slightly, Yuriko continued in the direction of the station. I turned around and watched her, then wound up following her. I wasn't sure what made me go after her like that. I guess it was an impulse. Gripping the strap of my bag, I hastened my pace.

Yuriko was wearing a black dress with short sleeves and black slip-on shoes, a black bag slung over her left shoulder. Her skinny neck and arms were disturbingly pale, and her black hair was tied back in a ponytail, just like when I met her at the symposium. She walked in a straight line, without changing the position of her head in space.

At first, I wondered what Yuriko was doing here, but quickly remembered how Aizawa told me that she lived only ten minutes or so from Sangenjaya Station. Yuriko crossed Setagaya Avenue, passed the karaoke center I just visited, crossed under Route 246, and ducked down a narrow lane. After several twists and turns, we came into a shopping arcade. A young group was shouting drunkenly in front of a convenience store, while across the way, outside some kind of a venue, a group of wannabe rock stars stood by dollies heaped with speakers and guitars, taking pictures on their smartphones. Yuriko marched right between them, practically brushing past them, as if she didn't even notice they were there. My eyes locked onto the back of her head. I followed probably twenty feet behind her.

The arcade ended at a three-way intersection, no one in sight. At the massive drugstore on the corner, they were closing for the night, rolling the carts of toilet paper and tissues and sunscreen into the store. Yuriko proceeded at a steady clip. From behind, she looked like she was either thinking about something very serious, or about nothing whatsoever. Unerring in their focus, her eyes pointed where her feet were taking her.

We came into a neighborhood, beyond the streetlights. Partway down a gentle slope, Yuriko stopped short, like something had occurred to her, then slowly turned around. I stopped walking too. From that distance it was hard to see her face, but judging from her posture, she had only just now realized I was following her. From maybe fifty feet away, Yuriko looked at me, and I looked back at her. I figured she was going to come up to me and ask why I was following her, but instead she turned around without a word and kept on going. And so did I.

I could see a park ahead, up on the left, beyond a modest structure made of brick. Out front there was a steel bulletin board, rusted where the white paint had flaked away, and a few flyers for events. Evidently the little building was a library. The park was a good size. Large trees cast deeper shadows over the ground. I felt a mild breeze against my skin, and the branches and the leaves and shadows swayed and shifted like they were alive. An empty swing set sat under a dim light. Toward the center of the park was a little hill, presided over by a noble tree. I couldn't tell what kind it was, but the dark branches and leaves, against the low and cloudy sky, looked like they had been cut out from black construction paper. As the road came to a T, Yuriko changed course and walked into the park.

We were only a few minutes away from the noise of the arcade, but it was quiet all around us. It was night alright, but on the early side. There should have been all kinds of noises, but it was oddly silent, as if the bark of all the trees, the dirt, the rocks, and the plenitude of leaves had sucked up all the sound and held their breath. Yuriko shot through the park to a row of benches on the far edge and sat down. I came close, but not too close, just watching.

She was the first to speak.

"Why are you following me?"

I gulped and nodded several times, but not as some kind of an answer. It was like my spine was faltering, unable to withstand the weight of my head. Half of Yuriko's face caught distant light, leaving the other half to cool in shadow. There was no color to her eyelids or her lips, and the freckles on her cheeks were nowhere to be found. Her pointy nose cast a dark shadow on the center of her face. I could feel sweat on my back and in my armpits. A throbbing pain pinched at my temples. My lips were dry.

"Is this about Aizawa?" she asked.

I shook my head without much thought but wasn't sure what to say back. It was beyond me why I'd followed Yuriko here.

"Did you want to talk to me about Aizawa?" Her face made a strange expression, hard to read. "The two of you have gotten pretty close, huh?"

I nodded noncommittally.

"He talks about you all the time," Yuriko said quietly.

"I'm not sure what made me follow you," I said. "But I know it wasn't about him."

"How do you know, if you're not sure?"

"Because he didn't cross my mind, when I was walking behind you."

Yuriko stared at me, narrowing her eyes.

"Are you feeling okay?" she asked.

"I was just . . . meeting with someone." I said. "A potential donor."

Now she really stared. Letting out a breath, she wagged her head from side to side.

"Did someone hurt you?"

I shook my head no. After another lengthy stare, Yuriko looked down at her knees, then slid to the end of the bench and leaned slightly, gesturing for me to join her. I sat down at the other end, clutching the strap of my bag.

"Has Aizawa told you anything about me?" she asked after a moment of silence.

"He said you helped him through a difficult time."

Yuriko let out a little sigh and smiled. "Did he tell you more? About that period in his life?"

I shook my head.

"I wasn't even trying to help him, but it's all he ever talks about. That's the only reason we're together," Yuriko said. "Did he ever tell you about his ex?"

I shook my head again.

"Aizawa tried to kill himself."

Yuriko folded her hands in her lap and fixated on her fingers.

"It was just before I met him. I don't know if he really wanted to die, or if something came over him in the moment, but he took some weird medicine, enough to kill him, and nearly died. Since he's a doctor, I'm sure it was easy enough to come by, but he still got it illegally. That was why he had to quit the hospital. He didn't lose his license, but things were pretty hard for him after that. Though I guess he was fragile to begin with."

"I didn't realize. I knew he was with somebody." My voice was unexpectedly hoarse. I cleared my throat. Yuriko nodded pensively.

"Well, they were supposed to get married. Everything was going well, too, until Aizawa found out that his father wasn't who he thought it was. Aizawa told her what he found out. He probably thought he couldn't keep something like that secret. And that was the end of that. I'm sure she struggled with it, but she ended up calling things off. She basically said she couldn't imagine bringing a child into the world when she had no idea who their grandfather was. Then her parents came along and said they would never recognize a grandchild if Aizawa was the father. After that, he left the job at the hospital. I think Aizawa really trusted her. It must have really hurt him. They'd been together for years, since medical school."

I thought this over.

"Maybe two years after that, he read about me in the newspaper," she said. "He wound up coming to one of our meetings. At first, it was hard for him. He barely said anything about himself, but he listened to everyone else. Maybe he thought he'd found a place where he belonged."

Yuriko blinked a few times, as if she was sorting through the air in front of her in some way only she could understand. When she turned a certain way, the whites of her eyes shone back at me.

"I know I said there was only one reason Aizawa was with me. But there's another. He felt bad for me."

"Felt bad for you?" I asked.

"Yeah," Yuriko said. "Not only because I don't know who my father is. He feels bad about other things that have happened to me. You read my interview, too, right?"

I didn't answer her.

"I've never told Aizawa the full story." Yuriko raised her jaw. "All I told him was that the man I grew up thinking was my father raped me. I haven't told him anything beyond what was in the newspaper. That in itself was a pretty big shock for him. When I saw how he took that, I didn't feel comfortable telling him the rest. I couldn't tell him that it didn't happen once or twice. I never told him how he invited other men to do the same. I never told him that it wasn't just at home. He took me to this abandoned lot by the river in his car, where other men came out of other cars. I could never tell him about the strange clouds that I saw as it happened, or how I could see other kids, probably my age, off in the distance, running around and playing."

I watched the side of her face.

"Why do you want to have a child?" she finally asked. A thick wind blew around us. The humid air caressed my arms. My hair fell across my face. Yuriko narrowed her eyes and looked at me.

"Do I need a reason?" I asked, speaking from the back of my throat.

"Maybe not," Yuriko said, laughing faintly. "Desire is a justification on its own. Even when it's something that hurts others, you don't need any reason. You can do whatever you want . . . It's not like you need a reason to kill somebody or have a child."

"I know it's unnatural," I admitted, "the way I'm going about things."

"The way?" Yuriko smiled. "It doesn't make the slightest difference how you do things."

"Sorry?"

"It doesn't matter. I'm not talking about genes or families or knowing who your parents are."

"What do you mean? What about all the people who are suffering?" I asked uneasily. " . . . Like you, and Aizawa."

"Look, I'm not saying it's not a little different for children of donors," Yuriko said. "It's not okay to set them or the entire family up for a future of counseling and therapy. But it's basically the same for everyone. That's what it's like to be born. If you stop and think about it, that's all life ever is. Like I was saying, the way you do it doesn't matter. What I'm asking is: Why do you want to bring a child into the world? What would possess you to do that?"

I was quiet.

"Let me guess," Yuriko said quietly. "You think giving birth is some kind of a miracle. The gift of life . . . "

"I don't understand."

"I'm sure you've given a lot of thought to how to have your baby, but have you really thought about what that really means?"

I looked at my own knees in silence.

"What if you have a child, and that child wishes with every bone in her body that she'd never been born?"

Yuriko stared at her fingers.

"When I say this sort of thing, people always feel sorry for me. Poor you, never knowing your real parents, living through years of abuse. No wonder you can't find anything good in life. I can see the pity on their faces. Sometimes, they'll tell me it's not my fault, tell me it's never too late. They'll start crying and hug me. They'll look me in the eye and say I can turn things around. These are good, kind-hearted people," she said. "Here's the thing, though. I genuinely don't think I've had a bad life. I don't need anyone's pity. Whatever it is I've had to live through, it's nothing compared to being born."

I looked at Yuriko's face. I replayed what she had said inside my head, in an attempt to fully comprehend what she was saying.

"You have no idea what I'm talking about, do you?" She exhaled through her nose. "It's really simple, I promise. Why is it that people think this is okay? Why do people see no harm in having children? They do it with smiles on their faces, as if it's not an act of violence. You force this other being into the world, this other being that never asked to be born. You do this absurd thing because that's what you want for yourself, and that doesn't make any sense."

Yuriko stroked her left arm with her right palm. Her arms were white against the sleeves of her black dress, or almost blue, depending on the angle of the light against her skin.

"Once you have children, you can't unhave them," she laughed. "I know how this sounds. You think I sound extreme, or detached from reality. Nothing could be further from the truth. This is real life. That's what I'm talking about—the pain that comes with reality. Not that anyone ever sees it.

"Whenever I say this to somebody, I can see it on their face.

It's never crossed their mind that bringing a child into the world could be remotely violent. Hey, everyone loves surprise parties, right? One day you open the door, and everyone's there waiting for you, ready to surprise you. Here are all these people you've never met, never seen before, congratulating you, big smiles on their faces. Parties are different, though. You can go back through the door behind you, but when you're born, there's no leaving. There's no door. There's no way back to how things were before. I hate it to say it, but not everyone likes surprise parties. Most people go around believing life is good, one giant blessing, like the world we live in is so beautiful, and despite the pain, it's actually this amazing place."

"I admit that bringing a new life into being is selfish and violent."

"You say that now," said Yuriko, "but that kind of proclamation hasn't stopped anyone else from doing it. People always find a way to justify their behavior. You tell yourself *that's the way it is*, then do whatever you want." Yuriko smiled wanly, then addressed me in a quiet voice, like she was talking to herself. "So, what is it? What makes you want to have a baby so badly?"

"I don't know," I answered automatically. Onda's grinning face swept through my mind. I pressed my eyelids with my fingertips. "I don't know. Maybe there's no real reason." I nodded slowly, out of steam. "I just have this deep-seated need to know my child."

"Everyone says the same thing," Yuriko said. "And I'm not just talking about artificial insemination . . . Everyone. They think babies are adorable. They want to try being parents. They want to see how their children will turn out. As women, they want to make full use of their bodies. They want their partner's genes to live on. Or maybe they're lonely and they want someone to look after them when they're old. Whatever the reason, it's all the same. Do you see what I mean?

"It's always about them. They're only thinking about themselves. They never think about the poor kid being born. No one gives a damn how that child is going to feel. Isn't that crazy? Once they've had a baby, most parents would do anything to shelter them from any form of pain or suffering. But here it is, the only way to actually keep your child from ever knowing pain. Don't have them in the first place."

"But—" I said. "But how could you know? If you don't go through with it."

"Right. How could you know?" Yuriko asked. "It's a bet, a gamble—but who wins, who loses?"

"Wait, what's a bet?" I muttered.

"The whole situation," she said. "You're betting that the child that you bring into this will be at least as happy as you've been, at least as fortunate as you've been, or, at a minimum, that they'll be able to say they're happy they were born. Everyone says life is both good and bad, but the majority of people think it's mostly good. That's why people go through with it. The odds are good. Sure, everyone dies someday, but life has meaning, even pain and suffering have meaning, and there's so much joy. There's not a doubt in your mind that your child will see it that way, just like you. No one thinks they'll pull the short straw. They're convinced everything will work out fine. But that's just people believing what they want to believe. For their own benefit. The really horrible part is that this bet isn't yours to make. You're betting on another person's life. Not yours."

Yuriko pressed her left palm to her cheek and sat there for a minute. The night was filled with an elusive color, not quite black or gray. The breeze brought the smell of rain. A car was coming down the road, too far away to guess what kind of person was inside. Pale yellow headlights drifted from right to left then disappeared.

"There are children," Yuriko said, "who are born into a

world of pain and die before knowing anything else, no chance to see what kind of place the world is. With no ability to speak for themselves, they're plunged into the most painful existence only to have it taken away. Life is pain. Did Aizawa ever tell you about the children's ward?"

I shook my head.

"Parents want to hear their kids say 'I'm happy I was born,' to hear their beliefs reinforced. That's why parents and doctors are always making new life, even though no one asked for it. And in the process, those tiny bodies are sometimes cut up, stitched back together, hooked up to tubes and machines, or bled dry. Lots of them die in overwhelming pain. When that happens, everyone's hearts go out to the parents. There's no greater sadness than that. The parents break down and cry, do what they can to overcome their grief, and thank the child. They're grateful to have had the chance to know them. They're truly thankful that the child was born, too. But what is that? Who, exactly, are they thanking? The child who knew nothing of life but excruciating pain? What gave them the right to have these kids, when they could easily wind up spending their whole lives in horrible pain, thinking of nothing but dying, every single second of the day? What could possibly make that okay? What made them so sure that things would never go that way? So certain that they wouldn't lose the bet? Is everyone that stupid? Tell me—what are parents actually risking? What's on the line for them?"

I was quiet.

"Here's one way of looking at it," Yuriko said after a pause. "Imagine you're at the edge of a forest, right before dawn. There's no one else around, just you. It's still dark, and you have no idea what you're doing there. For whatever reason, you make up your mind to walk straight into the forest. After walking for a while, you come to a small house. Slowly, you open the door. Inside, you find ten sleeping children."

I nodded for her to go on.

"All the children are fast asleep. Now, in that moment, in that small house, there's no joy, no pain, no happiness, no sadness. There's nothing, because all the children are asleep. So what do you do? Wake them up or let them sleep? The choice is yours. If you wake them up, nine children will be happy that you did. They'll smile and thank you. But one won't. You know this, before you wake them up. You know that one child will feel nothing but pain from the moment they open their eyes until they finally die. Every second of that child's life will be more horrible than death itself. You know this in advance. You don't know which child it's going to be, but you know that's going to happen to one of them."

Yuriko clasped her palms together in her lap and blinked once, slowly.

"If you bring a new life into the world, that's exactly what you're doing. You're waking one of these kids up. You know what makes you think doing that's okay? Because it's got nothing to do with you."

"Nothing to do with me?"

"Because you're not one of the kids inside that little house. That's why you can do it. Because whoever the child is, the one who lives and dies consumed with pain, *could never be you.*"

All I could do was blink.

"People are willing to accept the pain and suffering of others, limitless amounts of it, as long as it helps them to keep on believing in whatever it is that they want to believe. Love, meaning, doesn't matter."

Her voice had grown so soft that I could barely hear her speak.

"Do you realize what you're doing?"

The air was getting heavier, making the sweat covering my body even stickier. I thought I could smell bile. My stomach must be acting up, since I hadn't eaten any solid food the whole day, but I wasn't feeling hungry. Just the slightest rumbling in my chest. I touched my nose. The skin was oily. Greasy enough to make my finger slip.

"No one should be doing this," Yuriko nearly whispered. "Nobody."

It started to rain, but so gently you could only see it if you squinted at the lights. More like a light mist, really. For a while we just sat there, posted at the ends of the bench. Yuriko looked like she was either lost in thought or staring at the blank gleam of the pavement. Thunder crumbled in the distance.

As June turned into July, I came down with a serious fever.

The first night my temperature approached 103 degrees, then hovered around 102 degrees for two whole days. I was laid up for three more before it came down.

It'd been so long since I'd had this bad a fever that I didn't even feel it coming on. Then it was like my skull cracked open. Something was gnawing at my insides. It hurt so bad that even sitting in a chair was more than I could handle. The pain shot through my wrists and ankles. When I finally took my temperature again, the thermometer said 100.

The blinding summer sun spilled through the windows. I stepped outside. The heat was so profound I could feel it filling up my lungs, but on my way to the convenience store, I realized I was shivering. Inside, I bought some powdered sports drink packets and gel packs, then went to the drug store for a pack of vitamin drinks. By the time I made it home, I felt even worse. I changed into my flannel pajamas and burrowed under the comforter.

The first day was endless. In the throes of the fever, my sense of time sped up and slowed and even started to unravel. More than once, I lost track of when I'd come down with the fever, or even who I was or when all of this was happening. It seemed like I should visit the emergency room, but I wound up sitting it out in bed. I didn't even take anything. I remembered reading somewhere that a fever's just your body's way of battling a virus, so if you bring it down with medicine it's only going to last longer. I mixed up all the sports drink powder and drank some every time I woke up, then staggered to the bathroom, changed into fresh clothes and underwear, and went back to bed, until I woke again.

When the fever finally started to subside, I grabbed my cell phone off my desk. I hadn't thought to charge it, so the battery was at 13%. I checked my email. Just a bunch of ads and other junk. Nothing from Rika or Sengawa, Makiko or Midoriko, and definitely nothing from Aizawa.

Not like the world had changed while I was down with a fever. Of course it hadn't. Still, even if nothing changed, the thought that no one on the planet knew that I'd been seriously sick for almost a week left me feeling alien. I tried to ponder this as best I could with my exhausted brain, but I couldn't make the gears turn. Then something really strange came over me. Had I actually had a fever for the past week? It was just a passing thought. Of course I'd had a fever. I'd been in bed for days. There were sports drink packets all over the kitchen counter. Sweaty pajamas balled up in the corner of my room. If I stepped on the scale, I'd probably see I'd lost a couple of pounds, and if I'd had the nerve to look into the mirror, I bet I would've looked a little worse for wear. Still, though. The fact remained that no one knew that I'd been sick. Not like anybody would have argued with me if I'd told them. They'd just take it at face value. But nobody on earth could know for sure.

I was left with a weird sense of desolation, like a girl left standing on a corner in an empty, unfamiliar town. The orange sun would sink into the murk, while the telescoping shadows sidled up to her, as if they had something to say. Overcome with unspeakable terror, I could see the dark eaves of the houses, and the dull gray of the fences, and the cool refusal of the windows. Had I stood on that corner myself? Or was this just my imagination? At that point, it was hard to say.

While stricken with the fever, Yuriko came to mind repeatedly.

Arriving on a wave of recollection or through the dully glinting fragment of a scene, Yuriko was always wearing the black dress she wore that night and staring at the slender fingers folded in her lap. And like that night, I couldn't say a thing. Not because I couldn't come up with the right rebuttal—but because I saw what she was saying. Because I thought she probably had a point. Because deep down inside, I understood.

As I tossed and turned, there were so many times I felt like I should tell her this. But what was I supposed to say? Little shoulders, thin white arms. Kneecaps touching. She was like a kid herself. The sight of her convinced me I'd be making a grave error if I said what I had thought or felt. I could've just told her I understood. But would those words mean anything to her? Gazing into the darkness of the park at night, Yuriko pressed her cheek with her tiny hand. But no, I thought. That wasn't it at all. I'd got it wrong. She wasn't like a little kid. *She was a little kid.* The Yuriko who heard the door close behind that crew of shadows and the icy shudder of the lock, who saw the clouds through the back window of the car, drifting way up in the sky and changing shape before her eyes, was still a child.

She could hear the other children playing, even see them, way off in the distance. How could they be living in the same world? If the grass covering the river's edge could talk, what would it say? Growing its whole life in the same spot. Stuck there. What about her? What did she have to say? Staring off into the distance, Yuriko remembered the time that she got separated from her mother in the meadow. The smell of grass was almost suffocating. Crouching so she could get a closer look at all the shiny flowering plants, she blew their fronds and asked them: "What makes us so different, huh? Does it hurt to be you? Does it hurt to be me? What's it mean to hurt, anyway?" Jostling on the fragrant breeze, her new friends wouldn't answer her. Night came, bringing the darkness. The road into the forest even darker than the fields. Reaching out her little hand, Yuriko led me deep into the woods. Before long, we made it to a little house. Yuriko pressed her face against the window glass to have a look inside. She turned around looking incredibly relieved and beckoned to me, raising a finger to her lips and shaking her head gently. There were children sleeping in the house. Eyes shut, cuddled up and sleeping soundly. No more pain, she smiled. Here there's no more happiness or sadness. No goodbyes. Then she let go of my hand, opened the tiny door, and slipped inside. Laying down among the sleeping children, she closed her eyes as well. No more hurting. No more pain. At first her feet poked from the blanket, but I watched them shrink with my own eyes. The web of sleep around the children thickening with every breath. A warm, wet darkness wrapped around them. No more pain and no more hurting. None—but then there was an unexpected rapping on the door. Someone was knocking to a steady beat. The unabashed knocking shook the house, reverberating through the trees for miles and miles, until the whole wood echoed with it. Like someone hammering a wooden peg between intervals of silence, this person pounded on the door with a clear sense of purpose. They were only banging on the thin door of a tiny house—but it rang loud enough to shake the whole founda- tion, like a bell tolling the same time the whole world over. My eyelids trembled. I yelled for it to stop, but my voice had no sound. Stop. Please. Stop knocking. Don't wake them—but in an instant, I felt my own chest heaving and realized I'd been sleeping. I blinked, and way up on the ceiling was the same halo of light that I woke to every day. It was bright out, but I couldn't tell what time of day it was. I realized that my phone was buzzing. When I checked my phone, I saw it was Aizawa calling.

"Hello?" I said.

"Natsuko?"

Holding the phone, I heard Aizawa's voice saying my name, but I couldn't understand why I could hear his voice. It was like the space between my skull and brain had been filled in with a gummy substance, incapacitating me for the foreseeable future. I breathed slowly, blinking several times; there was a throbbing pain behind my right eye.

"I had a fever," I said. "Almost all week."

"Feeling better now?" Aizawa asked, sounding genuinely concerned.

"Yeah, I think it's over. I'm just sleeping. Hey, what time is it?"

"Did I wake you up? Sorry," Aizawa said. "It's 9:45 in the morning. Go back to sleep. We'll talk later."

I hummed ambivalently.

"Did you go to the hospital?" he asked.

"I think I've got it under control." My heart was still pounding against my chest, but my hands and feet had started feeling as if they were mine again, at least compared to how they'd felt a couple of days earlier. "I'm brimming with electrolytes."

Aizawa asked me several questions, but I couldn't really get the point of anything he said. Before I could process the meaning behind his words, Aizawa's voice—his voice—filled my ears and head. I felt like I hadn't heard his voice in forever. This realization crept over my scalp, making it tingle. We hadn't seen each other since the cherry trees . . . but that was spring, and this was summer. He'd sent me emails and texts—but I gradually lost the ability to answer.

"I'm okay now, I think. I just had to sleep."

"If you're feeling off, you should see somebody, get yourself checked out," he said, after which there was a period of silence. "—Should I let you go?"

"No," I said. "I have to get up anyway. Looks like my fever's gone."

"Have you eaten anything?"

"I couldn't earlier, but I bet I could get something down now."

"Well, in that case, give me your address. I'll pick up whatever you need. I'll leave it at your door," Aizawa said, but quickly added: "Only if you want me to. I'd be happy to do it. Or I could meet you at the station."

"Thanks."

"Hey, you sound a little better." Except he was the one who sounded relieved.

From there we talked about how things had been going for each of us. Judging from the way he sounded, he didn't seem to know that I'd seen Yuriko on that night two weeks or so before. Aizawa had been working non-stop, taking basically no time off. He told me the plot of a movie he had gone to see late one night. He never mentioned Yuriko, and I didn't ask about her.

He said he'd read my book a few times over, and that each time he'd discovered something new, adding to the list of things he liked about it. I felt a hint of passion in his voice, which told me that he really meant it. At first, I felt a little bashful, hearing him say all these things about my work, but soon it felt like we were talking about something created by someone else entirely. It was a lonely, painful feeling, as if all of this was ancient history—the novel that I'd written, the fact that it had been published, the fact that I was a novelist who wrote books for a living, and even the feeling of wanting to write novels in the first place—these were things that happened long ago, to someone else entirely.

I told him about how me and Makiko had got into an argument over the dumbest thing, but didn't go into details. It didn't even matter. It was so dumb. Nothing to fight about. And now I hadn't heard from her in almost two months.

"I bet she's worried about you."

"We almost never fight," I said. "So I don't know how to make things right."

"I can tell from the way you talk about her that you're really close," Aizawa laughed. "Have you talked with your niece?"

"We don't really communicate that regularly or anything. We text sometimes, but I haven't really talked to her about this."

"Maybe your sister didn't say anything . . . "

"Maybe," I said. "Midoriko's birthday is coming up, though. I told her I'd go back for that, for the first time in a long time. We'll go out to eat, just the three of us. Midoriko's really amped about it, so I'm hoping I can make it happen . . . "

"When's her birthday?" he asked.

"August 31st."

"Really? Me, too."

"You're kidding," I blurted. "August 31st?"

"Yeah. Last day of summer break. Well, I guess it's the same for your niece, even if we were born years and years apart."

"Crazy," I said, laughing.

Then came another silence. I remembered how a while back I stopped at the post office, on the way home from the grocery store to pick up some commemorative stamps. Not like I collected stamps or had anyone to send a letter to. Sometimes I liked to check out what they had, is all. This piqued Aizawa's interest.

"Is there a post office around there?"

"Yeah," I said. "A small one— diagonally across from the bike lot. They have some great stamps. You should check them out next time."

"Okay," he said. "Well, I'm sure they'll have them at the one near me. I don't think I'll be in Sangenjaya any time soon."

"What do you mean?" I wasn't sure if I had the right to ask

what I asked next, but I did it anyway. "Doesn't Yuriko live around here?"

"We haven't met up in a while. At least two months."

His voice was slightly quieter than before. Unable to come back with any kind of response, I kept my mouth shut.

I wondered whether following Yuriko and talking with her was behind this, but Aizawa had just said that it'd been two months. It'd only been two weeks since I'd run into Yuriko. I got the sense the two things weren't explicitly related, but the news still dimmed my spirits.

"You haven't even seen her at Children of Donors?" I asked.

"I haven't been going, actually," he said.

"Did something happen?"

"The last time you and I met it was the end of April," he said after a pause, but really quietly. "Remember how warm it was? The perfect combination of the best parts of summer and spring. It was beautiful. I'd been to Komazawa Park before, but when we went together, it felt like I was seeing everything for the first time. Nature all around, just walking, moving my arms, my legs, breathing, it was a memorable day for me.

"Right after that, though, I had trouble reaching you. At first, I assumed your work was probably keeping you busy. I didn't want to bother you, so I decided to leave you alone, but I sent you a few texts and a few emails that you never answered."

"Yeah."

"I figured maybe I'd offended you. I thought maybe I'd said or done something. I racked my brain but couldn't think of anything. Even if I didn't do anything, I figured that if you'd grown tired of meeting and talking, if your feelings had changed . . . there was nothing I could do.

"Around that time, we had our last meeting for April. There was a bit of a difference of opinion that day. It wasn't anything major, just something about the direction the group was taking. Still, that meeting gave me the opportunity to think. I suppose I hadn't really given it much thought before, but I'd been feeling weird about things, maybe for a year or so. In my head, these different things started to connect. The discussion we had that meeting pointed straight at whatever had been weighing on me."

"The group was weighing on you?"

"Not really," he said. "It had more to do with me than them. Their work is meaningful, of course. It saved me, to know that there were others, people like me, out there. That made an enormous difference."

I nodded.

"But at some point, I got confused," Aizawa said. "I felt like I needed my own space, so I decided to get a little bit of distance. Everyone at the group is great. They're all nice people. Still, I needed the space and time to think about my own needs, separate from the group. I was done. I had to make a clean break. So at that April meeting, I said that I wouldn't be back any time soon."

"What did Yuriko say to that?"

"Yeah," he said. "All she said was 'That's for you to decide.' Nothing else. I felt awful about it. I didn't feel like I had done anything wrong, really, and everyone gave me their blessing. There was no discord or anything, but I still had this awful feeling. And there was this guilt growing in me, especially when I thought about Yuriko."

I heard Aizawa breathe into the phone.

"But it wasn't hard for me, not seeing her, not talking to her. If anything, I felt relieved. What was hard for me . . . "

His voice grew even quieter.

"Was that I hadn't seen you in so long. That's what really hurt . . . "

I pressed the phone against my ear.

"I know that might sound totally out of line," he said, "but it's the way I've felt for quite a while now."

I took a deep breath, holding it, and closed my eyes. And then I let everything go.

What Aizawa had said was like a dream. Just like a dream, I told myself. Only it made me feel hopelessly depressed. I ran through what he had said a bunch of times and shook my head. It made me even more depressed. What if . . . what if I'd met him years ago, when I was younger. Why couldn't we have met back then?

The thought tore through my heart. If we had only met back then. But when, exactly? What would have been the right time? How many years ago? Ten? What if we met before I even met Naruse? What would have worked? Hard to say. All I knew I wished we could have met *before I got this way*. That's for sure. But there was nothing I could do about that now.

"Komazawa was really pretty, huh?" I said. "April 23rd. It was the perfect April day. Warm and breezy. I felt like I could have kept walking forever, that's the kind of day it was. For me."

I was choking up. I took a deep breath.

"I think I fell for you as soon as I read your words."

"My words?" he asked.

"From when you were searching for your father. 'The man I'm looking for is probably on the tall side with single eyelids. Probably a good runner. If any of this rings a bell . . . '"

I tried to remain conscious of my breath.

"For whatever reason, I couldn't forget what you said. Not like I can pretend to understand the way you feel, but those words kept coming back to me, the words of a person who only has three clues to figuring out half their story. This was before I met you. I kept seeing someone in my head, in this place without end, with no one else around. I couldn't forget you, but I hadn't met you yet . . . "

Something stopped me, but Aizawa waited patiently.

"These are just feelings. They don't really connect to anything. What you said just now was like a dream, but even if you want to see me, want to be with me, there's nothing I can do to make that real."

"What do you mean?"

"I don't have the right to be a part of your life in that way." I said. "I can't do normal things."

I shook my head.

"I can't do it."

Aizawa started saying something but I cut him off.

"The same goes for having kids. But I let myself get stupidly excited. I got carried away, like maybe I could do it. I was just being an idiot. I probably knew all along that I was being an idiot. But I let myself believe that maybe I didn't have to be alone, like maybe I could have this thing in my life, this special thing."

"Natsuko."

"But the truth is," I said, biting my lip, "it was always a dream. It could never be real for me. And to wake up, to really wake up, I think that's why I went to meet you."

"Natsuko—"

"This is it," my voice said, springing from the deepest part of me. "I'm done."

After hanging up, I spent about an hour gazing at the stains on the ceiling. Harsh summer light rippled through the curtains. My place was quiet.

When I finally got up, it felt like I was absent from my body. Or maybe like I was in someone else's body. I shuffled to the bathroom and took a hot shower. I let the water wet my hair and washed it with a palmful of shampoo, but even after multiple attempts, the accumulation of sweat and grime prevented it from lathering. In the mirror, I looked shrunken. My hips were thinner, and my ribs were faintly visible. All the spots and moles stood out.

I took my time drying my hair. It didn't want to dry. In my room I reclined on the beanbag and watched the ceiling, blinking repeatedly, then took stock of my room. White wallpaper. My bookshelves, and to the right of them, my desk, and the black screen of the computer that I hadn't touched in days. A cup of sports drink sitting by my bunched-up futon. There were used tissues and sweaty towels. Dirty clothes balled up by my feet. I rested my palms on my stomach and closed my eyes. The skin felt cool under my hands, no temperature. None of this stuff mattered.

I got up and went over to my desk. Sat down in my chair and leaned into the backrest. I put my pen into my penholder. Then I checked out the drawer. A pad of paper. My bankbook. Paperclips. The scissors Rie gave me, with the lily-of-the-valley on the handle. I found a notebook at the bottom of the drawer and took a look inside. There was the poem I had written ages ago—a seriously long time ago—when I was drunk. After staring at it for some time, I ripped it out of the notebook, folded it in half, then in quarters, then in eighths. Once it was too small to fold anymore, I stuffed it in the trash can.

16.
BURNING UP

Three days into August, I found out that Sengawa died. I was reading in my room when Rika called me, around two in the afternoon. "What do you mean?" I asked her. "How?" Rika said she only just now heard herself. The word "suicide" flashed across my mind, and close behind it "car crash."

Rika explained before I had a chance to ask.

"She died at the hospital. I had no idea she was even there . . . "

"She was sick?" I noticed that my voice was trembling. "You mean she was sick?"

"I don't have all the answers yet," she said. "All I know is she was diagnosed with cancer at the end of May. They admitted her right away."

"Late May? When we met at your place?"

"Yeah," Rika said somberly. "But it had already metastasized."

"What? Where was it?" I shook my head in disbelief. "You mean she didn't know until then?"

"It looks that way. Hey, Natsu, I'm getting a call. Let me call you back."

When she hung up, I stood there in the middle of my room. Then I looked at my phone, pressed the home button, and watched the screen until it went black again. I felt a dire need to call somebody, but there was no one.

I put my phone and wallet in my handbag, found my sandals,

went out in my pajamas, and wandered around the neighborhood. In under a minute, my armpits were wet and beads of sweat were trickling down my back. Some wispy clouds had dimmed the sunlight to a bearable level, but the summer heat was in full force. It clung to every inch of skin, like when you drape a wet bandana over your face. I felt disgusting.

I stopped at a convenience store, walked up and down each aisle, then left. I did this several times at different stores. I checked my phone compulsively, to make sure that I hadn't missed a call from Rika. I bought a bottled water at a vending machine and drank it under a tree. Then I tried calling Sengawa, but it didn't even ring. It just went straight to voicemail and an automated message. I walked around like that for probably an hour and went home.

Rika called me back at six-thirty in the evening.

"Sorry that took so long," she said. "There's a whole lot of conflicting information. It looks like no one has a real handle on it."

I nodded through the telephone.

"I wish I could tell you everything in the order that it happened, but I don't really have a grasp on it myself. Sengawa died last night, in the middle of the night. Multiple organ failure brought about by cancer. In May, they told her she had cancer in her lungs. She was in the hospital for a while, but then they let her go. About two weeks ago, she was admitted to another hospital, where she died."

"I don't understand," I shook my head. "When I saw her she was fine. You're telling me she had terminal cancer?"

"It looks like when they told her it was cancer, she didn't tell anyone—only a few people at work. So maybe like a month ago, I emailed her about something, still no clue she was sick. She wrote back like normal. At least I didn't feel like anything was different."

"She'd been off work for the last two months."

"Well, yeah. I talked to another writer she was working with. They had just started going over galleys together, in early June. Then Sengawa reached out to her, saying, 'I know it's horrible timing, but I'm going to have to hand you off to someone else for a little while. It's nothing major, but my asthma's been acting up and I need to take some time off.' So the writer went along with it. 'Get plenty of rest,' and all that. Sengawa said, 'Thanks. I'll be back by the end of summer.' She asked her to keep things quiet. She didn't want anyone making a big deal out of it."

I covered my face with my hands and exhaled into my palms.

"She was always coughing . . . " Rika said. "I thought she looked pale. I kept telling her to see a doctor. But she insisted that everything was fine, that she was getting a regular checkup and all. She said she looked pale because she was anemic, and she was taking medicine for that. She said the cough was just her asthma. She basically brushed me off, assuring me that she'd feel better once she finally took a break. She said I was worrying too much. But then when she went in for X-rays, her lungs had all these little snowballs."

"She was coughing all the time," I said in a low voice. "For some reason, I never really thought about it. She always made it sound like it was stress, or blamed it on her asthma."

"Yeah," Rika sighed. "After that, it spread to her brain, leaving her paralyzed."

"But—" I didn't know what else to say. For a while we just sat there, listening to each other breathe. I heard Kura saying something in the background, and a woman calling after her. Probably Rika's mom.

"I was just talking to her closest coworker," Rika said. "I guess she didn't know it was cancer, either. Sengawa hid it from her, too. She told her she had to be hospitalized for some routine tests, nothing unusual. Asthma, anemia. She told her it was nothing to worry about, though. She just had to spend some time at home, recovering. Sengawa asked her not to tell anyone, either. They'd been in touch while she was out of the office. The last time they talked was mid-July. She said nothing seemed off. It was a totally normal exchange."

"Is there going to be a service?" I asked.

"The family's keeping it small."

"Just family?"

"Yeah. It looks like they won't let anyone in without an invitation from the family."

"That's not what Sengawa would have wanted."

"I agree," Rika said. "But it came out of nowhere. They were just about to try something else, a different treatment. Then it spread to her head and other parts of her body. They were considering radiotherapy. There's no way that Sengawa or her family ever expected things to change so quickly."

"Yeah," I said.

"Natsu, when was the last time you spoke with her?"

"The last time," I said, staring at the wall, "was at your house. That was the last time I saw or talked to her."

"Same here."

"Are you going to go to the funeral?"

"I don't think so," said Rika. "It seems like a lot of people from work who were even closer to her than I was won't be going either."

I said nothing.

"I think some people from her work are going to put a service together once things calm down . . . "

"Yeah."

"I just . . . " Rika was sniffling. "I just can't believe it."

"I know."

"It really came out of nowhere. It's not the sort of thing Sengawa would want."

"Yeah."

"There's no way she wrote a will. I mean, she wasn't planning on dying."

"Yeah."

"She read everything of ours, and always had something to say . . . "

"Yeah."

"But didn't leave anything for us. Not a word."

"Yeah."

"It's just so sudden."

"Yeah."

"I'm sure she couldn't believe it, either."

I thought about Komi and Mom. Both of them had known that they had cancer, but failed to grasp how bad it was or get the care they needed. I guess no one bothered explaining what was happening. They died before they realized. Laid up in the one big room of our sorry excuse for a hospital, shrunken bodies hooked to the IVs. There one day and gone the next. I remembered the blue-black tiles outside the building, cold toes protruding from the sheets.

"It was just too fucking fast." Rika was about to cry. "If I wrote a scene like that into a story she was editing, she'd eat me alive."

"Seriously."

"Natsu," she said. "Why don't you come over? Come over."

"To your place?" I asked.

"Yeah, Kura's here. My mom's here, too. You should come. We can eat together." Now she was really crying. "Kura's here, too. We can have a nice big dinner."

"Thanks, Rika." I pressed my cheek with my right hand.

"Don't thank me. Just call a taxi and come over."

"I don't think I can."

"Just come."

"Thanks," I said. "But I think I need to be alone tonight."

*

For a while after hanging up, I stared out the windows. I made some food, but halfway through I started feeling sick. I took a shower and went straight to bed, towel wrapped around my hair.

It was only starting to get dark. The daylight gradually lost its edge, until my room was filled with bluish summer twilight. It made me wonder where the blue was coming from.

I closed my eyes and saw Sengawa. In every scene that I imagined, she was smiling. Why was that? It's not like we were always laughing. Most of the time, she looked so serious, talking about work and her idea of the novel; but now all I could remember was the times she laughed. Like when she giggled at the Christmas lights strung up all over Omotesando. I remember being surprised that she could laugh like that. Or the time she permed her hair. When I told her it looked great, she laughed like she was really happy, if a little bit embarrassed. I guess we had some laughs, I thought, gazing out my window at the evening blue.

Sengawa was dead. Everything Rika said was true. And now I had to figure some things out. I knew that. Unfortunately, my mind was in no shape to do so. Like I had been paralyzed from the neck up, blocking the parts of me that created my emotions, all the sadness and the torment, like I was no more than a living body. But that body was in pain. Not like I'd been punched or kicked or anything. I knew that I was safe there on my futon, but I was still in pain. My organs bloated in my ribcage, swollen and engorged, pushing on my muscle and fat from the inside; it felt as if any moment they might break skin.

I groped through the darkness for my phone, but when I looked through our text history, I couldn't believe my eyes. It felt like we had texted all the time, but she had only sent me seven messages.

All of them were concise blocks of text, only a few lines

long. Then it hit me. Strictly speaking, we hadn't actually ever worked together. We were in a holding pattern, just before the real work started, as the open-ended nature of our formless correspondence made so clear. It felt like we had seen each other all the time and talked about a million things, but how was I supposed to prove it? I realized that I didn't have a single picture of her. And what about her handwriting—while I had seen it on the mail and packages she sent, I hadn't kept them or retained the slightest mental image of her script. I saw her more than I saw almost anyone else. She was a good friend—in fact, one of my only friends. And yet I didn't know a thing about her. There was nothing left. The evidence was gone.

She came running up the stairs—the staircase in Midorigaoka Station, trying to catch me on the platform. That wound up being the last time that I saw her. While she was looking all around, trying to find me, we met eyes for an instant, but I had to look away. Why didn't I try to contact her? *I knew that she was right, and I was wrong.* What if I had let her finish, instead of running? It was early. We could've walked to the next station. Maybe then she would've told me she was sorry, admitting that she drank too much again. If we had made amends that night, maybe she would've let me know that she was in the hospital. We would've had the chance to talk. The thought of this made my heart sink. But who knows. She could just as soon have not wanted to contact me at all. She might have thought I didn't deserve to know the truth, that I wasn't worth it. Maybe the friendship was one-sided, and I didn't matter to her. Maybe I was just one of the many writers she had been forced to befriend as part of her job.

That time she called me late at night and we got drinks down in that basement-level bar. Sengawa was a mess. It was February, cold. My hair was wet. The bar was dark, candles flickering at the edges of the room. We talked and talked. The

bathroom equally dark. She hugged me. Had I hurt her without knowing? What did she want from me? Did she have
something to say? Or was this just a front? Had she actually
been angry with me? Mad that I was unable to write. I couldn't
finish the novel in time. She never had a chance to read it.
Maybe she had given up on me and was just going through the
motions. But regardless of whether she had actually been sin-
cere, Sengawa was the only one who cheered me on, who saw
potential in my work. She was the only one. Almost three years
earlier, on a summer day as hot as this one, she took time out
of her busy day to meet with me. To talk. That was three years
ago. But in three years, I had failed to give her anything sub-
stantial in return. She disappeared before I had the chance to
hear her thoughts.

I was up late, pondering these questions. Waves of regret,
nostalgia, loneliness, and more regret washed over me. It
seemed like I would never fall asleep. My body was heavy, and
my head hadn't cleared at all, but the longer that I stayed
awake the more alert I felt. It was as if the arteries and nerves
that linked my brain and eyes had swollen to an unnatural
degree. When I got up to use the bathroom, I couldn't help
but feel like someone was standing on the other side of the
front door. I thought that if I threw it open fast enough, I'd
find Sengawa. I actually tried it once, but obviously she wasn't
there.

Laying in the darkness of my bedroom with my eyes wide
open, there were times when things I knew I was imagining felt
real, like I could actually see them. It's possible that I was dozing off, but I was conscious that the weird scene around me
wasn't a dream but some kind of *recollection*. I was in what
seemed to be a restaurant with lofty ceilings, the big round
tables covered with white tablecloths. Nothing to eat or drink.
Sengawa sat beside me. I turned to face her, feeling both tear-
ful and furious, and asked her why she had to die like that,

without saying goodbye. Laughing nervously, she told me "Too late, Natsuko" and eyed me with concern. Rika sat across from us, crying her eyes out. For some reason Sengawa couldn't see her. Although Rika shared our table, she kept to herself, crying like crazy. On one side of her was Yuriko, holding Kura, and on the other side was Rie, holding up the silver scissors. Cutting something from a bright white sheet of paper. Some kind of floral design. Rika didn't realize anyone was there, but Yuriko patted Rika's back to comfort her.

"It's too bad."

Yuriko muttered this to no one in particular, like she was talking to herself.

"Maybe so," Sengawa said, smiling. "At least there's no more pain."

Rika put one arm around Yuriko, who was still holding Kura, and heaved her shoulders, crying with no sign of letting up.

I thought that I heard something in the kitchen, so I got up to check. My head was buzzing. My brain could've been shooting sparks. If vision is an interplay between your state of mind and whatever you see, my nervous brain was capable of seeing anything. It would've been perfectly normal to see things I couldn't normally see, or things that didn't actually exist. Except I'd never seen things in a state like this before. For a while after Mom and Komi died, I felt things stirring in the night and couldn't sleep. I scanned the room and checked behind closed doors. But I had never seen a ghost. When mom and Komi died, I never saw them again. They never visited me. This felt incredibly wrong, like an absurd injustice. For over twenty years, I hadn't seen or heard from Mom or Komi *because they died.* I wanted to scream at the top of my lungs. *Because they died!* I leaned against the fridge, checking every corner of the room for signs of life, but all was still. Not a sound.

What about Aizawa? I wondered what he was up to. I guess he'd be on call, working the night shift. He'd told me once that when he did house calls after dark, he almost always found the patient dead. And that was that, forever, because they died. Isn't that bizarre? I wanted to ask Aizawa how he felt. I wanted to talk with him about my feelings. How I'd never know what Sengawa thought of me but knew for sure that I'd lost someone special. It was all so sudden—but was she really special to me? Did I really feel that way? It was a scary thought. Did I really think that she was special? Really? What made her special? I didn't know. I didn't know! That's why I wanted to ask him.

I thought about how good it would make me feel to have Aizawa here right now. But that was impossible, and it made me want to cry. I was torturing myself. This was an emotional dead end. I was the one who told him that I couldn't see him anymore. That was the last time that I heard from him. To make matters worse, back in July, I saw him with Yuriko near the station, through the window of the Starbucks. I got the hell out of there before they noticed me.

Aizawa told me that he wished that he could see me, that not seeing me was driving him insane, but that was just a flight of fancy, or a whim. What he really needed, what I know he wanted, was to be with Yuriko. I was sure that's where his heart was. Aizawa was alive, or at least I thought he was, but if we never saw each other again, if I had seen him for the last time ever, in what sense was he alive?

My next thought caught me by surprise: was I still incapable of having sex? My pulse quickened and my face went hot. Were things as bad as they had been before?

I had convinced myself that sex would never work for me. What if things had changed? I thought this over, standing in the darkness of the kitchen. Then I pulled my shorts down to my thighs and put my hand inside my underwear, touching my vagina. Soft under my fingertips. A way inside of me. I put my fingers in. It felt like if I tried, they could go deeper. They went inside. This went nowhere. I tried using two fingers, tried being rough and being gentle. Nothing worked. I was a little wet, but that was probably just sweat from the heat. I wasn't actually aroused.

I stood there, pondering the question of sex. It went the only way it could. Every question had another question right behind it. What did it mean to be incapable, or for that matter capable of having sex? I was a grown woman, sexually mature. I knew I wasn't physically incapable. So what was stopping me? That wasn't how my body worked. That part of me, the part I had just touched, to see the way it felt—*it wasn't made for that*. It was a part of me, but that's not what it was for. I knew for sure. I'd had it forever. Of course it'd changed as I'd grown, but I'd had my vagina my whole life. No one expected me to use it as a kid, so why should I have to use it now? What's wrong with that part of me staying the way it's always been?

How come these things had to overlap? Why did caring about someone need to involve using your body? All I wanted was to have this conversation with Aizawa. To have him hear me out. So why was I obsessing over sex? Aizawa wasn't asking this from me. I was the one making this a problem. And why did I have to pick the night after Sengawa died to try and solve it?

It's for the best—Yuriko said to me. *She isn't suffering. And you—you're lucky that you've never been pushed over the edge. That part of you is still a child. Aren't you the lucky one. You have the body of a child. It can just be there. It can stay soft.*

Yuriko Zen. Still a child in her own right. Nose and checks of a young girl, a window into the night sky.

In the dark kitchen I shook my head, closing my eyes tight.

"Hey, how have you been?"

Midoriko was chipper. Her voice was comforting.

"God, it's so hot. You there?"

"I'm here, I'm here," I said. "I bet Osaka is on fire."

"Oh, it's insane. Every second I'm outside I feel like I'm gonna burst into flames," she laughed.

"I bet, same here. Hey, how's your job at the restaurant going?"

"Oh," Midoriko said. "It's wild, literally wild."

"What, what's going on?"

"Weasels." She sounded fed up.

"Weasels?" I asked. "In the restaurant?"

"Acting like they run the place. I don't even know where to begin. The whole thing has been crazy. It's crazy. The building we're in, it's gotta be pretty old. At least thirty years old. Well, before summer started, the place was kinda falling apart. We had to get everything fixed. Water, electricity, everything. That meant construction. Pretty serious construction, for the whole building."

"Oh yeah?"

"Our upstairs neighbor is super weird, though. She's all over the place, does reflexology, tells fortunes, a little consulting, all in one. It's all very 'new age,' you know? But yeah, we're in the same building, so she knows all about the construction. There are these notices posted all around the building. On this and this day, we're going to start doing X, Y and Z. Anyway, construction starts. It's pretty noisy, of course. I mean, you can't do construction without making some noise, right? But the lady upstairs, when everything got started, she ran downstairs, screaming like she thought it was the apocalypse. We were like, 'Everything's fine. It's just construction.' She muttered something to herself and left. The next day, though, the same thing happened. The same thing, all of it. At first, we thought she was probably trying to get under our skin or something, but it turned out she was serious. Hey, have you seen that movie, where that guy forgets everything right away, so he has to write it down, on paper and on the walls and stuff? *Memento*. Do you know that one? Have you seen it?"

I said I hadn't.

"Well, this was like one-day *Memento*, in real life. It was the craziest thing I've ever seen."

"Wait, what about the weasels?"

"Yeah, yeah," said Midoriko. "One day, out of nowhere, a couple of the ceiling boards broke off and this weasel came falling out."

"Into the restaurant?"

"Yeah, right where the customers sit and everything. Everyone went nuts. It's not like it's some high-end place or anything. I mean our ravioli is decent, but I don't care who you are, you're gonna flip your shit if a weasel drops in on you during lunch, right?"

"Oh yeah, for sure," I agreed.

"I mean, we have the canal right outside and the whole building is grungy anyway. I've seen weasels in the neighborhood before, running around in the middle of the night. I bet they were already in the building, though, and all the construction set them off or something. But it didn't just happen once. The weasels kept on coming. We blocked the hole the first one made, but they fell in from other spots."

"The weasels must be going crazy, too, trying to stay alive," I said. "It's good they weren't falling from the ceiling in the kitchen. If they fell into an open pot, they'd be soup."

"You're right about that," Midoriko said. "Anyway, my manager was losing his mind. He's like, I don't care how old the building is, how close the canal is, this is too weird. He got it in his head that the new-age lady upstairs was dropping weasels on us. He went upstairs to complain, but she said she had nothing to do with it, obviously. I mean, how could she? Have you ever tried catching a weasel? It's not easy."

"I can't even imagine."

"Still, though, my manager won't back down. He's convinced she's behind the weasels. So he calls an emergency staff meeting and walks us through this whole elaborate conspiracy theory—that the new-age lady upstairs has connections to some weird cult, that the whole amnesia thing was just an act . . . He was genuinely spooked, whispering the whole time like he thought the restaurant was bugged or something. I mean, he's obviously delusional, right? Anyway, it was an all-out war between us. Meanwhile, weasels keep falling on our heads. Our customers are all gone. I just wanted to lighten the mood a bit, so I said to the manager, 'We could always change our name to *The Leaning Tower of Weasel*.' But he wasn't keen on that, to say the least. He was like, 'Why the hell should we be the ones to change our name? That psycho upstairs should be changing hers.' I was just joking, but he was on a mission. He was like, next time a weasel falls in, I'm gonna grab it and send it back up where it came from. I'm gonna send them all back. So I said to him, '*Up goes the weasel*, get it?'"

"Nice one," I laughed. "But that sounds like a real disaster. Weasels can be pretty cute, but no one likes them when they're in the middle of a meal."

"Guess you're right about that," Midoriko sighed. "Anyway, Natsu . . . "

"Yeah?"

"It's almost my birthday," she cleared her throat exactly once. "You're still coming, right?"

"I'm planning on it, yeah," I said.

"But what about you and my mom?"

"What do you mean?" I asked. "Did she say something? Is she doing okay?"

"Well, she's okay. But it's clearly weighing on her, how you're not talking at all. She doesn't know what to say, or if it's cool for her to call."

"Yeah."

"She told me what happened. You really surprised her."

"Oh yeah?"

"Yeah, for sure," Midoriko laughed. "You remember that time when I was a kid? My mom and I came to visit. It was really hot, like it is now."

"Yeah, we stayed up late, waiting for your mom to come home."

"I was all worked up about my mom getting her boobs done. And now you're the one who isn't talking to her, Natsuko!" she laughed. "Forgive and forget. Come on, you're sisters!"

"I suppose you're right," I said apologetically. "You're totally right."

"Anyway, we'll see you in a week. Make sure you get on that train. We almost never get to see each other, and you promised. We'll be waiting for you."

"Got it."

"What day are you going to be here? You'll come for lunch on my birthday, right? Then spend the night with us?"

"Yeah."

"Okay, call me when you get into Osaka and see the train times. We'll meet at Shobashi. Then all three of us will go out for dinner."

When we hung up, I went out into the kitchen for a cold glass of water, which I drank standing at the sink. I went back to my room and over to the window, parted the curtains, after who knows how long, and peered outside. Leaves fluttered on the trees in front of the next building. Beyond them was the summer sky, where a textbook cloud, humungous and puffy, towered in the distance. I lost myself in its changing textures. The cloud had so many different colors. Parts were white, and other parts were gray, or tinged with blue, but as a whole it was bright white.

It had been twenty days since Sengawa died. Not long after, Rika called to tell me that from what she heard, the funeral had gone off without a hitch. The only people in attendance from the literary world were her immediate boss, an executive from the publishing company, and the female editor who she was closest to. None of her authors was invited.

"They said Sengawa looked pretty. Not skinny or anything."

"Yeah."

"Since the funeral was closed, lots of writers and friends are talking about doing something. I mean, it just doesn't feel real yet, right? It sounds like there'll be some kind of service, maybe in September or something."

"Okay."

"People are always saying how memorial services and stuff are for the living . . . "

"Yeah."

"I guess I've never been able to see the benefit," said Rika. "Whatever, I dunno."

I looked down into the street below. An old woman was coming up the mild slope, pushing her shopping cart with all her weight. She wore a white sunhat, a white open-necked shirt, and beige slacks. Nothing stood in the way of the afternoon sun. It was as if a camera flash had been drawn out indefinitely, and the trees, the asphalt, the word "STOP" spelled out on the street, the telephone poles, the old lady, her shopping cart, and all the different shadows had been captured in a giant photograph by the harsh August sun. How many summers had I been alive? The obvious answer was as many summers as my age; but for some reason I felt the presence of another number, a different, realer number somewhere out there in the world. I thought about this as I gazed into the summer glare.

Tokyo was cloudy on the final day of August. Clouds spread

in clumps across the sky, but bright blue peeked through a handful of openings, sending down shafts of light. I woke at six, pulled my old backpack from the closet for the first time in however many years, and packed two changes of underwear and socks and my toiletry kit. I must've had that bag for twenty years. It may have been beaten up, but I'd made sure to air it out once in a while. All things considered, it was in decent shape. I had a leisurely breakfast, just something simple, and a glass of mugicha, then got my stuff together and left the house.

I knew the easiest and fastest way to catch the Shinkansen was to go from Sangenjaya to Shibuya and take the Yamanote Line to Shinagawa, but I went out of my way so I could board at Tokyo Station, for two reasons: there were always tons of non-reserved seats, and I had only ever used Tokyo Station for trips to Osaka. I wasn't used to taking trains. Most days I rarely ventured further than the supermarket by the station. Besides, I'm easily disoriented. I knew that I would have a hard time navigating a bigger place like Shinagawa.

The summer air felt so good to me that morning. Though I was on my usual route, just walking the gray pavement to the station, the fact of having the street essentially to myself made me feel sharp, like when a freshly folded handkerchief is tucked into a pocket. I remembered how we used to do morning aerobics in the park during summer vacation, in elementary school. The poor kids showed up looking tired but excited. We were always wearing flip-flops. The rough sand of the playground stuck to our toes. Pigeons cooing in the background. The drainpipe, damp and cool, set in a corner of the park. Then in the afternoon, we splashed around. The smell of soggy dirt, blackened with moisture. I could have watched the spray cascading from the hose play in the light forever. Sometimes I could see Komi hanging laundry on our balcony. Watching her from a distance, pumping her arms and hanging up our clothes and underwear, without her knowing that I was watching. This was somehow both reassuring and unsettling—like she might be that far away for all eternity.

It was seven thirty when I arrived at Tokyo Station, for the first time in years. Even that early there were people everywhere, no different from the last time that I came. It felt like I had turned a corner and gone back in time, like when you're folding up a bedsheet and its top and bottom edges come together. People spilled into the concourse and slipped away in an endless cycle. The major difference from the last time I was there was the enormous number of foreign tourists, sunburned in their tank tops, dressed in little shorts and sandals like they were going camping. Their backpacks were so big that one false step would've sent them tipping backwards. The departure announcements were impossible to hear unless you focused hard on listening. There were so many different noises coming from the speakers.

I bought a nonreserved ticket bound for Shin-Osaka, where the Shinkansen pulls in. The train was waiting on the platform. I found the back of the line and waited for the doors to open. Inside, I sat down at a window seat. The train left the station soundlessly, as if pushed forward by a planetary force.

For forty minutes the Shinkansen shot ever westward through the sprawl of houses, warehouses and buildings, crossing a few big rivers in the process. I started seeing fields and empty lots. We passed through tunnel after tunnel. Soon we were in the mountains. Houses of all different shapes and sizes built into the hillside. On the empty paths between rice fields stretching off into the distance, I could see small trucks moving slowly. The black roofs of the plastic greenhouses threw back the summer light. Smoke plumed in the distance. I let the landscape pass before my eyes, preoccupied with an awareness there were things that I could see if I were dropped down like a pin along the road, or in the corner of that rice field, or along that riverbank—but I would never have a chance to see them. We're all so small, and have such little time, unable to envision the majority of the world.

Stepping off the train at Shin-Osaka, I felt humidity hit me like a wall. I had to laugh. I'd forgotten what the summers here were like. It's like a jungle. I took the stairs down from the platform, weaving through the bustling crowds. The second you're in Osaka, you feel it all around you. As I headed for my transfer, I wondered where this feeling came from. You'd think it had to do with overhearing people talk in a familiar way, but coming home after so many years, the strongest signals weren't linguistic. Maybe it was the way that people held themselves. How they made eye contact, how they walked. The differences were minor but conspicuous. It could have been their hairstyles or their sense of fashion. Or maybe it was all these things, a little bit of each. I watched the way that people moved and listened to the folks beside me talking. Once I was on the next train, I gazed out on the city through the windows. The train leaned into turns and rumbled down the tracks, uncomfortable reminders of the laws of gravity.

This didn't feel like any kind of a homecoming, laden with nostalgia. More like I'd shown up at the wrong house for a party that I hadn't been invited to. Disoriented, I felt a dim sense of regret. I checked my watch. 10:50. I'd told Midoriko that I was coming out to Osaka, as promised, but hadn't given her an ETA. Midoriko had said it'd be good if I could make it around seven. She'd meet me at the station after work, and then we'd all go out for dinner—I could've left the house midafternoon and made it there in time, but before the three of us met up I wanted to see Makiko alone, in order to apologize and set things straight between us. Makiko lived twenty minutes from Shobashi. Once I arrived, I'd grab a box of Horai pork buns, her favorite, and call her up, using the happiest voice I could muster. We could leave the house a little early, to grab some kind of little present for Midoriko along the way. It'd be great.

Unfortunately, the trip from Shin-Osaka Station to Osaka Station, and the final leg to Shobashi, hampered my enthusiasm. I wandered up and down the street, stopping repeatedly and looking back at nothing in particular. Before I knew it, I was standing in the plaza outside Shobashi Station, both hands tight on the straps of my backpack. It was getting hotter by the hour, and my sweat-drenched t-shirt stuck to my chest and back, both of which shed more sweat each time I exhaled.

For the better part of ten minutes I stood there, paralyzed and sweating, in the center of the plaza. I had to meet up with Makiko, but first I had to buy the pork buns. That was all I had to do, but another set of feelings, according to which I couldn't care less about Makiko or the pork buns, somehow got the upper hand, pulling me down. Shobashi was full of people. Coming and going, meeting one another, straddling their bicycles and talking loudly on the phone. When I used to work nearby, there was no shortage of homeless people by the station. People begging, laid out on the ground, or saying things I couldn't understand. Now all of them were gone. It looked like none of that had ever happened.

Beyond the station, I could see a sign I recognized—Rose Cafe—the light around the letters pulsing even in the daytime. Although I'd never been inside, me and Naruse used to use it as a meeting spot. Then out of nowhere I remembered Kewpie. The scam artist with the guitar, who got banged up one too many times. Makiko had said the last time she saw Kewpie was outside Rose Cafe. What was he doing there? Waiting for someone? Or maybe he'd been trying to decide where he would go, or what to do, and realized that he couldn't move. I could relate.

I walked into a sort of alley crammed with little shops. Before I'd made it very far, I was practically alone. The narrow distance between buildings made it feel much later in the day than on the plaza. The few people I passed were walking quickly. The udon counter that Mom used to bring us to at night was gone, replaced by a cell phone retailer. The ramen shop that was beside it had become the tiny franchise of a chain restaurant, and the bookstore next to that, where I used to come a little before work to browse the titles—it was nothing. The gray shutter was down, and a group of guys were sitting on the pavement outside smoking cigarettes or talking loudly on their phones.

On my last trip home, a few years back, I'd taken a bus to Makiko's from Shobashi Station. I probably hadn't walked down here in almost twenty years. A faded mouthwash banner hung askew outside what used to be the pharmacy. On the other side of an intersection, things were a bit noisier. There were adult establishments and pachinko parlors, long and narrow yakiniku restaurants. A bar in every building, and no space between the properties. A lot of them were open, but their signs were wasted on the empty street. It was hard to judge, since it was daytime, but there was almost no one here, at least compared to how it used to be. The place felt abandoned.

I continued through Shobashi in the summer heat. Atop the crooked telephone poles, a mess of power lines monopolized the narrow strip of sky. I decided to check out the building where the restaurant used to be. For old time's sake, I stepped into the lobby. Everything was different, with the exception of the elevator. A giant yellow sign fixed to the wall announced: "Relaxation for the Modern Man! DVD Rooms. Total Privacy. Entrance on F1."

I turned around and found the road back to the station.

There were a bunch of larger buildings on the other side of the street. One of them was the old hospital where Mom and Komi died. The hospital sign was branded in my memory. That was around the time the first convenience stores were popping up. One night, when Mom was already hooked up to the IV, just laying there, I told her all about the different stuff they sold at the convenience store near us. She was so tough and positive. Raising a frail arm splotched with purple bruises, she rubbed each of our hands and smiled. "You two must be exhausted. Go home and sleep." While Makiko and I were walking home, Mom died alone. I remember thinking "Mom and Komi lived around here their whole lives . . . " but caught myself. This wasn't true; Mom moved away once. From the time that she had Makiko at the hospital until I was about seven, we lived in that small town by the ocean. We were broke, so Komi took the train to visit us all the time. If Dad was home, Komi met us at the station, but if Dad was out, she came over to the house and cooked for us. Every morning, I always followed Mom out to the payphone she called Komi from. If it sounded like Komi was coming, I became totally fixated and ran down to the station, literally hours early, to sit down by the ticket gate and wait for her. When she arrived, I jumped into her arms. I loved her smell.

I looked up the directions to our old station by the harbor on my smartphone, to see how long it took to get there from Shobashi. You had to switch trains twice, but it was just twenty-eight minutes. That seemed impossible. I knew it wasn't far—or knew that now, but not when I was little. Back then, I chased down Komi every time she had to leave. Her house seemed so far away. Those visits kept us alive. I sobbed watching her go. But she had lived under thirty minutes away.

I could smell the harbor from the station. I hadn't been back here in thirty years. Not since the night the three of us escaped.

The inside of the station looked completely different, except for the two stairways to the left and right, outside the ticket gate. A fairly large crowd of people got off with me, chattering about the heat. They couldn't wait to make it down to street level. Back when we lived here, there was nothing but the harbor. It was only ever busy once a year, in summer, for the tall ships. About ten years after we left, they built this huge aquarium. It was a big deal. The harbor used to be a wasteland. Steely warehouses the length of city blocks. Waves battering the shoreline. Salty air. That's it. I remember the time dad told me everything was soon going to be levelled for a huge construction project. He'd had so many beers his face was like a red balloon. I asked how soon was soon. He laughed and said it would be done in ten or twenty years.

I paused on the landing of the stairs to watch the sea. The sweeping roof of the aquarium shone white with summer light. Beside it was a giant ferris wheel.

After we moved in with Komi when I was seven, sometimes I thought about the place we'd lived in until we had to run away. It always made me sad and sorry. Like everything we'd left behind was watching me—the gaunt stray dogs, the broken bottles, the gum spat out on the sidewalk. Stained futons, dishes piled in the sink, angry voices in the distance. Sometimes I felt like I had left myself behind. Like I was still in bed, beside my bookbag packed for Tuesday. Waiting for something. Confused about what happened, overlooked in all the chaos, unable to get up from where I was.

The busiest street in town was lined with taxis. It used to make me so afraid I held my breath each time I crossed it. Now there were loads of people here for the aquarium. On the other side, down on the corner, I saw an udon shop and recognized the name. This was the udon shop my classmate's family ran. I peered inside. It was lunchtime, and the place was packed. Everything about the street, besides the udon shop, had changed. Now it was one long row of gift shops for the tourists. Then again, it's not like I could tell you what kinds of

businesses or buildings used to be here. I went into a convenience store and bought two onigiri and a bottle of water. Then
I continued down the street, sweating every step of the way.

I checked my watch. Twelve-thirty. The sun was blazing
overhead. If you squinted, you could see a rainbow-colored
ring around it. Beads of sweat were dripping from my scalp
and temples. I could almost hear the sun scorching my hair and
skin.

Up ahead I saw a place I recognized. The little sign above
the door said "Cosmos." I drifted toward it, as if it had me in
its thrall. This was the lunch spot that my mom had worked at
part time. Komi had brought me here for lunch a few times,
when Mom was working. Seeing us walk in the door put this
huge smile on her face, like she felt safe. It filled my heart to
watch her zipping around behind the counter in her red apron,
answering enthusiastically when called, washing the dishes,
serving food. Komi looked at me and smiled. "Your mom's a
trouper." I nodded. She sure was.

I imagined myself opening the door to Cosmos and thanking them for hiring my mom. Telling them she had worked
there over thirty years ago. How I had visited a few times with
my grandmother, and how watching my mother hard at work
had almost made me cry. I thanked them for making me a ham-
burger I was almost too emotional to eat, but had eaten anyway. It had been so delicious. But there was no way I could do
it. I took a sip of water, stared at the door of Cosmos for a second, and walked over to a bench under a patch of shade to eat
my onigiri.

When I was finished, I sat and watched the people come
and go along the main road leading straight to the aquarium. I
looked around and noticed all the ways the town had changed
while leaving pockets of the town I used to know. It made me
wonder why my mother moved us out here in the first place.
How had it made her feel the first time that she saw this town

and smelled the salty air? Had it filled her heart with dreams and expectations for this new life with her family? I realized that I'd never asked my mom about her early life, before she was a mother.

What happened to the building that the four of us had lived in, me and Makiko and Mom and Dad? If it was still there, all I'd have to do is head back to the udon shop, turn right, and walk a couple of blocks. When we were living there, I think there was a yakitori spot next door, and an okonomiyaki spot this lady ran herself, and next to that a little artificial pond with all these giant goldfish. I remember how they swam, weaving through the dark green algae. On the corner was a greengrocer that must have been there since the war. They didn't have a register, just a basket bungeed to the ceiling where they kept the cash. They always let Mom put the shopping on her tab, but they never seemed the least resentful, and smiled and laughed whenever I was with her. The hair salon was close by, down a side street. The owner liked to tell you one of his old stylists had become a stunt-man, how if you watched carefully you could see him on TV. He always told you the same story, with the same absurd enthusiasm. At night, I went down to the ground floor of our building, by the izakaya, and sat down on the stoop outside the hallway, where I waited for Mom to come home from work.

I wanted to see it all again, but quickly reconsidered, knowing that there wasn't any point. I sighed under my breath. This wasn't why I'd come to Osaka. What was I doing out here? Brushing sweat off of my skin with a stiff finger, I watched the people walking up and down the street. The front of the building had been all tiles, brown and shiny. A strange brown for a building. I remember thinking how the tiles looked like caramel. If you went all the way down the hallway by the iza-kaya, you reached the stairway, by the metal mailboxes set into the wall. Was any of this still there? I was a little kid, no real possessions, but whatever I did have I had left behind, never to return. Could that place really be a short walk from the bench where I was sitting? It felt impossible, but there was only one way to find out. I guess the building could still be there. Who knows about the rest. But if the building was still there, what was I supposed to do? Why was I obsessing over this? There was nothing monumental about checking out a neighborhood you used to live in. So why was I in turmoil? I was terrified, though not entirely sure why. The thought of seeing our old building made me weak in the knees.

I went back to the convenience store for another bottle of water and drank it taking little sips. Then I went over to the bench again and let the scenery wash over me. I checked my watch. Just past two. I knew that I should probably make my way back to Shobashi and call Makiko, and while I'm at it, text Midoriko to say I'd made it to Osaka. That made the most sense. Except I couldn't leave the bench. I couldn't go.

Two girls wearing matching outfits, obviously sisters, swung their turquoise backpacks as they rushed to catch up with their mother. The first one jumped beside her and the second threw her arms around her waist. The three of them walked off together laughing. I watched them until I couldn't see them anymore, then wiped the sweat off of my face. I finally stood up and swung my backpack into place, then turned right at the udon shop, heading in the direction of our building.

One block away from the main drag, all signs of tourism disappeared. The street was quiet. The summer sun was indiscriminate, beating down on the deserted streets and buildings. I knew the way. I checked out every house and storefront that I passed. Some places looked remodeled, but it was mostly buildings that I'd never seen before. On the right there was a tiny empty lot that I was sure had been the laundromat. I spent a lot of rainy days inside there, sitting on the benches, surrounded by the smell of drying clothes, watching giant raindrops travel down the windows.

The greengrocer had turned into a little house. Its blue-gray exterior had such sharp lines it looked like origami. Hard to say how new it was. There was a steel door on the left. No curtains on the windows, but because the glass was frosted, I couldn't tell if anybody lived there. The cafe to the right was basically as I remembered it, except the shutter looked like it had been down for ages. I walked at a leisurely pace. No one in sight, and literally not a sound. As if the sun had swallowed all the sounds and all the people. On the right there was a metered parking lot without a single car. Right—there used to be a house here. People coming in and out all day. I couldn't tell you what they did inside, but the door was always open. They had a giant mutt. Her name was Sen. What a sweetheart. Always panting on the concrete by the door. One time I saw Sen giving birth to puppies. Popping out of her like glassy organs, slick and individually wrapped in cloudy film. Sen licked her newborn puppies clean. Eyes pinched shut, they yapped and bobbed their little snouts, searching for her teats. I remembered the smell of the doggie bed, the way their tongues hung from their mouths. The black tear stains around their eyes. I stopped to take a look around—and there was our old building, standing right in front of me.

I gazed up, taking it all in.

The caramel-colored tiles. The storefront on the ground floor, several iterations later. A pale green overhang I never saw before, where the sign for the last failed business had been painted over, making the characters indecipherable. The shutter patched with rust and covered with mildew. The building was so small. You could've barely parked a couple of bikes outside. There was a narrow entrance to the right, the hallway leading to the stairs to our apartment. I pursed my lips. I knew it would look small, but not this small. The entryway was barely wide enough to fit through. You almost had to turn your body sideways. The little concrete stoop between the sidewalk and the entrance, where I always used to sit, was the same concrete gray. I can vividly remember the day some guy showed up in work clothes and filled the crack in the pavement outside the entryway with concrete, to make a little slab. He told me to stay away until it dried. When he was gone, and I'd made sure the coast was clear, I held my breath and poked the drying concrete with my finger. I crouched down to investigate. It was still there: a tiny dent that looked like it might disappear before my eyes. Waiting for Mom, I used to lean against the caramel tiles and press my finger in the dent I made.

I took a breath and stepped inside.

The hall was dark and damp. The air had a mildewy edge. The building looked abandoned, standing up against the sands of time, like it was waiting to be torn down. The rusty metal mailboxes cut through the shadows by the stairs. The little stairwell. With every step I felt an old sensation rising from inside of me like goosebumps. I drew another breath and climbed the stairs. They could only fit one person at a time. Komi used to carry me upstairs on her back. Sometimes I played in the stairwell with Makiko or screamed and chased Mom up and down the steps. I remember watching my dad go down first, hands stuffed into his pockets, on one of the few occasions that we left the house together, as a family.

On the third floor was a door finished with a wood veneer. A tiny little door. I knew it well. I gazed at the imitation wood, full of memories, and turned the doorknob. The door was locked. I tried again. Locked for sure.

I wiped my forehead, rubbed my eyes. Gripping the knob, I tried jiggling the door. It wouldn't open. I tried knocking. The door rattled, creaking from its hinges. I knocked a little harder, like I was in a hurry, like I was being chased. Now I was really pounding. If I could open up this door, maybe I would find them. Coming upstairs, carrying my bookbag. Mom opening the door for me. Saying welcome home in her red apron. If I could open up this door, maybe I would see my favorite sweatshirt and my bookbag and my doll, where we laughed and where we slept, the little heated table that we sat around. The wood post where we carved our heights. The red plastic cups in the cupboard. I'd open up that window once and for all. Maybe everything would be the way it used to. I knew the answer, knew that it was no, but I knocked anyway. Banging down on the little door of our old house. What about Dad? Did he remember anything? After he up and disappeared one day. Wherever he was now, did he remember? Did he ever think about the years he lived with us? Did he remember us at all?

I sat down in the stairwell and tried to breathe. The floor was cracked. Everything was dirty. Muddy buildup in the corners. The air was damp, and the space at the top of the stairs was piled with trash. Cardboard crumbling with moisture. A dirty mop stuck in a faded plastic bucket. A stiff rag draped over the side. A black trash bag filled with who knows what. Everything covered in dust. Light coming through a tiny window lit up a corner of the landing.

I heard music. At first, I didn't understand. I sat up like I'd been punched in the arm and put my hand over my throat. It was my phone. My phone was ringing. I remembered I still hadn't said anything to Midoriko. I swung my bag off of my shoulder, undid the zipper, and found my phone.

"Hello? It's Aizawa."

"I know," I said, my voice unexpectedly hoarse. I gulped. "Natsuko?"

From the way he said my name, Aizawa sounded nervous.

"You really surprised me," I said, straight up. "I wasn't expecting you to call."

"Sorry about that," he said. "I'm a little surprised myself. I didn't know if you'd pick up."

"It was ringing, so . . . "

"Hey, Natsuko?"

"Yeah?"

"You sound a little funny. Everything okay?"

"Oh, I'm fine," I sighed into the phone. "You startled me is all."

"I'm sorry."

"No, I'm fine now."

"Is this an okay time?"

"Sure," I said. My heart was beating like crazy. I took deep breaths, hoping he wouldn't notice. I could hear Aizawa breathing on the other end.

"I know you said we wouldn't be seeing each other anymore, and . . . "

He sighed and cleared his throat.

"Since that day, I've thought a lot about it. About us not talking, and not meeting. If that's how you feel, well, you've already said as much . . . I'm not trying to change your mind, but I'd just like to say my part."

"Okay . . . "

"I'm hoping we could meet and talk . . . " he said. "That's why I called."

For a while we were quiet. It was so strange to be sitting in this stairwell after thirty years, listening to Aizawa and hearing my voice echo in the dark, familiar hallway. It felt like I was floating, caught in someone else's dream. I pressed the phone into my ear and blinked repeatedly.

"Hey," I said. "Isn't today your birthday?"

"You remembered."

"How could I forget?"

"I guess it helps I share it with your niece."

"That's not why," I laughed.

"Natsuko . . . "

"Yeah?"

"Have you been okay?"

"Me?"

"Yeah."

"These past two months—" I said. "I don't know, it feels like a lot has happened."

For another moment we were quiet.

"I'm where I used to live, a long time ago," I said brightly.

"Where you used to live?"

"Yeah. I told you about it, in the spring. The place we lived when I was really little."

"By the harbor?"

"That's the one," I laughed. "It's so much smaller than I remember, everything about it. I can't believe it. I'm sitting on the stairs, inside, and they're so unbelievably small. It's been like thirty years. No one even lives here now. Not surprised . . . "

"It's just you? On the stairs?"

"Just me. There isn't even room for someone to get by, that's how small they are. It's older now, and dingier, but it's the same old place. It's abandoned. Like a ruin."

"Hey, uh, Natsuko."

"Yeah?"

"For the past two months, I've been trying to figure out how I could see you again." Aizawa said. "I knew that you'd be in Osaka today. You told me so, last time we spoke."

I nodded.

"I thought that, if I were in Osaka today, and if you picked up the phone, maybe you'd be okay with meeting up with me. For just ten or twenty minutes," Aizawa clarified. "All I knew is that you'd be in Osaka today, though."

"Are you—" I said. "Are you in Osaka?"

"Just give me thirty minutes," he said. "That's all I'm asking."

When I hung up, the same silence prevailed. I sat there in

the stairwell, gripping the pull straps of my backpack. When I finally stood up, I took another look at our old door. I stared at the peeling imitation wood and at the numbers "301." I pressed my hand against the roughness of the wall and gave the door one final look, then took a deep breath.

Taking one step at a time, I made it to the bottom. I stood up straight and lifted my chin, looking straight down the hall. Sunlight spilling through the narrow entryway. I watched the light until my vision blurred with tears.

17.
NOT LETTING GO

The wind from the harbor hit me in invisible waves, leaving a tidal residue on my skin.

Aizawa met me at the station fifty minutes later. I was standing in the exact same place I used to wait for Komi as a kid. When I saw him at the ticket gate, it made me dizzy, like I couldn't stand up straight. Noticing me, he nodded slightly, then nodded again once he was through the turnstiles. I nodded back. We hadn't seen each other in four months. He was wearing a white long-sleeved shirt and beige trousers.

Heading nowhere in particular, the two of us went down the stairs and blended into the crowds on the main street. We started walking. For a while, neither of us spoke. I was on the left, and Aizawa on the right. I focused on the movement of my feet, but when I looked up, our eyes met. Instinctively I looked away, sending my eyes back to my footsteps.

"It's sudden, I know," Aizawa said in a low voice. "I went too far, didn't I?"

"No, no." I shook my head. "I just didn't see this coming. It's a little surreal, walking here with you. I can't believe I'm here with you."

"I get that," he said apologetically. "I'm sorry. I know I kind of forced you into this."

"It's fine," I said. "I'm just meeting my sister at seven. What would you have done if I wasn't in Osaka?"

"I don't know." He sounded troubled. "Turn around and go right back to Tokyo?"

"Sure, what else?" I laughed. Aizawa joined me. "Hey, can you smell the ocean?" I pointed at the aquarium. "The water's right down there. Not even a ten-minute walk. See that giant building? That's the aquarium. It's a huge tourist attraction. You see the ferris wheel?"

"I think I've heard about this place. They have some really rare species, right? Have you ever been inside?"

"Nope. I haven't been down here in almost thirty years."

"Has it changed much?"

"I don't know. The roads are the same. Some of the shops are the same, too. See that udon place?" I asked. "I know the family that runs it. That's their name on the sign. They had a son my age. I wonder if he's running the place now. Not like I could show my face in there."

"Why not?"

"We were so poor, we went to bed hungry all the time. We couldn't afford to go to the supermarket. The local grocer let us shop on credit, but that only went so far each month. When my grandma couldn't come and save us, my mom would place an order here. We didn't have a phone at home. So she had to use the payphone. She called and asked for two orders of plain noodles, for delivery. When they showed up at the door, I'd say my mom was out."

Aizawa nodded, eager to hear more.

"I'd say she didn't leave me any money, and that I'd tell her what happened once she was home."

"What did he say to that?"

"He'd look at me for a second, scratching his head, and ask how she had called if she was out, but always ended up leaving us the noodles. Once a restaurant is out with a delivery, there's no use taking it back. The noodles get soggy, and no one else is going to want them. If the food's warm, they'll leave it behind. That's what my mom said. It wasn't a good thing to do, she said, but someday we'd make it right. Once she got paid.

While all of this was happening, my mom would be up on the roof, watching the street below. Once she saw the udon guy take off, she'd come downstairs so we could eat. Their son, though, he was my age, you know? I could never face him now. I didn't realize it back then, but he was really nice to me. He must have known what was going on, but never called me out. That was so nice."

"Sounds like your mom was pretty great." Aizawa was impressed.

"Yeah," I laughed. "Whenever they turned off the electricity or the gas or the water, she knew how to fiddle with the valves to turn it on again. That really got us through."

"What a lady."

"She really was."

"You lived here until you were how old?" he asked.

"We left the summer I was seven, a couple of months after I started first grade."

"Was that near here?"

"The school?" I asked. "It's two blocks that way and all the way down. I remember taking pictures, after the first day of school, over by the gate. But that picture is gone, like all the rest."

"I'd like to see it," Aizawa said. "Your old school, I mean."

Falling in with the people heading toward the aquarium, we started off in the direction of the school. Almost all the shops were shuttered in the small shopping arcade along the way. I told Aizawa stories as they came back to me. That used to be the stationery store the school told us to visit for supplies. They had an old white cat. It was always sprawled out on the counter by the register. That empty lot where all the weeds are growing used to be a takoyaki spot. The place was always packed. They had a cute picture of Lum Invader from *Urusei Yatsura* on the sign. The old lady who ran the shop had painted it herself. She drew me Lum a bunch of times, like it was nothing. I used to think she was the one who created her. Next to that was the bedding store that got broken into that one time. It was a major neighborhood event. Everybody showed up at the crime scene. That was the first time I saw someone taking finger-prints, using that silvery powder. I told Aizawa how sometimes I still imagined the detective fluffing the posts with his big powder puff. He listened carefully to everything I said, nod-ding as I pointed out the buildings or the empty lots where buildings used to be. Once we made it through the arcade and crossed the street, I could see the school.

"This is the place," I said. "But I was barely here. I started in the spring, then we left that summer."

"I don't know," Aizawa said, gazing up at the school. "A couple of months can feel like a long time at that age."

"I was always getting bullied for being poor," I said. "There was this one girl who was really nice to me, though. She was poor, too. The other kids were always making fun of us, but she and I had each other."

"Yeah."

"I wonder how she felt after we vanished. I bet she was so confused. No explanation. One day we were gone. What was that like for her?"

Aizawa nodded.

"If that happened now, we'd have all these ways to stay con-nected. We could've texted or used social media. When we were kids, we didn't have anything like that. Besides, we were on the run. I couldn't exactly sit down and write her a letter, right?"

"Guess not."

"I thought about that girl a lot. I hope she's doing good."

Aizawa nodded sympathetically and wiped away the sweat with his handkerchief. The temperature was stifling, but despite the overwhelming heat and humidity, his hair was neat as ever, swept back like reeds in water. We crossed the street and stopped in front of the school. You could see straight through the lobby to the sunbaked schoolyard where we had gym. After standing there for a while, looking at the school, we started walking with the flow of people coming from the busy street. We were heading toward the water. It got more crowded as we went. Around a corner, we found ourselves by the aquarium. It was way bigger than I thought. I was awestruck.

"Look at this view," I said and sighed. "It used to be nothing but warehouses, as far as the eye can see."

"It's so big."

We walked up an enormous bank of stairs and went inside. Sweat chilled my skin.

"Whew, get a load of that AC," I said. "This place has its own climate."

"Tell me about it," Aizawa laughed. "What a cool place."

The aquarium wasn't out of control crowded, but there were people everywhere. Families, young couples. Kids running back and forth between the cafe and the gift shop. We got ourselves iced coffees and sat down on a bench to people watch. Some young people were pointing at the giant aquarium floor guide, so excited that they weren't sure where to start. Elaborate displays directed patrons toward the special exhibits. As a photo opportunity, there was a penguin with its face cut out, where two teenage girls were snapping pictures of each other. A group of schoolkids gathered around the station set up for the aquarium's official stamp. Whenever one of the kids slammed the big stamp in their notebook, there was a cry of victory. Helium balloons of starfish, seahorses, turtles and flounder bobbed and spun by the entrance to the gift shop. An old woman grabbed what must have been her granddaughter by the hand and commented on all the things that she was doing wrong.

"Have you been to a lot of aquariums?" I asked.

"Not really," he said. "Not like I have anything against them. They just haven't been a big part of my life. What's the best time for an aquarium? A hot day like today? Then again, I could see the appeal in a winter visit."

"I'd like to see the penguins in winter," I said. "That must be when they're in their element. I've only been to the aquarium a couple of other times, not like we're really in it now. We're just sitting in the lobby."

We sipped on our iced coffees, watching the people walking by and all the kids running around. Neither of us said anything. Aizawa looked like he had something on his mind, but he could just as easily have only been focusing on all the things happening in front of him.

"There's something that I want to tell you," he said finally.

I looked at his face.

"It's about Yuriko. Maybe it doesn't mean anything to you, but for what it's worth . . . " Aizawa nodded, looking me in the eye. "It's over."

He nodded softly, looking down at the cup of iced coffee in his hands.

"Things ended soon after the last time you and I talked on the phone, I guess two months ago. She and I met up and talked things over. I told her what I was thinking, what I'd been thinking for a few months at that point. I was as direct as possible. I told her there was someone else. Someone I'd rather be with."

My jaw dropped. I was staring at Aizawa.

"What'd she say?"

"She said to do whatever I had to do. Typical for her, I suppose. She didn't ask me who it was, or what came next. She didn't ask me anything."

"Then what?"

"Then . . . nothing." Aizawa sighed. "That was it. When I got quiet, she told me to stop taking things so seriously. She said she knew it wasn't going to last, so the sooner it ended the better."

Aizawa was quiet. I didn't ask him to elaborate.

We sat beside each other on the bench, not saying anything. The condensation on my iced coffee wet my palms. My sweaty body started to feel chilly. My skin was prickly; it almost felt like it was fizzing. Aizawa leaned forward, propping his elbows on his knees, and gazed down at the lid of his iced coffee. High up on the wall, a clock decorated with all kinds of different sea creatures said that it was half past four. An announcement echoed overhead. Groups of girls walked past us carrying bags from the gift shop. Prompted by nothing in particular, we stood up and walked outside.

A steam whistle blared off in the distance, like it was slicing through the thick membrane of heat lining the atmosphere. At the edges of the sea breeze you could detect a hint of summer night. The shadows were growing longer, and the light in the west appeared to take on richness. The very start of evening. Neither of us said a word, one footstep after another.

The ferris wheel I thought was still far off was right in front of us. I stopped and looked up to watch it spinning. The cabins, alternating white and green, rose up into the evening sky. Aizawa stood beside me, watching the cabins go.

"I wonder what this place looks like," I said, "all the way up there."

"I'm picturing the town, the ocean," said Aizawa. "But I bet it's mostly sky."

There weren't so many people lined up in front of the ferris wheel. When I looked over at Aizawa, he raised his eyebrows, asking if I wanted to get on. I looked up again. The ferris wheel was huge. Too big to take it all in. You could barely see the cabins at the very top. Imagining myself moving at that height made me feel dizzy. I gripped the straps of my backpack. Aizawa looked at me again, seeking confirmation. When

I nodded, he walked up and bought us a pair of tickets, then came back and gave me mine.

We went to the back of the line and waited for our turn. When a gondola arrived, the next couple or little group boarded as soon as the pair of female attendants flanking the gate gave them the okay. Soon it was us. Ducking down, Aizawa slid himself inside. I hesitated, unsure of my footing, but grabbed the bar beside the hatch and hopped in after him.

The ferris wheel revolved so gently that I wasn't sure if it was moving. Our cabin didn't rock at all, but we were rising. We sat across from one another, looking out our little windows. They must have been made from some special kind of plastic. If you looked closely, you could see that they were marred with countless tiny scratches, and that they were fogging up, however slightly. The cabin climbed into the sky, nudging its way up into the summer evening. The roof of the aquarium sank before our eyes, and the trees in the neighboring park and all the different buildings in the area were getting smaller. We had a clear view of the ocean. The water was a dark gray, something between ash and lead, striated by gentle waves. Scattered boats, like fingers tracing the surface of the ocean, left white wakes on the water, staying their course. Aizawa gazed off into the distance.

"When I was a kid," I said, "it never occurred to me this was the ocean."

"What do you mean?"

"I thought that it was something else. I obviously knew that we lived by the water. I could smell low tide and hear the waves. I mean, I knew it was the ocean, just not, you know, the real ocean."

"Real?"

"Like beaches in photographs or stories," I said. "Know what I mean? Sun shining over the blue water, white sand. I guess sometimes the sand isn't exactly white, but there's plenty of it. Waves crashing. You can walk right down to the water if you want and touch it, dip your toes in. I guess I always thought that was the ocean."

Aizawa nodded.

"This place was nothing like that," I continued. "The water wasn't blue, and there was definitely no place to dip your toes in. Just deep and dark, like a bottomless pit. When I was a kid, it always made me wonder. How can this be the ocean?"

"Does it make sense to you now?"

"To be honest, not really."

We continued our gradual ascent. As we took on elevation, the ocean changed in color and in breadth, and the horizon drew a faint line along the limit of the sky. High above us, in the haze, black birds were coasting on the air. White smoke rose from a factory in the distance.

"You can see so much up here," said Aizawa. "I used to go on ferris wheels all the time, with my dad."

"With your dad?"

"Yeah. My mother never cared for amusement parks. My dad didn't like the rides himself, but he still took me all the time. He'd wait in line with me, then hang out by the exit while I did the rides alone. Sometimes, if I looked down from the high point of the rollercoaster, just before the drop, and saw him down there, like a little speck, it made me really sad, but when he waved to me, I felt incredible," Aizawa laughed. "The only ride my dad would ever go on was the ferris wheel. I guess he liked them. At the end of the day, right before we left, we always rode the ferris wheel together. We saw so many different views, from all the ferris wheels at all the different amusement parks."

Aizawa rubbed his eyelids.

"You know the Voyager?" he asked.

"The Voyager? You mean the NASA probe?"

"Exactly," Aizawa said. "There's actually two of them.

Voyager 1 and Voyager 2. Both launched 40 years ago, towards the end of summer. Voyager 2 was first, then Voyager 1 went up about two weeks later. It's funny, we're basically the same age as them. They're still out there, the size of cows, floating through space 12 billion miles away."

"Whoa, 12 billion miles . . . " I said.

"The number is so big it doesn't even register, right?" Aizawa said. "I was reading this article that tried to put the distance into context. If you were on the Shinkansen, traveling 185 miles per hour, it would take you 7,200 years to reach these things. At that distance, if you said hello to someone on the phone, it'd take a day and a half for their response to reach you."

"Damn."

"Right? My dad talked about the Voyager program and the probes whenever we were on a ferris wheel."

I nodded.

"Everywhere they go, they take photos and send back the data. Pictures of moons or Saturn's rings, or those famous images of Jupiter and the Great Red Spot. They even took pictures of Neptune, in the deepest reaches of our solar system. After thirty-five years in space, the probes left our solar system behind. Just think about that. They've made it further into space than anything else we've ever created. It's been years since the probes completed their original mission, but they keep on flying, further away, maintaining contact with the earth."

"For forty years."

"Yeah," Aizawa said. "Hurtling through total darkness, toward Sagittarius. It's hard to grasp the distance between heavenly bodies, but in terms of time, it'll be another 40,000 years before the Voyager passes the next star. I say pass, but the two of them will barely come within two light years of each other."

"In 40,000 years," I said.

"Amazing, right? If I was sulking on the ferris wheel, not wanting to go home, or otherwise bent out of shape, like if I'd been fighting with a friend or Mom had yelled at me, my dad would say: 'When things get rough, just think about the Voyager.' He told me it was always out there, flying through the darkness. Not metaphorically. Literally there. At any given moment, somewhere on earth, it was directly overhead."

I nodded.

"Kind of a lot to tell a kid. But I think I understand what he was saying. We're always getting caught up in our problems, but what's 100 years? Human lives are so short. The whole of human history is nothing, up against the depths of outer space. I don't think he was trying to tell me I was going to die at some point or anything like that. It wasn't about me at all. More like saying there would come a time when the sun has fizzled out, when human beings and this planet no longer exist, but the Voyager would still be out there, drifting ever deeper into space."

I nodded.

"You know about the golden record?"

"What's that?" I asked.

"The Voyager is carrying a record filled with the sounds of our planet. Waves, wind, lightning, birds. Greetings in over fifty languages. Music from across the globe. Information about human reproduction, our anatomy, the way our bodies change. The colors as we perceive them, the things we eat, the things we care about. Our daily lives. Deserts, oceans, mountains, animals, musical instruments . . . Science, culture, everything. It's all on this record. There's a record player too, so you can hear it play."

I imagined a single record made of gold.

"Someday, if someone in another galaxy finds the probe, and they can make sense of that record, they'll get a sense of who we were. By that time, we'll be long gone, all of us. But at least we left a record. In that sense, our memory could live on.

That's how my dad saw it. Hearing him talk this way put me in a bizarre headspace. It reminded me that someday I'd be gone, just like everything around me. Sometimes it made me wonder if I was even alive. Like, what if this was all a dream in someone else's head, you know?"

Aizawa smiled.

"He used to tell me, 'People are strange, Jun. They know nothing lasts forever, but still find time to laugh and cry and get upset, laboring over things and breaking things apart. I know it seems like none of it makes sense. But son, these things make life worth living. So don't let anything get you down.' I was just a kid, but I think I knew what he was trying to say."

I nodded.

"When we were on our way home, I always thought about the space probe traveling through space, carrying all our memories, slipping further and further away."

Aizawa cracked a smile and looked out the window. Somehow we had made it past the top and were beginning our descent, like we were drawing a circle in the summer dusk that no one would ever see. We gazed out over the harbor, at the bands of blue spreading across the sky.

"When I think about you, I remember the way that felt," he said. "Every time."

I didn't respond.

"Once I met you, I realized," he said. "I'd been spending all my time trying to find my father, thinking that was my only hope of discovering who I was. I thought that if I didn't know him, I couldn't know myself."

"Yeah."

"As if I'm stuck being the way I am because I'll never find this man."

"Yeah."

"Maybe there's some truth to that, but now I have a sense of what's really at the heart of it. I realize what's been bothering me all along, ever since I heard the truth, is that I never got to tell my dad, I mean the dad who raised me, how I felt."

I looked at Aizawa.

"I wish I could've found out earlier, when he was still alive. I would've told him that it didn't change the way I felt, that he was still my dad, as far as I was concerned."

Aizawa turned his back to me, facing the window. The few clouds we had seen on our way up had been dispersed across the sky, and a gentle rosy glow was suffusing them, the way that ink might stain a dampened napkin. The light entered our cabin, casting a faint, quivering halo around Aizawa's hair. I went over to sit next to him and touched his shoulder. His back was broad and his shoulders were wide, but when I touched him, making contact for the first time, my palm connected with the boy he used to be, touching Aizawa as a child—like I was reaching out through space and time. The cabin clicked its way back down to earth. We shared a window, looking out over the harbor and the town, catching the remaining light so that they almost seemed to breathe.

We hopped down from the cabin, sunset pressing on our backs. I took a deep breath, filling my lungs with the summer twilight. The sea breeze caressed my skin; and as we walked back toward the station, it felt like we were plowing through the start of night.

Back on the main street, we saw the lights of the udon shop on the right and joined the steady march of people. As we approached the stairway to the station, Aizawa turned to me and spoke. His voice was gentle, but it hit me.

"Natsuko, if you're still considering having a child, how about having it with me?"

We kept on walking, heading up the stairway. Aizawa tried asking me again, speaking as softly as before.

"If you still want to have a kid, to have that presence in your life, I could—"

My heart was beating so aggressively I almost lost my footing, but I took one step at a time. We cleared the ticket gates and boarded the next train. Sitting quietly, we watched the sunset through the windows, slipping over the horizon.

"Natsu! You're here!"

When I parted the noren and stepped into the restaurant, I spotted Makiko and Midoriko sitting at a table in the middle of the crowded room. Midoriko was standing in her seat, waving me over. She smiled when she said my name.

"I see you, I see you!" I said, trying to play it cool.

Makiko was sitting straight up in her chair. From the way she bit her lip, it was hard to tell if she was grinning, upset, or about to cry. When I sat down at the table, she nodded several times and gave me a real smile.

We wound up meeting at this okonomiyaki spot in Shobashi. Makiko had already ordered a mug of beer, and it was half gone. Midoriko was drinking mugicha. Over the hot plate set into our table, the air crackled with the sounds of sizzling konjac and bean sprouts frying, and the sweet and savory aroma of okonomiyaki sauce undulated like a memory through the room. When my beer came, Makiko screamed happy birthday to Midoriko and we had a proper toast, clacking our glasses.

"I can't believe you're twenty-one," said Makiko fondly. "Look at how big you are."

"You're so young," I laughed. "Enjoy it while you can."

"I'll try," said Midoriko, grinning.

Makiko told us all about this new girl who had started at the bar, and how her plastic surgery was way too obvious. At first Makiko and all the other hostesses treaded lightly, since no one had the nerve to bring it up, but pretty soon the girl was telling everyone about the place she had her eyelids done and what it cost, or where she went to have the hyaluronic acid treatment for her chin, or where she went to have her nose remodeled. She made it sound like she was talking about makeup. Makiko had been taken by her frankness.

"It's so interesting. Her face is like a parade float. Everyone's like that now. I mean, what's there to be ashamed of?"

"Sure," Midoriko said, "but why would a girl who spends that much on her face start working at a bar like yours?" She took a bite of konjac. "There's lots of flashier spots with younger staff and better pay."

"I guess she used to work somewhere that paid pretty good, but they had a quota and the competition was too much for her. We're not like that. We let the girls wear warm clothes when it's cold out, and we try to make them feel at home. That's why they stick around. Besides, this girl works days at a nail salon." Makiko ate some bean sprouts. "Check it out. She did these for me earlier this week. Pretty cute, right?"

Makiko showed off her nails, done up in a pearly pink. She wiggled her fingers and we all had a good laugh. Midoriko talked about the Kripke she was reading, segueing into how things were going with Haruyama. It sounded like things were going well. She showed me pictures of a hike they went on recently.

"You guys are pretty outdoorsy, huh," I remarked.

Midoriko shook her head and said that Haruyama liked to write haiku, which meant he sometimes dragged her on these inspirational treks. I took another look at the picture. Both of them were smiling. Their youth was dazzling, like they were wrapped in light.

The server brought over the okonomiyaki and yakisoba. We divvied it up and focused temporarily on eating. For a few minutes, all we talked about was how hot or delicious all the food was.

"Hey, Midoriko, what happened with the weasels?" I asked.

"Oh," she said. "They're gone."

"Just like that?"

"Yeah. It was so weird."

"Did you have an exterminator come or something?"

"No, they just vanished."

"Out of the blue," Makiko said. "Gone."

"It was weird. The woman upstairs stopped bothering us," Midoriko said between mouthfuls. "It was like it never happened. They finished the construction, too."

"What happened?" I laughed. "Did they die or something?"

"Everyone's fine. I guess the weasels found somewhere else to live. Wow, this stuff is super good."

After dinner, we got on a bus and rode back to Makiko and Midoriko's apartment. It was a short walk from the bus stop. This was my first visit in years. When I saw their building down the street through the warm evening air, I felt something like a cross between heartache and reassurance. Our footsteps echoed up the metal steps. We spent the rest of the night watching TV and chatting away.

We took turns in the shower and then collapsed on a pair of futons, Midoriko sleeping between Makiko and me. We kept on talking, even once the lights were out. At times we laughed so hard it hurt, and Midoriko sat up and told us she was gonna lose her mind unless we stopped. I don't know how long we lay there talking, but eventually the pauses started getting longer, and we could hear Midoriko sleeping.

"What a hoot," said Makiko. "We should probably call it a night." By then my eyes had totally adjusted to the darkness. The plywood shelves, Midoriko's t-shirts hanging up to dry, the bookcase. All different shades of blue. A little after we said goodnight, I spoke again.

"Hey, Maki."

"Yeah?"

"I'm sorry," I said quietly. Through the blue of night, I saw Makiko turn to face me.

"No, I'm sorry," she said. "I should have heard you out. I know you must have thought it through before you told me. I was being dumb. I'm really sorry."

"I'm the one who should be sorry. I shouldn't have said what I said. There's no excuse."

"Natsu, I'm your sister."

I blinked in silence.

"I'll always be your sister," she said. "We're gonna be okay. We're in this together. Whatever you choose, I'm with you."

"Listen, Maki . . . "

"Let's go to sleep, okay?"

"Okay."

Gazing out the window into the darkness of the summer night, I felt myself remembering all kinds of things, entire conversations, but before long I was asleep. The sleep was like it had been cut out from a slab of clay, round and clean. I slept straight through the night. No dreams.

* * *

In the middle of September, I emailed Yuriko Zen using the address on the business card she gave me when we met. Starting off with an apology for writing her so suddenly, I asked if she was willing to meet up and talk. Four days later, she wrote back. We made plans to meet the following Saturday at two in the afternoon, in this little cafe toward the end of the arcade in Sangenjaya.

Showing up five minutes early, Yuriko looked even a little skinnier than she had been when we last met in June. When she appeared at the entrance, it was hard to say who saw who first. She wore a plain black dress, just like the last time, and walked toward me without checking the place out.

Taking a seat, she bowed her head, almost like a nod. I bowed back.

The server brought menus and water. I ordered iced tea, and Yuriko said that she would have the same. A piano sonata played at a tasteful volume in the background. It had to be a famous melody, the sort of thing that everyone has heard before, but I couldn't for the life of me remember the composer's name. For a while we were quiet, staring at our cups of water.

"I know this was sudden," I said.

After a brief pause, Yuriko shook her head. Sun streamed in through a window off behind us. The lights in the cafe were bright, but Yuriko looked pale. The freckles on her cheeks had blended with the shadows underneath her eyes, creating a peculiar set of colors almost like a bruise. Yuriko looked exhausted. She sat there quietly, waiting for me to continue. Eyes fixed on her fingers clasped around the water glass.

"I don't know where to begin," I confessed. "Honestly, I'm not even sure if it's okay for us to talk about this."

Yuriko looked up, ever so slightly.

"I just felt like I had to talk to you," I said.

"Is this about Aizawa?" she asked quietly.

"Yes," I said, "but it's also about me."

The server brought us our iced teas and asked us with a smile if she could take away our menus. We nodded yes and she excused herself, allowing us to return to our conversation.

"I've been thinking a lot about what you said in June, that night we talked in the park," I explained. "Even before, I was pretty sure I'd given a whole lot of thought to it, to why I wanted a child, to where those feelings were coming from. Wondering what gave me the right, since it's not like I have a partner, and I'm physically incapable of doing, you know, the deed . . ."

"Incapable?"

"I can't sleep with anyone. I can't get into it. Physically, I can't stand it."

I told her how I'd only slept with one guy, that we had broken up because of it and that I hadn't had sex with anybody since.

"When I heard about sperm banks, I started to wonder. Maybe this might work for me. Maybe I could have a child after all."

Yuriko stared.

"But I was only thinking superficially. That hit me when we spoke in the park. I'd lost track of what I wanted, but the more I thought about it, the more what you said resonated with me. I realized it could never be undone. I hadn't really thought about the consequences. Now what you said makes so much sense. Nobody gets to choose whether to be born."

I shook my head and sighed.

"I realized I was being selfish, even cruel."

Yuriko blinked at me, clasping her elbows.

"Without you," I said, "I never would have understood."

"Me?" she asked. Her voice was raw.

"Thanks to you," I said, laboring to get the words out. "I finally understand."

Yuriko turned toward the entrance. For a minute, she just sat that way. I saw the sharp lines of her chin, the blue veins in her skinny neck. I imagined the dark, luxuriant forest. The children snug inside a web of sleep, soft bellies rising and falling. Yuriko was snuggled up among them, eyes closed, hugging her knees, every single breath complete. Her little body safe and sound.

"Maybe this thing can never be undone. There's no way of knowing how it will turn out. Maybe I'll look back and realize it was all one big mistake. But as far as I'm concerned . . . "

My voice was shaking. I took a couple of breaths and looked at Yuriko.

"I'd rather fail than let it go."

We sat in silence, staring at our iced tea. A whitehaired man sitting behind Yuriko stood up. With the help of his cane, he headed for the exit.

"I guess you're having Aizawa's baby," Yuriko said.

I nodded.

Yuriko pressed her fingers on her eyelids.

"You know," she said almost inaudibly. "Aizawa's glad he was born."

I stared at Yuriko, not saying anything.

"I'm not like you," she said. "I'm not like either of you."

I nodded.

"Maybe I'm just weak," she said, smiling faintly. "But I can never accept life. Not if I want to go on living."

I shut my eyes, squeezing them so hard I swear I heard the muscles strain. Letting up a bit, I noticed something in my throat, a churning presence ready to spill forth. Lips pursed, I focused on my breath. Breathe in, breathe out. For a while, we said nothing.

"I read your novel," Yuriko said finally. "The one where everyone dies."

"Yeah."

"But they keep living."

"Yeah."

"It's hard to tell if they're dead or alive, but they're still living."

"Yeah."

"Why are you crying?" she asked.

Yuriko had been smiling, but then she narrowed her eyes, like she was hovering between laughter and tears, then looked at me, determined not to cry. In that moment, all I wanted was to hold her. To wrap myself around her. Not with words, and not with my arms. In another way entirely. In some other, undiscoverable way—I wanted to embrace her. To hold her skinny shoulders and her tiny back. All I wanted was to hold her. But instead I wiped away the tears and nodded.

"It's weird, isn't it?" Yuriko said.

"Yeah." I said.

"It's weird."

* * *

"I visited Sengawa's grave the other day."

Rika stirred her iced coffee with her straw. The ice cubes fell together.

We hadn't seen each other for two months. She was incredibly tanned, and her stark white dress was almost too bright to look at. She wore a small straw hat with a black ribbon.

"I know what you're thinking," she said. "Why bother? It won't do anything, right? But you can only visit the family so many times. I've never been a fan of graveyards. I always thought they were so stupid. Still do, actually. It's all a waste of money. No connection to the dead, no love, or none that I could ever see. Though I guess they give the living a place to go, when they don't know where else to turn. And there's nothing wrong with that."

"Yeah," I said.

"I asked Sengawa's parents for directions to the grave. It's past Hachioji, to the north. When I got there, I couldn't believe it. It was like five or six times bigger than anything I'd ever seen."

"What was, her gravestone?"

"Everything!" Rika laughed. "I mean, the stones themselves were big. The tall, fat kind. More like obelisks than gravestones. But so was the entire family plot. They have this whole space to themselves. I'm not even exaggerating. A group of schoolkids could have used it for a campout."

"She told me once about when she was younger," I said.

"Seriously?" Rika's bottom lip rested on her straw. "She never said anything to me."

"I guess she spent a lot of time in hospitals as a kid. And she had all these private tutors. Anyway, she spent a lot of time alone, and that was when she really started reading books."

"She loved to read," said Rika.

"I mean, she was an editor."

"I know plenty of editors who don't love to read," she laughed. "Sengawa honestly loved books, though. Books were her life."

The server brought me an iced herbal tea and gave us the check. Her fingers were clad with rings. I liked her smile. She went back into the kitchen.

From our seat over by the window, we could watch the people walking around Sangenjaya. People holding parasols and walking tiny dogs, pairs of schoolgirls wearing matching thick-rimmed glasses, mothers holding hands with kindergartners in uniform, all moving at their own pace. It was late July, ten-thirty in the morning, and the summer sun streamed down over the buckets of flowers, whatever they were called, outside the florists, who were opening for the day, and over the hand-written sandwich boards outside the bakeries, casting trim shadows on the pavement.

"I can't believe it's almost been two years," said Rika, gazing out the window. "On some level, there's a part of me that can't believe it, even now. I guess that's how it is, though, isn't it?"

We drank our drinks and watched the world outside.

"Can you feel it moving?"

Rika looked across the table at my belly.

"Oh yeah." I looked down. "Moving, kicking. This kid's ready to come out. I feel like I'm about to pass out."

"That takes me back." Rika laughed, raising her eyebrows. "I can't believe it's less than a month away."

"I know!" I said. "It's even less than that, though. Two more weeks."

"The last shopping list I sent you should cover just about everything, but I think you should just go ahead and get the cotton wipe warmer. Even though it's summer."

"The one that uses cotton wipes?"

"Exactly. It's a godsend," Rika said. "The warm wipes work so much better, trust me. So what did you decide for the crib?"

"Well, I wanted to put a couple of futons together and call it a day, but it looks like a real crib is the way to go. It turns out you can rent them for six months for almost nothing. I think I'm going with that."

"Cool."

"Clothes are good, bath stuff is good, diapers are good." I opened up the note file on my phone. "I bought a dozen milk bottles and some size one nipples, too. The formula can wait."

"I guess you can hold off on the stroller, too."

"Yeah, for sure. That's the sort of thing I can get used online."

"Hey," Rika said. "When's your sister coming?"

"She's coming on the due date and staying with me for a week. Then my niece is going to take her place."

"Oh, that's nice," Rika said. "Of course you know I'm here for you through all of this, but it'll be really good to have her there with you right after."

"Yeah."

"Wonder if it's a boy or a girl. I feel like not asking is pretty rare these days. When I was pregnant with Kura, from about two months in, I was dying to know, like, 'Come on, tell me.' My doctor must have hated my guts."

"Two months?" I laughed. "That's too early."

"Yeah. Anyway, I'm so glad everything is going well," she said. "That's all that matters. You haven't picked a name yet, though, right?"

"Not yet. I haven't even thought about it."

"Have you talked about all this?" Rika leaned a little closer as she spoke. "With your partner, or the dad. You know, the names you're considering, or when you're due?"

"We haven't talked about names, but he knows when I'm due. I told him as soon as I found out I was pregnant. He's in Tochigi now, so I haven't seen him in a few months. But we've been texting."

"Is his family up there?"

"Yeah. He's with his mom. She's not doing well and there's no one around to look after her. So he found work up there."

"That's not that far away, though."

"True. Still, the plan is for me to have the kid and raise them on my own."

"Right."

"And if they want to meet him down the line," I said, "that's fine. We both want to make that part as seamless as possible. Who knows what's going to happen, in terms of his role in the whole thing, but at least we've talked it over."

"That's great," Rika said.

She finished off her iced coffee and stretched like she was waking up. She took off her straw hat and scratched her head, making circles in her hair. Then she showed me her tanned arms.

"You'll be like me in no time," she laughed. "You realize how often I've been going to the pool? Ask the lifeguard, he'll tell you."

We paid and left the cafe and started walking toward the station. Rika said she had a meeting in Shibuya. I walked her as far as the ticket gate.

"Hey, how's everything with Okusu?" she asked me.

"Yeah, really good, actually. I think we're a good match."

"Glad to hear it." Rika sounded relieved.

"We just finished going over galleys together. It was really smooth."

"He really likes your stuff," Rika said. "He's perfect for you."

"I couldn't agree more," I said. "Thanks again for introducing us."

"Please. All I did was tell him how to reach you. Your work speaks for itself. I think you really won him over. This is really good, Natsuko. All good things."

"I know."

"Can't wait. Hey, I almost forgot about this stuff."

Rika peered into the shopping bag that she was carrying and told me what was inside. The back brace she wore after she had Kura. A few pairs of pajamas with a chest flap so that you could breastfeed. A bunch of tiny infant outfits.

"I'll text you tomorrow," she told me. "Get home safe."

She waved and went into the station. I watched her walk away until she disappeared around the corner.

I decided to have a baby with Aizawa at the end of 2017. We made some promises to each other. Neither of us was really interested in being in a committed relationship. I guess these weren't exactly promises, so much as ground rules, like a game plan for the future. I told Aizawa that I wanted to have the baby and raise them on my own. Down the road, we could talk about when and how often he would visit, but if we decided as a rule that it was better for him not to play an active role, we'd make sure that the kid could see him if they wanted to. I told him I would pay all of the medical bills and didn't want financial assistance. We could survive on what I made. It didn't have to be extravagant. Aizawa had his own ideas about the money side of things and proposed a few alternatives, but in the end, he respected my wishes.

Toward the end of February 2018, we visited an infertility specialist, under the pretense of being in a common law marriage. Luckily, we didn't need any specific documentation. All we had to do was show them copies of our family registers, to prove that we weren't actually married to anybody else.

I told the doctor I'd been trying to get pregnant for six months now, using the rhythm method, but we weren't having any luck. The doctor scheduled us a follow-up based on my menstrual cycle and ran an ultrasound, confirming I was ovulating properly. They ran tests on Aizawa too and saw no issue with his sperm. This was obviously a good thing—for this to work, his sperm had to be good and I needed to be ovulating—but since there wasn't any problem, I was scared that they were going to tell us to keep trying for a while, the old-fashioned way. However, contrary to my expectations, the doctor said that given my age and the fact that we only had one chance per month, and had been trying now for half a year, we should probably go ahead with artificial insemination. Eight months and five tries later, I finally got pregnant.

After seeing Rika off, I bought some food for dinner at the supermarket in the basement of Carrot Tower. If things went according to schedule, I should have two more weeks to go. My belly was huge. I couldn't see it getting any bigger than it was, but according to Rika, things kicked up a notch in the last week. I patted the distended area just below my stomach. Walking slowly with a parasol, I kept to the shade as best I could the whole way home.

Back in my apartment, I flicked on the AC and was pouring myself a tall glass of mugicha when my phone blew up. It was Midoriko. She and Makiko had been checking in with me all of the time, asking how I was feeling, if I needed anything, if there was any way that they could help. They were so sweet. Without fail, Makiko started off by saying that she barely remembered anything at all, since it was over twenty years ago, but this didn't stop her from remembering all kinds of things as we went along. She always finished off by stressing that although the labor was "excruciating," it was different for everyone, making it impossible to know how it would be until it happened, so I may as well not worry about it.

The plan was for Midoriko to relieve her mother and stay until her classes started up again. She sounded a little nervous about spending over two weeks with a newborn, and in Tokyo no less, but I could tell she was excited.

"What's new?" she asked cheerfully.

"Nothing. I feel the same as yesterday."

"Oh yeah? No pain?"

"Nope," I laughed. "I mean, there's a lot of movement. Maybe it's the head. Have you heard of the cervical os? Well, the baby's head keeps bumping into that. Once in a while it hurts so bad that sometimes I think I'm going to pass out, but the rest of the time it's fine. Except for when my legs cramp up at night."

"Oh my gosh." Midoriko was blown away. "What can you do about a leg cramp when your tummy's big like that?"

"Nothing. I can't do anything but wait for things to work themselves out naturally."

"That must suck," she said, even more stunned. "Um, are you still leaking?"

"That phase has passed, fortunately," I said. "Fine otherwise. Protein is good. Uric acid is fine. I was a little puffed up yesterday, I guess, but overall the doctor says I'm doing really well."

"Hey! That's great." Midoriko laughed. "So, what's it feel like? Having a baby inside you."

"It's not really what I expected," I confessed. "Kind of surreal. You know how I never got morning sickness? It didn't really click, even, until I started getting bigger. Even that, at first, sort of just felt like I was gaining weight. Eventually, though, I started feeling heavier, and realized that all kinds of things were changing."

"I bet."

"It's weird. I know it's me and everything. Like, my own body."

"Yeah?"

"But everything is harder, takes more time. It's almost like I'm dressed up as a cartoon version of myself. At first it was exhausting, but I've really gotten used to it. At this point, I'm at peace with it."

"That's amazing."

"There's been a few times, in the bathroom, when I've looked at my belly in the mirror, and asked myself like is this really gonna make it out? Can I actually do this? It only lasts a second, though. A moment of clarity."

"Wow."

"But that doesn't happen anymore. I guess I'm not afraid anymore, like I'm letting myself take up space. Like noodles in a pot of boiling water. Pretty soon they spread and fill the pot."

"I can see that."

"I always thought it was so funny. Once you hit eighty-five or ninety, you gotta figure you've got what, like five or ten years left to live, right? I mean, you know you're gonna die before too long. That's gotta be weird. Seriously, what's that feel like? To say to yourself *I might not be around this time next year.* Know what I mean? You know that you're not dying someday. You're dying *soon.* What do you think that feels like?"

"Wow, hard to say."

"Folks that age always look so calm. I wonder if they really feel that way, though. What are they really thinking?"

"I know."

"I mean, there's still a chance that I could die in childbirth, Midoriko. I know it's not the old days, and on some level I know it's going to be okay, but you never know. What if I have a hemorrhage? Anything could happen. All I'm saying is the possibility is real. This is the closest that I've been to death in my whole life."

"Yeah."

"But it's weird. Somehow it doesn't faze me. If I try to think about it, imagining the way that things will be after the fact, it's like I'm being wrapped up in a cushy blanket. I can't form a single complete thought."

Midoriko hummed pensively.

"Think about it, though," I insisted. "What if whenever you're like *Whoa, am I gonna die*, some substance gets secreted in your brain? Maybe that's what it's like when you're super old. Maybe it's like this every day. Even now, though, I feel myself sinking down into the pillows. Thoughts melting away."

"I don't think you're going to die, Natsu, but I hear you."

"It's strange, though, right?" I laughed. "I'm not afraid of anything."

I made it through the last week of July and into August. At that point I was waking up multiple times every night. In the mornings, even once I was up and around, it was like my head was full of fog. I spent most of the day flopped down on the beanbag with my eyes closed, dozing off. Around noon, the sun turned the curtains white, sending streaks of sunlight over the carpet. From my reclined position, I reached out to feel the sun, opening and closing my hands in its warmth. Even with the AC running, it felt as if the temperature was climbing steadily throughout the day. My armpits and my back were drenched in sweat. When I blinked, I swear that I could feel the summer swelling.

Then I felt it—a tension different from anything I'd felt up to that point. I clasped my hands over my belly, holding on for dear life. The tension was gone, like it had passed through me, but a few minutes afterwards I felt a presence swelling from the deepest part of me, coming in waves. Each time it grew stronger, until it finally registered as pain. I was a week ahead of schedule. I felt like it was still too early, but in terms of the

number of weeks it was within the realm of possibility. I realized it was really happening. I was sweating like crazy. My
heart was racing. I'd listened to the doctors, listened to Rika,
and listened to my sister, even though she claimed not to
remember anything. I'd read accounts of pregnancy and
childbirth and studied up online, but I'd forgotten all the signals, how to tell for sure if it was really happening.

The pain subsided. Exercising caution, I sat up and went
out to the kitchen, to pour myself a glass of mugicha, which
I drank instantly. For a second, I had been so thirsty that I
could've sworn my cheeks were sticking to my teeth.
Intervals, I told myself. I read somewhere that when you feel
a pain you've never felt before, you need to track how long
it takes before it comes again. To make sure I could stand up
if I needed to, I skipped the beanbag, sitting in a chair
instead, and watched the clock. The hands said three in the
afternoon, on the dot. Eventually the pain came back. It
seemed like it was happening every twenty minutes. I panicked, trying to remember what I was supposed to do, but it
was like the space behind my eyes and forehead, every nook
and cranny, had been packed with cotton. Everything felt
surreal.

Between bursts of pain, I texted Makiko and Midoriko:
"Hey, I think I'm going into labor . . . Talk to you later." I
texted Rika, too. Then I checked the duffel bag and tote bag
that I'd packed for the occasion, to make sure that I had my
wallet and my maternity notebook, and called the hospital. A
friendly nurse came on the line and heard me out. She said that
it was probably safe for me to watch things for a bit, but it was
fine to come now, if I wanted to. I told her I was on my way,
since I was alone and didn't think that I'd be able to move if
the pain got any worse.

By the time I got there the intervals were slightly shorter,
but the pain was noticeably worse. They took my things and

led me directly to a delivery room, where they told me that my cervix had dilated almost two inches and that my water had broken, although we had a ways to go. A team of nurses sped around the room. To measure the exact intensity and frequency of the labor pains, they laid a special pad over my belly, which at this point was so big that I could barely see beyond it, and slipped a heart rate monitor over my middle finger.

"How are you feeling, Natsuko?" an older nurse asked, smiling all the while. She had been looking out for me every step of the way. "We're going in. Everything good?"

The pain made it hard to speak. I nodded yes. The nurse smiled. Her whole face was a smile. She gripped my shoulder.

Over the next few hours, the intervals dropped down to fifteen minutes, then to ten. Each time the pain returned, the world went black. Then came a period of several minutes where I was coming to my senses, feeling the smoke clear, until finally I could see again. All the while, I panted, with my eyes as wide as possible, as if I literally had to pull myself together. When I felt the next wave swelling deep inside my belly, it was enough to make my knees shake.

The waves toppled me, each one stronger and bigger than the last, until I couldn't tell up from down. My eyes were open but I saw no light. I couldn't find the sun. I had to know how deep I was, but all my wriggling and writhing only made the screaming pain intensify. I heard a woman's voice trying to tell me something. As one of the waves was pulling back, I looked up at the clock. The hands said it was a little before ten. How could that be? I felt upset that it had taken me this long, and equally upset at how much further I would have to go. But then I heard something like laughter bubbling up from deep inside of me. It was a feeling I had never felt before. When I could move my hands again, the nurses gave me water, which I drank, hearing their reassuring voices spin away and circle back.

Around two in the morning, the bursts of pain were five minutes apart. I was roaring uncontrollably. I was certain this was as much pain as any human body could produce, but it would seem the pain had set its sights far higher. If it pushed further, past the limits of my being, could I survive? Would that be when I died? No, I don't think so. This was beyond painful. I felt it everywhere. What hurt? Was it my body? The whole world? I couldn't tell you for the life of me. But then— a voice tore through the heavens. I saw the face of the kind nurse. My eyes were open wide like I'd been slapped, and my belly—though at that point it was something else, a different entity, the center of the universe—rang with explosive strength. In a voice no one but me could hear I screamed relentlessly, pushing with everything I had. Next thing I knew—it all went white, as if my consciousness had escaped from my body. My body became liquid, lukewarm and spilling across the surface of the earth.

My head and body filled with blinding light, inside of which—I saw something expanding. Like a nebula, breathing without a sound, millions of years away. Astral mist and stars spun from the total darkness, twinkling in every color of the rainbow, breathing silently. I opened my eyes wide and watched the haze, the colors—breathing softly through the tears. I watched the light. Eyes wide open. I reached out and tried to touch its brilliance. Something was crying. Coming to, I saw my chest was heaving. I was on my back, and I was breathing. The nurses wiped my sweat away. My heart sent oxygen throughout my body. I blinked and heard a baby crying. Someone said it was four-fifty. A baby's voice rang through the air.

They placed the baby on my chest, wearing a little yellow hat. Its body felt so unbelievably small. Its shoulders, arms, fingers and cheeks were puckered up and red. Every inch of it was flush with blood. It screamed at the top of its lungs.

"Seven pounds, two ounces," somebody said. "A healthy baby girl."

Tears were streaming from my eyes, but what kind of tears were they? I felt something greater than the sum of all of my emotions welling up inside of me. A feeling that I couldn't name, though it still made me cry. I looked at the baby's face, tucking my chin to get a better look.

I saw her for the first time. She was unlike anyone that I had ever known. Unprecedented in my memory or my imagination. She was new to me. Her voice rang through her body, loud as anything. I called to her, speaking in a voice that no one else could hear. Where were you? You're here now. I watched her, this new baby girl, letting her cry into my breast.

THE END